Dead Man's Wake

Also by Paul Doiron

Hatchet Island

Dead by Dawn

One Last Lie

Almost Midnight

Stay Hidden

Knife Creek

Widowmaker

The Precipice

The Bone Orchard

Massacre Pond

Bad Little Falls

Trespasser

The Poacher's Son

Dead Man's Wake

Paul Doiron

MINOTAUR BOOKS
NEW YORK

This is a work of fiction. All of the characters, organizations, and events portrayed in this novel are either products of the author's imagination or are used fictitiously.

First published in the United States by Minotaur Books, an imprint of St. Martin's Publishing Group

www.minotaurbooks.com

Designed by Jonathan Bennett

The Library of Congress Cataloging-in-Publication Data is available upon request.

ISBN 978-1-250-86439-0 (hardcover)
ISBN 978-1-250-86440-6 (ebook)

First Edition: 2023

10 9 8 7 6 5 4 3 2 1

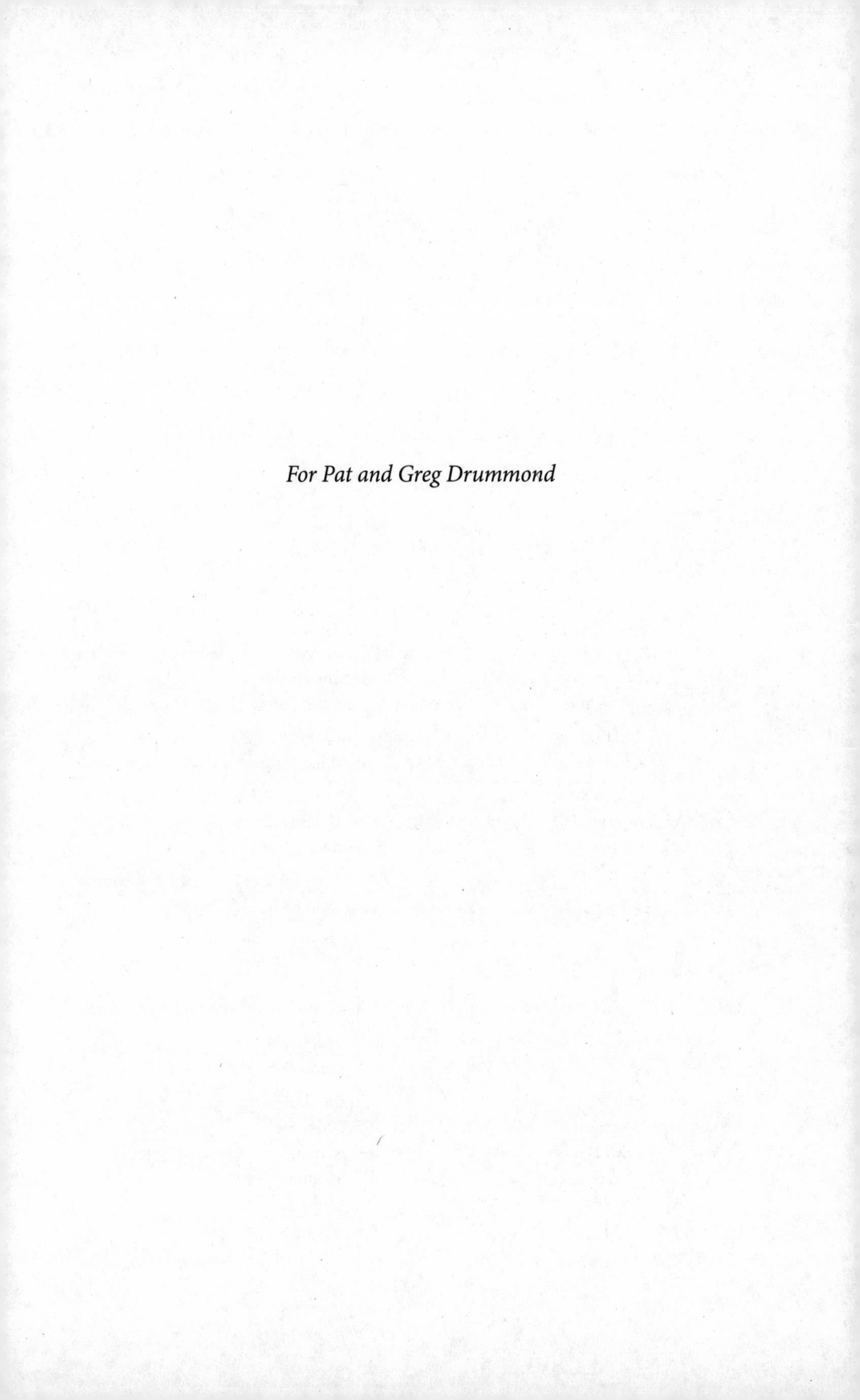

For Pat and Greg Drummond

Beware the fury of a patient man.

—John Dryden

Dead Man's Wake

I

It's a wonder that all marriages don't end in murder-suicides," said my stepfather's new wife, Jubilee.

Neil, my stepdad, nearly spit out his decaf.

It was the evening of Stacey's and my engagement party.

In the five years since my mom had died, Neil Turner and I had drifted apart. We had never been close to begin with, but he and Jubilee had decided to have a celebratory dinner for us at their lake house in central Maine, over the Labor Day weekend. They had invited Stacey's parents, Charley and Ora Stevens, who had flown down from the North Woods in their Cessna 182 bush plane. Now the six of us were gathered in the great room, enjoying our blueberry pie and coffee while a warm breeze ruffled the curtains.

"You might want to have another look at your will, Neil," Ora Stevens said apropos murder-suicides.

"He has nothing to worry about," said Jubilee. "I told him, after he proposed, that I wasn't after his money *or* his last name."

Jubilee Batchelder had been christened Julie, but the name hadn't been fabulous enough for her adult self. (It was a judgment with which I happened to agree, based upon our brief acquaintance.) And so, in college, she had become Jubilee.

She worked as a yoga teacher and massage therapist—she had met Neil on her table—and was closer to my age than his: a fact that had troubled me at first and still did to some degree. She was an attractive if not conventionally beautiful woman, lean from hot yoga and a pescatarian diet. Her most striking feature was a mass of honey-blond hair that would not be contained.

I guessed that Jubilee had been the creative force behind the design of this modernist mansion, as my stepfather was a bright but thoroughly conventional man, a graying tax attorney who dressed in ironed polos and pressed chinos and played a lot of golf.

Somehow the topic had gotten onto the dreaded 9-1-1 calls that cops termed *domestics*. Jubilee hadn't realized that Maine game wardens—which Charley had been before his retirement and which I still was—had the same arrest powers as sheriffs, that we served as an off-road police force when no other officers were available in rural corners of the state. We saw a lot of shit, in other words. When a warden rolled up on a house fully involved in a conflagration of violence, you could never predict the outcome.

"Finish your story, Charley," Ora instructed her husband.

Stacey's mother sat, as always, in her wheelchair, cupping a tumbler of scotch on her blanket-draped lap. She wore her snowy-white hair in a shoulder-length bob. Her daughter had inherited her high cheekbones and almond-shaped green eyes that, in Ora, were even paler and more captivating.

"It happened just up the road when I was a tenderfoot warden," said Charley, who never needed encouragement. "The Belgrade Lakes region was my first district, you see."

Stacey's dad was a wiry man with white hair clipped close to his head and a rugged face I'd heard described as "halfway between handsome and homely." As usual, he was dressed from head to toe in green, as if he'd spent so many decades in uniform—first as an army pilot in Vietnam, then as a warden in Maine—that it was impossible for him to imagine wearing any other color.

"One night," he continued, "I got a call from the dispatcher that a man was beating up his new wife over in Skunk Hollow. He gave me some lip when I arrived, but I wrestled him to the ground easily enough. But as soon as I slapped the cuffs on the husband, the wife began punching *me*!"

Neil was still off-balance from Jubilee's joke about all marriages going bad. "I'm not sure this is an appropriate conversation for an engagement party."

"I haven't reached *le dénouement,*" said Charley, who had learned French from Québécois loggers when he was a boy in the lumber camps. "The kicker was that the wife hit harder than her man! And then, when I had them both restrained, the newlyweds began making out."

Everyone but me laughed at the punch line.

I was distracted by an intermittent noise coming through the screen doors. Some idiot on a Jet Ski was still buzzing about the lake. There were other boats racing around, too, but the whine of the two-stroke engine annoyed me as when an unseen mosquito is moving about a darkened room.

"You're not working tonight, babe," my fiancée whispered knowingly.

"It's illegal to run a Jet Ski or WaveRunner after dark."

"This isn't your district. It's not your job."

"If he crashes, it will be."

Sensing the need for a change of subject, Jubilee said, "I'd hoped you'd bring your wolf with you tonight, Mike. I'm so eager to meet him."

"Shadow isn't the best houseguest," Stacey said, tucking several strands of long brown hair behind one ear.

I felt obliged to add, "He's actually a wolf hybrid."

"A high-content wolf hybrid," Stacey said, "meaning he's basically a wolf. You'd never know to look at him that he has any domestic dog genes in him."

"Who's watching him while you're away?" Neil asked.

"A friend's son who wants to be a wildlife biologist. They get along great."

"Shadow has another new friend," said Stacey. "A raven's started visiting his enclosure. It just perches in a tree and *quorks* at him conversationally. We don't know if it's a male or a female, but we're calling it 'Gus.' Show them the cute picture, Mike."

I was reaching for my cell phone when the Jet Ski revved its engine not fifty feet from Neil and Jubilee's dock.

"I need to step outside," I said, rising with difficulty from a sectional sofa that looked and felt like a roasted marshmallow.

Stacey sprang up, too. "I'm coming with you."

The night was humid. The smell of the lake wafted across the blue lawn and through the towering pines. We crossed the patio and proceeded down the granite steps between fading viburnums until we'd entered the shadows beyond the house lights.

The Jet Ski had zoomed off by then. But I could still hear its motorcycle engine up the channel.

We had made it to the end of the dock and were gazing at cottages strung like Christmas lights along the far shore. I fancied that above the odor of the pines and the lake, I could smell the smoke from the fireworks that had been exploding at irregular intervals in celebration of summer's last hurrah.

The lake had served as the inspiration for the play—and later the movie—*On Golden Pond,* and it retained some of the quaintness that summer people treasured and lobbied hard to defend against the realities of modern life. For instance, a mail boat continued to deliver letters and packages (now mainly from Amazon, I suspected) to mailboxes at the ends of docks.

"I have to say," Stacey said, "Jubilee isn't what I expected. When you said she was only forty and taught hot yoga—"

"I expected Neil had found himself a trophy wife, too."

"Instead, she's perceptive, funny, and altogether awesome. Oh, Mike, I know how much you wanted to hate her."

"I have it on firsthand authority from the Brothers Grimm that all stepmothers are supposed to be wicked."

Stacey affected her father's Maine accent. "Well, Jubilee *is* wicked—wicked cool!"

A loon announced itself in the near darkness. Its yodeling was at once comical and haunting. Farther out, several watercraft were racing about as if the lake were paved with wet black asphalt. One of the speedboats sounded positively rocket-powered. There were very few shoals or ledges at the center of Great Pond, but a fast-moving boat always risked striking a submerged log, especially when the vessel had the horsepower to outrun its own bow lights.

The Jet Ski was coming back. In the weak starlight, it was utterly invisible except for the pale, shimmering rooster tail ejected by the impeller from the rear nozzle. I feared for the safety of the loon we'd just heard.

But the personal watercraft turned sharply before it came within range of the dock lights, made a tight ninety-degree turn, and zipped off toward deeper water. It was headed for a humpbacked shadow a half mile or so out. Neil had earlier identified the wooded islet as Mouse Island.

I held my breath, waiting for the wake to arrive. When it finally reached us, the waves caused the floating dock to buckle so that we staggered against each other like the drunken newlyweds from Charley's story.

The fenders cushioning the pontoon boat from the dock rubbed and squeaked. In my peripheral vision, I saw Charley's moored floatplane rocking. It was an amphibious model, equipped with both floats and retractable wheels, that could land as easily on water as on land.

"Let it go, Mike," Stacey said as I glared at the retreating Jet Ski. "For me."

"OK."

She took my arm as if we were preparing to walk down an aisle. "If we don't go back inside soon, they're going to wonder if we're *shtupping*."

"*Shtupping?*"

I allowed myself to be pulled back to our party. We'd made it down the dock and had reentered the festive glow of the house when we heard the collision on the lake.

2

The noise was more of a percussive thump rather than the explosion of fiberglass and metal you might expect from a motorboat striking a hard object at fifty miles per hour. If Stacey and I hadn't spent so much time on the water, we might have failed to read significance in that vague thud.

She turned back toward the lake. "One of them hit something!"

"A log, maybe?" I began striding toward the end of the dock. "I just hope it wasn't a loon."

The Jet Ski was nowhere to be seen, but it had no running lights to reveal its location. As far as I could discern, there was only a single motorboat in the middle of the lake, due south of Mouse Island. Its navigation lights were barely visible, but I could tell it was slowing to a stop.

"Could that boat have hit the Jet Ski?" Stacey asked.

"The crash would have been louder. Both boats would've gone spinning, and the Jet Ski would have broken apart."

I worked in the Wildlife Crimes Investigation Division of the Maine Warden Service. My cases involved everything from busting poaching rings to solving hunting homicides to reconstructing boating accidents.

But before I'd become a warden investigator, I'd patrolled Sebago Lake, and one of my responsibilities was to police the considerable boat traffic that clogged the waters in the summer. I spent July and August writing dozens of tickets for speeding, safety violations, and boating while intoxicated.

Once I'd watched an Allison Grand Sport go airborne after it crashed into a swimming float off Frye's Leap. This was in broad daylight: visibility unlimited. The driver tumbled into the water, none the worse for wear, being as loose as a marionette from drink. But his speedboat lodged in a stand of pines on Frye Island. It hung suspended in the branches ten feet in the air, with the engine still running. I remember looking up at the spinning prop and the vibrating bottom of the V-shaped hull. The state didn't pay me enough to climb up there to switch off the ignition. That damned boat took forever to run out of gas.

I squinted now at the distant speedboat. "They're turning around to have a look at whatever they hit."

"Your eyes are so much better than mine."

"There it is," I said. "Proof of guilt."

"What?"

"They just turned off their running lights. They know they hit something. They're hoping to slip away in the dark."

I took off at a sprint toward the house, my footsteps loud on the aluminum-framed dock.

"Where are you going?" Stacey called.

"To fetch the keys to Neil's boat."

When I slid open the door to the great room, I was met by four startled, slightly puzzled faces.

"We heard a noise out on the lake," I explained. "One of the speedboats struck something. It circled back and immediately turned off its lights."

Charley just about vaulted from the chair. "I'd call that suspicious."

I looked at my stepfather. "I need to borrow the Leisure Kraft."

"I'll take you out there," he said, smoothing his polo as he rose to his feet.

I could hardly kick Neil off his own boat, especially after he'd given us a tour of the pleasure barge earlier, showing us its many amenities. The rectangular vessel reminded me more of a floating living room than a proper watercraft. It had padded seats, a dry bar, a sound system, even a refrigerator.

"Do you have an idea where the crash happened?" he asked.

"Half a mile due west of us. Near Mouse Island."

"That rock is no bigger than a fleabite—barely enough acreage for a house and a fishing cabin," said Charley.

Ora pulled a phone from the pocket of her white cotton shirt. "I am going to call 9-1-1 to tell the dispatcher to alert the local warden."

Neil was an attorney and cleared his throat as if preparing to address the court. "We don't have a warden here, I'm afraid."

"What's that?" Charley asked.

"This district doesn't currently have a game warden assigned to it," I explained. "The last one retired unexpectedly in May—throat cancer. And we couldn't get a deputy warden up to speed in time."

"And neither Belgrade nor Rome have municipal police officers," added Neil, meaning the neighboring municipalities, not the great cities of Europe. "The elected town councils pass ordinances, but no one enforces them. That's why the lakes association came up with the money to hire a constable." He, too, now reached for a cell phone. "I think I have Galen's private number in my contacts."

"Galen?" I said.

The name was unusual enough that I knew I'd encountered it before. I couldn't recall the circumstances. But the initial association was negative.

"Galen Webb is the lake constable we hired," Neil said. "The Kennebec County sheriff made him a part-time deputy so he could enforce state laws on the pond. If you call 9-1-1, he'll be the one they send out to investigate. Galen's a solid young man. Very polite and responsible. We've received few complaints about him all summer."

The Warden Service brass talked a lot about the importance of practicing courtesy, but it was my belief, having dealt with dozens of Maine's mouthiest scofflaws, that a law enforcement officer who receives no complaints whatsoever can't be doing their job responsibly.

"I need to get some things from my Scout," I said.

Before I could exit the room, Jubilee rose fluidly like the yoga teacher she was. She was wearing loose-fitting pastels and had a gardenia tucked behind her left ear.

"Is it possible someone was injured out there?" she asked with blunt perceptiveness. "A swimmer, maybe?"

She had given voice to a fearful possibility I hadn't permitted myself to speak aloud.

"We need to go," I said, leaving the question unanswered. "I'll meet you all at the boat."

"Are you staying here, Ora?" asked Jubilee. "If so, I'll stay with you."

"They don't have room for extra ballast, dear."

I was grateful that Stacey's mother recognized this was potentially a rescue—or worse, a recovery—mission and not a moonlight cruise. I had been afraid the whole party might want to tag along.

As I headed out to my vehicle, a vintage International Harvester Scout, I assessed the situation. The Leisure Kraft was propelled by a single 115-horsepower Suzuki engine. We wouldn't be engaging in any high-speed pursuits in that party barge.

I almost literally ran into Stacey in the dark outside. She was returning from the Scout with her medical backpack. She was an emergency medical technician, among other things, and always traveled with her trauma kit in case we came upon an accident.

"I would have brought your sidearm, too," she said. "But I don't have a key to the lockbox."

"That's all right. Can you see if Neil has a mask and snorkel. Flippers, too?"

"Will do." Light from the house touched part of her face. "I have a bad feeling about this, babe."

3

Neil couldn't raise Galen Webb. Maybe the lake constable recognized the name and number and decided he had something more important to do than take a call from a member of the association board.

I had remembered why I knew Webb's name.

He had recently applied to join the Warden Service. I was supposed to do his background check, but a bullet to the leg had sidelined me. The investigator who checked Webb's background didn't breach confidentiality, but he did make a pointed comment to me about "applicants who look great on paper and then you begin interviewing people who know them, and you realize that every closet in their house has another skeleton in it."

Evidently the Kennebec County sheriff, or whoever had vetted Webb for the constable job, hadn't stumbled upon his ossuary.

"I'm sure young Webb has his hands full, it being Labor Day weekend," Charley said as we left the no-wake zone. "He's probably already out here somewhere, chasing speeders."

"Let's hope he saw something," I said. "I couldn't even make out the boat's silhouette, but I could tell from the sound that it definitely had two outboards. I wish the moon had been up."

My friend pointed over my shoulder at the elongated hill above Neil's house. A cold glow was radiating into the sky, revealing the serrated edge of trees along the ridge. "It will be up soon, at least."

At that moment, someone at the north end of the pond decided it would be a good time to set off more fireworks: a fusillade of

Roman candles, followed by a burst of skyrockets. As a wolf dog owner, I wasn't a fan of explosive light shows that sent my animal into fits of panic.

We were crossing a channel of sorts between the shore and Mouse Island. Neil was no fisherman, but the salesman at the yacht dealership had sold him the most expensive depth finder in the Humminbird catalog. After we had moved past the steep drop-off along the eastern edge of Great Pond, the bottom was never more than twenty feet below our hull.

I moved to the squared-off bow and began shouting directions to my stepfather seated at the wheel. The center of the vast, open lake provided few guides to navigation. But Mouse Island continued to take shape to the northwest: an area of blackness without definition—more of a void than a place—between the glittering water and the star-filled sky.

Now that we were out on the pond, I was surprised by the dark swaths of shoreline. The fireworks and the racing boats had given me the false idea that summer was still in full swing in Belgrade. But now I had that nostalgic feeling of another season over, of time gone and irrecoverable. The kids who had come north to attend the camps that were institutions on Great Pond—Pine Island and Runoia and Bombazeen—had returned home, leaving darkened cabins and bunkhouses. Elsewhere, cottages stood empty; some already had their docks pulled up. Signs of human life were scattered, detached, and diminished from what I would have found a mere week before.

Stacey came up beside me. She'd put on her faded Red Sox cap. "I'm thinking we need to turn to starboard. Fifteen degrees, maybe."

"Neil, can you turn to starboard a touch?"

"Is starboard right or left?"

"Right as in 'right you are'!" said Charley. He had taken it upon himself to serve as first mate to our inexperienced captain.

"Where's Constable Webb?" asked Stacey, scanning from shore to shore. "I can't see a single boat now."

"At least the joker on the Jet Ski went in."

The half-moon was announcing its arrival by the minute. I welcomed its light, however faint.

A red cup floated past the pontoon boat. It was one of those disposable pint-size containers that are so popular at keg parties. I wasn't sure if it constituted evidence. Beer and boating are inextricably linked in the minds of many people. But the cup's random appearance struck me as potentially significant.

"Hold up."

"Kill the motor if you would, Neil," said Charley, anticipating my next words.

The pontoon boat continued its forward momentum. With the engine off, I asked my stepfather to come around in a circle.

Mouse Island was very close now: two hundred yards to the north. Charley had been correct about its diminutive size. I had brought my binoculars from the Scout, along with my rucksack and sidearm. The image that appeared through the lenses as I tightened the focus was blurred but showed a surprisingly long dock. It was hard to tell, but I thought a boat might be tied to one side.

The Leicas revealed the shapes of trees, both conifers and hardwoods, rising to a central hump. Somewhere amid the thicket must have been a house—perhaps more than one house—although the island was starved for acreage.

Charley had come up to join Stacey and me.

"When I was the district warden here, Mouse was owned by the Fenton family," he said. "The wife's name I forget, but I'll never forget Judge Coleman Fenton. He wasn't much older than I, but the Kennedys had gotten him installed for life in the Massachusetts judiciary. He never would abide a negative word about the clan."

The retired warden pilot couldn't abide hagiography of any sort, but he had a special disdain for JFK, who, in his opinion, had never received the blame he deserved for miring the U.S. in the swamps of Indochina. Charley rarely spoke about his time in Vietnam. But the mention of certain '60s politicians and bureaucrats could spark him like a match to dry tinder.

"Do you remember if the judge and his wife had children?" I asked.

"I believe so. Why?"

"I'm just wondering if the island is still in the family." I brought up the binoculars again and this time managed to focus them with the help of the moon. "There's a boat tied to that dock."

"I expect the judge is dead now," said the old pilot. "What an imperious SOB he was! I'm sure he did some good in this life, but it's a coin toss if Judge Fenton went north or south at the hour of his demise."

"It's weird that the lights are off in the house if someone's staying there," said Stacey. "It's not *that* late."

"They could be asleep," said Neil.

I thought of the recent roar of the motorboats and the booming of the fireworks. You would've needed more than a pair of earplugs to sleep through that commotion.

Stacey shivered beside me. "Something is wrong here."

Charley tilted his chin in the direction of the western shore, where a lighted motorboat was fast approaching. "That would be Constable Webb, I expect."

Stacey had begun using the headlamp in her EMT bag to scope the water around our boat. The light penetrated the surface by four or five feet, which took on a greenish-brown quality before it faded into grainy darkness. The color of the water reminded me of weak tea with the leaves floating around in the form of lake vegetation, churned up by boat propellers.

I aimed the beam from my powerful Fenix flashlight at the same spot, hoping to amplify the effect. I had the impression of a sandy bottom as if a shoal extended south of the island.

"What the hell?" Stacey leaned toward the water.

I followed her lead, hanging my upper body over the side. I brought my flashlight as close to the surface as I dared.

"Do you see something?" Neil asked.

"Maybe. What do you think it is, Charley?"

We were drifting over a spot between clusters of slimy rocks and beds of freshwater mussels. Above the sand, a pale object hung suspended, swaying at the outermost edge of the beam. Then the brighter underwater lights of the pontoon boat also touched the thing, and for an instant, there was a metallic shimmer.

Charley, being the only combat veteran among us, was the first to identify the object. He looked sadly at his daughter. "I wish you'd been wrong about your feelings."

Stacey put a hand to her mouth. "Oh no."

"What? What are you looking at?" Neil left the wheel unattended, and the boat listed as his weight combined with ours on the starboard side. "What is it?"

The object floating beneath the surface of the lake was a severed human arm.

4

The detached limb seemed to be scrabbling over the sand, but it was only drifting on a subsurface current.

Most people don't know this, but a variety of factors determine whether a body floats or sinks. Babies, for instance, will often bob along the surface since their fat-to-muscle ratio is so high. Weightlifters, by contrast, often have trouble keeping their heads above water despite their prodigious strength.

"Where's the rest of him?" Stacey whispered.

Beyond the stern, the shoal ended, and the bottom fell away into murky water that our lights were unable to penetrate. I moved quickly to lower the anchor, which caused a little burst of sand to erupt when it hit bottom—well away from the arm, fortunately. It was imperative not to disturb the crime scene.

"Once you get west of the island, there's a steep drop-off," said Charley, accessing memories of long-ago lake patrols. "There's a lot of motion under the surface. Currents will carry that arm over the edge in no time."

The limb was already drifting beyond our lights. My mind was running down a checklist of ways I might secure it.

Then I heard Stacey exclaim, "Dad!"

Charley had stripped to his underwear. With his clothes on, it was easy to forget how badly the former POW had been tortured during his imprisonment in the Hanoi Hilton; he stood straight as a rail, moved without a hitch in his step, and possessed remarkable range of motion for a man whose arms had been dislocated if not broken.

But now that he was nearly naked, the white razor scars and red craters left by burning cigarettes showed in their vivid awfulness.

"No, Charley," I said too late.

He was over the side before I could speak another word. He scissored his frog legs and dove for the bottom.

"No, no, no."

"What's wrong?" Neil loomed over my shoulder, smelling of sandalwood, whether from a cologne or some product in his hair. He was one of those wealthy professional men who always wore a scent.

I saw bubbles rise from Charley's nostrils as he exhaled to decrease his buoyancy.

"He's going to bring it up," I explained.

"Shouldn't he?"

Stacey kept her light on the zombie limb as it crawled toward the shadows.

Meanwhile, the other motorboat was drawing near. The man at the wheel had throttled his engine back to headway speed as he entered the safety zone around the island. But six miles per hour was still fast enough for the propeller to kill Charley if the outboard happened to pass over him while the old man was surfacing.

The captain of the craft hailed us in a reedy voice. "Is that Mr. Turner?"

Neil answered with a wave. "Galen?"

I moved to the bow. "You need to cut your engine, now! We've got a diver down."

Constable Galen Webb hesitated—unsure who I was, taken aback by a reprimand from a stranger—then complied.

For a game warden, learning to ID a watercraft is as important as a highway patrolman needing to recognize the make and model of a speeding vehicle. Galen's was a Crestliner deck boat, twenty or so feet in length. The vessel had been designed with a deep vee hull to slice through waves. The constable had fitted it with an aftermarket spotlight for night work, and he'd installed blue pursuit lights that troubled me. I hoped he wasn't fool enough to engage in high-speed chases across Great Pond, never having been trained in pursuits, from what I understood of his background.

Charley popped up between the two boats, holding his grisly trophy aloft.

The arm had been torn from the body above the elbow. I saw ragged flesh where the amputation had occurred and a pale stub of bone protruding from pink muscle. The shape of the limb, as well as its general hairiness, all but confirmed it had belonged to a man. The metal object I'd seen glitter was a watch on a steel bracelet fastened around the wrist.

"Dang!" said Galen Webb. "Is that a—?"

To keep the severed limb above water, Charley began an awkward one-handed dog paddle. He was heading toward the swimming platform at the stern of the pontoon boat.

I glanced around the Leisure Kraft and spotted a trash can that Neil had emptied when he'd tied up the boat earlier. He'd replaced the plastic liner, fortunately. The bag was the best I could do.

Stacey continued scanning the bottom with her flashlight. "Where's the rest of him? Can anyone see?"

Galen Webb fired up his spotlight and briefly swept the Leisure Kraft with the beam, blinding us all like deer in the road.

"Dude!" said Stacey.

From behind my raised arm, I said, "Could you turn that off, Constable? Or at least focus it elsewhere."

"Sorry! I'm sorry."

I pulled the plastic bag from the container and knelt at the stern, waiting for Charley.

"I wish you hadn't done that," I said softly as he drew near. I didn't want anyone else to hear me criticize him.

He blinked up at me. "Done what?"

I reached out with the bag held open so that he knew to thrust the severed limb inside.

"Retrieved the arm. We should have left it where it was."

He knitted his wet, weathered brow. "But the current was pushing it along. It would have been over the drop-off in no time."

I wrapped the arm securely in plastic, then knotted the top of the bag.

"I appreciate the heroic gesture, Charley. But it's evidence of a crime, and we shouldn't have disturbed it more than we had to. Where it came to rest might be important in determining where the collision took place. Before moving it, divers would have taken photos, placing it in situ."

My old friend looked up at me, and I saw the dawning recognition widen his eyes.

"I should've known better."

"Underwater crime investigation is a pretty esoteric discipline among the forensic sciences."

"I can mark the spot with a buoy if you can jury-rig one for me." His experience showed in the quickness with which he'd switched into problem-solving mode. "There's a quart beer bottle down near where I got hold of it."

"You would really have just left the arm there?" Neil said, aghast. Evidently, he'd overheard us. The color had managed to drain from his suntanned face over the past few minutes.

"Until morning, yes. Once we'd kept it from moving and marked the spot. You have bottled water in the fridge, right?"

"Yes. Why?"

"You'll see."

Stacey, meanwhile, was still rushing around the boat, continuing her quixotic pursuit of the man's corpse. "Did you see the rest of him, Dad?"

"Afraid not. But I can look around when I go down again with the marker."

Galen Webb called to us across the moonlit water. "Is it possible our victim is still alive?"

"No way," said Stacey. "Take it from an EMT."

Galen moved the white-hot spotlight over the surface of the lake.

"You won't find him floating," I said as I emptied the plastic bottle of its fizzing water.

"How do you know?" Galen sounded like he didn't believe me.

"Because dead bodies sink. It's the air in your lungs that causes you to float. After you breathe your last breath, down you go. Corpses only rise again when their insides decompose and create gas."

I screwed the top back onto the bottle, then tied two half hitches around the neck with a length of paracord. I handed the spool to Charley and said, "You need to let out enough line so the bottle floats to the surface."

"Ten-four!"

His head disappeared into the lake.

Galen's boat had come close enough that I could have leaped over a rail into the Crestliner.

For the first time since he'd arrived, I had a moment to study Galen Webb up close.

He might have been a teenager. The wispy mustache darkening his upper lip failed to dispel the notion. He wore sagging jeans, an inflatable vest over a loose shirt, and a black baseball cap with the word SHERIFF embroidered above the brim. Around his narrow hips hung a gun belt arrayed with special pouches and sheaths for all the tools of the trade: handcuffs, pepper spray, multitool, and so on. The pistol in the holster had the squared-off profile of a Glock.

"Maybe I could make circles outward from this position, spotlighting the bottom," he said.

"It would be better not to start the engine while Warden Stevens is submerged."

"Right! Of course."

I understood the constable's compulsion to act for the sake of acting. It had been my first instinct as a young officer, too. I hadn't yet learned that busyness isn't the same as progress.

"You could help me out by calling dispatch," I said.

"Sure thing!" Then he cocked his head. "How do I explain this, exactly?"

In fairness, it was a good question.

5

I told Galen to report a boating fatality. We had at least one person dead in the water. No ID of the boat involved. I said I'd contact the warden lieutenant assigned to the area myself. We would also be needing the bureau's dive team.

"Request that a death scene examiner meet our boat at Neil's house to take possession of the severed arm."

"You got it," Galen said a little too enthusiastically.

He was a young man new in his job and eager to please. He didn't seem to appreciate that this wasn't a training exercise. A real human being had been killed and dismembered, and the person or persons who had caused this poor man's death had escaped. Fleeing the scene constituted a criminal act.

The plastic bottle floated to the surface. It bobbed around for a minute and then strained against a current pushing it southward. Charley had done everything I'd asked to mark the location of where he'd found the arm.

The man himself emerged from the depths a moment later. I stretched out my forearm and pulled him onto the nonslip swimming platform.

"I didn't see the rest of the body down there, but if Neil wants to lend me his mask, snorkel, and fins, I don't mind playing Jacques Cousteau."

"Unfortunately, we don't have a flashlight that works underwater," I said softly. "Besides, I need you to bring the arm ashore and deliver it to the death scene examiner when they appear on the scene."

"What do you plan on doing, Mike?"

"I'm going to stay out here with Galen Webb until a warden boat arrives."

"Can't the constable transport the severed appendage?"

Even at Charley's advanced age, he always wanted to be at the center of the action. He was like a dog that can't stand being separated from his people.

"You understand chain of custody at least. I don't trust Galen with evidence this important."

"Did you examine the arm?"

"No."

"Mind if I have a look?"

"As long as you don't touch it again." I carefully opened the bag just enough to reveal the hand and wrist.

"That's an expensive-looking watch," Charley observed.

"It's a Rolex Daytona, the new model," said Neil, who was a collector of luxury timepieces and had gifted me with his old Seiko Marinemaster for my thirtieth birthday. "Those aren't easy to come by unless you have a relationship with a dealer or are willing to pay well above MSRP."

"No wedding ring," I noted.

"He took it off," said Stacey. "See that indentation beneath the second knuckle of his ring finger? Married guys think they're fooling women in bars, but we know what to look for."

Neil had a more trusting response. "Maybe he didn't want to lose it swimming. I know people whose wedding rings have slipped off in cold water."

"I recognize that watch!" Galen had used his paddle to maneuver the boat close enough to eavesdrop and get a glance at the wrist protruding from the mouth of the bag. "It belongs to Mr. Whitcomb. He and his wife own Mouse Island. I asked him once if his Rolex was real or a counterfeit, and he thought that was the funniest thing he'd ever heard."

"Are you sure the name's not Fenton?" I asked.

"Oh! I see how you might be confused. Mouse is owned by a lady named Dianne Fenton-Whitcomb. She's a member of the lakes association and a big-time donor. I've never met her in person as far as I know. I've only ever dealt with her husband. That boat tied to the dock belongs to Mr. Whitcomb. I'm a hundred and ten percent sure of it. He keeps it at Great Pond Marina. He's a cool guy. Very friendly and generous for a dude from Massachusetts."

I was about to ask him what he meant by *generous,* but Stacey interrupted.

"What's Mr. Whitcomb's first name?"

"He calls himself Kip." He smiled and reached up under the brim of his cap to scratch his acne-scarred forehead. "Gee, I just realized I didn't catch *your* names in all the commotion."

"I haven't properly introduced everyone," said Neil, collecting himself. "Galen, this is my son, Mike Bowditch. He's an investigator with the Warden Service. Mike, this is our lake constable, Galen Webb."

"Nice to meet you," I said.

"Privilege to meet you, Warden. Mr. Turner has told me a lot about you. Says you're a real hero."

Two things surprised me about this statement.

The first was that Neil had always referred to me as his *stepson.*

The second was that I couldn't imagine him *boasting* about me to strangers. I'd been under the impression that I was rarely in his thoughts, especially since his remarriage. Driving with Stacey to Belgrade, I'd expressed my misgivings that he and Jubilee had felt obligated to throw us an engagement party, even a private one.

"I don't think you're giving him enough credit," she'd said.

"All we ever had in common was my mom."

She'd laughed at that. "And you don't think that was sufficient?"

Charley had put his clothes back on in time for Neil to introduce him and Stacey, too.

"Do you know the names of everyone who owns property on Great Pond, Constable Webb?" she asked. "It seems like a pretty large lake."

"Call me Galen. Yeah, I've studied the membership roster of the lakes association. And I've got a copy of the property deed map for this lake as well as Salmon, Messalonskee, and Long Pond. I figured it would help me do my job better, knowing who's who out here."

"Good for you, young man." Charley, I could tell, was genuinely impressed by the young officer's can-do spirit.

"The info's already come in handy," Galen said, energized by the old man's approval. "I caught a father and his little girl trespassing on one of the islands, falsely claiming to be the owners. Those were my first arrests."

Stacey drew our attention to flashing blue lights coming from Neil's property, half a mile to the east on the mainland. "Looks like someone with a badge has arrived at the house."

"You'd better head back, Neil," I said. "Charley will handle everything with the arm."

My stepfather looked like he'd had the wind knocked out of him. "That arm . . . it's the most terrible thing I've ever seen."

I envied him his innocence.

"Galen, you don't mind staying out here with me, do you?"

"I'm at your service, Warden Bowditch," he said. "Just say the word, and I will do it."

"What about me, Warden?" said Stacey. "What are my orders?"

"I assumed you'd want to go back with Neil and your dad."

She shook her head in feigned amazement. "How can we be getting married, and you don't know me at all, Mike Bowditch?"

6

A bass jumped to our left. It sounded like a big fish. There are northern pike in Great Pond, too, some as heavy as thirty pounds, but the toothy predators rarely left the water unless they were hooked.

I retrieved my phone from my rucksack to make an overdue call.

The lieutenant in charge of Warden Division B was a man named Rick LaJoy, who worked out of the local headquarters in Sidney. He and his wardens would be backstopping me on this investigation. I assumed LaJoy would want me working as case manager, since I'd been first on the scene, but the man was something of a cipher, not just to me but to his own officers.

Physically, he was an imposing figure. Six feet eight inches tall. In school, I'd heard, he'd been invited onto the basketball team for no other reason than that he could swat down layups and pull down rebounds. He'd been born with a harelip that had been surgically repaired but that, forty years later, still afflicted him with self-consciousness and perhaps made him less inclined to speak. He had a habit of touching the scar with the tip of his tongue while engaged in quiet contemplation.

LaJoy was frequently engaged in quiet contemplation. He was a sphynx, impossible to read, the most reserved person I had ever met.

Charley summed him up best. "If still waters run deep, then Lieutenant Richard LaJoy is the Mariana Trench."

"Hello?" I said into the phone.

There was a long pause. "Yes?"

"Lieutenant LaJoy. This is Mike Bowditch."

"Yes?"

"I am on Great Pond. My stepfather owns a house here. There's been a boating fatality. A swimmer was apparently struck by a powerboat, and his arm was severed by the propeller, I'm guessing."

"I've heard the news."

I was tempted to ask how, then realized that word of the grisly accident must be spreading through law enforcement circles, given that a death scene examiner had been called to retrieve an amputated limb from a party boat fridge.

LaJoy seemed to be waiting for me to add information to what he already knew. Since I couldn't expect engaged responses, I decided to pretend that I was giving a speech to a remote audience. I started by saying, "Here's everything I know so far," and proceeded from there while the lieutenant listened in silence.

When I'd finished, he waited a whole minute before answering. "You didn't see the boat, then?"

"No."

A pause and then: "Shit."

A meteor flashed across the sky. It was gone before I could turn my head to follow its trajectory. The Perseids had peaked the previous month; the Orionids were weeks away. We had entered a period without major showers, when meteors were sporadic and, therefore, more surprising—even portentous.

"I'm here with the lake constable, Galen Webb. I'm in his boat at the moment."

"I know Webb. He's a promising young man."

The lieutenant's assessment went against the rumors I'd heard. If we'd been alone and not dealing with a death, I might have asked him what he knew about Webb that merited such praise.

"Send me your coordinates," LaJoy said.

"Will do. I haven't contacted the district attorney yet."

"I'm on it."

Then he hung up.

As I was texting him the longitude and latitude, I happened to notice a spiral of red cord dangling from the console beside the ignition. It was the boat's kill switch, sometimes called *the dead man's switch*. Its purpose was to stop the engine if, for whatever reason, the driver fell overboard. The idea was that Galen, in this case, would clip the stretchable cord to his person as a precaution against some mishap.

I motioned toward the coiling wire. "You should put that on."

His lips parted beneath his mustache in a disbelieving smile. "I'm not going to fall out of the boat!"

"I've known it to happen. A man trolling in Moosehead slipped and went into the water while his motorboat continued straight across the lake. We found it run aground in Rockwood. The divers recovered his body off Mount Kineo, a mile away."

When Galen could see I wasn't joking, he grudgingly clipped himself to the console.

"What's this?" Stacey was staring at the boat's fish finder.

It was a more expensive version of Neil's Humminbird. The glowing display showed a split screen. One half was a nautical chart of Great Pond, with our position south of Mouse Island indicated by a boat icon. The other half of the display was what had caught Stacey's attention. I understood why at once.

"You didn't mention you have sonar," I said to Galen.

"Pretty cool, isn't it? It's got down imaging, side imaging, dual spectrum . . ."

The same technology, in other words, that the wardens would use to locate the corpse of our missing man. The side-scan sonar employed by the dive team would be far more sensitive and offer better resolution and greater detail than Galen's fishing model. But the humble Humminbird gave us a valuable tool if we utilized it correctly.

"We can use your depth finder to plot a grid," I explained. "We're in seventeen feet of water here, beyond reach of any light. But CHIRP will reveal structure and irregularities along the bottom."

"Is that an acronym?" Stacey asked. "CHIRP?"

"It stands for *compressed high-intensity radar pulse*. See this shape off to our portside? It's clearly a sunken log."

Galen Webb leaned over the monitor. "What about this blobby thing?"

I peered closer. "Oh my God."

"What?" said Stacey.

Before the pontoon boat departed, I had asked Neil to borrow his snorkeling gear "just in case." I peeled my shirt over my head. "I need that mask and those fins. And it would help if you jury-rigged another buoy marker."

"Wait!" the constable said, swirling his finger over the pixelated shadow. "Do you think this blob is Mr. Whitcomb?"

"Only one way to find out."

The challenge was daunting. To reach the unknown object, I would have to swim straight down and then extend my arms; I needed to measure a distance of seven feet from the boat. From there, it was imperative that I maintain a straight line as I moved through the darkness, feeling my way through the silt and mussel shells. There were excellent reasons recovery diving was best left to professionals.

Galen offered me a big orange flashlight. "I've got a waterproof lantern if you want it."

Now he tells me.

"It won't be much help," I said. "I'll be basically diving blind down there, and this won't light more than a couple of feet at most. But I'll take it."

I didn't strip all the way down to my skivvies like Charley had; I left on my chinos against the cold water. I slid my bare feet into the fins, fastened the mask over my face with the snorkel to one side. When I sat down on the gunwale, Stacey instinctively moved to the opposite side of the boat for balance.

"I still need a marker."

"Here you go."

Galen handed me the end of a wet coil of rope. To the other end, he was attaching a fluorescent yellow ResQFlare. It was an electronic beacon used by vessels in distress. The floating light gave off three emergency flashes, and I knew from personal experience that the pulses would be visible for miles.

Stacey faced me across the boat, her arms spread along the gunwales to steady herself. "Don't get eaten by a pike down there."

I let myself fall backward into the black water.

7

The top layer was only slightly cooler than the air above, but the deeper I dove, the colder it got. I was glad for the assistance of the fins. A few kicks of my legs powered me into the darkness. The mask kept the murky water out of my eyes, but I might as well have been blind. I bit down on the mouthpiece of the snorkel, willing myself to descend into what my irrational mind perceived as an abyss.

Underwater, my hearing became acute. I heard feet moving around on the Crestliner. Beneath those thuds and clanks was the sonorous living presence of the lake. Then the dull sloshing gave way to pressure against my eardrums.

I swam with my arms stretched in front of me, one hand clutching the line, the other gripping the lantern. The glass of the swim mask had seemingly turned opaque. But I perceived a brief explosion of black glitter when I finally touched bottom. Silty sand blanketed the lake floor here: the accumulation of centuries of farmland runoff.

I figured I should be able to hold my breath for three minutes tops. In that time, I would need to find something to secure the line so that, after I resurfaced and dove again, I could return to where I'd left off searching.

With my bare chest pressed into the silt, I reached left, hoping to find a handhold to pull myself laterally. But I came away with nothing but a palmful of sand and decomposing plant matter.

The coldness of the water had raised goose bumps over my entire body, and I began to shiver.

Left again now, using my wingspan, to measure distance.

I am totally fucking this up.

This time, my hand closed around a stick, a broken branch of a submerged tree. I took advantage of the grip and pulled myself into what I prayed was my intended search lane. Divers called the line they used to maintain course a *jackstay,* but I had no such navigational aid.

It was hard, with the flippers, to creep along at a crayfish pace. But I feared missing the body if I shot forward too fast.

Then I felt something fleshy brush my shoulders and the back of my scalp.

I had expected, from the grainy image on the depth finder, to find that the cadaver had come to rest on the bottom. But I had forgotten the lesson I had tried to teach Galen about the variable movements of human remains underwater. The newly dead man hadn't lost all his buoyancy. Without meaning to, I had crawled under the floating corpse. Kip Whitcomb now seemed to be riding my back.

Air bubbled out of my snorkel in a reflex gasp.

In my panic, I released the boating flashlight Galen had given me. It had been designed to float if dropped in the water. I watched its pinwheeling light disappear as it rose to the surface.

I could have sworn the cadaver was animate; the undead thing seemed to be pushing me down with its weight, trying to drown me.

I rolled onto my back and felt the body with my left hand. Whitcomb, presuming it was Whitcomb, was floating facedown. I was glad of my blindness because I didn't care to look into the dead eyes. My fingertips brushed icy skin. He was, I realized, totally naked. Then I touched the pulpy stump where his arm had been, discovered the shards of snapped bone amid shredded tissue.

The current and the chemical process his body was undergoing had already moved him away from the scene of the collision. I could make a good case for letting go of the line, wrapping my arms around his torso, and bringing it up into the air, crime scene be damned.

Then I recalled a diatribe Sergeant Bill Boone, chief of the dive team, had leveled at me and my fellow investigators.

"Most public safety divers don't have the sense God gave a goose," he'd said in his East Texas accent. "Your victim ain't gonna get any deader than he already is, gents. Remember that an underwater crime scene is still a damned crime scene. I dare you to tell a family how you messed up a murder investigation because you wanted to bring up the remains quick and be the hero of the hour."

My lungs desperately needed oxygen. They demanded it.

Then I heard Boone shouting in my head. "*Decide, Bowditch!*"

My own buoyancy was causing me to rise against the drifting body. The contact of living flesh against dead flesh was at once intimate and repulsive. I felt for a bare leg and looped the slimy rope around the ankle. As a teenager, I had taught myself to tie knots blindfolded. I made a couple of half hitches to secure the beacon. Kaleidoscopes began to twirl behind my clenched eyelids. There was no time to double-check the knots. I had seconds left before I inhaled lake water or blacked out altogether.

I used the soft bottom of the pond to push up, feeling the slimy line brush me as Whitcomb continued his subsurface wanderings.

One kick, then another, and I was above water again. I spat out the snorkel to gulp air.

The Crestliner was behind me now. I peeled up the mask, breaking the seal. Treading water, I saw Stacey leaning out over the bow with an arm outstretched, although I was many yards away.

"What happened?" she asked. "We saw the flashlight pop to the surface and thought you were in trouble. I was ready to dive in after you."

"I got a fright is all."

"The beacon is moving," she said. "Did you lose it?"

"No, I tied the line around his leg. I think the flare is reaching the end of its tether. The rope should straighten out soon."

"You actually found the body?" Galen Webb sounded gobsmacked.

I had begun to shiver. "I did."

"Why didn't you bring him up?"

Chilled to the marrow, I felt no desire to explain myself to the young constable.

"He's not going far, and even if he continues to drift, we've got the flare to track him."

"I can't believe you actually found him in the dark!" said Galen, sounding younger than his years as his voice rose with excitement.

"It's how recovery divers conduct their searches, feeling their way to the corpse." I began to sidestroke toward the boat. "I don't see myself joining the dive team after this, though. Groping in the dark for a naked corpse is not an experience I need to repeat. Can someone give me a hand up?"

Stacey closed her hands around my wrists. She possessed her father's wiry strength. The boat began to tip, but Galen shifted his position, and I gave several awkward kicks with my fins. It was enough to get my armpits over the gunwales, and from there, I tumbled into the bottom of the boat.

"What a night." Stacey knelt to remove the flippers from my blue feet.

"And it's not even over."

"It's horrible, Mike. You need to find the sons of bitches that did this."

I pledged to her that I would. The person or persons who'd struck Kip Whitcomb while he was swimming must have known what they'd done. They had turned the boat around for another look. Their decision to run had been cowardly at best. You can never avenge any death in law enforcement; you simply can't. But if you do your job, you make punishment possible and show society that we are all accountable for our misdeeds. It's a reminder the world needs daily, unfortunately.

Galen didn't have a towel for me, so I had to content myself with dripping dry in the night air. My chinos clung coldly to my thighs. After a while, I pulled my Henley and socks back on and laced up my boots again. Both my shirt and my stockings were made of merino wool, which retained heat even when wet. It didn't make being soaked any more pleasant.

I told Galen to call in our coordinates to Lieutenant LaJoy. Rick could then pass the location on to Bill Boone and his team. The divers wouldn't begin their work until morning. I had always known night diving was dangerous. I now had a better idea of just how dangerous it could be.

Stacey continued to kneel before me, rubbing my wet thighs to warm them. "Could you see anything at all?"

"Nothing."

"What did you feel?"

"The stump where he lost his arm. Beyond that—"

"It's got to be Mr. Whitcomb," Galen said, eavesdropping again. "The island is right there!"

A child with water wings could have crossed the short distance between the Crestliner and the dock at the southwestern tip. We'd found the severed arm where the lake was shallower. The impact of the boat hitting the body, and the slicing motion of the propeller or propellers, must have given momentum to the severed limb. How far it had been carried away from the body spoke to the violence of the collision.

"What do you want to do now?" asked Stacey.

"Drink a gallon of hot coffee."

"I only have some Sprite," Galen offered. "But you're welcome to it."

"I was joking." I fixed my eyes on the constable. "Can you drop us at the Mouse Island dock? It's past time we had a look around."

8

He piloted the Crestliner alongside the dock, opposite Kip Whitcomb's runabout. Instead of tying the painter to a cleat, Stacey held the edge of the dock so that I could step out. I returned the favor, kneeling on the splintery planks, holding the boat by the gunwale, so she could come ashore.

"What about me?" Galen all but whined.

"I need you to keep watch on that ResQFlare and tell any wardens who arrive to wait for my signal before landing here. If something bad happened, I don't want a bunch of boots trampling the evidence."

His response took me aback by its unexpected arrogance. He'd been so accommodating, almost obsequious, before. "Isn't that for a detective to decide?"

"It's certainly not for the lake constable. You told me you'd follow my orders, Galen. I'm giving you one to watch that beacon."

He wouldn't back down without a fight. "You've never set foot here, but I have. Whose observations are going to be more useful? Yours or mine?"

"In that case, I'll take advantage of your knowledge," I said, feeling myself growing more and more resentful of the punkish attitude. "Before you go, what more can you tell us about Kip Whitcomb and his wife . . . ?"

"Dianne," he said sharply. "Dianne Fenton-Whitcomb, according to the lakes association."

"You said you never spoke with her."

"No, but . . ."

"What?"

He smoothed his little mustache with his thumb and forefinger. "I knew Mr. Whitcomb from around town. He showed me around the island once. How many tours did he give you?"

"Was he usually out here alone, or did he ever bring company?" Stacey asked before I could bite his head off.

Galen Webb had a lopsided grin. "Company? Yeah, I guess you could call them that. My mom might use a different word."

"Whitcomb brought other women here?" I said. "Why don't you get over your hurt pride, Galen, and stop jerking us around and tell us what you know. Should we be looking for a female companion or not?"

He dug his hands into the pockets of his jeans, forcing them even lower down his hips. "I didn't see him this weekend, so I can't tell you. But the guys at Great Pond Marina probably know if he had someone with him. That's where he parks his car. Do you want me to call them and ask?"

"Be my guest. And ask them if they got a name or any other identifying information on whomever he might have brought with him to the island."

After he'd left us, Stacey asked, "What was *that* about?"

"Galen applied to become a game warden this past winter but was shot down by the hiring committee—something about his temperament being unsuited to a career in law enforcement. It makes sense he has a chip on his shoulder. Did you get the same feeling I did, that he was deliberately withholding information about the owners?"

"There was definitely something he wasn't sharing with us."

I shined my flashlight into the runabout tied to a pair of cleats beside us. The dock might have been weathered and sagging and in need of replacement, but the boat was a luxurious indulgence. Some might have said that the Chris-Craft Capri was too good for these waters. It possessed a fiberglass hull, but its bow was covered with varnished teak, its steering wheel was wrapped with leather, as were the two chairs behind the dash, which had been designed in a retro manner with dials and displays recalling the heyday of ostentatious runabouts in the 1930s.

"Fancy!" said Stacey while I snapped a photo of the registration and texted it to dispatch for identification. "How much do you think one of these goes for?"

"More than my house."

"Soon to be *our* house."

Aside from some smashed bugs on the windscreen and a few curling birch leaves that had drifted into the cabin, the boat appeared spotless, as if it had come directly to the island from the marina without so much as a detour.

My cell chimed with a text replying to my inquiry about the boat's registration.

"It belongs to Whitcomb, all right. Get this. His first name is Kipling!"

"I can't say I've met one of those before."

"You've never met a Jubilee, either."

"It's a weekend of firsts."

"No wonder he went by 'Kip,'" I said. "The dispatcher says he lived in a town in Massachusetts called Medway. I don't know it. Do you?"

"It's south of Boston, near Foxborough, I think. It's a wealthy suburb, which means he was probably loaded. I guess the boat told us that."

"Or he wanted people to think he was rich. This runabout could be heavily financed."

"He owned an island in one of the toniest lakes in Maine, Mike."

"According to Galen, the deed is in his wife's name. Dianne Fenton-Whitcomb must have inherited Mouse Island from her parents."

Stacey turned the beam of her headlamp to the shore where a gap between the trees indicated a path wide enough to haul building supplies and carts full of provisions up to the house.

"We should be looking for the woman he was with," she said.

"From what Galen told us, it seems safe to conclude she wasn't his wife."

"Could she have ran over him? Maybe she hit him accidentally with his own boat?"

The Capri had an inboard engine, invisible to the naked eye above the waterline. Nevertheless, I squatted down and probed the stern with my light. I saw no damage, nor signs of blood.

"If the man who brought you to 'his' private island disappeared while swimming, wouldn't you call for help?"

"Me, yes. But if I had a jealous husband at home, I might be paralyzed with second thoughts. And we can't be sure she's safe, either. Her body might be out in the lake, too, for all we know."

"I say we knock on the door and see who's home."

The light from her headlamp bounced as she nodded her agreement.

But we hadn't made it ten feet into the trees when we heard the roar of yet another motorboat racing toward the island. We watched its lights grow brighter until it swung alongside Galen Webb's Crestliner.

Indecipherable shouts, a man's questioning voice, came from the strange craft. Fainter replies followed from Galen.

Then the unknown powerboat gunned its engine and made a line for the dock. My first thought was that it belonged to Lieutenant LaJoy or some other warden. Then I saw that the boat wasn't any model in our fleet but rather a flat-decked fishing boat made for nuzzling into the shallows in pursuit of trophy bass.

We advanced back down the dock to catch the stranger's line and knot it around a cleat.

Our lights revealed a man of late middle age, wearing a navy windbreaker over a Hawaiian shirt, relaxed-fit jeans, and flip-flops. He had ginger hair that was making a quick retreat from his forehead and a stony chin that would break your fist if you managed to land a punch on it.

When he tossed the painter to Stacey to make fast, I saw the badge on his belt and a holstered Heckler & Koch handgun. I didn't have to see the back of his jacket to know it said STATE POLICE across the shoulders.

Before I could ask what Roger Finch was doing here, miles north of his designated barracks, he glared at me with disbelief. "I should have known you were involved in this shit show, Bowditch. What's that that line from the Dirty Harry movie? 'People have a nasty habit of getting dead around you.'"

"It's good to see you, too, Detective."

9

I could never decide whether Roger Finch disliked me or only pretended to dislike me. The truth was, I doubt he gave me much thought except on those occasions when I'd blundered into his way. In each of our previous encounters, I'd forced him to question the path he'd been pursuing. The detective was a man who hated to depart from a predetermined route even when presented with proof that he was headed in the wrong direction. Especially when presented with proof.

He gestured with his thumb toward the lights of the Crestliner, anchored along the seam where the shallows dropped into the depths. "That kid tells me you found the body. Why didn't you bring it up?"

"That kid is the lake constable," said Stacey. "He's a deputy sheriff."

I didn't share her desire to defend Galen's honor, so I contented myself with answering the question. "The area is a crime scene, even if it's underwater. Where the corpse ended up will help determine where the collision took place."

"He said it was drifting."

"We can still make certain calculations based on physics and the lake's hydraulics."

Finch shook off his windbreaker and tossed it in his bass boat. His face shone with perspiration from the unseasonable humidity. "Forensic mapping. I get it."

"How is it you got here before anyone else?" I asked.

He ran a sweaty hand through his hair. "My wife and I rent a cabin up at Mosher's Sporting Lodge on North Bay every Memorial Day and every Labor Day. We spend the weekend fishing for pike."

"Fly fishing?"

He pushed air through his teeth at the absurdity of the suggestion. "We use bait. Some people actually want to catch fish and not show off their beautiful casting. What's the name of our victim?"

"Kip Whitcomb."

"And he owns this island?"

"His wife does—Dianne Fenton-Whitcomb."

"Sounds like the name of a law firm. Is she up at the house?"

"We haven't been there yet. We don't know who's there and who isn't. But Constable Webb believes Whitcomb came out here with a woman not his wife."

"That's pretty ballsy, using your wife's island for your private love nest." Finch reached down for what I realized was his murder bag: the kit that contained the forensic items he used at homicide scenes. He tossed me a pair of vinyl boot covers. "In case we need these at the house. I assume you've got your own gloves."

"What about me?" said Stacey, more surprised than affronted.

"You're staying here. It's bad enough I've got to bring Bowditch, but at least he's a warden."

"And this is my investigation," I said, preparing to tell him that Stacey would be accompanying us.

"For the moment."

Not for the first time, she saved me from my anger. "It's fine, Mike. I think I'll stretch out on the dock and do some stargazing while I wait for reinforcements. Maybe I'll get lucky and see some bats."

We kissed goodbye, and I followed Finch down the dock to the benighted shore.

"Will your partner be joining us?" I asked as he motioned me ahead of him. I had the more powerful flashlight, it was true.

"Pomerleau? Yeah, she's on her way. I can't say she'll be happy you interrupted her weekend with her husband and kids."

It was another of his feinting jabs. Finch could have made it to the Olympics if ball-busting were a competitive sport.

Detective Sergeant Ellen Pomerleau outranked her partner despite being younger than him, and Finch didn't need to be a chauvinist to be unhappy with the situation. He'd paid his dues and had done good work, mostly.

"Are we sure it wasn't the wife who ran the guy down? If I die the same way while swimming, have a look at Allison. Be sure my old lady has an alibi."

"Galen Webb says Dianne doesn't come to Maine anymore," I explained.

"Why, I wonder."

The pine needles in the path had been disturbed and scattered by foot traffic, but the ground beneath them was so hard I couldn't detect actual prints. I did spot a pair of shallow wheel ruts leading down to the water and back; Whitcomb must have used a handcart to carry his groceries and bags from the runabout up to the house. I sidestepped these reflexively. Finch couldn't see the marks and so he trod on them.

"You realize you get to deliver the death notice to whoever's home," he said. "It is your investigation, after all."

That was why he'd wanted me to go first. The coward didn't want to be the one to knock at the door with nightmarish news.

It had to be a trick of the light, something about the way the pines wrapped the building in shadows, but the house seemed to loom before me as if it hadn't been there until I raised my eyes from the forest floor. That the windows shone like black mirrors when my light touched the glass only added to the creepiness.

It was a two-story clapboard cottage, built in the old Maine summer style with no foundation. Instead, it was raised up on supports with a crawl space walled with broken latticework. A steep set of stairs ascended to a porch that ran along the front. The house was in such disrepair I might have thought it had been abandoned if I hadn't known better. The steps were crooked from roots bulging beneath them. The clapboards were warped and weathered. Asphalt shingles lay where the wind had tossed them, accumulating moss.

It had been another bone-dry summer in Maine. Half the evergreens around the lake had turned rusty or dropped their needles altogether. And my first thought, looking at the dried-out ruin, was: *This place is a tinderbox.*

My second thought was: *Why is the front door open?*

"Who leaves a door wide open when they go for a swim?" I asked, ignoring the obvious answer. "Unlocked, yes. But ajar like that?"

I took the lead going up the unlevel stairs. Stopping on the porch, I poked the flashlight beam through the front door, where it found first a table with an extinguished kerosene lamp and then the rest of the room beyond. The odor was of musty furniture, a chimney choked with creosote, and brittle paper from ancient paperbacks.

"Hello?" I said in the loudest voice I could manage short of shouting. "This is the police. Is anyone home?"

Finch rapped with his big fist against the doorframe. "Police!"

"Do you think this qualifies as exigent circumstances?"

"If a dismembered body and an open door don't justify us going in, I don't know what does. That doesn't mean we won't be reamed out by the AG's office if something goes sideways. But I'm not going to wait here for two hours for a judge to sign off on a warrant."

The doormat was made of rough fiber for scraping the mud and sand off your feet. It had a motto printed on it:

I'D RATHER BE LOST
AT THE LAKE
THAN FOUND AT HOME

The same kitschy décor continued inside. I spotted a framed cover from *The Saturday Evening Post* showing a fisherman squinting at the fly he couldn't see well enough to tie onto his leader while trout jumped around his hip waders.

"Hello?" I called again as I stepped inside and swept the low-ceilinged space with the light.

The beam stopped seemingly of its own accord on the dinner table. There were two place settings. Between them was a platter of overturned oyster shells and smaller plates wet with mignonette. Crackers spilled from a cutting board on which was a crumbling hunk of blue cheese. In the center of everything was a guttered candle and a half-empty bottle of tequila beside a pair of shot glasses.

"Two people, it looks like," I said. "A man and a woman."

Finch sighed. "Or a man and a man. Or a woman and a woman. These days—"

"I just meant it looks like a romantic dinner. They made a pretty good dent in that bottle of Código tonight."

"That explains the stupid decision to go for a moonlight swim in a boat lane."

"It's like a scene from the *Mary Celeste*."

"Who's Mary Celeste?" Finch asked.

"Not *who*. *What*. The *Mary Celeste* was a brigantine discovered adrift and deserted off the Azores. She was the original ghost ship."

"Well, this place feels like a haunted house, I'll give you that," he said. "What I still want to know is, where's the mystery woman?"

"It might be time we got a warrant if we intend to keep searching."

"You do that. Meanwhile I'm going to have a look upstairs in the bedrooms."

I hesitated.

"Since when did you become a Boy Scout, Bowditch?"

"All right," I said.

The funny thing was that Finch made me go first.

10

The lowest step groaned as I planted my boot on it.

A staggered series of family photographs hung along the staircase. The frames and glass were coated with dust, making them appear even older than they were.

The first picture showed a man and woman of late middle age posed in front of this same cottage in its glorious, unrecognizable heyday. The father was clutching the hand of a little girl who looked to be about three years old. The mother was holding a baby of indeterminate sex.

If Charley hadn't told me Coleman Fenton had been a judge, I might have guessed it from his unforgiving expression alone. I have read in novels of eyes as black as coal, but his truly were. His hair was also black and slickly parted. His eyebrows were heavy and black. He was a powerfully built man who looked capable of personally delivering whatever punishments he handed out.

His wife was an ash blonde—pretty, but sad in a way her smile couldn't conceal. Maybe *sadness* was the wrong word. There was something off about her expression, as if her sorrow went deeper than a passing emotion.

The little girl was as dark-haired as her dad but possessed a doll-like beauty. Her wide-eyed face was utterly symmetrical. She looked too perfect to be real.

The baby was just a baby—eyes and mouth scrunched.

"Are you going to stand there all night?" said the detective.

I could feel his breath on my neck as he tried pushing me forward. There would be time to examine the other portraits, I decided.

The doors along the upstairs hall were all shut except for the one at the end, which would have had the best view of the lake before the trees had closed in.

More kitsch on the walls: A taxidermied salmon with an actual cigar wedged in its mouth. A *Bambi* movie poster with crosshairs drawn with a marker over the head of the iconic fawn.

I couldn't help but wonder whether it had been Coleman Fenton who possessed the ironic personality or his pallid wife. My money was on the judge. As someone with a perverse sense of humor myself—though not to this extreme—I recognized how it tended to appear in people prone to arrogance.

"Hello? Is anyone there? This is the police. Are you all right?"

"There's no one here," pronounced Finch.

"Then we should get a warrant."

"Not until we ID the missing girl." He edged past me through the door of the master bedroom.

His own weak flashlight revealed an unmade bed. The top sheet and blanket lay in a heap at the bottom as if kicked aside in the throes of passion. The fitted sheet was sodden with perspiration that smelled of sex and perfume.

"At least he went out with a bang," said the detective.

"That's classless, Roger."

"So's cheating on your wife. Have a look at this."

At first, I thought Finch was indicating a coffee mug on the bedside table. The cracked cup was a souvenir from a historic boys' summer camp on Pine Island, at the south end of Great Pond.

But, in fact, the detective was pointing at the saucer beside the mug. In it were two wedding rings: one large and gold, one small and silver.

"Christ," I said.

"What?"

"Two rings, two swimmers. Whitcomb is dead, but the woman might not be. We need to start a full-on search. There might be a person out in the pond who is injured or on the verge of drowning."

"Do you still think we should have waited for a warrant?" Finch moved around the bed, pulling on a pair of nitrile gloves. "Here's the luggage. And their phones. And their wallets. We need to know who we're looking for."

Finch opened the woman's pink wallet first. It looked like a knockoff of some designer brand. He removed a lone Visa and a T.J. Maxx card before locating a driver's license. His expression transformed from smug indifference to utter surprise. He licked his lips as if they'd gone suddenly dry.

"Who is she?" I asked.

He held out a Maine driver's license from which a brown-haired, brown-eyed young woman stared intensely. Gina Randazza, age twenty-two, had chosen not to smile for the photographer at the DMV. She wore a jeweled stud in her nostril and a defiant expression.

Her height was given as five feet; her weight was ninety pounds. She lived on a street in the nearby city of Waterville, where I had attended college, a street in a seedy section of town where Colby students never visited. She had a restriction on her license. An asterisk meant she had been convicted of operating under the influence of intoxicating liquors—or OUI in Maine parlance.

Finch finally managed to speak. "I know her."

"You do? How?"

"I mean I know her piece-of-shit husband. He's a biker named Joey Randazza. The guy's a career criminal and member of a second-rate motorcycle club, the Direwolves. They're an affiliate of the Outlaws. Maybe you heard of the Outlaws? One of the Big Four motorcycle gangs?"

"How do you know Randazza?"

"We had a run-in on Route 27 this spring," he said almost dreamily. "Gina was on the back of his Harley. He was with four or five of his crew and their women when I pulled them over for speeding through Belgrade Village. It was close to midnight, and they got off their bikes and surrounded me. I came close to pulling my piece before they backed off."

"Does Joey own a boat?"

"If he doesn't, one of his brother bikers does. Fuck, he must have killed Whitcomb. Gina, too, probably."

"We don't know her husband had anything to do with this. We don't even know she's dead, Roger."

"So where the hell is she?"

His entire affect had changed before my eyes; the swagger and jokiness were gone. Detective Roger Finch looked uncertain, even afraid as he reached for the man's wallet on the bedside table.

The billfold was made of burgundy cordovan. Finch popped it open and revealed several hundred-dollar bills, a Mastercard Black Card, and a platinum AmEx.

He smirked when he located Whitcomb's driver's license. He all but tossed it at me.

In life, Kipling Whitcomb had stood six feet one inches tall and weighed 175 pounds. He was thirty-five years old. He lived on Charles Lane in the town of Medway, Massachusetts. I wouldn't have described him as handsome, but he had a full head of chestnut curls, imploring eyes, and a broad smile. He reminded me of an over-eager spaniel.

Two cell phones lay side by side on a bureau. One was the latest, greatest iPhone; the other was an old Android in a sparkly protective case. Both were undoubtedly locked. We would need to secure a warrant for the cyber guys to breach the passwords and extract whatever relevant information might be stored on them.

Finch had by now moved on to a purple carry-on bag. He knelt beside it and tugged at the zipper.

"We should definitely get a warrant for that," I said.

"Why?"

"Because we have enough information now to confirm we're looking for two people. Whitcomb we've found, deceased. But as long as we're unsure about Randazza, she has a right to privacy."

"We found her bag open," he said, then unzipped the little suitcase, exposing its contents. I saw folded clothes. A makeup bag. "See? Everything was in plain view."

"No, it wasn't." It was a strange day when I was the officer in the room arguing we needed to stick to the rules.

I hadn't realized the window was cracked open until I heard an outboard approaching the island. There was no view of the dock through the trees. But I was certain I heard a man shout my name from the newly arrived boat.

"I need to get down there," I said. "Zip that bag back up, Roger. You know how Pomerleau feels about warrantless searches. Don't put me in an awkward position with your partner here."

Finch, on his knees, returned my command with a glare. I had no doubt he would rifle through the suitcase as soon as I'd left the room.

11

By the time I reached the shore, the boat I'd heard approaching had come alongside the dock. I had expected to find Stacey greeting the new arrivals, but she was nowhere to be seen.

Where the hell is she?

The boat was a standard-issue Lund, a newer version of the one parked on a trailer in my yard. This craft had been assigned to Lieutenant Rick LaJoy. The tall man had already stepped onto the dock to take the hand of his passenger, a woman whose ivory-colored hair I would have recognized from a mile away. There was no mistaking Finch's partner, Detective Sergeant Ellen Pomerleau.

"Hello, Mike," she said. "Happy Labor Day."

"Sorry to bring you out for this, Ellen."

"It's not you I blame. As soon as I heard Roger had raced out here from Mosher's, I had no choice but to change out of my jammies."

The moonlight brought out all the qualities that made Ellen Pomerleau such an unusual and interesting-looking woman. She was spectacularly pale, almost devoid of pigment, with hair more white than blond. Scientists hadn't invented a cream strong enough to protect her skin from ultraviolet radiation. Her eyes were photosensitive to the point where she often wore shades indoors.

Her natural pallor was intensified by her choice of clothing, which was always black. For tonight's lake cruise, she had chosen a black suit with black leather sneakers. The inky outfit made her trim figure appear even more skeletal.

LaJoy hadn't uttered a word but stood silent as a monolith. He was the tallest man in the Warden Service by several inches. As someone who isn't short, I always found it odd looking up at the underside of his jaw.

"Has the lieutenant brought you up to speed?" I asked Pomerleau.

"I'm assuming there have been new developments. But yeah, this sounds like a grisly one. When you get around to writing your memoirs, you can title this chapter, 'Death and Dismemberment on Golden Pond.'"

"You're betting I'll live long enough to write my memoirs."

"I'll take the under on that bet," she said.

"Where's Finch?" LaJoy asked in the deep bass voice you would expect out of a giant.

"Up at the house. There's a woman missing, too. Our victim's companion. Her name is Gina Randazza."

"Did you say *Randazza*?" asked Pomerleau.

Her knitted brow told me that she knew about her partner's run-in with a biker of that name.

"Finch thinks he knows her husband," I said, hoping to draw information out of her.

But Ellen wasn't going to tell tales out of school. "What's Roger doing while you're down here?"

"Your guess is as good as mine."

She cast a worried glance in the direction of the house. "Who'd you get to sign off on the warrant?"

"We haven't," I said flatly. "Not yet. The door to the house was wide open when we arrived."

She sighed and let her head drop so her chin touched her clavicle. "I'm going to remedy that. Excuse me while I make a call."

When I turned back to the lake, I found myself staring at Lieutenant LaJoy's Adam's apple.

"What's the latest?" he asked.

I did my best to offer him a full account of everything that had happened since Stacey and I had come ashore on Mouse Island, omitting only my dispute with Finch over the need for a search warrant. He listened with the silence of a literal stone.

"Did you speak with Webb on your way past his boat?" I asked innocently.

"Briefly."

"You said you knew and admired him before, and I have been wondering why you said that."

"His family belongs to my church. I've flown with his father many times. The Webbs are good people."

"I suppose you know his application to join the Warden Service was rejected. Based on what I've observed tonight, it was for good reason. The guy is in dire need of an attitude adjustment if he hopes to have a career in law enforcement."

"Maybe we should focus on the boat accident and the search for Mrs. Randazza instead of Galen Webb."

The lieutenant was right. My beef with the constable was insignificant compared with the challenges facing us.

"First we should clear the island," I said. "But if we don't find her, we need to light up this lake."

"I've got a dozen wardens on the way. What have you learned about the boat that struck our victim?"

"Nothing, I'm afraid."

Great Pond covered something like eighty-three square miles in area. There were hundreds of houses, cottages, and cabins along the pond. Some of these properties had boathouses where the damaged vessel could be easily hidden until it was repaired. Or the fleeing boater could have made for a public landing, hauled out their watercraft, and towed it down the road. By now, they might be so far from Belgrade there would be no chance of ever connecting them to the crime.

"We'll take it in steps, then," said LaJoy. "First priority is locating Mrs. Randazza."

There was no irony in his use of her married name. The God-fearing lieutenant was an upright man, and he didn't consider it his place to pass judgment on the actions of a woman who couldn't defend herself. Rick LaJoy was a better man than I.

"I'm going to make a search of the island perimeter," I said.

"Good idea. You mentioned Stacey was with you."

"I don't know where she's gone."

"Maybe you should find her first then."

I heard a loon calling from the direction of Neil's camp, perhaps the same harassed bird Stacey and I had heard before.

LaJoy must have caught me listening to the eerie song. "In Britain, they call them *divers*."

"What's that?"

"Common loons. The colloquial name for the species in the UK is *northern diver.*"

For Rick LaJoy, two sentences were half a monologue. I felt like this statement should have opened a window into the man—he'd read my expression correctly, he'd traveled abroad, he knew his birds—but it would take more than an ornithological aside for me to gain insight into him, I concluded.

The lieutenant surprised me once more by detaching his gaze from mine and moving it to a spot above my head and somewhat to the right. "Hello, Charley."

I spun on my heel to see a small silhouette emerge from the shadows. Then a cloud that was partially obscuring the moon drifted away, and the grinning mug of Charley Stevens was revealed.

That my friend had returned to the scene made perfect sense. The retired warden's face should have appeared in the dictionary beside the word *curious*. Also, *unflagging, audacious,* and *contrary.* What I couldn't fathom was how Charley had gotten out to the island. Neil's Leisure Kraft was nowhere in sight. Nor did my stepfather possess a canoe or kayak that the old man might've borrowed.

I located the answer in the form of a white oblong leaning against a pine trunk.

Jubilee's stand-up paddleboard.

I would have wagered the old pilot didn't even know what the acronym SUP stood for, and yet he had crossed half a mile of open water, in the dark, on a piece of epoxied foam, to reach a place he had no place being.

"What are you doing back here?" I asked.

"I figured my institutional knowledge might be of some help to the investigators."

I turned to the lieutenant. "Charley was once the district warden here."

"I know," said LaJoy with what might even have been a smile. "He'll always be famous for catching that hermit."

His phone buzzed, and he released it from the clip attached to his belt. When he lifted the glowing screen to his face, it revealed the scar from his repaired harelip.

"It's a text from Finch. He's found drugs."

"Of course he did," I said beneath my breath. "In Gina's carry-on, right?"

"LSD and pot. Small amounts."

"Pomerleau's going to be ripshit he didn't wait for a warrant."

"I'd better get up there."

Charley and I watched LaJoy stride on his long shanks into the darkness without need of a flashlight. Most game wardens possessed excellent night vision. And he seemed to know intuitively to avoid the main path lest he disturb whatever evidence the CSI team might find there.

"LaJoy's not much for conversation, is he?" I said.

"Maybe not, but he's one of the best wardens I had the privilege to work with."

"I cannot believe you paddleboarded here."

He cracked a smile that would shame a jack-o'-lantern. "It's not much different from paddling a canoe from a standing position. I'm surprised young people even consider it exercise."

12

Not what you expected for an engagement party, I reckon."

My chinos and underwear were still damp from my swim and growing more uncomfortable by the minute. I wished I'd packed a change of clothes in my warden's rucksack.

"How is everyone doing back at the house?"

"Ora went to sleep. She learned long ago that waiting up for a warden to come home is an exercise in futility. But Jubilee was awake when I left."

My gaze moved in the direction of the mainland, trying to pick out their dock light. "How's Neil faring?"

"He disappeared as soon as we tied up at the dock. Having that arm aboard his boat did a job on his nerves. I offered to take the helm to pilot us across the channel, and he didn't put up a fight. Most men are worried about seeming tough. I respect one who's not afraid to show he's rattled."

Neil couldn't have been less like my biological father in that respect.

As a teenager, I had often wondered what my mom saw in the bland attorney—besides his wealth, patience, and social status. I wondered how she didn't grow bored with him. The former Marie Bowditch possessed a wild, willful, and passionate soul. She had been Cathy to my late father's Heathcliff, to use her own favorite (if inaccurate) literary analogy. So why choose Neil? It didn't occur to me that simple goodness can be irresistibly attractive—especially when you've known so little goodness in your life.

"How did the handoff go with the medical examiner's office?" I asked Charley.

"I hope that wasn't an intentional pun."

I rubbed my tired eyes. "I think this night is beginning to catch up with me."

"All the forms were signed and dated, if that's what you're worried about."

"Chain of evidence matters more than when you were my age."

"I don't envy you that part of the job." He peered into the shadows between the near pines. "What's become of Stacey in all this excitement? That girl is usually in the thick of everyone else's mischief."

"I left her here when Finch and I went up to the house. I honestly don't know where she might have gone."

"This is a small island on which to lose your fiancée."

"She's *your* daughter. Where do you think she might have gone?"

He chuckled at me. "I haven't noticed any tracks from the dock to the outhouse, unless she followed a wayward path there."

"Where else is there to go?"

"There's another cottage on the back side of the island, a log cabin. The judge called it his fishing camp. It faces northeast across the channel toward Camp Machigonne."

He was referring to one of the historic kids' camps that ringed the lake. Presumably Machigonne was closed up for the summer now and unattended. Under the circumstances, I thought it was unlikely we'd find any witnesses to the boat accident on the mainland.

"Does Stacey know about this cabin?"

"I don't see how she could."

"So why would she have gone there?"

"Maybe we should go ask her."

A pine-needle path led around the Fenton house and through the thicket that covered nearly all of Mouse Island. Moonlight fell upon the ground in luminous patches where it was able to penetrate the treetops. We couldn't tell if Stacey had come this way or not, but it seemed worth a look.

It took us all of three minutes to reach the cabin, the island being so small. Unlike the main building, this one had been built out of rough logs with oakum wedged between the cracks. Orange needles lay so thick atop the roof it looked like the pelt of some Muppet. What windows there were had been shuttered against the weather and against trespassers who might find their way onto the island. (Certain ice fishermen and snowmobilers were notorious for breaking into camps, giving a lot of outdoorspeople an undeserved reputation for petty crime.) No light leaked out through the gaps.

"She's not here," I said.

"No, but what do you make of this?"

He squatted down so his headlamp was level with the door. A rusted padlock hung from the latch. The lock was open.

"I doubt Stacey did this," I said, leaning over his shoulder. "Lock-picking isn't in her skill set."

"Are you sure of that? The girl is resourceful."

In fact, I wouldn't have put it past her to have learned safecracking in her travels.

The old man straightened up like a spring uncoiled. "Would you say that the circumstances here still qualified as exigent?"

"If you're going to touch anything, put these on." I handed him a pair of nitrile gloves from my rucksack.

An acrid smell rushed out of the cabin when he pulled open the heavy door. It was even stronger inside. The stench was like a punch in the nose.

Mouse Island was properly named. Mice have a special fondness for nesting in unused appliances like propane ovens and refrigerators. Generations of rodents had stunk up the cabin with their accumulated droppings.

Charley didn't even flinch, he was so focused on the room revealed by my flashlight. Cobwebs hung from the rafters, some filled with dead cluster flies. A half-inch of dust lay on the knife-scarred table where Judge Fenton had filleted the trout and salmon that had once been abundant in this lake. The initials *CJF* had been carved with boyish bravado into the wood long ago.

To me, everything appeared undisturbed, but not to Charley. He squatted on his haunches again and ran a finger along the floor. He raised it to show me that there was minimal dirt on the pad.

"It doesn't appear from the needles out front that Whitcomb's been here in ages. Certainly not this weekend. So why is the floor clean? And why was the lock jimmied?"

"How do you know the lock was jimmied?"

"Because the end of the shackle is shiny, and the keyhole is scraped free of rust by whoever used a pick on it."

Charley stroked his large chin, which was shaped like the toe of a boot. He was in the habit of touching it when he fell into thought. It was another of his old-fashioned mannerisms.

"What are you thinking?" I asked.

He grinned and slowly raised a finger in the air to signal he'd had a brainstorm. Without a word, he scurried outside and began scanning the forest floor until he found what he'd hoped to find. He held aloft a small pine bough fashioned into a makeshift broom. The branches of young conifers are notoriously hard to break or twist off. The end of this one had been sawed with a small blade. Charley shook the bough, precipitating a flurry of dead needles.

"Whoever broke into this place brushed the ground with this sprig to cover his backtrack."

"It could just be a trespasser," I countered. "Galen mentioned that it was a problem all over the Belgrade Lakes—people camping on islands they don't own."

"Could be."

"But you don't believe it."

"A wise man once said that coincidences are God's way of telling you to pay attention."

I knew Charley Stevens well enough that I didn't need to guess the name of the wise man. He was standing right in front of me.

13

My cell phone buzzed. It was Stacey at last.

"I just finished a circuit of the island," she said. "I figured *someone* should check the shoreline in case Whitcomb's companion had crawled out of the water, injured or half-drowned."

"Where are you now?"

Charley recognized how my voice and facial expressions changed when I was speaking to his daughter. His eyes crinkled with amusement.

"I called Galen and asked him if he'd ever seen Whitcomb swimming around the dock. He said no. It's too near the channel, he said. Boats are always speeding back and forth there, sometimes towing water-skiers, tubes, or planer boards."

I turned my face from the phone. "Charley, do you remember where the Fentons used to swim when you patrolled the lake?"

"Southeast corner of the island, facing the channel between Mouse and Stony Point."

Stacey had overheard her father's answer. "There's a flat rock here for sunbathing. On one side is the shoal. I'm guessing it stretches south to the place where we recovered the arm. But on the other side is a spring hole deep enough for diving. My headlamp beam can't even touch bottom."

"We'll be right there!" Charley took off as if a starter's pistol had fired.

"Don't get lost," Stacey purred in my ear.

The island was so compact that getting disoriented would have been impossible. We'd barely taken ten steps before we caught sight of her headlamp, shining in our direction now like a beacon.

We pushed through the underbrush and found her standing above a rock that was as wide and flat as a mattress.

"Why am I not surprised that you're here, Dad?" Stacey said.

"The night was young, and I thought I could be of some assistance to Mike's case."

She cocked her head. "He has all the assistance he needs, thank you very much."

And with that, she turned her head so that strong white beam from her headlamp shined upon the stone.

Clothing was heaped on the rock. A pair of boxer briefs and a thong lay on the rock as if quickly discarded.

"So they *did* go skinny-dipping," I said.

"No shit, Sherlock. It was a sexy getaway on the lake. Skinny-dipping is de rigueur on a night like this."

"So they went into the water here," I said, thinking out loud. "And yet we found his arm fifty yards to the southwest and his body another twenty yards beyond that." When I shined my light into the shallows, a school of minnows darted willy-nilly beyond its edge. The water on this side of the rock was clear down to the soft sand. "There's some current flowing through the channel, but it's not particularly strong. It's not like a stream. They didn't get swept away, in other words."

"You're wondering why they decided to swim toward the boat traffic," Charley said.

"Maybe they were drunk," Stacey said.

I had forgotten that they didn't know what Finch and I had discovered inside the house. "They seemed to have polished off half a bottle of tequila before they decided to go for a dip."

"People lose all common sense when they're sufficiently sluiced," Charley pronounced.

"There's something else," I said. "Finch says he found LSD and pot in Gina's bag."

"Your tone of voice sounds like you don't believe him," said Stacey knowingly.

"It's not that. I told him to wait for a warrant to search her luggage. But I knew he planned on ignoring me as soon as I went out to meet LaJoy's boat. Pomerleau's here, by the way, Stace. She confirms that Finch had a run-in with Gina's husband a few months ago. He's a minor-league outlaw named Joey Randazza."

"You're not accusing Detective Finch of planting—"

"No," I said. "I've never heard anything about Roger being dirty—Ellen wouldn't work with him if he was—and besides, it's not like he came out here from his fishing lodge with baggies of drugs in the eventuality he might like to incriminate someone."

"So they were probably drunk *and* high," said Stacey. "How does that change the calculus of the situation?"

"If Gina gave Kip the hallucinogens that caused him to drown . . ."

"You suspect she might have fled?" Charley asked. He sounded doubtful.

"Or her husband kidnapped her after he polished off Whitcomb," Stacey suggested.

Around the lake now, I noticed a handful of boats spotlighting the shore. Some of them were undoubtedly the wardens Lieutenant LaJoy had summoned to search for the missing woman. Others might have been volunteers who'd heard the news through the Great Pond grapevine.

"Let's head up to the house to tell the detectives what Stacey found," I said.

As we approached the cottage, I was shocked to see a strong light flickering through the door. Someone had decided to ignite a kerosene lamp to guide the evidence response team to their destination. Maybe they didn't think the white-hot lantern held any evidentiary value. But as dry as the island was—tinder and kindling everywhere—I found the decision perplexing. It wouldn't have taken Mrs. O'Leary's cow to kick over that lamp and set the whole island ablaze.

14

Pomerleau, Finch, and I spent the next forty-five minutes in calls with our superiors, then with representatives of various state and federal agencies that might have a stake in our investigation. Between us, we probably woke up a dozen people, the last of whom was the public information officer for the Maine Department of Public Safety.

When an off-duty warden retrieves a severed arm from a storied Maine lake, you can bet journalists will descend like carrion crows.

Death and dismemberment on Golden Pond.

Pomerleau might well have predicted tomorrow's headline.

Charley arranged by phone for Galen to transport him, Stacey, and the paddleboard back to Neil and Jubilee's lake house. Her announced plan was to get some sleep. His plan was to commandeer Neil's Leisure Kraft to begin cruising the pond's eastern shore, searching for any sign of Gina Randazza.

The constable stared hard at me when he arrived at the dock to pick up his passengers. He must still have been smarting from the dressing-down I'd given him.

"I've got news if you want to hear it," Galen said with a sour smile. "I called the owners over to Great Pond Marina. Mr. Whitcomb arrived yesterday, so he got a late jump on the holiday weekend. His Mercedes is still parked there. The owner said Mr. Whitcomb left the marina alone. That means he must have picked up his girlfriend somewhere along the shore."

He was intent on proving his instincts and initiative to me. I had to give him credit for reaching a plausible conclusion about Kip's female companion.

But Galen wasn't done. "The folks at the marina told me Mr. Whitcomb bought and sold real estate. He was always inquiring about properties on the lake that might not yet be on the market, they said. And there were rumors he might make Mouse Island available."

This tidbit struck me as interesting. Given the high prices Maine properties were commanding, especially waterfront properties, a lot of people with deep roots in the state had decided the time had come to cut them. But the constable had been clear that the deed to Mouse Island was listed in the name of Dianne Fenton-Whitcomb. It was the legacy left by her parents. What were the odds she would wholeheartedly approve her cheating husband selling off her birthright for quick cash?

In any case, I had to admit that the constable had partly redeemed himself in my estimation. But I still worried about his maturity and emotional stability and wasn't inclined to trust him with important tasks.

"How long do you think you'll be?" Stacey asked me before she stepped aboard Galen Webb's Crestliner.

"I can't predict."

She nodded. "Let me know what happens. OK?"

I watched the boat putter off, leaving an invisible cloud of gasoline fumes in its wake. The benzene rush, combined with the adrenaline steadily departing my bloodstream, left me feeling light-headed.

I went up to the porch to join LaJoy and the detectives.

A judge had signed off on the search warrant Pomerleau had submitted. The next item on her to-do list was contacting the dead man's widow, Dianne Fenton-Whitcomb. The notification would be doubly awkward since we couldn't be certain of our victim's identity until the dive team brought up the body. You hate to tell someone their spouse has been dismembered and drowned, and then they show up alive, having run off to the market for potato chips and a six-pack of beer.

"The Medway police chief is going to their house with one of his officers," Pomerleau said. "Chief Dannenhauer says he knows the Fenton family well. He used to play golf with the judge before the old man died."

Smart move, I thought. Death notifications should be made in person whenever possible.

Pomerleau continued: "He's going to call us after he's delivered the news. I've emailed him the warrant to give her, but I've also asked him to put the widow on the phone so we can answer any questions she has about the scope of the search."

"I'd like to be part of the conversation," I said.

Finch looked up from a granola bar he was tearing apart with his strong teeth. "It's not the time to grill her about her husband's infidelities."

I felt my face flush. I wanted to defend myself against Finch's slur of insensitivity. Then I realized that, from his perspective, I was going to be more of a hindrance to their homicide investigation than a help. My reputation had a bad habit of preceding me.

For an officer whose job was to stop poachers and sort out the whys and wherefores of accidental deaths, I had been entangled in an inordinate number of murders and manslaughters over my career. It was no wonder that members of the state police Major Crimes Unit saw me as someone unable or unwilling to stick to my lane.

A detective friend, for instance, had recently presented me with a deerstalker cap as an engagement present. The tweed hat was of the kind famously worn by Sherlock Holmes. The gift was meant as a joke—but I got the message.

While I waited now for Pomerleau's phone to ring, I consulted with Lieutenant LaJoy on the plans he was formulating to search the lake for our missing person. Warden boats had already begun to converge on Mouse Island. Their intersecting wakes caused Finch's candy-colored bass boat to bump repeatedly against the dock.

"They need to hang back to avoid running over her," I cautioned LaJoy. "The last thing we need is another dismemberment."

He peered down his nose with those unreadable eyes. "I've ordered my wardens to establish a cordon around the island, east to Stony Point. We need to seal off the crime scene."

"Since the divers won't be able to search until daylight," I said, "what do you think about calling in a K-9 trained in finding drowned bodies? We have Gina's clothes to put the dog on the scent, at least, and a skilled team can do this work in the dark, without having to wait for the sunrise."

"Any suggestions?"

"I can call Kathy Frost if you'd like. Maple, her Belgian Malinois, is hands down the best cadaver dog in the state."

"I'd prefer an active-duty warden."

Kathy Frost had been my field training officer and very first sergeant. Decades ago, she had founded the bureau's K-9 team. Most notably, Kathy had been the first female officer in the history of the Maine Warden Service and had served with distinction until a shotgun blast to the abdomen had cut short her career. Recently, she'd received the Legendary Maine Game Warden award, putting her in a pantheon where Charley Stevens had long reigned as the god of mischief.

"You know she's always ready to volunteer," I said.

"It seems an imposition when we have wardens who are paid to do the job."

"We don't need a handler and a dog who are still learning the ropes. We need the best team we can get. And that's Kathy Frost and Maple."

LaJoy scratched the scar from his harelip. "Just don't twist her arm."

I resisted the urge to smile. The lieutenant had no idea that I had never once won an arm-twisting contest with Kathy.

Before we could continue the conversation, Pomerleau beckoned to me. I think. She had Dianne Fenton-Whitcomb on the line. The death notification had happened more quickly than I had expected.

The detective added me to the teleconference.

"Yes, I knew my husband was in Maine," Dianne Fenton-Whitcomb was telling Finch. Her voice had a shakiness to it that I attributed to shock. "He goes up there a lot in the summer. He's been the only one who uses the place since . . ."

We waited for her to complete the sentence, but she left it unfinished.

"Chief Dannenhauer was unclear why you're unsure the body you found belonged to my husband. How can you possibly be confused? Is Great Pond suddenly awash with corpses?"

"We are in the process of recovering the body from the lake bottom," Pomerleau said patiently. "If everything goes smoothly, the warden divers should have it up by midmorning."

"You don't need to mince words with me, Sergeant. Why is there a question around the identity of your victim?"

Interesting that she knows to address Ellen by her rank, I thought. Most civilians didn't.

"We believe the body we've found was struck by a speedboat while swimming."

"Kip? Swimming?" Dianne Fenton-Whitcomb managed a dry laugh.

"Your husband doesn't swim?" I blurted out.

Pomerleau and Finch scowled at me, but it was too late. Now I had no choice but to introduce myself.

"This is Mike Bowditch, Ms. Fenton-Whitcomb. I am an investigator with the Maine Warden Service. I work on reconstructing boating crashes and consult with prosecutors to determine whether criminal charges should be filed against the operator."

"Our conservation officers in Massachusetts do the same," she said in that quivery voice.

Her knowledge of these obscure aspects of law enforcement convinced me that Dianne Fenton-Whitcomb had some background working with the criminal justice system.

"Does Kip wear a Rolex, Ms. Fenton-Whitcomb?"

"Yes, a platinum Daytona. Why?" I heard an intake of breath. "Are you saying you found Kip's *arm*?"

Her intelligence was formidable. I wasn't sure I could have made the leap to that conclusion myself.

"This will be hard to hear, but it was detached during the collision," I said. "We've located the rest of the body in deeper water, but it's unsafe for our divers to bring it up until they have light to work with."

Silence.

"I have so many fucking questions," Dianne Fenton-Whitcomb said finally. "But what is it you wanted again, Sergeant? Permission to search my family's cottage?"

"We've already obtained a search warrant, ma'am," said Finch, forgetting his own admonition that I be sensitive to the widow.

"What do you expect to find inside that will tell you who ran over my husband?"

"We don't know," said Pomerleau. "But there's something else."

Dianne Fenton-Whitcomb anticipated what was coming. "Kip was with another woman."

The detectives and I were momentarily at a loss for words. None of us had expected her to throw the fastball.

"Yes, he was," said Pomerleau finally.

"Why can't this woman tell you what happened then? I would think she had a front-row seat to the whole bloody thing."

"The woman is missing," I said.

"She ran off, you're saying?"

"We don't know where she is."

Now it was the wife's turn to take a pause.

"Who is she?" she asked after a moment.

Pomerleau and Finch exchanged glances. Dianne Fenton-Whitcomb had boxed them into a corner.

"Does the name *Gina Randazza* mean anything to you?" Pomerleau asked.

"No. How old is she?"

"Ms. Fenton . . . ?"

"If you think you're protecting my feelings, you're not. I just want to know how old the bitch is."

"Twenty-two."

"That's the youngest yet!"

Finch was resolved to regain control of the interview. "Obviously, you have a lot of questions, ma'am. And we have questions for you, as well. What makes the most sense is that we have another conversation in the morning after the divers have done their work. This has got to be a shocking situation. You'll need time to process it."

"Do you think?" She let out a hoarse laugh. "And you're going to need me to ID the body. Neither Kip nor I have family in Maine, so it will have to be me. I'm assuming it can be done remotely once you've brought up his corpse. I'm unable to travel for medical reasons, so if you want to interview me, you'll need to drive down here to Medway."

"We sometimes use videoconferencing for these conversations."

"Whatever."

"We're sorry for your—"

"You have my permission to tear the house apart. Your officers shouldn't worry about being delicate with my possessions. I won't complain if they trash the place. I have no intention of returning to Maine. My father's cottage ceased to mean anything to me after he passed away. Ironically, Kip had recently been pushing me to sell the island. He even had an agreement at one point, but I made him cancel before the closing. Maybe if I'd let him go through with the sale, he'd still be alive."

15

Kathy Frost didn't pick up the phone. I wasn't altogether surprised. Not being on call 24/7 was one of the prime perks of life in the private sector.

Since her retirement from the Warden Service, she had found work as a K-9 consultant to public safety agencies around the globe, teaching dog handlers and their dogs to conduct rescue and recovery missions. She also volunteered in disaster areas and war zones, from Haiti to Ethiopia. She was always traveling with her Belgian Malinois and might be abroad again, I realized. But I left a message anyway in the desperate hope she was home.

I texted Charley, asking him to swing by Mouse Island to pick me up. There was little for me to do except get in the way of the evidence response team. I figured I could at least ride along with my friend while he explored the shore in Neil's pontoon boat, looking for signs of Gina Randazza.

When Kathy called me back, I almost didn't believe it was her. Hearing her voice filled with me with more joy and relief than I would have expected.

"I can't say I ever found a stray arm before," she said after I'd explained the situation. "Not while I was a warden, at least. I tripped over arms and legs in some places in Africa I'd prefer to forget."

"It's the missing woman I'm hoping Maple can find for us."

"It's kind of a sad commentary on the Warden Service that you have no other choice but to drag me out of retirement for this."

She let out a yawn. "If it was anyone else asking, Grasshopper, you know what the answer would be."

It was her nickname for me when her job had been to teach the secrets of being a successful warden to the greenest rookie in the service.

"I really appreciate it, Kath."

"I won't need to bring my own boat, I hope."

"You can ride along with Charley and me on my stepfather's Leisure Kraft."

"A party boat? Why didn't you tell me that at the get-go? Just make sure the cooler is full of PBR."

She was joking, of course; she had lost her spleen when she was shot, along with pieces of several inner organs required for the processing of alcohol.

I gave her the directions to Neil and Jubilee's place and told her to call or text when she and Maple arrived.

By the time I'd finished with Kathy, Charley had motored out to the island. The old man could still go for hours—days, it seemed—without rest when there was a mystery to be solved, especially a person missing. There were so many boats tied up to the dock now that he couldn't get close to the landing. Instead, he directed me to that flat stone where we'd found the discarded clothing. I stopped at the house to sign my name to a form saying I was borrowing one of Randazza's dirty socks for the cadaver dog to acquire her scent. The CSI person put it in a bag for me and made me promise to return it, untouched. Kathy would only need to open the bag for Maple to get the whiff she needed.

Detouring around some evidence techs photographing the couple's unmentionables, I hopped from the rock onto the swim platform of Neil's pontoon boat. Charley was a natural waterman and had managed to back the Leisure Kraft six inches from the shore and hold it there as if tethered by a mooring line.

Since last I'd seen him, my friend had managed to acquire a powerful DeWalt handheld spotlight.

"Your stepdad has all sorts of fancy tools down cellar," he

explained. "Most have never been used. It's like walking down an aisle at Home Depot."

"That's Neil Turner in a nutshell."

Charley moved us away from the island at trolling speed. "He might not be the most practical-minded man, it's true, but what he lacks in horse sense, he makes up for in enthusiasm and kindness."

I was too tired to discuss my stepfather's unsung virtues. "How are things back at the ranch?"

"Everything's as quiet as kittens. Why don't you take the light while I plot a northerly course. I figured we might circumnavigate that point that was part of Camp Machigonne."

"I'm grateful for everything Neil's done for me. I really am," I said, returning in spite of myself to the subject of my stepdad. "There was a time, after my mom died, when I thought he was drifting out of my life, and I told myself I didn't mind. But maybe I was the one drifting out of his life. I don't know."

My old friend let those words float in the air between us. "I wouldn't beat yourself up over it although I know you do."

"It's how my mom raised me."

"But she's gone now and you're a grown-up about to be wed. You have the choice not to wear a hair shirt every day, if you don't mind my saying."

To be known that well had always scared the shit out of me.

Charley must have felt my unease. "I've been thinking about our missing girl," he said after a long pause.

Stacey would have jumped down his throat for using that word to describe the legally adult, married Gina Randazza, but he was a man from a bygone era and always would be.

"What about her?"

"I'm wondering where she is."

"Isn't that why we're searching?"

He let out a chuckle. "I can't see how a boat could have killed them both."

"What do you mean?"

"I don't know about your experiences taking moonlight swims.

But except for the occasional clinch, I always kept a little distance between me and my gal. You can't hug someone and tread water is what I mean. So that boat would've had to hit them during mid-embrace, and I can't see how that would have happened."

He had always encouraged me to visualize the moments before death occurs, but I hadn't been following his advice.

"And you and Stacey didn't mention hearing a shout or a scream," he added as behind us, a generator started up on Mouse Island, to power the searchlights. "If they saw the boat coming, wouldn't one of them have given a cry?"

"Judging by the tequila bottle and the drugs, I'd say they were both probably plenty wasted."

"Assume for a minute that the boat strikes Whitcomb but misses her. What does she do after her boyfriend gets run over?"

"Swims back to the island."

"Then what?"

"We already discussed the possibility she took off."

"How though? The runabout is still there, and the keys are on the bureau. No, she never made it back to the house."

We had crossed the channel and turned north to follow the shore. I switched on the spotlight and trained it on the trees that had marched down to the lake to sink their roots in the water.

"She didn't have to be run over. She simply might have panicked and drowned."

"Doubtful. The girl on the driver's license looks like a fighter to me."

"You can't *know* that, Charley. I'm willing to bet that Bill Boone and his divers will find Gina's drowned body somewhere near Whitcomb's. They were both shit-faced, stoned, and maybe tripping. He got struck by the boat because he was out of his head, and she panicked and went under."

He grunted his dissatisfaction with the banality of my theory.

We had idled past the last cottage, and now the spotlight revealed sandy beaches and, beyond them, grassy spots beaten down as thin as carpets by hundreds of feet. The grounds were open and parklike.

The beam caught the window of a cabin off in the pines; the glass threw the light back at us as brightly as a signal mirror.

"Is this Camp Machigonne?" I asked.

Before he could confirm what I already knew, we heard a crash ahead where a cluster of alders and black huckleberry had been allowed to grow up. I zeroed the spotlight on the brush but too late to see what had gone charging off into the forest. It had sounded very large and heavy, whatever it was.

"A bear?" I offered.

"A bruin wouldn't have listened to us talking and decided to wait until we were right on top of him to make his retreat. Could have been a young moose, but they sound . . . clumsier." The elusive man had been a legend in the Belgrade area before rookie warden Charley Stevens had captured him at considerable risk to his own life. Far from being an amiable camp robber, the cuddly bearded man had turned out to be a murderous psychopath.

"That poor feller died in prison some years back," Charley said with sincere sadness.

"He tried to shoot you with your own gun!"

"In my experience, people act more out of weakness than malice. That man was just another lump of mortal clay, same as you or me. He received his earthly punishment, but what happened to him in the hereafter is beyond my capacity to know and my right to judge. I hope he found mercy because I'm going to need clemency myself when the hour of my own death rolls around."

16

Charley gave me the last of the coffee in his thermos, but it wasn't enough to resuscitate me. Nor were my wet clothes going to dry of their own. I needed a shower and a power nap or I would be useless when Kathy Frost arrived with her cadaver dog in a couple of hours.

As we cruised back to Neil's dock, I found my gaze attracted to the spotlights and bobbing headlamps of the wardens and other searchers probing the shallows and the shore for the missing woman. In my early years on the job, guilt would have kept me in the field to the point of collapse. But I would need my wits in the morning. I was the case manager on the boat crash, and it was my job to locate the operator of the watercraft that had killed Kipling Whitcomb.

Probably I would need to send warden teams dock to dock around the lake. I'd tell them to look for any damage to boats still in the water or signs that one had been hauled out in a hurry the night before. I'd encourage them to chat up the cottage owners and renters, not just asking if they'd seen anything suspicious but appraising their reactions. Sometimes a guilty person is surly and standoffish. But just as often they are eager to be of assistance and have lots of questions for the officers about what is known and not known about the crime.

Stacey and I hadn't planned on staying the night—my house was an hour's drive to the east. I never liked the idea of leaving Shadow either. We had recently begun going on leashed walks together along the river in preparation for a life beyond his pen. And I hated to interrupt our routine.

But it would have been stupid to drive home only to turn around an hour later. And Jubilee had made up one of the spare rooms for us. (Charley and Ora had the guest cottage since they'd always intended to stay longer.) I said a yawning good night to my future father-in-law as he tied up the pontoon boat and made my way to my personal vehicle, parked beside Jubilee's yoga studio.

In the quiet of the night, I heard the teeming crickets that heralded summer's end in Maine. Noises from Mouse Island and the search boats echoed across the channel. A barred owl howled like a monkey up the ridge behind me.

In my International Harvester Scout, I always packed a field uniform, having been called in on too many days off that I no longer traveled unprepared. As an investigator, I normally dressed in plain clothes, with only a badge on my belt and a holstered SIG P226 to identify me as a law enforcement officer. I didn't miss the weight of the plate vest or the duty belt worn by patrol officers, but sometimes I did miss dressing up like a real warden. It must have been the little boy in me, still wanting to wear a uniform.

Stacey didn't awaken as I entered the darkened bedroom and crossed to the attached bathroom. She didn't even wake up at the sound of the shower or the fan sucking the humid air up into the ductwork. It was only as I crawled under the covers beside her that she opened her eyes.

"What happened?" she murmured.

"Nothing worth getting up for. Kathy is coming with Maple at 0500. I'm hoping to get a little sleep before she arrives."

She mumbled something about being happy to see Kathy and then she was asleep again. I was right behind her.

I awoke exactly two hours later to find her gone from the bed and the bedroom.

After dressing in my uniform and creeping downstairs, I was surprised to find Jubilee in the kitchen cracking eggs in a cast-iron pan filled with tomatoes and other vegetables and spices, most notably garlic, the smell of which assisted in awakening me.

"Where is everyone?"

"Stacey went down to the lake. She woke up and couldn't get back to sleep, she said. Neil told me it was a bad scene out there. He's still sleeping the sleep of the just. I haven't seen Charley or Ora yet."

"Hopefully, they will both sleep in."

"It's weird seeing you in uniform," she added, wiping her hands on her apron. "I've seen photos before, of course. Neil is proud of the one taken on the day of your swearing in. You're wearing a red jacket and a fedora."

"That's our dress uniform."

"To be honest, you're the first person I've ever really known who works in law enforcement," she said, and I could tell she'd prepared the next part. "You don't get many cops coming in for Reiki. I'm hoping, as we get to know each other, you can help me understand what drew you to this sometimes-violent line of work."

I cleared my throat.

"You must already think I'm a crazy leftist kook," she said, sensing my discomfort and now obviously distressed to have been the cause of it. "Because I'm a massage therapist and teach yoga and have a DEFUND THE POLICE bumper sticker on my car."

I hated the sticker but decided this was the wrong moment to explain why it offended me so deeply.

"No, I don't think that."

"Really?"

"I think you're a gold digger who married Neil for his money."

It took her a minute because my deadpan was so good. Then she let out a riotous laugh.

"You nailed me," she said. "I'm all about the Benjamins."

The kitchen door opened. It was Stacey, looking as tired as I felt, but no less attractive in my eyes.

"What did I miss?" she asked when she caught us grinning.

"Mike and I were discussing misleading stereotypes. But what I'm really interested in is hearing how you two found each other. Stacey, I want you to tell me the moment you fell in love with Mike."

"I wish it were more romantic, but we were climbing Katahdin, and Mike was ahead of me on the trail, and he reached back, smiling, to help me up a boulder, and I felt this electricity in his touch. I didn't want to let go of his hand."

"That's totally romantic!" Jubilee said. "What about you, Mike? There must have been a moment it happened for you."

I was already thinking of the night I stayed with Charley and Ora at their old place on Flagstaff Pond. I'd just met the Stevenses, who seemed too good to be true, and I'd slept in the room Stacey had once shared with her estranged sister, Anne. There were framed photos of the two around the cabin, as girls and teens and young women, and even though I'd been in love with someone else at the time, I had felt a shiver go through me when I saw Stacey in those candid portraits. The uneasiness, I now realized, was because it was the first time I'd sensed intention in the universe; that there was such a thing as fate, and it meant for me to be with this green-eyed woman.

"I think I loved her before we ever met."

Jubilee clapped a hand over her heart.

17

After eating, I went upstairs to brush my teeth. When I returned to the kitchen, I found Stacey reading emails on her phone. Jubilee had gone into her studio to practice her yoga, she said. Neil still had not awakened. But I saw lights on in the guest cottage, meaning Charley and Ora were up.

Then I filled a forty-eight-ounce thermos with coffee, emptying the just-brewed pot.

"Do you think that'll be enough to get you through the morning?"

Stacey was used to my prodigious thirst for coffee, exceeded only by her father's. But it still baffled her how I could consume so much.

"I'll have you know coffee is high in antioxidants," I said.

"So are blueberries."

"When they develop a strain of blueberries high in caffeine, let me know."

Through the open windows, I heard a big vehicle coming down the driveway. It was five o'clock sharp. Punctuality had never been one of Kathy's virtues when we'd worked together, but I had to believe that working in the for-profit world had forced her to adapt.

A moment later she appeared at the screen door.

Other women considered Kathy Frost tall, and it was true she'd been a basketball star for Presque Isle High School, three decades earlier. But it was common now to see teenage girls who loomed over her. She had sandy hair that she'd begun to have professionally styled, just as she'd added business suits to her closet. But in her sardonic, freckled face, I still saw the same wisecracking teacher who'd held my hand during my first rough year in the Warden Service.

"What a dump," she said, looking Neil and Jubilee's palatial house up and down.

"Yeah, it's definitely a fixer-upper."

"Given your stepparents' impoverished circumstances, it was good of them to host your engagement party."

We didn't hug because we didn't hug. But if a handshake can communicate love and respect, ours did.

Stacey, however, embraced her. Kathy received the gesture stiffly but not without welcome. I looked for a mug to fill with coffee from my thermos, but she was ready to get down to business.

"So last night, you watched a speedboat run over a swimmer, retrieved a dismembered arm from a lake, and located a dead body in the dark by skin-diving until you felt a corpse?"

"That about sums it up."

"Never change, Grasshopper. Never change."

"It's good to see you, Kath."

She turned to the door without ever really having come inside. "I've got to let Maple out."

The Belgian Malinois was a beautiful animal, shaped like a small German shepherd but sleeker, with a black muzzle and a syrup-brown coat. Maple's eyes were alert and intelligent, and if Kathy hadn't been present, she would have leaped up on my chest to greet me. But the dog had been impeccably trained and waited now for her handler's nod. There was no jumping, just some enthusiastic tail-wagging and a very sloppy lick on my face when I crouched to her level.

Charley appeared in the doorway of the guesthouse, holding a steaming mug of coffee.

"If it isn't the newest legendary Maine game warden! And her faithful pooch."

"Are you still alive, Stevens?"

"Some mornings, it's a question whether the spirit will rise before the body does. How are you, Kathy?"

"Ready to work."

"That's the stuff!"

Kathy moved to the lift gate of her Bronco and dragged out a red bag filled with gear. She knelt on one knee and fastened a blaze-orange search vest around the compliant Malinois's shoulders. Kathy herself was dressed for a summer hike in zip-off pants and a khaki shirt with rolled-up sleeves.

"You have an item of the missing girl's clothes, you said. We're going to need that."

"What else?"

"Just Maple's nose."

18

Neil came down to the dock to see us off. I could tell he desperately wanted to join our expedition, but we were already pushing the capacity of the boat; Maple needed the freedom to run around the deck chasing any microscopic particles that might rise through the water column into the heavy, humid air.

The sun had risen above the ridge behind us, but the shadows were lingering beneath the pine-studded hill. The surface was still flat, with an almost oily sheen. Mouse Island positively glowed across the channel.

Through my binoculars, I spotted state police boats still moored to the dock and a handful of warden boats moving about the water—not aimlessly, exactly—but I knew everyone was waiting for the dive team to appear. LaJoy had texted me that no one had located any trace of Gina Randazza.

Whitcomb's runabout was gone. The evidence team must have towed it to shore during the night for further inspection.

To my surprise, Galen Webb's Crestliner was anchored where it had been when I'd last glimpsed it. The constable was so gung-ho to prove himself he'd stood vigil over the ResQFlare and the body beneath. When I was twenty-three, I would have done the same thing. I didn't like to reflect on how progressively hard it was becoming for me, at the grand old age of thirty-two, to pull all-nighters.

"Is Mom sleeping in?" Stacey asked her dad.

"She's feeling under the weather. Just a sore throat. I'm sure she'll be fine with another hour or two of rest."

As a paraplegic, Ora Stevens was susceptible to a number of ailments and afflictions, mostly minor, but all worrisome in their potentiality. Her husband and daughter affected not to worry. But of course they did.

Neil cast the line off to Stacey. He was dressed for golf at the club outside Belgrade Village. The course was one of the highest rated in the Northeast and many of his law partners and friends from Portland were members. It had been one of the chief draws to building a place on Great Pond.

Charley took the helm, with his daughter acting as mate. Kathy meanwhile watched Maple's every move. My job, as I saw it, was to ensure the search was conducted in an orderly manner that didn't risk leaving any water uncovered, especially around the shoals and in the channel. Grid searches were like mowing a lawn except that you couldn't see the spots you'd missed, so you needed to take care from the get-go.

The logical place to start was where I'd found Kip Whitcomb's armless corpse.

Galen popped up as we neared his anchored boat.

"Hey!" He'd lost his ball cap, and his hair was comically mussed. "Any idea when the divers will be here?"

I checked my watch. "Not for another hour at least. They prefer to do recoveries in full sunlight if possible."

"Right," he said as if this was something he'd forgotten.

With Maple leaning her upper body so far over the bow she seemed in danger of falling, she began to twitch her nose as dogs do when straining after a distant scent. She lapped at the air with her tongue, too.

"What exactly is she smelling for?" I said softly.

"You don't need to whisper, Mike. She's using her nose, not her ears." Kathy preferred wraparound shades, the kind worn by Major League outfielders. She began applying sunscreen to her long neck. "Do you know what *autolysis* is? It's the first stage of decomposition, beginning two to four hours after death. The process gives off olfactory traces Maple can detect, although it's a lot easier when we're dealing with someone who's been dead longer, twenty-four to forty-eight hours. That's when the body enters the putrefaction stage."

I accepted the bottle of sunscreen she offered. "How deep underwater can she smell?"

"I've read about K-9s indicating cadavers over thirty meters down, but I've never experienced anything like that with one of my dogs."

Maple darted around the corner of the bow, claws clicking on the deck. Then she leaped onto one of the cushioned seats. Her tail swept right, then left.

"Is she—?" I asked.

"No." Kathy wiped her greasy hands on the sun gaiter around her neck. "She's going to reorient herself a bunch of times. Keep in mind there are other things down there. No doubt she's already picked up the odors coming off Whitcomb's corpse. An inexperienced or badly trained K-9 will have trouble differentiating her target from extraneous smells. But Maple shouldn't give us any false positives if she's on her game today."

After a while, all conversation ceased.

I wasn't sure what I had been expecting. My prediction that we would find Gina's drowned body not far from Whitcomb's wasn't panning out. As we moved farther away from that point, I began to doubt we were on the right track.

Maple's enthusiasm wasn't flagging, at least. And Kathy was keenly focused on the dog's every nose twitch and tail flick.

The sun grew hotter, and I asked Charley to raise the canopy. I found bottles of Evian in the fridge and refilled the folding bowl Kathy had brought along for Maple before offering drinks to my human companions.

My phone buzzed, but I let it go to voice mail.

Messages of different kinds began piling up in my digital mailbox. The only text that interested me came from the dive chief, Bill Boone, who said that he and his team were launching their specialized boat from the public landing adjacent to Great Pond Marina. I was cheered to learn they would be arriving soon. Once they were on the scene, I didn't expect it would take them long at all to bring up Whitcomb's body.

Bill Boone was one of the Warden Service's last swashbucklers. Law enforcement has always had a lower tolerance for big personalities than you might guess from watching prime-time TV. And the widespread vilification of cops had driven a lot of departments to purge their rolls of problematically "colorful" officers, even if those same officers happened to be good at their jobs. Union protections forbade outright firings, but few police appreciated being moved to desk jobs, excitement junkies least of all.

It was a small miracle that Boone was still in the field, but people must have said the same thing about me.

We'd been searching for over an hour when I said, "I want to change tactics. We've been using the spot where Whitcomb went down as the point last seen. But the last place we have proof of Gina's presence was that rock where Stacey found their clothes."

Behind us, I heard the engine of a motorboat approaching at speed. I recognized the vessel at once. The big gray boat was the largest of several operated by the Warden Service dive team. The others were basic Boston Whalers with winches in their bows to lower and raise sonar units and remote-controlled cameras. The ship of the line had an enclosed aluminum cabin with a Garmin dome radar mounted to the top and doors that opened outward from the hull with ladders for the divers to climb aboard.

I counted five people aboard—one more than I'd expected.

Usually, a dive boat had a crew of four: a warden at the controls, two divers, and a tender, whose job was to keep tabs on the officers below, especially if they were using surface-supplied air instead of scuba tanks and their lives depended on the umbilical connecting them to their oxygen.

I brought my binoculars up and saw a woman in the cabin conversing with the warden driving the boat. All I could see of her was that she was wearing a sun hat.

The dive boat came up alongside Galen's Crestliner.

It occurred to me that Bill Boone was going to ask the constable to be his chaser. When divers are down, protocol requires that another boat be available to protect the safety of the underwater operators by chasing off curiosity seekers and oblivious boaters who might get too close to the scene.

As much as I would have liked to watch Boone and his men in action, we had our own job. The arrival of the divers made me feel pressured for Kathy's sake. I had imposed on my friend to interrupt her holiday weekend. If Gina's remains were below, I wanted Maple to be the one to find them, not the dive team.

With Stacey as spotter, we crossed the shoal and turned around the eastern side of the island. From the water, the flat rock looked small and insignificant, with just a faint path leading toward the house. Loosestrife and rice cutgrass grew in the loamy spot where we'd found the underwear.

Fifteen feet from the rock, Maple began glancing over her shoulder at Kathy. She did this several times, growing more and more agitated by the second. Finally, she let out a bark.

"Charley, cut the engine," I said.

As we drifted past the rock, Maple rushed to the port side of the boat, her eyes fixed on a spot too deep for the sunlight to penetrate. She barked again, worried that we hadn't gotten her message.

"You found her, girl," Kathy dropped to her knees to congratulate her search partner and reward her with a treat.

Maple, for her part, began glancing from one of our smiling faces to the next, growing more and more excited by our reactions. I couldn't remember the last time I'd seen a living creature in such a state of ecstasy.

19

Two common mergansers shot by on whistling wings. The surface of the lake was warming from the heat of the late-summer sun. Mirages rose wraithlike on the shore across the channel, near the place where Charley and I had startled that big unknown creature in the bushes the night before.

I didn't want to risk dropping a marker that might have disturbed the spot where Gina had come to rest. Instead, I recorded the longitude and latitude in my GPS. I snapped photographs for reference and even recorded a quick video.

Not that Boone was likely to need this information. I had no doubt he'd find the corpse within seconds of descending to the bottom.

"I feel like I should be relieved," said Stacey, collapsing on one of the seats. "But I'm not. I'm heartbroken."

Kathy cracked open a can of Coke from the cooler. "Recovery isn't like rescue. You don't get that rush of having your wildest hopes confirmed. It's more a worst-fears scenario. We've established that a young woman has died. There's nothing to feel good about."

I had a feeling she was quoting from one of the speeches she gave when she trained dog handlers.

"At least we found her quickly, so her family won't spend days hoping in vain," I said.

My attempt at consolation didn't provoke a response from my comrades.

Kathy sat down at last on one of the cushioned benches. She

scratched Maple between the ears. The dog thwacked her tail against the deck.

"Now what?" Stacey asked.

"Should we stay here?" I said to Kathy.

"There's no current, so she won't be moving. If you've got the location recorded, Mike—"

"I wouldn't mind watching the divers at work," said Charley, which surprised none of us.

We all stared at Kathy, mindful of the time she'd already volunteered. We needed her permission to linger now that Maple had completed her mission.

She pretended to check her watch. "I have a little time."

I knew my old sergeant as well as she knew me.

For all her jaded talk, she wants to see the divers bring up the bodies as much as we do.

Neil didn't have a VHF radio, so I had to call Boone to tell him we'd found the missing woman. I got his voice mail, meaning he was already underwater.

The dive boat had anchored in the deep water north of the improvised marker. The flashing flare was pulling on its line to the south, revealing a current that was invisible at the surface. The idea, I gathered, was to get as close to the spot where the body had come to rest without sitting right on top of it.

Thirty yards separated us from the flag in the water signaling that divers were at work. We set up in the shallows, due south of the dock, and the bottom was visible beneath our hull. The sand appeared green through the algae-tinted water.

The tender was watching the bubbles floating up from the bottom. Boone and his partner had chosen to use their scuba tanks. It made sense under the circumstances. The lake was relatively warm, and the divers knew the location of the corpse, which meant they shouldn't need to spend hours submerged.

The unknown woman emerged from inside the cabin of the dive boat. She was solidly built, dressed in a jumpsuit similar to those worn by forensic techs, with a wide-brimmed hat to shade her face and neck.

"That's Leah Doumit," Kathy said. "What's the new ME doing here?"

"I've heard she's doing a lot of this," I said. "Getting out in the field."

"Kudos to Dr. Doumit," added Stacey.

In addition to her own staff, Maine's chief medical examiner employed something like thirty-five physicians to officiate at death scenes. Any one of these doctors had the training to oversee the recovery of a submerged corpse. Doumit's predecessor wouldn't have been caught dead on a dive boat when there was another round of golf to be played and a gin and tonic waiting at the nineteenth hole.

I stood in the bow and called across to her. "Dr. Doumit, I'm the warden investigator on this case, Mike Bowditch."

She leaned against the gunwale as if to see and hear me better. "The Warden Service assigned you a party boat?"

"This is my stepfather's boat. He has a house on the lake."

"Good for him."

"One of your people picked up the victim's arm at his home last night."

"I examined it before I drove out here. You should have known better than to bring that arm up, Warden."

The tender raised his eyes from the line he was using to stay in touch with the divers below. He made a face she couldn't see. I think it was an expression of sympathy.

With Charley on board, I felt a need to defend my friend, if not myself. "It was a spur-of-the-moment decision. But I made sure not to disturb the body under your boat."

She seemed to make a point of not responding. If I was fishing for praise, I would receive none.

"We think we've found the second victim around the island," I said.

"You *think*?"

"My K-9 indicated over a spot on the eastern side," said Kathy.

Dr. Doumit leaned forward, peering through her dark glasses at the woman in the shadow of the canopy. "Is that Kathy Frost?"

"It is."

"I attended one of your video talks. Very good. Very well organized."

A black head, as round and wet as a seal's, popped up beside the boat. The diver was wearing a neoprene hood. He removed his regulator and loosened his mask to drain water from the bottom. I recognized his sandy-blond mustache. It was the dive chief, Bill Boone.

"He's down there, all right," I heard him tell his line tender. "The one-armed SOB."

20

When Boone spotted me standing aboard the Leisure Kraft, he exclaimed in a Texas drawl, "If it isn't Mike Bowditch."

"Hello, Chief!"

Bill Boone was a Maine native (he'd be the first to tell you), but he'd grown up in Galveston when his father, a fourth-generation lobsterman, had fled the state without explanation to find work on shrimp boats under an assumed name. Rumors abounded that Bill's dad had double-crossed some Down East drug smugglers. He must have gambled they wouldn't find him in East Texas. Since he had perished by falling off his shrimp boat on a calm night, it seemed he'd lost his bet. But this brief sojourn down South explained Boone's unlikely drawl, which he seemed determined to maintain even having returned to Maine as an adult.

He swam the distance between our boats and hung off the swim platform by his gloved fingers. His bronzed face was wet, and his mustache was dripping at the corners. Boone was one of the few wardens who wore facial hair; usually a mustache made it hard to get a tight seal on a dive mask, but he'd learned various tricks, like shaving a line under his nostrils, that solved the problem.

"I hear you were the one who found our vic," he said. "Why the hell did you bring up that arm, though? I thought I taught you better than that."

"Don't blame the young feller," said Charley. "I was the one who got carried away."

"The site's pretty much fucked, evidence-wise, but I appreciated your marking the spot with that Poland Spring bottle. Tying that ResQFlare to the body was inspired, if I say so myself. We couldn't have asked for a more visible buoy."

"The line's still attached, then?" I wanted my moment in the sun.

"It is indeed," Boone said. "Your boy budged a little, but the knot held. What most folks don't realize is a submerged corpse moves in four phases. Settling to the bottom, movement along the bottom, ascent to the surface once decomposition sets in, and drift along the surface."

"You're forgetting the final descent." Kathy stepped forward into the sunlight.

Boone shrugged off his scuba tank and raised it for me to take. The steel cylinder was mostly full of air so it weighed thirty or forty pounds, maybe more. I set the heavy, dripping tank on the deck, against one of the cushioned benches.

Using the swim platform as a chin-up bar, Boone lifted his entire body out of the water, twisting in midair so that his butt landed on the boat with his legs hanging in the water. From there, it was a simple matter to swing his flippered feet over the edge and rise to standing. He stood in a self-made pool, his heavy weight belt around his hips and a big smile on his handsomely tanned face.

He removed his glove and extended his hand to Kathy. "You must be Kathy Frost. I'm Bill Boone. It's an honor and privilege to meet you."

Instead of rolling her eyes at his chivalry, which was what I would've expected, she stepped forward to shake hands.

Boone was a short and husky man, and no one would say he looked good in a wet suit. But he didn't lack for self-confidence. He was a veteran navy frogman who had fought in multiple war zones before he was honorably discharged from the SEALs, having obtained the rank of chief petty officer, and unlike his publicity-seeking brothers, decided to return to Maine and take a low-paying job with the Warden Service.

Maple moved forward, sensing from her handler's body language that the new arrival was a fellow pack member to be greeted.

"That's a beautiful pooch," he said, making the word sound vaguely lurid. "What's her name?"

"Maple," said Kathy.

"And she's here to help us?"

"She already has."

Boone twitched his dark-blond eyebrows.

"We gave Maple an item of Gina Randazza's clothes," I explained. "She just indicated at a spot on the southeastern edge of the island. We believe it's where Gina and Whitcomb entered the water. She's down there, Boone. I'd bet money on it."

He passed his blue eyes from the Malinois to mine and then turned his admiring gaze on Kathy.

"Well, damn," he said. "That's one well-trained dog."

"What's going on over there?" Dr. Leah Doumit shouted. "Are we bringing up our victim or not?"

Boone put on his best Southern manners. "Excuse me, Kathy, I have work to do. But you all are welcome to stay and watch the show."

And with that, he picked up the scuba tank, strapped it back onto his back, and jumped feetfirst into the lake.

21

While we were waiting for Boone and his partner to surface with Whitcomb's body, I noticed Galen Webb's chase boat floating in the channel in the path of a rowboat. I raised my binoculars for a better look. He was speaking with a woman who was clearly trying to approach the dive scene.

From a distance, she presented herself as a grab bag of descriptors: face white with zinc sunscreen, sunglasses, ball cap, short hair, maybe? She seemed visibly upset that the constable was keeping her from approaching the island. Galen didn't seem to be having much luck pacifying her.

Extrapolating from the position of the rowboat relative to the eastern shore, I reasoned that the agitated woman must have come from one of the cottages near Neil and Jubilee. What accounted for her outrage? If her goal had been to row out into the lake, she could easily have avoided our cordon.

Does she know something about Whitcomb?

I made a mental note to call Galen and ask him what she'd wanted.

Stacey offered me a bottle of water, but I hadn't yet finished my thermos of coffee.

"You need to hydrate, Mike."

"Coffee's a liquid."

She was staring at the dive scene. Her sweaty brow was knitted.

"I dived a lot in the Keys when I was in Florida," she said. "The most gruesome thing I ever came on was a goliath grouper swallowing a seven-foot-long moray eel in one gulp. I can't imagine going down in the dark after a human body."

"It's not an experience I'm eager to repeat."

"They've got him!" said Charley.

I looked up and saw the line tender and the rescue diver reaching over the gunwales for a human-size bag made of yellow mesh.

Most people assume that recovery divers bring a corpse to the surface before putting it in a body bag, but that was no longer the case. The once-common practice had fallen out of favor for two reasons: it was disrespectful for the deceased to be displayed to anyone with binoculars, and more importantly, it violated the standards of evidence recovery, since lifting a corpse through the water column was all but guaranteed to wash away whatever trace evidence might be clinging to the skin, hair, and clothing.

Boone and his partner had raised the body bag up on their own. But once Whitcomb's body broke the surface, it took four men to lift his corpse aboard. Water drained through the mesh as the two men set the bag down inside a conventional black bag for transport.

"Is it Whitcomb?" I called.

The dive chief turned his ruddy face our way. "Unless there are two dead men missing an arm in Great Pond, I'm going to say yes."

"How does he look?"

"Like a spiral-sliced ham."

Boone was always such a smart-ass.

Dr. Doumit bent over the corpse before they finished wrapping it, doing a quick examination.

I wondered what she could tell from a cursory inspection. I assumed cause of death was self-evident. Whitcomb had been at or just below the surface when the boat ran him over. If he were already dead, his body would have begun sinking as soon as he breathed his last breath.

The divers passed up their tanks and fins, then clambered up the ladder on the dive door with the help of the line tender. They quickly retrieved their lines and the floating red flag with the white stripe. Boone had been right that they could move quickly when they wanted to.

I watched him accept a phone from the tender. Seconds later, my cell buzzed. It was the man himself.

"You want to lead us to the spot Maple located our missing gal?"

"Happy to," I said.

I rose from my comfortable seat and approached the captain of the party barge.

"Charley, they want us to lead the way to Gina's body. I'm wondering if you can stop at the dock to let me off."

"Why do you want to go ashore?"

"I'll have a better view of the recovery from the land."

He frowned, and I knew it was because he wanted to join me.

"I'm coming, too," said Stacey.

The old pilot tossed Kathy a self-pitying look. "Kathy?"

"Maple and I won't desert you, Charley. We'll stay on the boat."

The dock posts had been wrapped with the requisite CRIME SCENE tape. The sagging yellow bands extended to the shore, where they were knotted around trees.

As Charley brought the Leisure Kraft to the dock, Stacey and I leaped onto the unsteady planks. I heard a crack beneath one boot and realized I'd broken the slat with my weight. I was fortunate that my foot hadn't gone through.

"I need to use the facilities," Stacey said. "You guys have it so easy on the water. I'm past the age where I'll hang my butt over the edge to do my business."

A flock of cedar waxwings, traveling in tight formation, descended into the treetops of the pines. They were sleek, crested birds, loud and gregarious, with bandit masks and tails that looked as if they'd been dipped in yellow paint, easily among the most charming and beautiful of bird species in Maine.

The night before, there hadn't been a trail from the dock to the diving rock, but the crime scene crew had made one, tramping back and forth to record and then bag the clothes Whitcomb and Randazza had left behind.

The pontoon boat kept pace with me the whole way, and I heard Maple bark as she detected again the smell of her target rising as microscopic gases through the brown-green water.

I stepped out onto the flat rock and gazed down through my polarized lenses, hoping the angle of the sun might penetrate deep enough to reveal a shape, but the water was too deep and murky. As expected, I was going to have a courtside seat for the recovery. I waited as the driver of the boat maneuvered his way close to the shore and found myself nearly knocked over by the fumes roiling up from the big engine.

Stacey appeared at my side, her throat and cheeks rosy from hurrying.

"You didn't mention the house doesn't have a bathroom. I went all the way upstairs looking for one."

"Wasn't there crime scene tape up?"

"Yeah, but that wasn't meant for me." She pressed her hand against her breastbone and affected an air of innocence. "My future husband is the case manager on this investigation, I'll have you know."

"I wouldn't try that line on Finch."

"Oh, I won't." Then the smile left her face. "Kind of creepy seeing the family portraits along the stairs."

I was only half listening to her and made a mumbled noise in acknowledgment. I was watching the dive boat. It had just lowered its anchor. Boone and his partner were checking each other's air supply, hoses, and fasteners as professional divers are taught to do. The tender threw out the buoy with the warning flag.

"Did you notice the mother has a walker in the last portrait in which she appears?" Stacey continued. "Her teenage son had his arm around her as if to prop her up."

Her daughter, Dianne Fenton-Whitcomb, had alluded to a significant health problem in our conference call. I wondered if some disease might run in the family. I would need to revisit the house to examine the family photos. Under the circumstances, I couldn't help but feel curiosity about the high-powered Fentons.

"You didn't mention Dianne used to have a brother," Stacey added when I didn't answer.

"Why do you say *used to have*?"

"He doesn't appear in the final two pictures. It's just Dianne and his Satanic Majesty, the judge. It made me wonder if the brother died. He would have been in his early twenties, I'm guessing."

"He might have been away at college."

"I don't know," she said. "It's hard to explain, but in the photos he seems more absent than that."

Before we could continue discussing the unknown, possibly tragic, fate of the youngest Fenton, we were interrupted by simultaneous splashes. The recovery divers had let the weight of their scuba tanks pull them backward in into the pond.

22

The dive boat had anchored fifteen feet from shore, providing my first close-up look at our new chief medical examiner.

Leah Doumit had pushed the brim of her hat back from her forehead, revealing hair that was grizzled and also a bit frazzled. She hadn't removed her fashionable shades. But the face beneath them was a picture of resolute concentration.

She had secured Kip Whitcomb in a vinyl bag folded almost like an envelope around the inner mesh the divers had used to bring him up.

I yearned to look upon the corpse I had touched in the blackness of the lake bottom. I felt I was owed a look, if I was being honest with myself. But my prurient curiosity was the last thing that mattered at the moment. Later, perhaps, I would have the opportunity.

"Would you mind my watching the autopsy?" I asked Dr. Doumit.

At first, I wasn't sure she'd heard me. Then she removed two foam earplugs from her ears. As a physician, she was aware of the damage exposure to outboard motors can have on one's hearing.

I repeated my question.

"I might not get to the postmortem for a few days." Her voice had a resonant, nasal quality as if it echoed in her sinus cavities. "We have a backlog, and the holiday weekend always brings in crash victims and other unfortunates."

I put on my most charming smile. "Is there any way I can persuade you to expedite this one?"

"No," she said with such finality, I had to concede that my charm offensive had been routed.

A large dragonfly landed on the gunwale of the dive boat. Stacey had been teaching me to identify the fast-flying predatory insects.

"Is that a Canada darner?"

"Lake darner," she said.

"How can you tell?"

"Lake is bigger."

Boone's partner appeared above the surface holding a whiteboard on which he had made a rough sketch of a body floating facedown with her elbows bent. Drowned bodies always seemed to end up in that same posture. He spat out his regulator and handed his drawing to the tender.

"She's wicked small," he said. "Looks more like a kid."

A series of flashes now emanated from the water below. Boone was taking evidence photos. More than anyone, he'd pushed the Warden Service to adopt best practices used by the premier underwater crime-scene investigators in the world.

"I had my share of pirate shit in the SEALs," he'd once told me over beers. "Guys who just want to act fast and fuck the rules. Frogmen are my blood brothers. But the culture of the teams has gotten more and more toxic. It's all the hero worship."

"I'm surprised you didn't take your pension and move to Cozumel or wherever the diving is gnarly," I'd said.

"I'm allergic to retirement." He had licked Budweiser foam from his mustache. "I'm one of the people who needs a purpose, and I figured I could do some good, especially when I saw how outmoded Maine's diving protocols were."

Boone poked his head up now. His expression, beneath his cowl, was uncharacteristically sober.

"Hand me the bag," were the first words out of his mouth. "She's such a wisp of a thing I can bring her up on my own."

This time, I was well positioned to observe the recovery process.

Boone brought the mesh bag down to the bottom, where, presumably, he had a method of easing the corpse onto the sheet before securing the ends. He was down for all of two minutes before he returned with his burden. I saw bare skin through the lattice that made me think of a water nymph caught in a net.

The dive chief passed her up to the waiting men above, water from the bag draining down his powerful forearms.

Dr. Doumit supervised as they laid the wrapped form onto the larger black bag spread out beside the vinyl mummy that was Kip Whitcomb.

The medical examiner had finally removed her sunglasses. She wore readers now that made her look almost professorial. She knelt beside the yellow bag and peeled the edges back to reveal the naked body of Gina Randazza. The line tender recorded everything.

I understood why both divers had remarked on her slightness. She had narrow hips and a small behind. Her skin was mostly pallid, blue with undertones of lavender, from the coldness of the spring where she'd come to rest. Livor mortis had already begun, darkening her forearms and knees where the blood had drained into the extremities. She wore a gold anklet that glittered when it caught the sun.

I saw no sign of the massive gashes that had disfigured and dismembered Kip Whitcomb.

"I'm going to turn her over now," Dr. Doumit said, addressing herself not to us but to the video recorder.

Stacey gripped my shoulder.

The medical examiner was now between us and Gina's upper body. But we had a clear view from the waist down. She wore a ring in her belly button and had waxed her genitals. Taken with the flatness of her stomach and the thinness of her legs, the lack of hair only added to the impression of her being prepubescent.

"Oh, no." The line tender involuntarily let the camera lens drift from his subject. His mouth had gone slack.

"What is it?" Stacey asked.

Without turning, Dr. Doumit said gravely, "As I understand it, you're handling Whitcomb's death. Is that right, Warden Bowditch?"

I felt a foreboding in the simple request for confirmation.

"I am investigating how he came to be struck by a boat," I said, "and whether it caused his death."

Still without facing us, the ME now asked, "Who are the detectives handling Gina Randazza's death?"

"Ellen Pomerleau and Roger Finch."

"I suggest you get them on the phone."

"Why? What do you see?"

"Whatever suppositions you've been working from need to be reexamined," she said.

"Care to clarify?"

Dr. Doumit finally turned her head to look back at. She realized that she had been blocking our view and shimmied on her knees away from the lifeless woman.

"Take a look at her throat."

She pushed aside wet strands of Gina's hair to reveal what were unmistakably strangulation marks.

23

Whitcomb strangled her," Stacey said, her tone somewhere between a question and an accusation.

"These handprints were clearly made before or at the time of death," said Leah Doumit.

"How do you know?" I asked.

"You wouldn't see the appearance of extravasation here if someone had done this hours after death." She registered the blankness with which I greeted these words and continued. "There would be no inflammation at these points if her heart had stopped. Postmortem, vascular pressure ceases, and gravity begins to act on the blood. Which is why we're seeing livor mortis—pooling of the blood—in her hands and feet."

I rubbed my jaw and became conscious that my stubble was approaching beard length. The Warden Service encouraged its investigators not to shave; the less we resembled conventional cops, the easier we could work under the radar. But it made me feel unkempt and unprofessional.

"But strangulation wasn't necessarily the cause of death?"

"I won't be able to say for sure until I get her on the table. Does she have water in her lungs? She might simply have been held underwater until she drowned. Or cause of death was something entirely different. For all we know, these marks were caused by aggressive consensual sex play."

Boone and his partner had removed their air tanks and flippers and climbed the ladder while I was distracted. The dive chief was unbuckling his weighted belt while the other man closed and secured the dive door.

"Bill, could you do me a favor?" I asked. "Can you put your hand close to Gina's throat?"

"Don't touch her," snapped Dr. Doumit before Boone could react.

"I want to get a sense of the size of the hands that made those marks," I tried to explain.

"I'll have precise measurements for you in my autopsy report," said Dr. Doumit, whose doubtful expression suggested she had reservations about this unshaven warden investigator. "Which will be done sooner rather than later now. I'm moving this woman to the front of the line."

Stacey stood beside me. "What's going to happen now? With your investigation, I mean?"

"It's just become two investigations. The detectives need to figure out what happened to Gina while I try to track down the speedboat."

The medical examiner had finished closing the body bag around Gina. Two black bundles at the ME's feet.

"Will you start the engine, please?" she said to the boat driver. "The longer these two cadavers are exposed to the heat, the harder it'll be for me to determine how and when they died."

Boone and the other wardens waved as they set off, but Doumit was fixing her hat for the ride home.

As soon as their boat was clear, Charley moved the Leisure Kraft in to pick us up. It was apparent from his and Kathy's grim expressions that they'd overheard our ship-to-shore conversation with the dive boat.

"Now where?" Stacey asked.

"I vote we return to Chez Jubilee," said Charley. "Kathy might want to hit the road."

And he wants to check in on his sick wife, I realized.

As he throttled up the engine, I reached for my thermos and the last precious drops of coffee it contained. Then I collapsed onto one of the cushioned seats.

It was another beautiful morning. Bass were rising to dragonflies and damselflies. The smaller fish jumped clear out of the water in pursuit of their airborne prey. The breeze wafted the odor of the sun-dried pines down from the ridge and across the flat lake.

This was the indifference of nature fully manifest, I thought. Human tragedies made not even the faintest of impressions upon the larger living world. It suggested something Jubilee had said the night before, one of those charming, left-field pronouncements she had a penchant for making.

"We're all just along for the ride, you know? Humans, I mean. That's the miracle of life, that we get to experience this moment together, and then our time is over, but everything goes on, and it's all right. We're not meant to understand."

Ora had finished her thought: "It's enough that we're moved to wonder."

"Yes! Yes! That's exactly right," Jubilee had exclaimed.

Now as we motored out into the channel, I cast one last look at Mouse Island, doubting I'd ever visit it again.

"Damn," I said.

Stacey had curled up beside me. "What?"

"I'd meant to have another look inside the Fentons' house before we left. You got me curious about those family photos. Not that they have anything to do with Whitcomb killing Gina and then getting run over while taking a post-murder swim."

"It would be a hell of a thing if the two deaths were unconnected," said Charley from the helm.

"Maybe someone murdered them both?" Stacey suggested.

"How?" I said.

"Drugged something they ate or drank," said Charley. "Then dragged them to the lake to drown."

"Why strangle Gina first?"

"Because it was her husband who did it and he was blind mad she was having an affair?" Kathy said. But there was no conviction in her voice.

"A violent husband doesn't sedate his wife and her lover before he kills them," I said. "Not Gina's husband anyway. Finch described him as a badass biker."

Stacey didn't enjoy playing detective, but she sometimes had insights that suggested an aptitude for the job.

"He might have drugged them if his plan was to make it look like Whitcomb killed her," she said.

Kathy scratched Maple behind the ears. "That's one way to distract the cops from looking at you—present them with an open-and-shut case."

A shadow passed over the pontoon boat. Then I heard a high-pitched whine.

What I had mistaken for an eagle turned out to be a remote-controlled drone.

Maine law enforcement increasingly used them to assist with searches for missing people or with mapping large-scale crime scenes, and my first thought was that someone in a position of authority had dispatched a boat with a drone operator to survey Mouse Island and its surrounding waters.

"There he is."

I followed Charley's outstretched arm and pointing finger up the channel in the direction of Otter Island, Mouse's larger neighbor.

An aluminum fishing boat floated off Stony Point. In it, a man stood operating a control device. Another person was manning the engine. The glare coming off the water made it impossible for me to make them out, even when I zeroed in my binoculars. But I felt sure they were either journalists or social-media opportunists.

Their appearance made me realize that Galen had disappeared while we'd been watching the divers recover Gina. I would have expected the young constable to check in with me before leaving the scene. But maybe his ego was still bruised from my treatment of him the night before.

"If Webb was around, I'd have him chase that idiot off."

"Under what legal pretext?" Charley asked. He was usually so impetuous, and yet every now and again, he would act his age and become the voice of reason.

"Under the pretext that he's an asshole."

The drone swooped toward us, then hovered fifty feet off our portside and a hundred feet in the air. Four spinning rotors held it in place. I felt certain a camera was mounted on the bottom, trained on us.

"It shouldn't be against the law to shoot those things down," said Kathy, rising to her feet. "You're not a bad marksman, Grasshopper. I'll give you a hundred bucks if you plug that bloody thing."

"Maybe if I weren't in uniform . . ."

Suddenly, I heard laughs around me. Maple let out a surprised bark.

I didn't understand what was happening. Then, out of the corner of my eye, I saw Stacey standing with her feet spread apart, flipping the drone the bird.

"The department fired *me,*" she said. "What do I care what your superiors think? Eat shit, trolls!"

24

I waited until we were ashore to call Pomerleau and Finch. There was no one on the party barge I worried about overhearing my conversation with the detectives, but discretion was a muscle I rarely exercised, and it was overdue for a workout.

While everyone trooped up to the house—or, in Kathy's case, prepared to depart—I grabbed a chair on the lower patio. Neil and Jubilee's landscape designer had chosen different-colored flagstones to create a patchwork effect and surrounded the space with plants that would bloom in succession from spring until fall. Purple coneflowers were closing out the season; in a week, they would go to seed and draw sparrows and finches by the dozens.

I slouched in the chair, stretching my legs out across the stones.

"Dr. Doumit already called us about the marks on Gina's neck," said Finch, sounding peeved.

You can never win with this guy.

"How did the death notification go?" I asked.

"Which one? Oh, you mean the cuckolded husband, Randazza? He wasn't home. And the only number I found was disconnected."

"So what did you do?"

"I knocked on his neighbors' doors, but I didn't tell them why I needed to see him. I ended up leaving a note with my name and number and told him to call me ASAP. I'm going on the record with this. Joey Randazza killed his wife and her lover. Him and his biker friends."

Finch's knee-jerk suspicion of the husband wasn't entirely

misplaced; women are most often killed by their domestic partners. But making premature assumptions of guilt was always a mistake. I couldn't help but wonder if there was more to the story he'd told about his run-in with the Direwolves.

Pomerleau was, by all indications, part of our conference call, but she hadn't yet spoken a word.

I watched a bluet damselfly alight on my boot. "We should meet. Don't you think?"

"Why?" Finch asked.

"To coordinate our efforts. I'm pursuing a negligent homicide case against the boater. You have a murder to solve. We need to discuss who's doing what."

"That all makes sense, Mike," said Pomerleau, finally announcing her presence.

"Is something else going on I should know about?"

"We're over at the marina where Whitcomb parked his car. The tow truck that was supposed to haul it to the public safety garage broke down. Can you believe it?"

"Why don't I drive so we can hash this out in person? If you think you're going to be there for a while."

"How much progress have you made locating your hit-and-run boater?" Finch demanded.

He wanted to goad me, and he succeeded. "Not much. I've been too busy finding your victims. I'm going to talk with LaJoy about holding a press conference. Maybe someone got a good look at the speed demons who were out on the lake last night, and we can start narrowing it down. I'll see you in thirty."

I put in a call to Rick LaJoy.

The dive chief had already briefed him on the bodies, which saved me some time, and he agreed to arrange a press conference later that afternoon at the public landing across the cove from Great Pond Marina. We were desperate and needed tips.

"I can't be there," I said. "You understand why."

"Because you don't want to be in the public eye as an investigator. Lots of people already know who you are, Mike."

"It doesn't mean I should be standing in front of cameras. I look different from my clean-cut days. But it's in no one's interest for me to become even more recognizable."

"It's your call about the conference."

"You're up to speed on everything. There's no question I could answer that you can't, Rick."

"Like I said, it's your call."

The lieutenant seemed to think I was trying to beg my way out of an unpleasant job, but I had meant what I'd said. LaJoy could believe what he wanted about me, I decided.

I went up to the house to let my once and future family know where I was going. As expected, no one was eager to accompany me to a series of bureaucratic briefings with the state police. The grim discoveries of the morning had been draining enough.

I paused only long enough to use the bathroom, refill my thermos with coffee, and grab a day-old bagel. Then I hit the road.

I drove the Scout up the steep drive and the even steeper hillside. I hadn't spent much time in the Belgrade Lakes region and found myself surprised by the heights of the watersheds between the lakes. A drop of rain falling on a ridgeline could flow east to Salmon Lake or west to Great Pond depending on which way the wind was blowing. It was an utterly haphazard-seeming landscape.

This impression was reinforced by the many pits of gravel and sand carved into the hillsides. Some of the excavations were truly massive, like something you might see out West. A bulldozer at the bottom of one open mine looked as small as a Tonka toy from the road above.

I was also distracted by thoughts of Shadow. The name of Randazza's motorcycle club, the Direwolves, had inevitably made me wonder how he was holding up in my absence. The boy who cared for him was a good guardian. But I missed my dog.

Lost in thought, I took a wrong turn and found myself at the public landing instead of the marina across the cove.

The mistake turned out to be fortuitous. I arrived in time to see Bill Boone and his divers securing their big boat onto its trailer. The only other vehicle present was a Kennebec County sheriff's cruiser. I realized at once that the launch was closed and the deputy's job was to keep out any recreational boaters who hoped to access the lake. I'd been assigned menial tasks like this myself back in the day.

As I made a loop around the parking lot, I rolled down my window and hung my arm out to have a friendly conversation with Boone. The dive chief had stripped off his wet suit and was now wearing a black T-shirt with a warden shield on the breast, fatigue pants, and black boots. He had some of the thickest wrists I'd ever seen; around one was a sailor's bracelet like those you can buy in beachfront tourist traps, and around the other was a chunky dive watch with an orange dial.

"Are you stalking me, Bowditch? Do I need to take out a restraining order against you?"

"I missed the turn for the marina."

"It's the next one down," called the deputy, who was leaning against the hood of his Ford Interceptor with his arms crossed. I had never seen a man looking so bored.

"I see Dr. Doumit is already gone."

"She's a fast worker. And a fast driver. I'm surprised the deputy didn't write her up when she floored it out of the lot."

I had so many questions for the medical examiner, starting with whether I could attend the postmortem she conducted on Kip Whitcomb. She'd never told me if I was welcome at the autopsy.

"You said Whitcomb looked like a spiral-cut ham."

"His back and shoulder did. The side missing the arm."

"Did Doumit say anything as she looked him over?"

"Only that you don't usually find a severed limb before you find the body from which it was detached."

"She didn't offer any preliminary conclusions?"

Boone smoothed the ends of his golden mustache. "You want to know if he was alive when the boat struck him?"

"Exactly."

The former SEAL could play the country bumpkin with such conviction I sometimes forgot what an educated and eloquent man he was.

"On the ride out to the dive scene, she told me that the arm was definitely taken off by a prop. The fracture to the humerus and the abrasion above the wound suggests mechanical cutting and enormous splitting power. She said it was consistent with other boat propeller injuries she'd seen."

"Were you a corpsman in the SEALs, Bill?"

"No, but I was a corpsman in the navy before I went to BUD/S. What gave me away?"

"Your anatomical expertise. What else did Doumit tell you?"

"That the wound might not have been instantly fatal. Whitcomb would have exsanguinated in a matter of minutes—no doubt—but cause of death might have been blunt force trauma to the head or spine. Or he might have lost consciousness and drowned before the boat appeared on the scene. A postmortem should settle the matter, though."

The sound of approaching motorcycles caused us to break off our conversation and turn in the direction of the road.

Three men on Harleys drove loudly into the parking lot. None of them wore helmets. None of the bikes had regulation exhausts. Their engines were deafening.

The deputy, to his credit, stepped in front of the lead bike, stretched out his arms like Jesus on the cross, and held his ground, trying to force the motorcyclist to a stop. When the biker failed to do so, he leaped aside and fell in the dirt.

25

The lead biker had a longish black beard and a black bandanna knotted over his head. The combination gave him a piratical aspect. He wore a sleeveless gray tee that exposed sun-bronzed arms mottled green and orange with intertwined tattoos. His quads bulged through jeans that were as dusty as the Harley-Davidson he was straddling. His boots had steel toes, perfect for kicking men in the ribs.

Having accomplished his goal of humiliating the deputy, he brought his Harley Nightster to a stop and looked down at the prone officer.

"Where's Finch?" he shouted.

The deputy scrambled to his feet. He was older and softer than the other man, and looked like one of the veteran officers who usually work at courthouses escorting defendants to and from the bar. But you can't always guess the size of a man's heart from the flabbiness of his gut.

"Sir, I need you to turn off your engine."

"Where the fuck is Finch?"

I cast a glance at Boone, who already looked pissed off. We'd both been in brawls, and neither of us relished them. The rest of his dive team was gathering behind him in anticipation of trouble.

"Fucker left a note on my door! I heard he's been asking about my wife."

This, then, was Gina Randazza's husband.

I had suspected Finch's moral disengagement might come back to bite us, but I hadn't imagined it would happen so soon. The detective had said he never mentioned Gina to the neighbors, but I didn't believe him.

The other two bikers made a semicircle around the deputy, using their revving engines to project unity and menace. They both wore leather vests with the same wolf's head insignia on the chest.

It made me think once more of Shadow.

The overweight officer wasn't going to allow himself to be cowed by these thugs. "I said turn off the engine. All of you."

Boone leaned toward me. "Are they going to run him over, pull out concealed weapons, or just start whaling on the dude?"

"None of the above." I directed my next words at the bikers. "You heard what the deputy said!"

One of the others, not the leader, revved his engine as a fuck-you. It caused his exhaust pipe to give off a flatulent noise.

But something about my bearing persuaded Randazza to shut off his engine. He shoved down the kickstand and swung his body off his aggressively styled Nightster. He was a medium-size guy, four or five inches shorter than me, but he looked to be in shape, and he balanced like a boxer on the balls of his feet, radiating the sneaky composure that police learn to recognize in fighters who make a habit of hitting first and hitting hard.

His buddies followed his lead, shutting off their Harleys and dismounting.

One was tall and lean, with ropy muscles. He had a shaved head and wore a mustache of Wild West proportions. White scars were visible through the shadowed stubble on his skull as if he regularly shaved his head while intoxicated.

The other was short, paunchy, and red in the face. No doubt he would be the first to draw a concealed weapon in a fight. Men like him were the reason revolvers had been nicknamed *equalizers*.

"Where's Finch?" Randazza sounded as parched as if he'd driven across the Mojave.

"I'm Warden Investigator Mike Bowditch. You can talk to me."

He smelled heavily of chewing tobacco and stale perspiration. "Where the fuck is Finch?"

"Mr. Randazza—"

"Why is he asking about Gina? I heard cops were investigating a couple of murders."

"Let's find someplace private to talk."

"Not until you tell me what's going on. Has something happened to Gina? She's not picking up her phone, and she's not answering my texts."

There was no way out of it: the unpleasant task of giving the death notification had fallen to me.

"Your first name is Joe. Is that right, Mr. Randazza?"

"People call me Joey."

"I have some bad news, Joey. The worst there is. Gina is dead. These men are members of the Warden Service dive team. Earlier this morning, they retrieved your wife's body from the water off Mouse Island."

"Where?"

"Mouse Island. It's close to the eastern shore."

"Near that kids' camp that just closed," the biker with the shaved skull muttered.

Joey Randazza didn't hear him. "Where is she? I want to see her."

"Gina is being transported to the offices of the chief medical examiner in Augusta for examination. We can arrange for you—"

"No! It's a mistake." He removed his sunglasses, revealing dog-brown eyes surrounded by pale circles where the skin had been stopped from tanning by the shades. "Gina's staying with her sister in Nashua. You must have found some other girl. Gina's out of state."

The two other bikers exchanged worried glances. I could sense the anxiety coming off them.

Boone produced a cell phone and held it out. He must have snapped a picture of the dead woman's face before Dr. Doumit had closed the body bag.

"Is this Gina, Joey?"

His lips began to tremble. I remembered Finch's conjecture that Kip and Gina had been murdered by her jealous husband. But if Joey and his goons had done it, they were excellent actors.

He took several ragged breaths. He rubbed a greasy hand across his brow and left a black mark there.

"Yeah," he said hoarsely. "It's her."

I lowered my voice. "We found your wife's clothes, phone, and wallet on Mouse Island. We believe she was staying at a cottage there."

He seemed almost grateful to have an excuse to become angry. Rage is an easier emotion than grief.

"Whose cottage? She doesn't know anyone with a cottage on Great Pond."

"Do you know a man named Kip Whitcomb?"

What happened next, I should have seen coming. I should have trusted my intuition that he was a dangerous and dirty fighter. I should have kept a safe distance.

But I hadn't.

Joey Randazza clocked me in the side of the face with a terrific right hook.

He knew how to throw a punch, too, turning his hips, keeping his elbow close to his body, powering the blow with his shoulder muscles as well as with the strength in his upper arm.

I dropped to my ass.

26

By the time I got back to my feet, Bill Boone had Randazza flat on his stomach with his arms twisted behind him. The biker was trying to make a fight of it, but he was a puncher and a kicker who did his best brawling on his feet. Joey had no answer for an opponent who was trained in grappling on the ground and knew how to use pressure points to cause excruciating pain.

The left side of my face ached from my temple to my cheekbone. My eye had become a cascade of tears.

I heard the deputy on his radio calling for backup.

"Can I have your cuffs, Mike?" Boone asked calmly as if I weren't reeling.

His divers had drawn their SIGs on Randazza's buddies, both of whom now held their hands high over their heads.

With one eye squeezed shut, I found my handcuffs in their case on my belt and handed them to Bill, who snapped the restraints on Randazza with a single, fluid motion.

I would have a black eye, of course. There was no question about that, even if I found a bag of ice in the next ten minutes. The real injury was to my sense of myself as a seasoned lawman.

"He really got you good," the deputy said unhelpfully. "Talk about a sucker punch."

I felt like a sucker, that much was true.

I squatted beside the still-writhing Randazza, pinned beneath Boone's knee. The side of his own face was red and dimpled from the gravel into which it had been pushed. Dust adhered to the sweat above and below his ear.

"Assaulting an officer is a Class C felony, Joey," I said. "That's a guaranteed year in prison, minimum. Whether I ask the DA to press charges depends on how fast you get your shit together. What'll it be?"

Boone was searching the man for weapons and contraband. He found a Beretta Bobcat and a Karambit fighting knife.

The divers made a similar haul off Randazza's companions: handguns, knives, and a baggie of opaque white crystals that sure as hell weren't rock candy. Whatever happened with Joey, the tall cowboy with the facial hair was looking at a mandatory minimum for possessing methamphetamine in a sufficient quantity that suggested intent to distribute.

The only one who interested me was Joey Randazza. I will admit to having mixed emotions about the man; I resented being made his personal punching bag, but I understood his anger. In less than a minute's time, he'd learned that his wife was dead and that she'd had a secret lover.

Unless he's acting . . .

"From that punch, I take it the name Kip Whitcomb means something to you."

In the same dry voice, he rasped, "I sold him a fucking bike."

"Whitcomb purchased a motorcycle from you?"

"My old Fat Boy. I put it up for sale online, and he came out to see it. The son of a bitch came to my shop when Gina was there. Twice!"

It wasn't my place to interrogate him, I had to remind myself. The detectives were investigating the murder of Gina Randazza, not me.

I had to figure Finch and Pomerleau had heard the deputy's call for backup and would be here in minutes.

With my fingertips, I explored my cheekbone and decided the bruise didn't go as deep as the bone. "I'm going to see if I can find a bag of ice."

"There's one in the boat cooler," said Boone.

I nodded in acknowledgment but directed my words at Randazza. "Sergeant Boone is going to put you in the back of the deputy's nice, air-conditioned cruiser so you can collect yourself. Detective Finch and his partner are en route, and I'll leave it to them to continue this conversation with you."

Still blinking tears out of one eye, I wandered back to the boat trailer. I took a look at myself in the mirror of the truck to which it was attached. The side of my face was glowing, and my eyelid was already swelling as if from a beesting.

I heard sirens approaching down the forested lane that connected the public boat launch with Sahagian Road.

Randazza wasn't the only one who needed to calm down. I scrambled up into the boat and found enough ice to make an igloo. I pressed a bag of cubes against my face and returned to the site of the melee.

Several police cruisers had pulled into the lot with lights flashing. I made for the unmarked sedan driven by Pomerleau and Finch.

I glared at Roger as he exited the vehicle. "I found Gina's husband for you."

"What's with the cuffs, guys?" Ellen asked, her pale skin looking almost transparent in the direct sunlight. "What's going on? What happened to your eye, Mike?"

"I walked into a tree."

"Did this tree have a fist?" Finch asked.

I grabbed his upper arm. He tried to shake me off. But when he could see how angry I was, he allowed me to drag him out of earshot of the others.

"What were you thinking, leaving that note for Randazza? You had to know he'd make the connection between our search and his missing wife."

"I didn't say she was dead. I said he should call me. How was I to know he'd ride out here with his gangbangers? What did you say that made him punch you? You must have pissed him off."

"Don't try to make this like I screwed up." I pressed the bag of ice harder against my face, which was beginning to burn from the cold. "Is that why you chickened out of giving the death notification in person? Because you were afraid to give him bad news without backup?"

"Fuck you. I didn't chicken out of anything."

"I wonder if your partner will agree when I tell her how I nearly got coldcocked."

Finch lowered his eyes as if to inspect the shine on his Cole Haans.

27

I told Pomerleau that I wanted to have a private word with her.

Afterward, she told Finch she wanted to have a private word with him.

Only when the detectives had finished their personal dispute did she beckon me across the parking lot.

"How did Randazza know to come looking for us here?" she said.

"The search has been all over the news and social media. We had a drone filming us after the divers brought up Gina's body. Joey didn't have to be a genius to make the connection between Roger's card and his missing wife. What would you conclude if a homicide detective came looking for you?"

Finch was massaging his arm where I'd squeezed it. "We need to get that asshole into an interrogation room, Ellen. I'm telling you he was behind those two homicides. Him and his crew."

"On what evidence are you going to arrest him?" I asked.

"We'll bring him in for assaulting you and go from there."

"I won't be your cat's paw," I said. "Randazza may be a prick, but it was Whitcomb's name that set him off. It wasn't a personal attack on me as a game warden."

"Your eye tells a different story," Finch said with a sneer. "Joey Randazza has a criminal record as long as my dick. Assault. Stalking. Criminal threatening. Burglary. Possession with intent to distribute. Do you want to read his file yourself? Would that be enough to change your mind?"

"Any felonies?" Ellen asked, readjusting her sunglasses on the bridge of her nose.

"Nothing but misdemeanors. He must have one hell of a lawyer."

"We can't even get him on unlawful possession of the firearm?"

A line of perspiration slid down Finch's cheek until it reached the precipice of his jaw. "No."

"Then he's committed no new crimes."

"He's the leader of a motorcycle gang!"

"A minor-league one," she said. "Look, Roger, I wouldn't want my daughter dating a Direwolf, but I'm not going to violate my own ethics to begin a baseless interrogation."

"You're just going to ignore that he's a dirtbag?"

"Until he gives me a reason to consider him a suspect, I'm going to treat him like I would any family member of a murder victim."

Finch reacted with disgusted silence as she released Randazza from the back of the cruiser and unlocked his handcuffs, handing them back to me. She introduced herself as the lead detective investigating his wife's death and then asked if he wanted a bottle of water, which he accepted. And when she asked if he would be willing to answer a few questions about Gina, he shocked Finch by saying he had nothing to hide.

The biker rubbed his wrists where the cuffs had pinched them. "I already know what you're thinking—that I had something to do with this. But I was riding with my boys yesterday in the White Mountains. That's why I didn't get the message until late, because the signal was crappy."

"And 'your boys' will confirm where you were?"

"Yeah, they will. And if twenty witnesses ain't enough, there's a waitress at a brewery in Gorham, New Hampshire, who will remember me. But I'm not into fat-ass white girls."

Finch peeled his damp shirt away from his underarms. "Plus, you're a loving and faithful husband."

"Gina was my wife. Yeah, we had problems. Who doesn't after they've been married a few years—"

"By few, you mean . . . ?" Finch asked.

"Three."

I knew this was supposed to be Ellen's interview, but it was already clear that her partner intended to highjack it, so I decided to cut in before he continued with his taunting questions. "Where did Gina work?"

Randazza studied my swollen eye as if it were had nothing to do with the punch he'd thrown. "She worked as a colorist at a hair salon in Waterville. She made good money. The rich girls from the college all go there."

"Did you know any of the women she worked with?" Pomerleau asked.

"She didn't like me dropping in," Randazza said in a voice that I was coming to think was perpetually hoarse. "But yeah, she mentioned some names. Girls she went drinking with after work. I wouldn't call them *friends*. She always came back from the bar saying what stupid sluts they were."

Ellen, I was certain, was going to ask for the names of these women, but Finch couldn't keep from interrupting. "Why didn't she like you dropping by the salon? Was she embarrassed by you?"

The question seemed to baffle Randazza. "Why would she be?"

Finch made a show of rolling his eyes. "Because you're twice her age and a career criminal."

"I'm a business owner, prick."

He explained that he'd inherited an auto repair shop in Oakland from his father. He'd gotten into some trouble in his late teens and early twenties, it was true. Maybe he'd been too trusting of the people he associated with. But if the detectives had seen his record, they knew he'd never been convicted of a felony.

"I want to hear about your stalking conviction," Pomerleau said. "In light of what happened last night, it raises a lot of questions for us."

"That was Gina."

"You stalked your own wife?" Finch said.

"We weren't married at the time!" Randazza shook his head as if it was the dumbest question he'd ever heard. "She was playing hard to get, is what the story was. When I kept showing up at her apartment, her stupid roommate told her to call the cops on me. Then after I pled out on the charge, Gina called me in tears saying how she really loved me. Et cetera, et cetera."

"How and when did you meet Kip Whitcomb?" Ellen asked.

"He stopped at my place because he'd seen I was selling a Fat Boy I'd restored. I don't know what you've heard about Whitcomb, but the guy had *midlife crisis* written all over him. I said sure, take it for a ride, and he did. Two days later, he was back with an envelope full of cash. I signed over the bike to him on the spot."

I was curious about the Harley Fat Boy Whitcomb had purchased. The detectives had found his parked Mercedes easily enough. Where was the motorcycle?

"What else can you tell us about him?" Ellen Pomerleau had a way of asking questions that might best be described as clinical.

"Typical Masshole. Treated me like I was some ignorant hick who'd be impressed by how rich he was. Said he had a camp in Belgrade, and he wanted to own a Harley he could ride when he was in Maine. I don't remember Gina talking to him. If she was there, which she must have been at least one of the times, I didn't even notice."

"Clearly, you're not the jealous type," offered Finch.

"Women don't leave me. I leave *them*."

"Not this time."

Randazza's smile slowly melted as the reality of the situation registered, perhaps for the first time. Maybe Gina hadn't officially ended their marriage, but she might as well have stuck a stake through its undead heart. Her smug, self-centered husband had been so confident in his alpha male status that he'd missed the infidelity happening under his nose.

"Are you wrapping up, Detective?" Pomerleau asked.

"Do we have somewhere else to be?" Finch loosened a polyester necktie that I suspected was the only one he owned. "Tell us about this trip you took with your 'boys' over the weekend. Whose idea was it for you to go, Joey?"

The biker paused, then looked down at his wrists, at the red scrapes left by the cuffs.

"It was Gina's idea," he said. "She said she wanted to go visit her sister in Nashua, so why shouldn't I go riding with the guys. I still can't believe she was fucking around behind my back. I thought I knew who she was."

He was on the verge of breaking down and didn't want us to see him cry, so he asked to use the outhouse.

After he'd left us, Pomerleau sighed. "Do you still think he's putting on an act, Roger?"

Finch, staying true to his bulldog nature, refused to relent. "You already know what I think."

"God forbid you should ever change your mind. What's your assessment, Mike?"

The cynical voice in my head had gone quiet.

"I think he's telling the truth—at least about Gina," I said at last. "He didn't know she was having an affair until I told him. And if you're being honest with yourself, Finch, you agree with me."

The detective spat on the ground. It was as close to an admission that I was right as we would get.

Randazza was such a lowlife. He made such a wonderful suspect. It was almost a shame to cross him off the list.

28

While we waited for Randazza to return, it came to me that this was the same boat launch where LaJoy would be holding the press conference. He had wanted water in the background, but the only part of the lake that was visible was an unclean channel leading around Hersom Point to Belgrade Village.

I checked my watch. I didn't want to be caught here when the television crews began rolling up in their vans and SUVs.

For that reason, I hoped we were done with the interview. But Randazza had some questions of his own when he reappeared.

"What's going to happen to my riders?"

He meant the two luckless men who'd followed their leader into the cold embrace of the police.

Finch got another laugh out of that one. "What do you think is going to happen to them? One has a bag full of meth, the other is a felon packing an M&P Shield. They'll be spending a little time away from home."

Randazza reached into his pocket and removed a packet of chewing tobacco. He plucked out shreds of Red Man and stuffed them into his mouth. His heavy beard hid the bulge in his cheek.

"When can I see Gina?" he asked thickly.

"You can see her after the ME has completed the autopsy," Pomerleau said.

"Don't you need my permission to cut her open? I'm her fucking husband."

"Not in the case of a suspicious death," I said.

Randazza studied me again, doing his best to hide his curiosity. Finch was another dumb cop intent on busting him. Pomerleau he'd pegged as a soft touch whose ethics and kindness he could manipulate. I was an unknown quantity, and he didn't like unknown quantities.

"You were the one who found Gina?" he asked in his buzz-saw voice.

I nodded, not wanting to get into the nitty-gritty.

"Am I supposed to thank you?" he said.

"That's up to you."

He dribbled a thread of tobacco juice onto the gravel. Not exactly an expression of gratitude.

I reacted with equal rudeness. "There's something puzzling me, Joey. Maybe you can clear it up. We told you that Gina drowned with Whitcomb, but you haven't asked us for any details about what happened."

"I figured they were wasted," he said. "People who are drunk or high drown all the time."

"The circumstances don't interest you at all?"

"Circumstances?"

"Where it happened? When it happened? How it happened?"

He tightened the bandanna around his head. The odor of old sweat came off him as he raised his arms.

"Gina betrayed me. I don't give a flying fuck how she died. I only hope it was painful. I ain't paying for the fucking autopsy, either."

We watched him walk back to his Harley and mount up. He churned up a cloud of dust and pebbles, peeling out of the parking lot.

"I could have gotten something out of him if you'd let me," Finch told his partner. "He's not half as smart as he thinks he is."

I might have said the same about him.

Pomerleau said they'd be in touch. Finch, grinning, wished me luck at the press conference. I decided not to tell him I wouldn't be attending. They didn't speak to each other as they returned to their car.

The other officers had all departed, leaving the Harleys of the two Direwolves in custody, to be retrieved later.

Boats glided back and forth along the channel, barely disturbing the tame mallards that were everywhere in the village. Children laughed, someone turned up a hip-hop tune. Two people were dead, but life went on.

My moment of solitude didn't last a minute.

Dust raised by the detectives' cruiser was still settling back to earth when a rusty Subaru rolled into the lot.

Galen Webb opened the driver's door while a young woman emerged from the other side. For a minute, they busied themselves removing an infant from a car seat in the rear. When Galen spotted me, he frowned and whispered something to his wife as she positioned the baby in a sling across her chest. They walked over to where I was standing.

"I guess we're early for the press conference," he said.

"Only by an hour and a half."

He had showered and shaved and was dressed in what passed for a constable uniform: black polo tucked into khaki cargos.

"Warden Investigator Bowditch, this is my wife, Grace, and our little boy, Coleman."

Grace Webb was taller than her husband. Her blond hair was pulled back in a bushy ponytail. Her face was round and pretty, with widely spaced eyes, and she had the whitest teeth I had ever seen.

"Galen's told me so much about you." She extended her hand. "May I ask what happened to your eye?"

"Gee!" her husband said. "I didn't even notice. That's quite a shiner. What happened?"

"I walked into something." It wasn't technically a lie. "Galen was very helpful last night, Mrs. Webb."

She bounced the baby while she gazed admiringly at her husband. "He still hopes to become a warden someday. We both pray it will happen. He was badly mistreated when he applied."

"Grace!" Her husband winced. "Don't say that."

The subject was yet another I didn't want to discuss so I put on a bland smile. "Did you say your baby's name was Coleman?"

The proud mother flashed her porcelain smile. The infant had lost whatever hair he'd come with at birth and resembled a nearsighted and grumpy old man. I waggled my finger, thinking he might take it. But he only slobbered onto his food-stained onesie.

"He's a cute little guy," I continued. "It's quite a coincidence. I hadn't heard of anyone being named Coleman before yesterday."

The mother parted her lips and waited expectantly for me to explain.

"The judge who used to own Mouse Island was named Coleman Fenton," I explained.

"His son, too," added Galen.

Grace gave her husband a disappointed look. "You didn't tell me that. Here, I thought it was an unusual name. I didn't realize it was common."

"I wouldn't call it *common,*" I said with a friendly smile. "I bet when Coleman goes to school, he'll be the only one in his class."

"We're going to homeschool him," said Galen quickly. "At least until he's old enough to attend Temple Academy. The public schools around here . . ."

"Do you have children, Warden Investigator Bowditch?" Grace asked.

"Not yet."

"Coleman is the greatest blessing Galen and I have been given. Of course, we hope to have more if the Lord wishes."

I checked my watch again. I had more than enough time to leave before the lieutenant and the media people from the Department of Inland Fisheries and Wildlife arrived.

"What kind of questions will they ask us?" Galen said. "I've never done TV before."

The naïve young man thought he was going to be standing on the podium beside LaJoy, fielding questions from the media scrum. Part of me thought I should leave it to the lieutenant to break the news to the constable. I hated to disappoint him in front of his adoring wife. But I knew I had a duty.

"This conference is going to be Warden Service only, Galen. You won't be answering questions."

The sudden flash in his eyes took me back to the night before, when he'd showed a quickness to anger. It troubled me just as much now as it had then.

"I'm the lake constable, deputized by the sheriff to police all the Belgrade Lakes. No one knows the waters better than me."

"That's undoubtedly true, but—"

"I probably saw Mr. Whitcomb more than anyone this summer. I was all around that island this weekend, checking boats and so on. But because I ain't a warden, nobody cares what I have to say, like none of the other stuff mattered?"

"Relax, Galen," I said. "None of this is personal."

He spun around on his wife. "What did I tell you? They've got a black mark next to my name!"

"Galen, I'm sure that's not true."

"I wasn't good enough to be a game warden. And now I'm not good enough to stand beside them."

It wasn't merely frustration rising to the surface. He was working himself into a state of real rage.

"Maybe it would be best if you went home, then," I said sternly.

Grace caught her breath.

But the constable puffed out his narrow chest. "Maybe it would. Come on, Grace."

"Galen?"

"We're leaving!"

She cast me one last pleading look, but I was relieved they were going. LaJoy would have a difficult enough job without having to care for Galen's ego, too.

Again, I remembered the cryptic comment of the warden investigator who had told me about the skeletons in the young man's closet. The more I thought about the phrase, the more puzzled I was. The Kennebec sheriff would never have deputized him if he had so much as a history of speeding.

Galen Webb seemed like a well-meaning man, a loving husband, and a caring father. He came across as the opposite of someone like Joey Randazza. But I'd learned to stop trusting appearances long ago.

29

The descent from the paved road to Neil and Jubilee's camp was steep and narrow, with protruding rocks the size of softballs. I wondered how Neil didn't bottom out in his Audi every time he drove down the hill. I was somewhat surprised not to find their car in the dooryard. The house seemed eerily quiet. When I announced myself upon entering, there was a pause, and then Ora answered weakly from the great room.

As soon as I poked my head in, she gripped the arms of her wheelchair. "Mike! What happened to your face?"

Even though it was tender, I had managed to forget the injury as I ran through my plans to search for the hit-and-run boater.

"The same old, same old," I said.

"Who hit you?" Her voice sounded scratchy, painful.

Sunlight usually flattered Stacey's mother, bringing out the ethereal paleness of her eyes. But now it also accentuated the translucence of her skin, so thin I could trace every blue vein.

"It was Gina Randazza's husband, after I gave him the death notification. He hadn't known she was cheating on him, and he lashed out at the messenger."

"That's very understanding of you, Mike."

"It's your husband's positive influence. Where is everyone?"

"Neil and Jubilee went into Augusta for groceries, and Stacey took the paddleboard out for some exercise," she explained. "Charley's off on a walkabout."

She had a book of poems tented on her lap, but I had the feeling I'd awakened her from a nap.

"How are you feeling, Ora?"

"Tired." She managed a closemouthed smile that didn't put me at ease. "I didn't expect you back this morning."

"I'm kind of in a holding pattern. Lieutenant LaJoy is doing a press conference asking the public for tips about boats speeding around Mouse Island yesterday. There's bound to be a bunch of calls for me after."

"I expect you'll be chasing a lot of false leads."

"That's what usually happens. There's a flurry of activity after something like this. But it won't surprise me if I'm working the crash on my own in a few days."

"What do you mean?"

"There's always another emergency coming around the bend. People will continue to commit crimes or get lost in the woods. More boats will crash or overturn in rapids. And we'll need to shift our resources to deal with the new crisis. Sometimes I think working in law enforcement is like sailing a leaky boat. You can bail and bail, but there will always be more water coming in."

"It makes me sad to hear you talking so pessimistically, Mike."

"Where do you draw the line between realism and pessimism?"

"I don't have to tell you that's a rhetorical question."

She hadn't exactly scolded me, but I got the message that I needed to get out of my own head.

Smiling to reassure her, I asked if I could get her anything, some toast or tea, but she said she was fine. She seemed obviously unwell to me, but not in a way I could easily define, and it seemed rude to press her about it. I left her alone with her book: a collection of poems by Mary Oliver.

In the kitchen I started another carafe of coffee brewing and toasted another bagel that Jubilee had ordered by the dozen from a famous New York deli. I smeared on some cream cheese and gravlax, thinking how the last salmon I'd eaten was of the landlocked subspecies: *Salmo salar sebago*. I'd caught the three-pound fish on a Black Ghost streamer on the West Branch of the Penobscot River.

I took my lunch onto the porch to look for Stacey, but she had paddled out of sight.

I decided to check in on my wolf.

Shadow was at my home in Ducktrap, under the watchful eye of a local boy named Logan Cronk. I texted him asking for an update and a photo. He responded quickly, saying the wolf had eaten a whole mutton leg I'd cadged from a slaughterhouse. Then he'd retreated into the coolness of the trees to digest his meal. Logan asked if I wanted a picture of Shadow's new raven friend, Gus, and I said sure. Twenty seconds later, a grainy image of a black bird perched atop a beech tree arrived on my screen. I thanked Logan and told him I wasn't sure when I'd be home but would keep him posted. The boy didn't mind. His favorite thing in life was sleeping in a tent outside Shadow's pen, taking observation notes in practice for his future career as a wildlife biologist.

Ora was asleep again when I looked in on her, and my phone was momentarily quiet, so I decided to go looking for Charley.

I found him in the dooryard, standing beside my Scout, wearing the deerstalker cap I'd been given as a joke engagement gift. He looked supremely pleased with himself in the Sherlock Holmes hat.

"What do you think?"

"You look ridiculous."

"And here I thought I bore a strong resemblance to Basil Rathbone. That's quite a mouse someone gave you."

"I'd rather not talk about it."

He nodded, having taken a few knocks himself in the line of duty. "I was thinking you might like to go for a ride with me."

"Where?"

"Down the road to Camp Machigonne. I thought it might be useful to explore that beach where we heard the bear crashing around last night."

"You don't really think it was a bear," I said.

"Only one way to find out."

I figured my phone would work as well at the camp as it would at the house, so I might as well take a ride with my friend. The camp was half a mile down the road. And there were houses between Neil's place and the gate with views of the channel and Mouse Island. We could stop at one or more of them to ask the residents if they'd seen anything noteworthy in the days and hours leading up to the two deaths.

I had assumed that Charley had put the cap on for my amusement, that he'd been playing the clown, but he continued wearing it without any trace of self-consciousness.

Camp Machigonne occupied an entire point of land jutting northwestward into Great Pond, ten acres in all. The dirt road, shown on my GPS screen as two double lines, ended at a gate.

Three signs greeted us. I put the truck into park and leaned forward against the steering wheel to read them. The first was the old billboard announcing to campers that they'd arrived at historic Camp Machigonne, founded in 1895, and emblazoned with the crest of two crossed tomahawks.

The second was a friendly message directed at everyone else who wittingly or unwittingly found themselves here:

NO TRESPASSING
Without Written Permission
CAMPERS & THEIR GUESTS
ONLY!
ALL OTHERS WILL BE
TOWED AT THEIR OWN EXPENSE

The third sign belonged to a commercial real estate company that specialized in expensive waterfront properties. It happily declared the camp under contract. But it included its own warning against unlawful trespass, lest anyone get the wrong idea about the new owner welcoming uninvited visitors.

The "gate" was a length of anchor chain stretched across the dirt road from one steel post to another. A padlock hung from one end. Even through the dusty windshield, I could see tire prints pressing down the pine needles.

"Someone's in there now," said Charley.

"How do you know?"

The old man pointed toward the tracks I'd spotted. "A big dually left those, going in. But it hasn't left yet. See?"

He was referring to one of those six-wheeled pickups favored by stonemasons and landscapers. It would have taken me crawling around with a magnifying glass to reach the conclusion he'd reached with a single glance.

To avoid blocking the gate, I pulled the Scout into a patch of goldenrod, aster, and orange hawkweed. The truck spooked several monarchs off the blossoms on which they'd been feeding. The butterflies remained airborne until we'd moved clear of the vehicle, then returned to the flowers to suck up more nectar for their long migration south.

Charley grasped the right post and hopped over the taut chain. Despite his age and the many injuries he had suffered, he remained as nimble as a man in his thirties. I felt compelled to demonstrate my own agility by doing the same. Never mind that there was a well-worn footpath around the gate.

The first building we passed was a one-room office where campers and their families must have been greeted. Next to the welcome cabin were two larger structures devoted to arts and crafts.

"Does it look the same as it did?" I asked.

"A little shabbier. That log cabin we passed is listing like a drunken sailor. If it wasn't going to be torn down, they'd need to jack up the whole shebang to rebuild the supports."

As Charley led me through the camp, I couldn't help but remember my first visit to Great Pond. Years earlier, my friend had flown me to the lake for a day of pike fishing after I'd confessed to never having caught one.

That spring, I had been suffering from a case of undiagnosed post-traumatic stress syndrome following a manhunt I'd been intimately involved in. Charley Stevens alone had recognized my malady and had brought me to Great Pond to begin a course of nature therapy. Not that he ever used that term. Charley simply believed that time on the water with a fly rod would be healing for my heart, head, and soul.

He had been correct in that regard.

The area around the bunkhouses was more parklike than forested. The lower branches of the pines had been lopped off over the years, and the brush had been regularly cleared to provide views of the shining lake. The fallen needles that covered the ground were so heavily trod upon by children's feet that they seemed almost interwoven—a russet carpet.

I spotted something red in the shadow of a cabin and bent to have a look. It was a basic Swiss Army knife, appropriate for a young user. Knife blade, nail file, and folding scissors. I wondered about the boy who'd dropped it and whether he would even miss what should have been a souvenir of his weeks in the Maine woods.

I had never even visited Camp Machigonne, let alone attended it, yet I seemed to feel more nostalgia over its closing than my friend did.

My reflective pause had allowed Charley to disappear around the corner of another bunkhouse.

When I caught up with him, he was standing beside a claret-red Ram 3500 with his palm pressed flat against the hood. There was no one in the truck, which did indeed have dual wheels on both ends of its rear axle for carrying heavy loads.

"Is the engine still warm?" I asked.

"Yeah, but it's a hot day, so I can't tell you how long it's been sitting here."

"Can't or won't?"

My friend showed me a big grin. He loved nothing more than showing off his deductive powers. In that instant, I decided to gift him the deerstalker cap. Lord knew I had no plans to wear it.

I peeked into the Ram's second row and saw two matching Callaway golf bags, both with full sets of clubs.

"I take it there's no golf course on the camp premises."

"Not so much as a putting green," said Charley.

I glanced around through the scaly pines. "So who are they, and what are they doing here?"

He rose and clapped me between the shoulder blades. "One mystery at a time, young man. One mystery at a time."

30

We located the little beach and the tangle of puckerbrush growing above the undercut bank. It was the spot where we'd heard the noise the night before, no doubt of that. But a new sign was nailed to an adjacent tree trunk. NO TRESPASSING.

"That wasn't here last night."

Charley squatted on his heels and peered under the bushes, then sprang up and climbed the grassy bank, disappearing behind the shrubs.

"It wouldn't have mattered if the sign was here or not," he called. "Not to the trespasser we frightened."

I followed his voice and found him leaning over a massive pile of bear shit.

"You were right about the bruin," he said, pushing the brim of the deerstalker back from his weathered forehead. "Sometimes I forget what an expert teacher I am. I take great pride in your having learned to identify a bear from sound alone."

"You really need to give yourself more credit."

He let out one of his signature guffaws. Charley laughed like I imagined Abraham Lincoln had laughed.

"I was hoping it was an illegal camper," I said. "So far, I'm short of eyewitnesses to the events on Mouse Island."

"After that press conference happens, you'll have more witnesses than you ever wanted."

"And how many of those people will have seen what they claim to have seen?"

"Sounds like you're in a state of *flusteration.*"

As often happened with Charley, I wasn't sure if he'd dragged the strange word out of some bygone era or had coined it on the spot.

It felt like old times, having my eccentric mentor beside me on a case.

"I need to figure out what's going on with Galen Webb. He's obviously angling for a job as a warden, so he's eager to prove himself. Plus, he was all over these lakes this weekend, checking boaters around Mouse Island. It seems like he should have come up with the names of a few speedboat owners for me to check out."

"How certain are you he's not pursuing his own covert investigation? Could be he's making private inquiries. If he identifies the offender himself, it'll prove what a mistake the Warden Service made in not hiring him."

"Shit, I didn't think of that." It seemed like the sort of boneheaded stunt the young constable would pull. "I was warned the guy had character issues."

Charley pursed his lips and let his gaze wander out across the glistening lake.

"What?" I said.

"I thought you knew young Webb's story."

"I was told Galen was denied a job because he had skeletons in his closet. But I didn't get the details."

"He struck and killed a boy whose ball bounced in front of his car."

"When was this?"

"When Galen was sixteen."

"If it was an accident, I can't see the hiring committee holding it against him."

"There were no witnesses, but Galen's dad was friendly with the trooper who responded to the call—they were members of the same flying club."

"I can see the Warden Service finding that problematic. But as grounds to reject him, it sounds . . . "

"You haven't heard the rest. When the polygraph administrator asked the young man what happened as part of the screening process, the test results indicated stress, which looked a lot like deception."

"Is it a surprise that being asked about the worst moment of his life would freak him out?"

"Galen's chart looked like a seismograph reading of the great San Francisco earthquake from what I heard."

I scowled at my friend. "How do you know this and I don't?"

"I still try to keep an ear to the ground."

"Meaning you're a gossip."

He shrugged to admit the label might fit. "Webb is busting a boiler to prove the wardens made a mistake. But I wouldn't be so quick to fault the hiring committee. I'm a good judge of character normally, but I can't read that boy at all, and I find that worrisome in a person, especially one carrying a badge and gun."

Off in the trees, someone began hammering: a staccato rhythm.

Then another carpenter joined in from a slightly different spot.

"Even money those are our golfers, putting up posted signs." Charley began striding toward the source of the first blows.

I caught up with him a hundred yards away where the waterline curved around a point to make a sheltered cove from which campers must have launched a thousand canoes over the decades.

A woman dressed in golfing attire was punishing a tree by nailing a sign to it with furious intention.

In the woods Charley moved with a practiced quiet that came from a lifetime of stalking deer. He got within fifteen feet of the golfer's back, when he decided it would be rude not to announce himself.

"Excuse me, ma'am."

The woman jumped a foot in the air. She swung around with the hammer raised, her eyes wide, and for an instant, I thought she might charge my friend to deliver a death blow.

Instead, she called out in a gravelly voice, "Rob, we've got trespassers!"

Charley seemed taken aback by the almost manic violence in her expression. "No, we're not trespassing. Which is to say my colleague here isn't, legally speaking. I apologize for startling you."

My late mother, I suspected, would have described the woman as "handsome." She wasn't unattractive, but the years had robbed her face of any softness it might once have possessed. She wore a blue golf skirt and a sleeveless blouse that revealed the muscular legs and arms of a CrossFit addict.

The sight of Charley in his silly Sherlock Holmes cap was causing her alarm to dissipate fast.

"Who are you supposed to be?" she sneered.

"Charley Stevens, Maine Warden Service, retired."

A man came lumbering between two cabins, also carrying a hammer upraised.

He was barrel-chested with a dark crew cut and a grizzled goatee. His eyes were intensely blue. He wore a black polo tucked into black golf shorts. The one discordant element to his appearance was a sleeve of tattoos that crept up his biceps, under his shirt, and halfway up his neck.

"What is this? Who are you?"

"Maine game warden, sir. I'd appreciate you both lowering your hammers."

"This is private property," the woman growled. "There's no trespassing here."

She used the hammer to point at a sign to that effect on a distant tree.

"Those prohibitions don't apply to law enforcement officers in the act of conducting a criminal investigation," I said.

As I was dressed in an actual uniform, complete with a fully loaded gun belt and a warden's badge sewn into the outer fabric of my ballistic vest, I provoked a different response than did my white-haired friend.

"OK, you're a game warden, but he said he's retired." The woman had been paying attention. "What criminal investigation?"

"Two people died in the lake last night, off Mouse Island. That's about half a mile from here."

"Who were they?" the woman demanded.

The press conference would begin soon, and I saw no point in playing coy. "One of them was a man from Massachusetts named Kipling Whitcomb."

"You're shitting me!" the woman said, almost with delight.

"You knew him?" I asked.

The lumbering man seemed to feel a need to assert some authority lest we think his wife was the dominant partner. "Before we say anything more, I'd like your name please, Officer."

"My name is Mike Bowditch. I'm an investigator with the Maine Warden Service." I found business cards for both of them. "And you are?"

"Rob and Robyn Soto," he said.

"We're Realtors," she added.

Charley scratched an ear. "Rob and Robyn! You two must have been destined to find each other."

Neither of the Sotos seemed remotely charmed by Charley's affect.

"How did you know Mr. Whitcomb?" I said.

The wife answered, "Our client tried to buy Mouse Island at the same time he purchased this camp. Kip Whitcomb led us on for weeks, negotiating the price up and up. We assumed he was operating in good faith. After we finally settled on a price, he came back and told us his wife had quashed the deal. The island is in her name, it seems."

"You're talking about Dianne Fenton-Whitcomb," I said.

"That sounds right."

"Who is the new owner of the property, by the way?"

Robyn replied with a close-lipped smirk, "Horse Point LLC."

I took the unsubtle hint that she wasn't in a sharing mood. "You don't want to compromise your client's privacy. That's understandable. But I assume you don't have the same qualms about Mr. Whitcomb's. Is there anything else you can tell us about him?"

"He had an office in Boston and lived somewhere outside the city. He said he did some investing, as well as selling real estate. Come to think of it, he never had an assistant answer his phone, which should have been a tip-off he was blowing smoke up our asses about the extent of his business operations."

"And you never met his wife?"

"No," said Rob. "The last conversation with him was when he told us he was backing out of the deal. Robyn hung up on him."

"Damn right I did. He wasted hours of my time. Kip and I had three or four lunches, trying to hash this out. Expensive lunches."

Her husband cast a questioning glance her way, as if these fancy lunches were news to him.

"It sounds like you came away from these talks genuinely disliking him," I said.

"What kind of question is that?" she said. "I hope you're not implying—"

Her husband interrupted to offer an unprompted alibi. "We were at home in Portland last night. We had friends over for dinner and to watch the fireworks over Casco Bay. Our house is on the Eastern Prom."

"Where we live is none of their business," said Robyn. "And they still haven't explained what they're doing here."

"We're searching the shoreline for whatever pieces we can find that help put the jigsaw together." Charley was affecting an exaggerated version of his natural accent, as he tended to do with supercilious people. "I don't suppose you've seen anything unusual around Mouse Island on prior visits here."

Rob passed the hammer back and forth between his meaty hands. "Like I said, we live in Portland. We're not here on a regular basis. We only drove up this morning to put up signs along the water."

"Your job responsibilities include personally nailing up NO TRESPASSING signs?" I asked, incredulous.

Robyn let out an audible sigh. "We got a call last week from the lake constable that people were throwing parties here and roaming around drunk and high, probably looking to steal whatever isn't nailed down. We specialize in exclusive properties, which means we go the extra mile for our clients. So we drove up here on our day off to put up these damn signs. Does that explanation meet with your approval?"

Rob decided he didn't want to come off as a total jerk. "We also wanted to play a round at Belgrade Lakes Country Club."

"Why'd you say that, Rob? Jesus, what's wrong with you?"

"I take it you're a Marine, Mr. Soto," said Charley.

"Former Marine. You?"

"I did a stint in the army," said the combat veteran and former POW. "But I happened to notice your tattoos. The crossed swords. And that bulldog on your arm—it's the Marine mascot."

Robyn leveled another glare at me. "Are we done here?"

"Have you discovered anything this morning to indicate someone was on the grounds of the camp last night?" I asked.

"There might have been trespassers," she said, swinging the hammer underhand as if to exercise the muscles in her forearm. "We'd have no idea if there were. That's why we're putting up these signs *on our day off.* We have a security company coming this week to install cameras around the property. The last thing the new owner wants is for some drunk redneck to set fire to these cabins."

"Isn't Mr. LLC planning on tearing them down, anyway?" I asked.

If she got my joke, she didn't appreciate it. "It's a matter of liability."

"Mr. Whitcomb's companion was named Gina Randazza," said Charley. "Does that name mean anything to either of you?"

"No," the husband said. "Should it?"

"So it wasn't his wife who died then?" Robyn said, showing that her facial muscles were capable of forming a smile. "I can't say I'm surprised. Five minutes with Whitcomb and I knew he was a sleaze. It was obvious he was used to having women throw themselves at him."

Her husband had lost a little color. "What exactly did Kip say to you over lunch, Robyn?"

"It's not a conversation I want to have in front of these men."

"It sounds like you should be looking for a jealous husband." Rob pointedly avoided looking at his wife. "Either this Gina's or another woman's. If Kip Whitcomb was such a gigolo."

"We need to finish putting up these signs." Robyn began tapping her palm with the flat of the hammer. "We can't legally stop you from searching the grounds, but I think I'm correct in saying you need a warrant to search the buildings."

"Not if you give us permission on behalf of the owner," I said.

"I don't think that's going to happen."

"May I ask why?"

"I don't have to answer that," said Robyn smugly. "I'd like the name of your commanding officer in case we discover you exceeded your authority here. What is his name, please? Your commanding officer?"

I gave it to her. His phone number, too.

31

The shoreline at the north end of the camp was a beautiful mixture of fields and sand beaches, more open than the rest of the wooded property. August had burned the lawn brown except in the shadows of certain pines where a few black-eyed Susans and blue asters stubbornly persisted. The roughhousing boys of the late, unlamented Camp Machigonne must not have been inclined to pick flowers.

Charley and I continued exploring the point until the Sotos had left for the golf course. I knew it was petty, but it was important to me that the power couple not think they had chased us off.

"Did you know the Sotos were from Portland?" I said after they had gone. "They have a house on the Eastern Prom."

"You can't let people like that get under your skin."

"You mean she didn't irritate you?"

"My epidermis was too thick for her proboscis to penetrate."

We'd come to an outcrop with a distant view of Mouse Island, half a mile to the southwest. None of the Fentons' buildings were visible from this direction, not even the fishing cabin.

"It doesn't look like we're going to find any witnesses here," I said. "LaJoy will be starting the press conference soon. I should begin getting calls immediately. What should we do in the meantime?"

"We can always knock on some doors. We passed a few houses with views of the island. Who knows what the occupants saw?"

As we drove back down the Point Road, the first home we came to was a ranch-style residence on the lakeshore. I slowed to an idle for a better look.

It was sided with blue clapboards, faded from a thousand summer afternoons, and the roof was so thoroughly covered with dead pine needles, you might have assumed the shingles themselves were orange. The house would have looked modest anywhere, but compared with the luxurious homes I'd seen on Great Pond over the past twenty-four hours, this one seemed downright seedy.

"No vehicles in the dooryard," Charley said from the passenger seat. "Let's keep going."

"It doesn't necessarily mean no one is home."

"True."

"And it would help to know if anybody's recently occupied the place. If it's already closed up for the year, then we can probably check it off our list."

We hadn't taken five steps down the rutted and root-tangled driveway before a dog began to bark inside the house.

"Hmmm," Charley said unhappily.

He planted both of his big boots on the welcome mat to rap at the screen door. The noise his fist made against the thin aluminum carried through the trees and probably far out onto the water.

In response, the barking dog inside upped its volume. Gauzy shades hid the interior of the house from view. We waited for the sound of footsteps.

Absently, Charley began to hum a tune.

"Is that 'Home, Sweet Home'?" I asked.

"This place isn't as humble as it seemed at first glance." He pointed toward the cone-laden boughs overhead. "Those cables are all new."

I had mistaken the building for an old summer camp. The flaking paint had thrown me off. But in addition to the new wires, we found a generator on the side of the building that looked as if it had also been recently installed.

A brand-new deck had been constructed along the entire back of the house. The wood was unpainted and unstained. The only pieces of furniture were an expensive-looking chaise longue for sunbathing, an Adirondack chair, and a matching side table positioned to support a book and a gin and tonic.

The sliding porch doors, from waist level down, were smeared with dog spittle. The pooch finally made its appearance when it heard us mount the deck. It scratched against the door and knocked itself against the glass as if determined to either break through the obstacle or crack open its skull. As it was a French bulldog, bat-faced and all muscle, I feared the door would give out first.

"You see a lot of those Frenchies these days," said Charley. "I've always said beauty is in the eye of the beholder."

"This one is a proper watchdog."

"If it gets through the glass, I'll be one step ahead of you."

Behind us, we heard a woman call from the lake. "Hello? Hello?"

We turned and saw a rowboat approaching from the north, following the shoreline as if she, too, had just come from Camp Machigonne.

She was the worst rower I had ever seen. Her strokes were totally out of sync. The blades of the oars skipped across the surface if they caught the water at all. Some missed the lake altogether.

Like many Maine summer people and tourists, the woman was wearing an outfit assembled entirely from the L.L.Bean catalog. Beneath an oversize life vest that could have kept an NFL lineman afloat, she wore a blue pullover made of some sun-resistant polyester and tan shorts woven from some similarly synthetic material. Her face was white with zinc sunscreen, and her hair was cut very short beneath her cap.

"I've seen her before," I whispered. "I spotted her talking to Galen near the dive scene this morning."

"She needs a rowing lesson if she plans on venturing out where it's windy, or she'll capsize for sure."

We made our way to the dock. The whole contraption was on wheels for easy removal before the winter ice closed in.

"I'm sorry if we scared you," I called.

"You didn't," she said in a friendly voice. "It says *Game Warden* on the back of your vest."

It felt nice to be greeted with warmth after the reception we'd received from the Sotos.

On the principle that it's better, as a cop, never to reveal everything you know, I pretended I hadn't seen her speaking with Galen.

"You've probably heard there was an incident off the island across the way. Two people died."

As the stern of her rowboat bumped the dock, she dropped the oars. She didn't throw us a line. I had the sense she was waiting for us to tie the boat up for her.

"Yes, I know. It sounds horrible."

Now that I was looming over her, I could see that she had a button nose. Outsize sunglasses hid the rest of her face. Her hair was very short and very red. She was wearing both an engagement ring and a wedding ring but gave off the vibe of a person alone and on their own.

"Your house looks straight across at Mouse Island. We were wondering if you saw or heard anything last night."

Charley dropped to his knees to catch the bow of the rowboat before she drifted away.

"Thank you." Then, raising her head, she said, "But I'm confused."

"How so?"

"I told the other officer I saw everything. I've been waiting hours for you to call me. I'm Shawna Miskin. Did he not tell you I was a witness?"

32

The dog's name was Matisse.

We sat on the deck, or rather, Shawna Miskin sat on the deck while I leaned against the rail and Charley stood with his arms crossed, his feet a shoulder's width apart. The bulldog whined from behind the spit-stained glass.

"If I let him out, he'll hump your legs," she explained with no trace of embarrassment.

She had removed her life vest, revealing a surprising amount of cleavage, especially when viewed from above. Her shirt was unbuttoned nearly to her sternum. I kept my focus on her face, which was so thick with zinc sunscreen she might have been wearing greasepaint. It made for a comical contrast with the va-va-voom display below.

"You claim you told Constable Webb that you'd heard the collision?" I said for the record.

Dark blue irises peered out of the white mask at me.

"Not exactly. What I heard was everything that happened before."

"As in . . . ?"

She motioned with her head. "Mouse Island is right there. It's hard to miss what goes on. They were playing music for a while, the couple. Spotify must have a 'music to fuck by' channel. The music stopped. Then came the argument."

"Argument?"

"Around nine o'clock, they started yelling at each other. I only heard bits and pieces. She sounded very drunk, and at first, he seemed to be trying to calm her down. But she just got louder. I heard her say, 'Tell your wife.' Then he started shouting, too, telling her to shut up."

"You're sure it was nine o'clock?" Charley asked.

"Yes, why?"

"Just curious why you made a note of the time."

"Oh!" She let out a nervous laugh. "I was doing the dishes, and there's a clock on the stove in the kitchen. It's an hour slow, like no one ever set it ahead in the spring. I couldn't figure out how to set it. I've gotten used to making mental calculations."

"Were you alone?" I said.

"I'm sure Matisse heard. But good luck getting a statement out of him. I shut my windows because I was sick of it," Shawna said. "Then I opened them again because I was worried things might turn violent out there."

"If you were worried, why didn't you call the police?" asked Charley.

"I didn't hear glass breaking or anything. Couples have fights. How do you know as a stranger when to intervene? Now I wish I had, of course."

I found no reason to disbelieve the woman. She seemed to have no motive to lie. In my work, I dealt with many people claiming to have witnessed crimes who were desperate for attention and willing to say anything. Shawna seemed intelligent, specific, not overly emotional but not coldly remote, either. The fight between Kip Whitcomb and Gina Randazza had obviously troubled her.

Dog-day cicadas were whining in the pines around us: a high-pitched, torturous sound. Late summer was their season to mate. If I didn't already have a headache, the annoying bugs seemed intent on inducing one.

"Can you describe the collision, Mrs. Miskin?" asked Charley.

He, too, must have noticed the wedding and diamond engagement ring she wore so proudly.

"I didn't actually hear the boat hit them. I must have been in another room or gotten distracted. I'd also put on an audiobook. But I feel like you're ignoring what I'm telling you about that man getting violent."

"We're not ignoring it," I explained. "It's just that he didn't run over himself. And at the moment, we're focusing on the boat crash."

She raised a pinky to her mouth to chew on the cuticle. I had the feeling she was considering her next statement.

"Obviously, I wish I'd gotten a look at the boat," she confessed. "But between all those roaring engines and the fight that couple was having, I needed some peace. That man sounded like a brute, I have to say. I believe he might have slapped her to stop her screaming at him."

I tried to keep my expression blank. She seemed disproportionately focused on Kip Whitcomb's anger. Why did she keep returning to that subject?

"Could you describe for us any boats you saw yesterday? It could help us narrow down our search."

"Before sunset, one of those cigarette boats, I think they're called, cut through the channel. It was mostly red with two big engines on the back. It nearly swamped the dock with its wake. Why are boats that powerful even allowed on fresh water?"

I tried not to reveal my excitement at this information. I'd thought I'd heard two engines. There couldn't have been many cigarette boats on the lake, to say the least. I would have been surprised if there had been two.

"Are you sure the boat was red?" I asked.

"Red and white is probably a better description of it."

"Did you happen to notice the person or persons in it?"

She picked up a water bottle she'd carried with her from the rowboat. She carefully unscrewed the cap and took a swig. Again, I had the feeling of careful deliberation.

"Mrs. Miskin?" Charley said.

Having swallowed the water, she cleared her throat. "There were two young men in the boat."

Now we were getting somewhere. "Could you identify them?"

"No."

Her answer had come too quickly.

"Were they teenagers, early twenties . . . ?"

"Sorry."

I exhaled and turned to survey Mouse Island from the sundeck. The eastern side of the island was clearly visible, including the spring hole where we'd found Gina's body, as well as the shallows extending to the south.

"What about other boats?" I said. "You didn't notice any other watercraft out there yesterday?"

"There are always people fishing in the channel, especially around twilight." She widened her eyes at me. "Wait, there was a man on a Jet Ski. He was hooting and hollering. Drunk, I'm sure."

"Did you mention any of these boats to Constable Webb this morning?"

"No," she said. "I suppose I should have, but I was concerned about that woman on the island. I wanted to know if she was all right. I hadn't heard yet that she was dead."

Again, she had managed to circle back to Kip's alleged mistreatment of Gina. No one outside the investigation knew about the strangulation marks we'd found on Mrs. Randazza's throat. No one except the killer, of course.

"What were you listening to?" Charley asked out of nowhere.

"Excuse me?" she said.

"You said you were listening to an audiobook. My wife, Ora, is big on them, too. She's always reading one book and listening to another."

She nibbled a while at another cuticle. "*Madame Bovary.*"

"Is that the one about the lady who throws herself under the train?"

Her smile was indulgent if not patronizing. "You're thinking of *Anna Karenina.*"

"I'm not much for reading myself," he lied. "I don't have the patience for anything longer than *Reader's Digest*. I don't suppose I could impose on you to use your washroom before we depart."

She rose quickly to her feet. "Matisse will be all over you, and I'll have to restrain him and—"

"I've never minded an enthusiastic dog. And I wouldn't ask if it weren't such a pressing need. A man my age with an enlarged prostate—"

"Fine, yes. I'll go inside the house with you."

When she slid open the door, the French bulldog jumped halfway up Charley's chest. Most people would have shrunk away or batted him down. But the old man did something entirely unexpected.

He caught the animal beneath his front legs, lifted him all the way up to face level, and planted a kiss on his wheezing, wet nose.

The dog went limp.

Matisse now began to whine and wag his stubby tail. In an instant, the strange man had gone from threat to new friend.

Charley allowed himself to be licked across the face several times in what owners of the breed must term a *french kiss*. He carried the kicking dog into the house, followed closely by Shawna Miskin, who slid the door closed behind her.

I found myself alone on the deck.

Shawna would have had an unobstructed view of the illuminated Leisure Kraft while Charley retrieved Whitcomb's severed arm. She hadn't mentioned watching us. She only wanted to discuss the ferocious argument she'd allegedly overheard.

I had turned off my phone for the interview and now decided to check it. The press conference must have concluded because I had twenty-eight voice mails and twenty-two text messages.

I searched the web for "Shawna Miskin" and found several mentions, none with images, however.

There was a listing on a professional networking site for a Shawna Miskin, identifying her as a self-employed human resources consultant. I didn't recognize the names of the Boston firms where she had worked before starting her own business. Her profile page said she had attended Tel Aviv University, where she'd received her bachelor's and graduate degrees (in liberal arts and conflict resolution, respectively). Then a decade spent working for a now-defunct NGO. It was an interesting résumé.

As I was musing over her past (assuming this was the same woman), it occurred to me what Charley was really up to. Under normal circumstances, when a homeowner was reluctant to let him inside, the old man would have used a nearby tree to relieve himself. He was undoubtedly looking to snoop.

Shawna Miskin was almost certainly standing guard outside the bathroom door, however. Perhaps holding Matisse by the collar.

I grabbed the sliding door. "Excuse me, Mrs. Miskin?" I called.

"Yes? What?"

"There's something I need to show you out here."

33

I had no idea what excuse I was going to cook up.

But it didn't matter.

When she opened the sliding door, the French bulldog bounded past her legs onto the deck.

"Matisse! No!"

The Frenchie came toward me, twitching his stub of a tail, believing I was another new friend. Suddenly, he halted. He lowered his head between his shoulders and snarled out of one side of his mouth. I knew exactly what had prompted this defensive reaction, because I'd experienced it many times with other dogs. Matisse had caught the smell of the wolf on me.

I had a canister of pepper spray in a holster on my belt, but I didn't want to use it under any circumstances. The animal was on his home turf and rightfully afraid. Bulldogs have strong bites, however, and the black eye was my one allotted injury of the day. So instead of making an aggressive move, I took two steps back, being careful to avoid eye contact and speaking in a calm voice.

"It's OK, Matisse. I am not going to hurt you or your mom."

The dog growled at me. He made sure I saw his teeth.

Shawna lunged for Matisse and got her hands in the armpits under his front legs. "He never does that!"

"It's OK."

"I'm putting him inside."

The door was still halfway open. She used her back to create a wider opening. Holding the struggling dog outstretched like a toddler who had dirtied his diapers, she disappeared into the house.

I had wanted to give Charley a few minutes to peek around—not knowing what he was looking for or why but trusting he had a solid reason to look.

The curtain behind the door was peeled back by a slender hand, and then the door slid open again.

Charley came out first, looking at me with a mischievous grin and raised eyebrows.

He discovered something, the old bastard.

"Is this your house, Mrs. Miskin?" he asked over his shoulder.

"God, no," she said. "I rented it online."

"What are the owner's names?" I asked.

"I got it through Airbnb, so you can contact them there if you need to confirm anything. I don't remember their names."

I offered my friendliest smile at this obvious lie.

"The address here is enough for the report. Also, your name and home address. And we'll want a phone number for you."

Shawna Miskin then did another unexpected thing. She reached into the pocket of her field shirt, causing the cleavage to become momentarily more visible, and withdrew a driver's license. It showed her face looking exactly as she did now: same age, same haircut, minus the white zinc, but with artfully applied makeup. I'd been correct in guessing she was attractive under the sunscreen mask.

It was a Massachusetts license, listing her home address as India Street in Boston. She was thirty-eight years old. Five feet seven (the same height as Stacey) and 130 pounds (10 pounds heavier).

I snapped a picture of the license and typed in the phone number she gave me.

Charley was looking at me with raised eyebrows.

"We noticed you don't seem to have a motor vehicle," he said. "We weren't even going to knock on your door, thinking no one was home."

"Of course I have a car," she said and laughed. "I ran over a big rock on my way down the hill and tore a hole in the skid plate. It's being repaired at a shop over in Oakland. They sent a tow truck to pick it up and will deliver it tomorrow, after the holiday weekend. I'd like to know how anyone can function in this area without a car. My first night here, I tried to get a meal delivered, but apparently, Grubhub or DoorDash don't recognize the Belgrade Lakes as part of the civilized world. The guy repairing my car told me there's a pizza place that won't deliver to your house but will meet you at some crossroads. That's as close as you get to delivery in Belgrade."

"How long do you plan on staying?" Charley asked. It was the kind of question that, coming from me, would have sounded invasive, but his age and accent let him get away with it.

She sat down in the Adirondack chair again, but this time only perched on the edge. "Through September."

"It's my favorite month of the year in Maine," I said, but I didn't have Charley's disarming charm.

She merely stared at me.

"You might feel like we're grilling you," I said. "But it's standard for us to get as much information as we can from someone who's witnessed a crime. We don't know what might end up being important."

"Like what I'm doing here alone? I'm a consultant. I can work from anywhere with a cell signal and a laptop."

Somewhere out on the lake behind us, in the direction of the island, two loons began to wail simultaneously. Then one of them changed its call to something resembling a yodel, followed almost at once by the other bird.

"That's not good," murmured Charley. "When two loons call like that during the day, it usually means trouble."

"Are they fighting?" Shawna asked with genuine interest.

The retired warden enjoyed teaching people about the outdoors, and he now adopted a professorial tone. "More likely one is warning the other about some danger—another loon encroaching or maybe an eagle flying over—and then they whip each other into a panic."

"You mean like human couples do? Someone told me once that loons mate for life. Is that true?"

"I'm afraid not," Charley said.

"That figures it was a lie." Shawna let out a bitter laugh. "Monogamy is such a pipe dream. What does it say about humans that we live inside a cultural institution for which we're evolutionarily maladapted?"

I wondered if Charley had come to the same conclusion that I had: that Shawna Miskin was a peculiar person and, perhaps, not an altogether reliable witness. She was an enigma if nothing else.

"Is this your first visit to Maine, Mrs. Miskin?" I asked.

"When I was a kid, I attended Tripp Lake Camp in Poland. It's a happy memory of a better time in my life."

"What made you choose Great Pond?"

"I saw the movie filmed here and remembered how peaceful it seemed. I needed peace."

Jubilee had referred to this romanticization of the lake as "Golden Pond syndrome." I didn't bother telling Shawna Miskin that the movie was actually filmed on Squam Lake in New Hampshire.

She hadn't mentioned her husband, but neither had she objected to us calling her *Mrs.*, which didn't mean anything on its own, but coupled with her cynical remark about monogamy, and the fact that she was wearing her engagement and wedding rings, raised some questions about her life in Massachusetts. Asking them might be a bridge too far, though. We'd intruded enough to determine she wasn't altogether truthful, but her romantic life was none of our concern.

The loons were still at it.

"I know exactly what that place is," she said, letting her gaze wander out over the lake. "Or was."

"Mouse Island?"

"It was obviously Whitcomb's love nest. In the two weeks I've been here, the guy has brought out two different women."

Every person you interview—let alone interrogate—is different. With each one, you need to find the right approach. Letting Shawna Miskin rhapsodize had worked initially as she talked herself into contradictions. Now it was time to be direct.

"That's odd."

A fearful look came into her eyes. "What's odd?"

"You used Kip Whitcomb's last name just now. Before, when you were telling us about the argument on the island, you referred to him only as 'the man.'"

"What are you implying?"

"I'm wondering why you pretended not to know his name earlier."

"I didn't pretend anything. I simply forgot." She stood up then like a person in a meeting signaling that it was officially concluded. "Do you have a card you could give me in case I remember something else? Since my memory is so clearly faulty."

I produced another business card. She tucked it into her pocket next to her driver's license. She took the opportunity to fasten her top buttons, too.

"About those other women you saw—" Charley began.

"I didn't get a good look at them," she snapped.

I thanked her for her help and said I would be in touch. She replied with a nod. I told her I might need a written statement for my report, and she agreed to provide one, but with no great enthusiasm.

"State police detectives might also want to talk with you."

"But I've told you everything. I have nothing more to add. I was joking about my memory being faulty."

One thing I had learned about interviews: honest people might not enjoy telling the same story over and over, but they usually acquiesced. It was only liars who feared giving multiple statements to the police. It's difficult keeping track of the things you make up, and you risk contradicting yourself when you can't fall back on memories of actual events.

"It's possible there was something I forgot to ask about," I said.

"I can't see how that's possible."

"You should expect a call or visit from the state police in any case."

She followed us down the steps as if she needed to be sure we'd left. Matisse must have heard or smelled us through a screen window because he started barking again, this time with the same aggressiveness he'd shown me when he'd smelled Shadow on my uniform.

At the top of the driveway, well beyond Shawna Miskin's ability to hear, Charley turned to me with a conspiratorial expression.

"Didn't she say she was planning on renting the place for the rest of the month?"

"Through September."

"When I snuck inside to use the john, I saw she had her luggage in the hall. Five big suitcases and the dog crate, too. Seems an odd place to store those items if you ask me."

"It wouldn't be the only lie she told us," I said.

"She definitely knew more about Whitcomb than she let on, although I don't see the point in her playing dumb."

"People lie to investigators all the time, Charley."

"They usually have a reason, though. I'll be damned if I can figure out what caused Shawna Miskin to mislead us." Then he grinned and pulled on the brim of his deerstalker. "The thing that's been on my mind is that she didn't make a single comment about my cap or your black eye."

"Maybe it's because she has better manners than we do."

"That's a low bar!"

34

The next two houses had clearly been vacated and locked down for the winter. Both had chains up across their driveways, and one had anti-theft shutters rolled down over the windows. It seemed like overkill to me unless the cottage contained a collection of priceless Ming vases, which raised the inevitable question: Who furnishes their Maine lake house with Chinese urns?

Charley and I hadn't spoken since we'd returned to the road, but we'd both been mulling over our interview with Shawna Miskin, and now I said, "I'm thinking of something else I should have asked."

"Just one thing?"

He didn't mean it as a dig, and I didn't take it as one.

"Joey Randazza owns an auto repair shop in Oakland. What are the odds he's the one who towed her car?"

"That's easy enough to check. But I would let the woman be for a while."

"It seems potentially important, though. It would connect Randazza and the lake. If he came to her house, he might have seen something on the island and—"

Charley rested a gnarled hand on my shoulder. "The inside of your head is worse than a bat cave with all the thoughts you've got fluttering around."

"One less bat screeching in my ear would be nice."

We'd now reached my stepparents' house. Inside the great room, we found Ora reading aloud to Jubilee. She was a frequent speaker at the Unitarian Universalist church in Eastport and knew how to project her voice when called upon. But she sounded raspy now.

"'Summertime, oh summertime, pattern of life indelible, the fade-proof lake, the woods unshatterable, the pasture with the sweet fern and the juniper forever and ever, summer without end; this was the background, and the life along the shore was the design, the cottages with their innocent and tranquil design, their tiny docks with the flagpole and the American flag floating against the white clouds in the blue sky, the little paths over the roots of the trees leading from camp to camp and the paths leading back to the outhouses and the can of lime for sprinkling, and at the souvenir counters at the store the miniature birch-bark canoes and the post cards that showed things looking a little better than they looked.'"

"That's beautiful," Jubilee said. "Who wrote that?"

"E. B. White," Ora said, removing her reading glasses. "It's an essay he wrote about a visit he made with his son to a sporting camp on Great Pond."

"Mosher Camps," I said.

I knew "Once More to the Lake." I had read the essay first in a college writing class at Colby but had returned to it again in recent years. The reason I'd reread it was the same reason I chose not to disclose E. B. White's real subject now. For all the melody in the sentences Ora had read, "Once More" was a doleful essay about the wheel of time.

"Where's Stacey?"

"Down at the dock on her phone," said Jubilee.

"How are you doing, Boss?" Charley asked. Concern darkened his face.

"I'm just having another of my spells." Ora turned her tired eyes to mine. "We watched the press conference, Mike. Rick LaJoy isn't one for public speaking. The bureau would be wise to keep him off camera."

"No one mentioned that Gina Randazza was strangled," said Jubilee. "Why did they omit that information?"

"The focus was finding our hit-and-run boater," I said. "We're going to need tips, and it's best to have a single message."

"And the staties still can't say for certain it was Whitcomb who throttled the girl," added Charley. "Until that question is resolved, they won't show any cards they might be holding to the killer."

"Gina isn't my case, in any event," I said. "The parameters of my investigation begin and end with Whitcomb's naked body being torn apart by our unknown boater."

"There's a coldness to that language that doesn't become you, Mike," Ora said.

Jubilee remained quiet but nodded along in assent.

"You're right, Ora." I kissed her cheek. "Thank you for reminding me to be better."

"That'll be my daughter's full-time job soon enough," said Charley.

"I think I'll go find her."

Jubilee's description of my fiancée chatting on her cell didn't jibe with who she was. Stacey didn't disdain social media and technological triumphalism as passionately as I did, but she believed in being present in every moment of her life. No one I knew went chasing after distractions less than Charley and Ora Stevens's daughter.

As it happened, I'd simply drawn the wrong conclusion, because I found Stacey stretched out in the sun, wearing a bikini top and shorts, doing research on the internet.

Before I could ask her what she was reading, she leaped up and pressed her warm fingertips to my swollen face. "Baby, what happened to your eye?"

"Joey Randazza."

"He got into a fight with you?"

"Finch flubbed the death notification so I had to tell him about Gina. He lashed out when I asked if he knew his wife was having an affair with Kip Whitcomb. It's almost like Roger's afraid of the guy."

"But why did he *hit* you?"

"Generalized anger and grief."

"As if you needed another injury. I worry about you, babe. You've taken so many hard knocks in your life. When you're forty, you're going to look like one of those ex-linebackers who can't walk or form a coherent thought."

"You underestimate my supernatural resilience. What are you reading?"

She returned to the chaise longue while I pulled up a patio chair.

"I've been researching the Fentons. Well, I started with Whitcomb, but there's not much about him online. He sold high-end real estate and seems to have moved into venture capital after Judge Fenton died. Most of what I've found are society photos. He and Dianne at fund-raising dinners for Democratic politicians, silent auctions, et cetera. This was before she was diagnosed with malignant multiple sclerosis."

"Dianne has Marburg?"

That explained why she'd stopped coming to Maine. The rustic cottage was not remotely handicapped accessible.

"She and Kip became major donors to the National Multiple Sclerosis Society. The most recent photo I found of her looks like she aged ten years in two. She's not much older than me, but she was using a cane."

I flopped back in my chair and asked her what more she'd learned.

"Before he became a judge, Coleman Fenton was really big in Massachusetts politics," she said. "He wasn't a politician himself but had his hand in everything, it sounds like. There was a huge outcry from the Republicans when he was appointed to the federal bench, because even though he had a law degree from Harvard, he'd never tried a case. Then when he got his lifetime appointment, he became a scourge on both parties. It sounds like the power went to his head, and he reveled in exerting it over anyone unlucky enough to find themselves in his courtroom."

"What about the rest of the family?"

"There's not much online about his wife, Claire, other than older society photos. She was directly related to one of those Boston Irish politicians. I'd figured Fenton was a Brahmin, but he seems to have been the gold digger who married into prestige and money. Anyway, Claire Fenton died young of MS, too. And the judge never remarried. They had two children, Dianne and a boy, Coleman Jr."

The morning had been so crazy I only now remembered the conversation the detectives and I had had with Fenton-Whitcomb the night before.

"Pomerleau was supposed to arrange a videoconference with Dianne. I don't know what happened. But the sense I got from her over the phone is that she's still a formidable personality despite her illness."

"She was on the fast track for a high-powered career. Harvard and Harvard Law. Four years in one of Boston's top firms and then a job as an assistant United States attorney. Who knows where she would have landed if she hadn't gotten sick?"

"Dianne and Kip seem like such an odd match. The picture everyone paints of him is kind of a schemer."

"Maybe he reminded her of her dad," Stacey said. "Some girls go for that."

By which she meant herself. Charley and I were cut out of the same piece of goods, to use his expression.

"You haven't mentioned the brother," I said. "Is he dead like you thought?"

"No, he seems to be alive, but there's not much to mention. I found something about him going to West Point, which seems significant given the family's Harvard connection. The judge was on the board of the Harvard Corporation, which oversees the university's finances."

"And money is power."

She ignored the cliché. "You would've thought his son and namesake would have followed in his footsteps. Strange that he chose the army instead. Cole Jr. almost became an Olympian while at West Point. He was on Team USA in the modern pentathlon before he took a fall from a horse. The five sports are fencing, freestyle swimming, equestrian show jumping, pistol shooting, and cross-country."

"Sounds kind of badass."

"George S. Patton was an Olympic pentathlete. Cole doesn't seem like the luckiest guy in the world. That fall cost him a career as an army officer. Evidently, he next took part in the motorcycle race that used to be called the Dakar Rally but failed to finish because of mechanical problems. I found a mention of him in his sister's wedding announcement as a junior official in the Defense Department, duties unknown. Then a press release announcing he was a partner in a cryptocurrency start-up, which went bankrupt. The last mention I found of him was working for a Turkish bank, of all things."

"Sounds exciting. But I guess it explains why he's not a regular visitor to the family island. I've got to say I'm impressed with how much you've learned about the Fentons."

"I know it doesn't help your investigation, but you know how other people's families can be so enthralling—especially when money and politics are involved."

"I'm serious, Stace. You're really good at research."

We often pulled faces or deadpanned when we bantered, but now she gave me a look that managed to combine disbelief and affront.

"When we met, I was working as a wildlife biologist. What exactly did you think I did, Mike?"

The question landed harder than Randazza's punch. But I knew this wound was self-inflicted.

35

Before I started listening to the multiplying voice mails on my phone, I put in a call to LaJoy to ask if there had been any new developments. I didn't mention the bad reviews I'd heard of his press conference, and he didn't bring it up except to ask what kinds of tips I was getting.

"I'll let you know when I start listening to them."

"It almost seems like you don't want to find this boat," he said.

"Why do you say that?"

"Because instead of canvassing the lake, you've been focused on whether Whitcomb killed Gina Randazza."

He was partly correct; I wasn't following the playbook for hit-and-run boat accidents. I should have been dispatching teams of wardens to visit docks. But as usual, I wanted to believe my brain could find a shortcut.

Stacey had gone up to the house to check on her mom, leaving me to watch the action out on the lake. A man in motorboat was pulling two squealing, screaming girls on a wakeboard. The girls were louder than the engine.

"What if I told you that I found a witness who claims to have heard Kip and Gina fighting at nine o'clock last night?"

"Did she see the boat that ran over him?"

"No. But she told me a cigarette boat was tearing around the lake yesterday afternoon."

"Cigarette boats—or boats that people mistake for them—aren't common on inland waters. It seems like Galen would have mentioned seeing one on Great Pond."

"Then we may have found an important clue."

"What do you mean?"

"The boat may be new to the lake. It was either recently purchased by a Belgrade resident, or it was brought to Great Pond for the holiday weekend."

"Makes sense," LaJoy admitted.

"I'm going to call Pomerleau and tell her about my interviews this morning, and then I'm going to follow up on the calls and texts. I'll be in touch if I get any decent leads."

"Be in touch anyway," he commanded.

"Understood."

Ellen seemed less excited about the information I had dug up about Whitcomb than I'd expected. I had the sense of her half-listening. She didn't ask any follow-ups about Shawna Miskin, for example.

"Whatever happened to your video call with Dianne Fenton-Whitcomb?" I said.

"She canceled. She was having a bad day, health-wise. She said that if we wanted to interview her, it would be better if we came to her house in Massachusetts. That's a long down-and-back. We're talking about seven hours, total, on the road. Today is obviously out, and tomorrow morning, Leah Doumit is doing her postmortems on Whitcomb and Randazza, and I need to be there for those."

"Me, too. At least for Whitcomb's. We still don't know if he was alive when the boat hit him."

Silence on her end.

"Is there something else bothering you?" I asked.

"That run-in Finch had with the Direwolves—there was more to it than he admitted. He really lost it with those guys. Called them pieces of shit, et cetera. If a trooper hadn't rolled up in time, someone might have gotten shot. The trooper is the one who told me this. He said it was almost like Roger was trying to provoke a fight."

"I should take what he says about Joey Randazza with a grain of salt, then?"

"More like all the salt in the Dead Sea."

I watched one of the girls on the lake slip off the wakeboard as her father made a tight turn in the motorboat, obviously at her insistence.

I'd read something about how kids like to be scared in a particular way. They want to experience a sudden fright and then the reassurance of an adult swooping in to tell them everything's OK. Surprise, fear, and then soothing support.

As a child, I had never had someone provide that conditioning. I wondered if it explained why I didn't properly feel the fear that I should. Bravery might be my own maladaptation.

I had put off listening to the voice mails as long as I could, so I stretched out on the chaise longue—or tried to stretch out before I realized that patio sofas hadn't been designed for men wearing gun belts and body armor. I returned to my chair.

I went through the texts first, since they were easy to skim:

- A few solid leads about a long red boat glimpsed on the lake before dark.
- A complaint about how the sender's tax dollars were being wasted investigating the deaths of out-of-staters.
- Someone reporting a reckless speedboat on Mousam Lake this morning, two hours south of Great Pond.
- Lots of worry expressed about boats and loons.
- Accusations against neighbors who owned Jet Skis and had a history of rowdiness.
- Profane assaults on the Warden Service for cheap pinches we'd made of friends and family members for poaching and other petty offenses.
- Someone claiming to have seen the incident offering baroque details of Gina Randazza's decapitation and Kip Whitcomb being "thrown like a rag doll" in the air.
- Another disgruntled taxpayer.

Having endured the texts, I felt even more reluctant to subject myself to the recorded calls. But it was the job I had signed up to do.

The first messages hit the same notes as the texts. There were people from the community trying to be helpful even if their information was next to useless. Many callers were deeply concerned for the welfare of loons. A woman who'd been kayaking at dusk reported a red boat that had nearly swamped her. A man, who might have been the same one who'd sent the text, wondered why his tax dollars were being used to "rescue" Massholes. I wondered where he'd gotten the idea someone had been rescued.

I was unprepared for the eleventh voice mail.

"My name is David Kwan," said a man in a calm, even tone. "I was a passenger in the boat that struck Mr. Whitcomb last night off Mouse Island. My friend Kyle McAllister was driving, but he refuses to come forward. The boat is a red Sunsation Dominator. The registration numbers on the side are ME 1124 ZW. I don't want anyone else being blamed for what happened. This isn't a prank. I am telling the truth. When you call back, I may have to screen you because I'm staying in the McAllisters' house, and Kyle is watching me closely because he's afraid I'll call the police, and I am scared of him."

36

Because I didn't have my laptop with me to check the boat numbers, I tried calling a woman I knew in the Licensing and Registration Division, forgetting that the office was closed for Labor Day. I hadn't wanted to bring in LaJoy before I could verify some of the information David Kwan had provided and had a chance to speak with the self-confessed accomplice myself.

"He provided you with the boat registration?" LaJoy asked. His voice gave nothing away, but I assumed he was also struck that a civilian would anticipate our needing that information to vet his claim.

"He comes across in the message as intelligent and sincere."

"Not a prankster?"

"Who knows? You held a press conference asking people to come forward, and this guy came forward. Let's check the numbers and see if he's legit."

LaJoy came back less than a minute later. "White-and-red Sunsation Dominator registered to John McAllister of Waban, Massachusetts."

"Kwan said his friend who was driving the boat is named Kyle McAllister. And the one thing consistent in the messages I received was that a red boat was speeding around the lake at dusk last night."

"How do you want to play it?"

"I'm going to call Kwan back and get an address. And then I'm going to pay him a visit."

"Just don't spook him."

I moved to a quiet spot under the sentinel pines that separated Neil's property from his neighbor. Pitch was oozing white through the scales of bark, so I was careful not to lean against one of the trunks. I hit the callback button but landed immediately in David Kwan's voice mailbox.

"David, this is Mike Bowditch. I'm an investigator with the Maine Warden Service handling the fatal boating incident last night on Great Pond. I appreciate your coming forward with information. It's very difficult to do and takes a lot of courage. I've been able to confirm that the boat you mentioned belongs to John McAllister of Waban, Mass. But I need more information to proceed. I'd like to speak with you as soon as possible. You can call or text me back at this number."

My phone chimed less than thirty seconds later. My screen showed a text message from David Kwan.

> I had to sneak into the bathroom. Kyles watching me. What info do U need for a search warrant?

I was taken aback by the reply. It was one thing for Kwan to anticipate our needing the registration number of the boat. But he had proceeded straight to the subject of a search warrant as if he were a lawyer.

> To start I'd like a little more info. Who are you? And where are you?

Forty-five seconds later, photographs of a Colby College identification card appeared, front and back. I had attended Colby myself, but they had tweaked the design in the ten years since I'd graduated. The photo showed a kid with a square face. His hair was short, black, and styled with some sort of pomade or cream that gave it sheen. He wore large round glasses with wire rims.

The card was helpful in establishing his age but short of the information I most wanted: where to find him and more importantly, the boat.

Kyle mcAllister killed a man last night & I'm the only Witness! i'm afraid for my life here

Give me the address and I will be there as soon as I can.

With a warrant?

He seemed unusually stuck on this subject.

Photos of the damage would help. Where is the boat now?

Inside the boathouse. On a lift. Doors R locked. You cant see it from the water. Dont you need a warrant to search?

Again, he responded before I could form a response.

He's calling me. Knows i'm on my phone!

Where are you David?

I thought I had lost him, but David Kwan surprised me with one last message.

3 Hoyt LN

I copied and pasted the address into the Maps app and saw that the home was on the far side of the lake. Between me and David were miles of open water and several islands, including Mouse. I would need to circle Great Pond—a drive that could take half an hour—to reach the McAllister house. What might happen to him in the meantime?

The problem was that he hadn't given me enough of anything.

Not enough specific details to prove he'd been in the boat that had struck and killed Kip Whitcomb. Not enough physical evidence to secure a search warrant of the property. I couldn't even be sure he was a guest in the McAllister house, let alone that there was an actual Kyle McAllister contemplating homicide.

People, for whatever reason, pull pranks. They report nonexistent bombs in schools. They call the Coast Guard claiming they're on board a sinking sailboat at sea.

I believed David Kwan, but my own belief wasn't sufficient according to the standards of proof required by the state of Maine. Nor was I ready to set myself up as the dupe of the year. I couldn't confidently summon the state police or the wardens to an emergency that might be entirely fanciful: the creation of a disturbed young mind.

I had to go myself.

But that didn't mean I had to go alone.

37

I knew I couldn't keep Charley from coming with me. As soon as I told him what was up, he became a dog straining against his leash.

I had expected Stacey might want to come, too. She shared her dad's near-fatal attraction to dangerous scenarios. I had begun rehearsing lines to dissuade her since, despite her many competencies, she was not trained in law enforcement work, and we didn't know the situation we would encounter across the lake.

Instead, she fixed her father with a look. "I'll stay with Mom."

Charley rarely blushed, but color bloomed along his throat.

"Is there something you two aren't telling me?" I said.

"She's fine," Stacey insisted. "But Neil is playing golf, and Jubilee is meditating in her studio. Someone should hang out here with Mom."

We considered borrowing the Leisure Kraft again. The party barge didn't have the most powerful engine, but it could get us across the lake. Ultimately, it wasn't the way I wanted to roll up on a potential crime scene, though.

Charley never went anywhere armed. He'd shot and killed one man in his career as a game warden and hoped to die before firing another shot at a human being. He believed that guns were generally more dangerous to the people carrying them than to potential attackers: a belief proven true in study after study, but hardly applicable to a man like himself, who was both a combat veteran and a lawman who'd trained with pistols and long guns over the course of decades.

"If you change your mind," I said, "my Beretta is in the glove compartment."

The route curled counterclockwise around Great Pond, along the pine and oak ridges, crossing eventually into the abutting town of Rome.

A sandhill crane threw a big shadow across the road as it glided south toward the swamp. The tall birds were related to vultures, I remembered.

And then, if my thoughts weren't morbid enough, we passed an unofficial sign welcoming us to the township with the motto:

ALL ROADS LEAD TO ROME

"What's so funny?" Charley asked.

"I had an English professor who read the proverb as a metaphor for the inevitability of death. No matter which road we follow, it leads to the same destination."

"Sounds like an amusing chap. You say this Kwan kid is a Colby student himself?"

"So he says."

"What about his friend McAllister?"

"I don't know. I haven't had time to do anything but grab you and jump in the Scout. What would help is if you could give Pomerleau a call for me."

I handed him my cell phone.

"Mike's at the wheel and wanted me to pass along the breaking news," he explained to the detective.

He ran through the information I had shared with him, even managing to quote parts of the texts from David Kwan he'd glimpsed on my screen.

"She wants to know why you had me call her instead of Lieutenant LaJoy."

"Because we might need troopers."

Suddenly, the phone chimed in Charley's hand. "Now what could this be?" He paused to examine the text.

I glanced at him out of the corners of my eyes, determined to stay focused on the winding road, given the speed at which we were traveling.

"That son of a gun Kwan actually did it!" he said at last. "It's a picture of the underside of McAllister's cigarette boat. It shows a scraped lower unit and an aluminum prop all bent to hell. The blade shows signs of scoring, consistent with a bone scratching through the paint. I've only ever seen this kind of damage on an outboard that ran over some hard object in the water."

"Send the photo to Ellen."

"Done! Now she says she wants to talk with you."

He put the call on speaker.

"What do you think?" I said. "Is it enough for a warrant?"

"Depends on the judge on call. There's a new moonbat on the district court bench who likes to make us go the extra mile. But the odds are good we'll get one of our old reliables. Do you want me to write up a warrant for you and run it past the DA?"

It was Monday afternoon at the end of a holiday weekend, and the traffic departing Belgrade Lakes was heavy with vehicles loaded with canoes and kayaks or pulling boat trailers.

"If you would," I said. "I'm about to turn down the Mountain Road and should be at Hoyt Lane soon."

"If there's a search warrant in the works, I hope I don't need to remind you to hold back and wait for a coordinated response."

"That depends on whether we hear gunshots inside the McAllister house."

"That's not funny, Mike," the detective snapped.

"Who said I was trying to be funny?"

38

I proceeded slowly down the forest lane with my headlights off despite the deepening shadows. I wish I could say we moved stealthily, but the V-8 engine sounded in my ears like rumbling thunder.

The compound, named Evermore according to a sign at the head of the road, came into view before I was ready for it. I had expected a single house, but the McAllisters seemingly owned an entire point of land. There were multiple shingle-sided buildings. The quick impression I had was of an old sporting camp remodeled and updated to serve as a retreat for a big family or one that entertained loads of guests.

"You might want to stop here," cautioned Charley as he leaned over the dash.

Too late.

I had just turned the key off in the ignition when I heard something between a scream and a shout.

The door of the main building, the former lodge, burst open, and a barefoot man, naked from the waist up, came running toward the truck. He seemed as crazed with panic as a person fleeing a burning building. And when he stepped into a shaft of sunlight, I saw blood from his hairline running to his jaw.

"Help!" David Kwan said. "He's trying to kill me!"

As I stepped from the Scout, my eyes moved from the running man to the open door of the big house behind him. I fully expected to see a lunatic come charging out with a carving knife. But no one emerged.

Ten feet from my vehicle, Kwan threw himself down on the pine needles. He lay sprawled for a few seconds, then rolled over. His concave stomach fluttered beneath his rib cage. Russet needles stuck to his bloody face and sweaty chest. His big eyeglasses were askew.

"David?" I asked, more for the record than because I thought he could possibly be anyone else. "What's happening?"

"Kyle has a knife!" he panted. "He caught me in the boathouse. Did you get the photo I sent?"

"We got it," I said.

"You can't let him destroy the evidence."

The engine of the Scout was still ticking, and I could feel the heat coming off the hood.

Charley had removed the deerstalker and tossed the cap on the front seat. His white hair was sticking up like he was some decrepit punk rocker. He stood over the prostrate young man with a curious look on his face. If pressed to name the expression, I would say he appeared peeved.

"I'm not sure how he'd do that," he said. "Destroy evidence."

"Where is Kyle now?" I asked.

"Still in the boathouse, I think." Kwan's voice was ragged, as if he'd run farther than the thirty yards between the front door and the Scout. "He said he was going to take a shower. He lied so I would let my guard down. I didn't hear him until he was right behind me in the boathouse. He grabbed a fishing knife and slashed at my face."

Charley squatted on his haunches beside Kwan. "Let me have a look at the wound."

The cut looked to be about two inches long but not particularly deep. Lacerations to the head bleed heavily because the face and scalp have so many blood vessels so close to the skin. There wasn't a thing about gashes, punctures, and slashes I hadn't learned from hard personal experience.

I grabbed my first aid kit from behind the seat. It contained hemostatic gauze that would stop the bleeding. Now I wished Stacey had decided to come along. Simple wound care didn't require an EMT, but I hated being distracted from what Kyle McAllister might be doing in the boathouse.

Charley rose to his feet again and brushed his palms although he hadn't touched the ground, let alone the blood on Kwan's face. "That knife was wicked sharp. You must have excellent reflexes. Or you got lucky."

"Luck?" Now tears began to run rivulets through the red smears. "Are you crazy? I watched my best friend run over a swimmer and kill him. And then when I told him he needed to call the police, he threatened and attacked me. I feel like I've been trapped in a nightmare the past twenty-four hours."

Kneeling, I cleaned the thin wound and wiped it with an antiseptic pad from which Kwan flinched. Then I applied the clotting gauze and some tape to hold it in place.

Charley had remained uncharacteristically solemn and silent. He removed a pack of Beemans chewing gum from the pocket of his T-shirt, pushed three pieces into his mouth, and began working on them with his jaw.

"What do you want to do?" I asked him.

"Nothing."

"What?" said Kwan, sitting up. "Kyle could take a hammer to the propeller or something. You need to stop him."

"Without a search warrant in hand, Warden Bowditch here would risk the case being dismissed before it even went to trial."

"He attacked me! What about that?"

"Is anybody else inside the house?"

"No."

"Then he poses no further danger to anyone but himself."

Kwan rose unsteadily to his feet. He was taller than I'd estimated, as tall as I was, but probably thirty pounds lighter.

The Colby student made another desperate appeal. "You guys need to go in there."

"I'm surprised he didn't keep chasing you," Charley offered. "He hasn't even shut and locked the door on us. That's unusual when someone doesn't want the authorities barging in."

All at once, I understood why the old pilot was treating our perfect witness with such callousness. Because David Kwan was too perfect.

I am such an idiot.

In my wonder and relief at being presented with an answer to a potentially unsolvable mystery, I had forgotten the old saying: "Beware of honor students bearing gifts."

"He's not coming to the door because he's inside the boathouse, destroying evidence," said Kwan.

Right on cue, Kyle McAllister chose that moment to make his highly anticipated appearance. He shambled up the doorway and paused at the threshold: a towheaded dude with a foppish haircut, soft features, and a nearsighted squint. His clothes were loose and rumpled, but you could tell that beneath them, he was even bonier than his classmate.

"Who are these people? What's going on, David?"

He had the foggy air of someone who had awakened a minute before.

"Game wardens. I've told them what happened, Kyle!"

That woke him up. "You did what?"

"I told them that we hit that swimmer with your dad's boat."

McAllister leveled a finger at his friend. "Did David tell you *he* was driving?"

During my first year as a game warden, I'd pulled over a car rocketing along a forest road one night. When I approached the vehicle, I found that the two teenagers inside had both scrambled into the back seat. It was impossible to determine which of them had been behind the wheel when they sped past at ninety miles per hour.

Something similar was about to happen here, I feared.

Kwan implored me through his big, round glasses. "I can't drive a boat! I can't even drive a car."

"Exactly!" said Kyle McAllister. "I never should have let you behind the wheel."

"He was the one who killed that man. I can prove it."

"How?" Charley was intrigued.

Kwan turned his back to the building and whispered, "I never touched the steering wheel. You won't find my fingerprints on it."

"What is he telling you?" Kyle called.

"Charley, can you stay with Mr. Kwan for me?"

He folded his arms and nodded gravely.

I crossed the dooryard, stopping only when McAllister showed signs of bolting into the house.

"Kyle, here's the deal. You've confessed it was your father's boat that struck Kipling Whitcomb in the water off Mouse Island last night—"

"Wait! Who?"

The response took me back. "Kip Whitcomb. He and his wife own the island."

For an instant, he seemed to show relief. "I thought it was Mr. Fenton! I knew him when he was a counselor at Pine Island Camp."

"His wife's original surname was Fenton." I rested my hands on my gun belt, assuming a more authoritative posture, and lowered my voice to sound more commanding. "Right now, state police detectives are en route with a warrant to search the premises for evidence that confirms your family boat was involved in the hit and run. You've already admitted to committing crimes by not reporting the accident and leaving the scene. You can help yourself on those charges by letting me into the boathouse." I threw in a lie to help things along. "We've stationed wardens in a boat on the lake to keep you from driving it off, and obviously you won't be towing it anywhere."

"I need to call my dad." He sounded very young now.

"Where is he?"

He pinched his tear ducts to stop the flow. "Back home in Waban."

I kept my voice hard: "There's something you should know, Kyle. We have a third witness to the crash who doesn't lie."

"Who?"

"I'm talking about your boat. Top-of-the-line outboards have what are called engine control units. They're basically black boxes for motors. We can connect a computer to the unit, and it will tell us the engine's rpms at any given time, and if they changed, for instance, in response to a collision."

He rubbed his eyes fiercely and straightened up to defend himself.

"David's lying about what happened. He told me not to call the cops. He said there were no witnesses, we could have the boat removed and fixed without anyone knowing. He said it would ruin both our lives when the story came out—even if it was an accident. I wanted to call you. But David can be real persuasive."

He certainly is.

"So you'll let me in?" I said. "You'll show me the boat?"

Kyle McAllister took several breaths. His wet eyes moved from me to David Kwan standing beside Charley in shadows already darker than when we'd arrived. Then, without another word, he stepped back through the door. I heard the lock click and a bolt slide into place, barring the way.

39

"Charley, I need you to watch David!"

I yanked my phone from its pocket as I circled the lodge, making for the water side of the property.

I hit Redial. "Ellen? Did you get the warrant?"

"I'm getting it. We've asked for access to the boat, the boathouse, anyplace he keeps the keys—"

"Has the judge signed off on the search? Is it in effect now? That's all I need to know."

"Verbally, yes. We were lucky to get—"

"I have to get inside that boathouse. Kyle McAllister has just confessed. Charley Stevens is my witness. But the stupid kid locked himself in now, and I don't know what he might try to do to destroy evidence."

"Wait, Mike. We're only ten minutes out at most."

"I can't wait."

The setting sun reflected off the lake. Its last light brought out the greens, reds, and golds along the far shore.

Between the house and the boathouse was a raised boardwalk. I expected to see Kyle McAllister rushing down it to stop me, but he must have been trying to call his dad and hadn't guessed, in his panic, what I might do. Or he might already was inside the boathouse, finding a hammer to take to the bent prop.

The door to the boathouse was locked. Through a dusty windowpane, I could see the shape of a boat suspended above the water. I didn't catch sight of Kyle, which didn't mean he wasn't in there.

I could likely have breached the door without consequences. The prosecutor would reprimand me and make noises about risking the search being thrown out in court. But it wouldn't be the first time I'd been chewed out by a DA, and I had never yet torpedoed a criminal case.

But given the ambiguity of the moment—between the approval of the search warrant and its delivery—I decided on a lower-impact option than breaking down the door. I picked my way along the building, which projected on piers over Great Pond.

I trailed my right hand along the clapboards to keep my balance since there were slippery stones beneath my boots. The wooden shingles of the boathouse were crusted with the husks of dragonflies and damselfly nymphs that had crawled from the lake to hatch. Having transformed into winged creatures, the insects had left behind the shells of their former selves.

When I reached the waterline, I began wading, first up to my knees, then up to my crotch. My phone was waterproof, and I didn't care that my gun got soaked. (I could always clean and oil it later.) But I did remove my Fenix flashlight from its small holster and put it in my mouth, holding the cylinder clamped in my teeth.

I found myself up to my neck in the still-warm lake. Then I was over my head, which was a familiar experience in my life.

The inside was webbed with shadows. The sole window, the pane in the upper door, let in a gray haze. And there was a sliver of luminescence between the boat doors and the surface of the lake.

The trapped air was heavy with gasoline fumes. But my nose detected another chemical odor as well. Chlorine bleach.

When I pushed the button of the Fenix, three thousand lumens of light punched through the darkness, and all the secrets of the boathouse were revealed to me.

The structure had two doors and two berths, with a central walkway in the middle and boardwalks along both sides. It had been designed to hold two boats. I had come in through the vacant bay.

I stuck the flashlight between my teeth again and reached up to grab hold of the walkway along the near side. Using the strength of my upper body, I pulled myself out of the water until the heel of my boot found the edge.

My sudden surfacing had disturbed a fishing spider. It skittered on legs three inches long across the back of my hand and jumped into the water. Dock spiders made their homes on swimming floats, too, and preyed on minnows and tadpoles. The little monsters probably accounted for more children's nightmares than any giant arachnids outside the stories of J. R. R. Tolkien.

The Sunsation Dominator had been raised on a cradle via a mechanical lift. The paint job was white with aggressive red slashes. It would have been a cliché, but not untrue, to describe the color as bloodred.

Shedding water, I inspected the lower units first. The engines were Mercury Magnums, capable of delivering 350 horsepower to their propeller shafts. I had zero doubt that this boat could surpass one hundred miles per hour.

I followed the harsh bleach smell to the hull and the props. It seemed to me as if someone had doused the blades with chlorine. Such an act constituted tampering with evidence. It also proved that the person or persons involved had guilty minds. Good luck claiming in court that they thought they'd hit a log.

Of course, McAllister's father and his father's attorneys might argue that the dumb boy had been trying to kill whatever milfoil—an invasive plant choking Maine's lakes and ponds—might have gotten tangled in the screws.

I walked along the sides of the cigarette boat, examining the hull for anything that might look like a dent. Were human bones hard enough to damage the fiberglass composite used by high-end boatbuilders?

Seeing nothing, I returned to the engines for another look.

I didn't expect to find physical evidence linking the Dominator to Whitcomb's corpse.

Traces of hair, blood, or skin would have washed off as the boat sped back to its secret hiding place.

But as I moved the flashlight beam over the lower unit of the left engine, I noticed that one of the propeller blades had been bent with signs of scoring in the black coating. More damning, a small, pale speck was embedded between the nut and the washer that locked the prop to the driveshaft. I leaned closer, careful not to touch the hull. The smell of chlorine burned my nostrils like poison gas.

A piece of flesh?

At that moment, the door creaked open, and I saw Kyle McAllister backlit. His arms hung at his sides. One hand still gripped a glowing phone.

"How did you get in here?"

"The lake."

"Oh, right." His gaze fell to the puddle around my wet boots. "My dad said not to talk to you. He said not to let you in until his lawyer could call your DA."

"How old are you, Kyle?"

"Twenty-one."

"And you're a student at Colby with David?"

"I just graduated. I've been living here all summer."

"I'm guessing this isn't the first time you called your dad to bail you out of a bad situation. Judging from the looks of this place, I know he can pay for expensive lawyers. But expensive lawyers lose cases every day. And your dad can't serve a prison sentence in your place."

"Is it too late to tell you what happened?"

"Not if you tell the truth."

40

We sat at a table on the porch, overlooking the lake. I'd persuaded him to silence his phone after his father kept calling. I turned on my recording app and began my interview.

Kyle McAllister had spent every summer he could remember on Great Pond. He'd attended Pine Island Camp, down near the south end, just as his father had, and his grandfather before him. His family had owned another property outside Belgrade Village into his teens, at which time his dad had purchased this former sporting lodge and had it renovated as a family compound.

"This lake is in my DNA," he said. "Like literally. I was conceived here, my mom says."

His parents had gone home to Massachusetts at the end of August, leaving Kyle alone with his friend and classmate David Kwan to celebrate the holiday weekend.

The two young men had thrown a party the night before the accident. The guests had been underclassmen from Colby, already on campus for the semester but with the weekend off. Kyle had given rides in the Dominator to whoever wanted them, but his dad had made him promise never to let anyone else behind the wheel.

Kyle now admitted to drinking beer and doing Fireball shots on both nights. He'd rented a keg from a place in Waterville called Joker's. He'd smoked a lot of weed, too.

"What about David? Did he drink and take drugs, too?"

"He can't handle alcohol. He says certain people from Korea have the same problem. His face gets all flushed and hurts."

All their guests left Sunday morning, leaving the two friends with one last day and night to clean up the house.

After dinner—leftover pizza—Kyle and David had gone out for one final ride in the speedboat. People staying around the lake had set off fireworks all weekend, and the friends wanted to watch them from the water. David said Kyle was too wasted to drive and he wanted to try piloting the boat home himself.

"He was right about how messed up I was."

"David told me he doesn't have a driver's license."

"Yeah. That's true. I guess I should've thought about that beforehand."

I paused, waiting for him to continue. In the quiet, I heard nighthawks passing overhead, their calls an insect-like buzzing.

"I know the pond really well," said Kyle. "Even fucked up, I could tell David where to go so he didn't run us up on rocks. I've never in my whole life seen anyone swimming off the west side of Mouse Island, day or night. It would be too dangerous because of all the boats and Jet Skis there."

"Did you notice anyone staying on the island?"

"I saw a boat tied up to the dock. There might have been lights on in the house. I can't remember."

"So David was at the wheel, speeding back and forth in the deep water. Then what happened?"

"We heard a thump and felt a shudder go through the boat, and I knew we'd hit something."

"You didn't hear any calls or screams beforehand, like someone trying to warn you?"

"How could we?" he asked. "Over the sound of the engines?"

"Describe the sound you heard."

"It was like a thump and then maybe another thump afterward. I knew we'd run over something. It didn't sound hard, like a ledge or a log. I was afraid it was a loon. That's why I told David to turn around and go back. He was already scared and said we should take off for home. But I couldn't stand the thought that a bird might be alive and suffering. I don't like to see anything in pain."

"What did you find when you turned around?"

"Blood in the water," he said.

"Anything else?"

"There was some other . . . stuff, pale flecks floating in this red cloud. The light wasn't great coming from the boat."

"Were there feathers?" I asked.

"No."

"So you knew it wasn't a loon?"

"There was so little blood, though. David said it was probably a beaver or an otter, but he doesn't know anything about animals. He's a totally urban person. David opened the throttle before I could get myself together to stop him. I was seriously messed up, like I said. I have been wasted ever since."

"What happened when you got back to the boathouse?"

David said to leave the boat in the water. But Kyle wanted to see if there had been damage, so he'd raised the Dominator up on the lift to have a look at the hull and propellers. He saw the blades were bent and there were scratches in the composite, and he was simultaneously afraid of what they'd hit and of how his dad would react to the new boat being damaged. Then David returned from the house with a gallon of Clorox, which he started splashing all over the outboards and hull.

"Did you ask him what he was doing? And why?"

"I didn't have to."

When they got inside, David downloaded an app on his iPhone so they could listen to the local police scanner, but there wasn't any chatter about people reporting an accident on the lake. Kyle eventually went upstairs and passed out, while David stayed up listening.

Kyle didn't wake up until late the next morning, and then the first thing he did was vomit. At first, he couldn't find his friend, and then he found him at the boathouse. David had lowered the Sunsation into the water.

"I asked him why, and he said I should try the engine. He said he'd tried it himself, and it didn't sound 'right,' whatever that meant. He said my dad would notice. So I climbed down and started it up, and everything sounded the same to me. Then he said, 'What about the wheel?'"

"He told you to take hold of the steering wheel?"

"Yeah, why?"

There had been no way for Kyle McAllister to overhear the conversation we'd had outside with David Kwan. And every word he'd uttered had only reinforced the extent of his cluelessness.

David Kwan had heard the news about an unknown boat striking a swimmer off Mouse Island. He had calculated the odds of the Sunsation Dominator, a distinctive boat in any waters, being identified. And he had worked up a plan to exculpate himself. It started with cleaning the steering wheel to remove any trace of his having driven the boat. Then he'd arranged to have his hungover buddy handle the wheel. The only fingerprints on the leather would belong to Kyle McAllister.

No doubt he'd watched the press conference carefully. He'd written down the phone number of the warden investigator, and then he'd called me to confess he'd been an unwilling accomplice to a case of criminally negligent homicide. At that point, he had only to wait until the first officers appeared on the scene to run out to meet them, half-naked and bleeding.

"Do you own a fishing knife?" I asked Kyle.

"Me, personally? No, but there's probably one in the boathouse. My dad likes to fish for pike when he's up here in the spring."

"Have you ever handled his knife?"

"Maybe. I don't know."

"What about last night or this morning?"

"No."

An image took shape in my imagination of a shadowy figure slipping into a bedroom where his friend lay sleeping. He is holding a knife in a handkerchief or towel. He reaches down for the sleeper's hand and—

41

As the sun sank behind the mountain above us and the evidence response team crawled over the boat, I briefed Pomerleau and Finch on everything we had discovered since arriving at the compound.

"You were a lot more scrupulous about search warrants when I was the one searching," Roger chided me.

"The circumstances here were different. I made a judgment call."

"A self-serving one."

The grimace on Ellen's face told me she shared her partner's misgiving. But I knew that even if the McAllisters' attorneys could somehow get my search thrown out—which I doubted—it wouldn't help them with their biggest problem: David Kwan's damning testimony.

To speed things up, I played my recorded interview with Kyle McAllister for the detectives.

"What do you want to do with them?" I asked.

"That's up to the DA," Pomerleau said. "Let's discuss what we have to hold them on."

"That McAllister kid pretty much admitted he knew it was a human being they'd run over," Finch said. "Whether he was driving or not, we have him on failing to report a fatal accident."

"But what about Kwan?"

"David Kwan says he didn't know what they'd hit," I said. "He claims he came forward immediately as required by statute. He seems to be a quick study when it comes to Maine law."

"Let's go talk with the boy genius," Pomerleau said.

We found David Kwan sitting quietly on the steps of one of the log cabins that made up the Evermore compound. Someone had found clothes for the half-naked man; he now wore a dapper button-up shirt, khakis, and boat shoes. His slender hands rested, one on top of the other, on his narrow lap. His travel bag lay at his feet, ready to go. He had the manner of a person waiting for a taxi to the airport.

Before I could launch into introductions, Kwan had an announcement prepared: "He's lying about me."

The words came out of his mouth so fast it was like they'd been dammed up.

"He said I was driving the boat, right? There are two problems with that assertion. First, he wouldn't have let me. Ask anyone at the party Saturday night. His dad made him promise never to let another person behind the wheel of his precious Dominator, and he didn't. Second, I wouldn't have driven that thing even if he'd offered. I don't have a driver's license, remember?"

"That's not a requirement in Maine," I said. "It's perfectly legal to operate a motorboat without a license here."

"Well, I didn't know that. But what proof do you have that I ever drove the boat?"

I had expected this question and was ready with my trap. "What proof do we have that *Kyle* was driving the boat?"

"His fingerprints should be all over the steering wheel—if he didn't wash them off."

"He said you tricked him into handling the wheel this morning," I said.

His eyebrows rose an inch up his brow. "That's what he *would* say, though. Right?" He scanned our faces searching for sympathy. "I'm feeling a little ganged up on here. I was the one who reported the accident. You wouldn't even be here now if I hadn't called Warden Bowditch. I get that it's complicated—sorting out who's telling the truth from who's lying—but it should count for something that I came forward of my own volition and basically incriminated myself, too."

"That's an interesting choice of words, Dave," said Finch.

"I didn't mean it literally. Look, I'm about to start an internship with an investment bank in New York. When what happened here gets out, the bank might decide I'm damaged goods. And I haven't *done* anything that deserves being punished."

Pomerleau had put on what I thought of as her "mom" affect. Her body language relaxed, and her face became unnaturally expressive for her. She was going to let Finch throw the hardballs. "You make some good points, David. But we're going to need a formal statement from you before we can let you go."

He held up his cell phone. "I've prepared a written statement I can email you."

"When did you do that?" I asked, amazed.

"While I've been waiting. I remember everything clearly. Why don't I text it to Warden Bowditch since I have his number, and he can share it with everyone?"

His chutzpah brought a laugh from Finch.

But Kwan's calm confidence would not be broken. He looked down at his phone and hit Send, causing my own cell to chime.

I held the device up before me, opened the document, and saw that it ran for hundreds of words.

"How much trouble is Kyle in, legally speaking?" Kwan asked.

"First-degree manslaughter. Negligent homicide," Finch said with the sort of relish he reserved for these moments. "And you're facing the same, Dave."

"Me?"

"You two kids can't get off by pointing fingers at each other."

Kwan sighed, removed his glasses, and examined the lenses for dust or smudges. Finding nothing, he returned them to his nose. "You're not going to arrest me."

He stated the situation as a matter of fact.

"The problem is, the DA might want us to hold you as a material witness," said Pomerleau. "But I think we can avoid that by being honest with each other."

"I am being honest, and you won't hold me as a witness, either, because I have provided a statement."

Finch dug a hand between the buttons of his shirt and scratched his chest. "Which we need to read before—"

"I have no prior record and nowhere to run. I'm starting an internship with a Fortune 500 company this week and have signed a lease on an apartment in Brooklyn."

"No one told us you'd passed the bar exam, Dave," said Finch.

He shrugged off the gibe. "After I helped you and answered your questions honestly without a lawyer present, there's no way a prosecutor is going to charge me without evidence. So you can hold me, but it would be a bad look for the state of Maine if you come down harder on the Korean kid than on the heir to the McAllister estate."

He had reduced us all to silence.

"And as far as a civil suit goes, I'm not worried about that either," he offered as an addendum.

None of us had mentioned the threat of a civil action.

"And why aren't you worried about being sued, David?" asked Pomerleau with a curiosity we all felt.

"Because Kyle is going to be the focus of the case. If he goes to trial, he becomes the target for a civil action. There's no point in Mr. Whitcomb's family chasing me for money I don't have. Kyle has a trust fund worth millions. Plus, there's the insurance policy Mr. McAllister keeps on the boat. If you were an attorney looking to score big for your client's family, who would you go after?"

Pomerleau couldn't hold in her real emotions any longer. "Wow."

"You think I'm being a prick," Kwan said. "But put yourself in my place. Kyle's family's lawyers need to make me an alternate suspect, and they'll go to any lengths to keep him out of prison. They're the McAllisters. I'm a scholarship student from Jersey. All I'm trying to do is protect myself."

Just then a familiar voice spoke from the trees: "A fishing knife didn't make that cut on your head."

Charley had drifted away while a trooper escorted Kwan into the house to retrieve his belongings. Stealthy as ever, he had returned now without any of us having noticed.

Kwan cleared his throat. "Excuse me?"

"The cut's too thin and clean. The blade that made that wound was razor-sharp."

"Kyle came at me with a knife. It had an orange handle."

"You mean like this one?" Charley produced a forensics bag containing a fillet knife. It had already been numbered to be taken into evidence.

"That's it. Unless he washed them off, you'll find Kyle's fingerprints on the handle. I guarantee you will."

Like the detectives, I had been dazzled by his self-confidence and intelligence.

"He didn't wash them off, because he never knew he handled it," I said, grasping the importance of what my friend was saying. "Because he was passed out when you snuck into his room with the knife. What did you do, close his hand around the grip?"

I could feel the detectives growing confused.

"The problem is you didn't test the edge first," said Charley." A knife this dull, you would have to saw the edge back and forth to draw blood. Which isn't consistent with the wound on your head."

"Prove it."

"You don't think the CSI folks can compare that fillet knife with the width of the laceration on your head?"

Kwan adjusted his glasses. "I've decided not to press charges against him for the assault. He's my friend, and he wasn't in his right mind. Basically, what happened last night freaked him out, and he's been self-medicating. Kyle's facing enough problems without me adding to them."

"That's extremely generous of you," Finch said.

"What I'm saying is you can forget about the knife."

I would have paid to watch the show he was putting on for us. "Ever since we first communicated, David, you've been directing me where to go and what to look for. I don't think it's a coincidence that everything you mentioned incriminates Kyle and exonerates you. And I doubt the prosecutors will believe it's coincidence, either."

It had grown increasingly dark around us. Automatic lights began popping on outside the buildings, synchronized to timers. Across the lake, the alpenglow that had illuminated the ridgeline—a golden light upon the highest treetops—was dwindling fast. Sunset was mere minutes away.

Kwan rose to his willowy height, clutching his bag by the handle. "I'm done talking to you."

"Where do you plan on going?" Finch asked.

"I have already called a friend from school to pick me up. I got a text from him a while ago that he's waiting on the road."

The presumption would have shocked me if I hadn't known kids like David Kwan at Colby.

"Can you believe that little shit?" Finch said as we watched him walk off.

Pomerleau shook her head. "He's not getting away with anything."

I wasn't so certain.

Before I could express this doubt, an unexpected noise came from the neighboring estate. It sounded like a blast from some wind instrument. But the musical moan sputtered out quickly.

Soon the same sound began to echo from other locations around the lake.

"They're blowing their conch shells," Charley explained to us. "It's a nightly ritual on the Belgrade Lakes. Everyone comes out at dusk and blows a tune. Tonight's the coda because it's the end of summer."

"What do you mean?" I said, confused. "Summer ends on September 21."

"No," Charley said. "This is the end."

42

Charley and I got a late start for home. I had to make a few calls for the Dominator to be removed from the boathouse and trailered down to the division headquarters where a boat accident reconstruction expert could make a formal inspection.

"Unfortunately, I can't be there in the morning," I told LaJoy afterward. "Dr. Doumit is doing her autopsies at the same time tomorrow. I can always read the inspection report and call the reconstruction analyst with questions. But I need to see for myself what that engine did to Kip Whitcomb's body."

I wondered if the lieutenant would have a problem with my priorities.

"Everything hinges on whether Whitcomb was alive when the Dominator ran over his body," I added.

"Fine," LaJoy said. "I'll cover for you at the reconstruction."

In the Scout, heading back to the lake house, Charley said, "I would think you'd want to be there for the examination of that boat."

"I do, but Pomerleau wants me to accompany her down to Medway tomorrow after the autopsies. If you were in my place, wouldn't you want to speak with the widow?"

His smile was his answer.

"It's not like it's going to be some fun road trip," I went on. "The day after Labor Day, there will be a stream of cars heading south. The turnpike from here to Massachusetts is going to be one big logjam."

In the light of the dashboard, I saw Charley crack another, even more mischievous smile.

"Why drive when you can fly?" he said. "I'd be happy to take you two down in the Cessna if the detective is amenable. There's a pocket-size airport down the road from Medway. Shouldn't take us more than an hour's flying time. I'm sure the local police would happily send a cruiser to take us to the Fenton house."

Charley Stevens was a canny bastard, I had to hand it to him. He knew his offer was too good for Ellen Pomerleau to refuse. And by piloting us to Massachusetts, he could continue to insinuate himself into my investigation.

Neil appeared in the doorway as we approached the house. Except for a pair of moccasins, he was still dressed for golf.

"My God, Mike, what happened to your face?"

I'd nearly forgotten the damage Joey Randazza had inflicted on me.

"It's nothing," I said.

"When have I heard that before? I remember you coming home from school looking like that once."

It was a time in my life I disliked revisiting. My biological father had been an enthusiastic brawler. He went out at night in search of reasons to throw punches. The high school fight I'd gotten into, by contrast, had happened when I'd tried to protect someone weaker than myself.

Fortunately, Neil felt no desire to linger on the subject.

"Galen Webb is here to see you," he said. "He's down at the dock talking with Stacey."

The mere mention of the constable was enough to trigger a nerve in my backside. "Did he tell you what he wants?"

"He might have told Stacey. She's been passing time, giving him a tour of the Cessna. His dad's a pilot, and he grew up around planes, you know."

As Charley and I made our way through the house, Jubilee called from the kitchen to ask if we wanted iced tea.

"No, but I'd take some coffee if you have any."

"Iced?"

"God forbid," said the old pilot, for whom coffee was an abomination if served any way other than hot and black.

Through the windows in the great room, I saw the Cessna tied to the dock now, bathed in the glow from the single lamppost at the end. Stacey must have completed her tour of the plane because she was sitting on one of the floats, dangling her long legs into the lake. Galen Webb, meanwhile, had climbed back into his Crestliner, which was floating free in the darkening water beyond.

I wondered what he'd wanted to tell me. Maybe the constable had come here, belatedly, to tell me about his conversation with Shawna Miskin and make amends. I hoped he had.

Once we were outside, Charley peeled off to check on Ora, who was napping in the guesthouse. It was a further demonstration of his concern for his ailing wife. Normally, he would have rushed down to the dock to crow about his Cessna. He could talk for hours about that plane.

Descending the steps, I called, "Hello, Galen. What are you doing here?"

The voice that rose toward me was loud with anger. "You don't think I'm a real police officer, do you."

"What?"

"Maybe I haven't gone through the Criminal Justice Academy, but I'm a sworn deputy in the Kennebec County sheriff's office."

His face was flushed under his ball cap. The redness made his small mustache seem somehow smaller.

"Have I offended you, Galen?"

"I heard you were up at the McAllisters' place making an arrest. I got a call from a neighbor of theirs who wondered what all those wardens and troopers were doing there. That's how I heard about it."

"It's not my job to update you on my activities, Galen."

He pretended not to have heard me. "How did you figure out it was the McAllisters' boat?"

Not so long ago, I had been like Galen Webb: arrogant, insubordinate, self-pitying. Maybe I didn't like to be confronted with my former self, but I responded sharply.

"You just said you worked for the sheriff. Why don't you ask him?"

"Screw you."

I tried taking a breath. I reminded myself that he'd worked tirelessly and had kept vigil all night over Kip Whitcomb's corpse. I remembered how proud his wife had been of him and the cuteness of their baby. I wanted to give this young man a chance to come clean about his undisclosed conversation with Shawna Miskin.

"I spoke with a woman who said she overheard Kip Whitcomb and Gina Randazza arguing before the collision. She claimed she told you about it, and you shrugged her off. You didn't think that a witness was worth reporting?"

He all but spat the words at me. "I don't know what you're talking about."

"I saw you talking to Shawna Miskin in a rowboat when you were the chaser for the dive team. Are you going to tell me that didn't happen?"

"You think I'm a fuckup!"

"I didn't say that!"

"Galen?" Stacey said with more kindness than I was feeling.

But he had already started his engine. Stacey and I watched the Crestliner turn away and cruise at headway speed until he was legally far enough from the shore to gun the engine.

43

Charley and Ora didn't join us for supper that night. She now had a slight fever, he said, and so he was going to make her some broth and toast in the guesthouse kitchen. Stacey didn't speak at the table except to compliment Jubilee's linguine con vongole.

"I got the recipe from a guy I lived with in Naples during my vagabond years." A heavy blond lock had escaped the mass piled atop her head and fell fetchingly down the side of her face. "He was *uno aitu cuoco* at a trattoria."

Neil glanced sideways at his wife as if he might not have heard of this Neapolitan lover before. After a pause, he said, "I always find it strange eating seafood at the lake. It seems wrong somehow."

Jubilee smiled over her wineglass. "We're not that far from the ocean, relatively speaking."

My stepfather had taken a shower and now sat with his wet hair slicked back from his tanned, handsome face, dressed in chino shorts and a polo shirt with the collar popped the way he must have worn it at Phillips Exeter Academy.

I had made it clear to them that I couldn't discuss the investigation, but with Stacey barely speaking, I felt compelled to carry the conversation.

"How was your round?" I asked Neil out of politeness.

"Belgrade is a tough course. Clive Clark designed it. I'm sure that doesn't mean anything to any of you, but he designed Eagle Falls outside Palm Springs, where they hold the Frank Sinatra Open Invitational." Neil realized at once that this accolade meant nothing to the three non-golfers in the room. "As designers of golf courses go, the man is a true artist."

A stray memory found its way into my thoughts. "I don't suppose you saw a couple there, Rob and Robyn Soto? They're real estate agents. You might know them from Portland."

He set his fork down on his plate. "I know the Sotos."

"What do you know about them?"

"They are clients of my firm, so it wouldn't be appropriate for me to talk about them. Not personal clients of mine, but it doesn't matter in terms of legal ethics." He touched his napkin to the side of his beer glass, which was sweating condensation. "Why do you ask?"

"Charley and I ran into them this morning up at Camp Machigonne. They were personally putting up No Trespassing signs along the waterfront on behalf of the new owner. I've met yellow jackets who are friendlier."

Neil suppressed a smile. "That's a good one."

"I got it from Charley."

"They're developing that entire point of land?" asked Stacey sulkily. "I assume there won't be public access on the property."

"There isn't public access now," said Neil. "Nothing will change."

"Nothing ever does," said Stacey.

To head off a debate about the private ownership of land and the redistribution of wealth, I leaned my elbows on the table. I turned from Neil to Jubilee. "It never occurred to me to ask if either of you saw anyone suspicious lurking around Mouse Island."

They shook their heads no.

"The rumor going around the lake is that Whitcomb killed the poor woman," Jubilee said. "I had a yoga class this afternoon, and my students wouldn't shut up about that girl being strangled."

The detail had been made public by someone who should have known better.

"I can't confirm or deny anything."

"Mike never accepts the official version of events, anyway," said Neil. "When he was a boy, his mother bought him the collected Sherlock Holmes stories. It was a toss-up what he wanted to be: a modern-day Holmes or a modern-day Hawkeye from *The Last of the Mohicans.*"

Stacey pushed her chair from the table. "Excuse me. I need some air."

Neil looked stricken. "Did I offend her?"

"She's worried about her mom," said Jubilee, then turned in my direction. "Does Ora have any underlying conditions, aside from her spinal injury, that might cause her immune system to be especially compromised?"

"Not that I'm aware of."

"Now that you mention it, there was someone suspicious," said Neil out of the blue.

"What's that?"

"Someone suspicious lurking around the island. He was there last week, not on the island but close to it."

"What did you see?"

"It was before twilight, and there was a man fishing alone near the island. What struck me as odd was that he was using a bobber, the way a small boy might fish. He seemed to be just sitting there like he didn't even have bait on the hook."

This didn't strike me as suspicious except in retrospect, knowing that two people had later died in those same waters.

"What kind of boat was he in?"

"Just an old canoe. But I haven't gotten to the suspicious part."

Jubilee brought her palms together in a silent clap. "Go on."

"I wasn't really paying attention to him. I was listening to NPR. But at one point, I happened to glance in his direction again, and he seemed to be gone."

Now it was my turn to set down my silverware. "I'm not following you."

"The boat was still anchored there, but I could no longer see him sitting in it. The fishing rod was still rigged, leaning against a thwart, but he was gone—or seemed to be. For a minute, I wondered if he'd fallen into the water."

"Why didn't you mention this before?" I asked.

"Because it was last week when no one was staying there, and it didn't have anything to do with Whitcomb." There were moments when the lawyer in him surfaced—he didn't like having his intelligence challenged—and this was one of them. "And besides, when I came back from the other room . . ."

This was his lifelong euphemism for the bathroom.

"When I came back from the other room, he was there again in the boat. He must have been bent over or working on something in the canoe. Maybe he'd caught a fish. In any case, he paddled away a few minutes later."

"In which direction?"

"North, headed up the channel."

Toward the vacated Camp Machigonne, I thought.

"Can you describe him physically?"

"He had on a baseball cap and sunglasses, I think."

"But you said it was nearly dark."

"They might have been regular eyeglasses with photochromatic lenses. Now I feel foolish for having mentioned this at all."

The door opened behind us. It was Charley and Stacey.

Jubilee looked up. "How's Ora doing?"

"She has a fever, and her lymph nodes are swollen," said her husband. "Listen, Mike—"

"It's been decided," Stacey announced. "I'm flying you and Ellen to Massachusetts tomorrow."

Charley wasn't put off by the interruption. "We decided it would be best for me to stick around the hacienda to tend to Ora. Stacey's as good a pilot as her old man. It you're back before dark, Ora and I can fly home then."

I knew how much he'd wanted to be present for the interview with Whitcomb's widow. But I also knew how devoted he was to his wife. There was no greater priority for him than Ora's health and well-being.

We ate our desserts at the table that night in relative quiet.

Later, after we'd gone to bed, Stacey wanted to make love. I'd been tired enough that I could have fallen asleep in seconds, but she took the initiative, and my body responded. Afterward, we lay in the dark with the window open, feeling the late-summer breeze on our exposed skin.

"I'm worried about her," she confessed finally. "This has been happening more and more frequently. Her getting mysteriously sick."

I reached for her hand. "I know she had a cancer scare before."

"Don't say that word. It's one of those words, like *divorce,* that can't be unsaid. I think I'd sense if something were seriously wrong. We have this bond, you know."

"What can I do to help you?"

She rolled onto her side for me to hold her from behind, and that was how we fell asleep, curled together that way.

44

I awoke before dawn and couldn't get back to sleep. Four-star hotels should have rooms as comfortable as my stepparents' guest suite. But my mind was instantly working on my investigation.

Without waking Stacey, I got up to use the bathroom. We'd forgotten to pull the shade. The window faced the guest cottage where Charley and Ora were staying.

To my surprise, I glimpsed Charley stepping out of the glow of the exterior lights and disappearing into the predawn shadows. He was headed up the driveway in the direction of the road.

I hastily pulled on the jeans and chambray shirt I'd worn the night before and slipped from the bedroom.

The sun wouldn't be up for half an hour, but it was already announcing its arrival. The pieces of sky visible through the trees were a luminous gray. After a string of dry weeks, we would finally get some rain, it seemed. The shapes of songbirds—chickadees and kinglets and migrating warblers—flitted silently among the boughs as if afraid to break the stillness with their songs.

I had no clue where Charley might be going at that early hour. He wasn't one to walk for exercise, as his usual outdoor activities burned more calories than he consumed.

I made my way up the drive in the direction of the sand-and-gravel pit that had been excavated out of the western slope of the ridge. Like the birds, I felt reluctant to break the silence. I couldn't bring myself to call out his name.

Minute by minute, the forest was growing brighter, and when

I reached the road, which had been cleared of all overhanging branches and boughs by the power company, I found myself in a faintly lighted corridor.

The road was privately owned and heavily posted, and I hadn't seen a single walker since we'd arrived. I scanned the scuffed sand along the shoulder for recent footprints. I soon relocated our tracks from the day before.

Then I spotted a signature boot print made minutes earlier: the impression of a Vibram sole, men's size nine.

Found you.

I switched into stalking mode. He seemed to be headed toward Camp Machigonne, but I made sure to inspect the dusty goldenrod and faded ragweed that grew along the gravel to make sure he hadn't left the road. It was a good thing I did because he'd cut unexpectedly toward the lake.

Pushing through the weeds, I disturbed a very large toad that had stopped for a breather in one of Charley's footprints. It hopped once, then paused; hopped again, then paused. Toads have a curious notion that if they remain still, they are cloaked in invisibility.

Then a voice shattered the stillness: "Game warden! Stop where you are and raise your hands above your head!"

Charley had circled around and crept within ten yards of me without my hearing so much as a twig snapping.

"Damn it, Charley," I said. "Where did you come from?"

He was wearing the deerstalker again and had a foraging bag over his shoulder, which he used when he was in the woods collecting mushrooms and edible plants. "I was out picking some herbs and roots for the Boss. She's still feeling poorly and wants to make her special tea."

"Yes, but what are you *really* doing?"

He pushed back the brim of his silly hat. Then the bottom of his face cracked open in one of his grins.

"I thought I'd peek in on Shawna Miskin. She's gone, by the way."

"Gone? Gone where?"

"Back down to Massachusetts, I expect. I think she was already planning on vacating the premises, and our arrival at her door spooked her into starting off at once."

"How have you come to that conclusion?"

He turned toward the dirt road and beckoned with a crooked finger. "Follow me and all will be revealed."

Charley was right. Shawna Miskin was gone for good.

The first proof came in the form of distinctive tire marks. Sometime after we'd left the rental, a wrecker had arrived, carrying something heavy on its flatbed. The truck had lowered its burden to the ground. Then both the wrecker and the small car it had been carrying had exited the driveway in succession.

The second proof was the condition of the ranch house. The little house was locked up with the blinds drawn, the doormat shaken free of dirt, and the sundeck swept clean of pine needles.

"Why did she run?"

"I have a few ideas." Charley reached into his foraging bag. "I found a nice stash of ripe blackberries. You want some?"

"How about you spit out that canary you swallowed instead."

"Do you remember the story Shawna told us about how she came to rent that place? How she'd chosen Great Pond because of that movie being set here. Like it was all a whim?"

"Yes."

"I emailed the owners last night, exaggerating my current connection to the Warden Service."

"You misrepresented yourself. You impersonated a law enforcement officer."

Charley popped a blackberry from his foraging bag into his mouth. "I was careful in my wording. Anyhow, the owners live on the West Coast and must be night owls, too, because there was a message from them this morning. They claim Shawna Miskin told them a different tale."

"Go on."

"Shawna, as we shall call her for the moment, told the owners that she was willing to pay extra to rent this particular house. They broke an agreement with another client because she offered cash on the side. She had her heart set on this property for some deeply personal reason."

"Why do you always drag your explanations out? Can't you just tell me?"

"I like to create a little suspense. The reason, Shawna said, she absolutely had to stay here was because she'd been a guest on Mouse Island some years ago and had fallen in love with the location."

"A guest on Mouse Island? She pretended she barely knew the name Kip Whitcomb—" I wanted to smack my forehead with the heel of my hand. "Her name isn't even Shawna Miskin, is it?"

He tapped the pocket in which he kept his smartphone as if to indicate the use he'd recently made of it.

"It's the one she gave them, but the address on her license isn't residential unless she lives at an Irish pub. I expect we'll find out her story was a lie from start to finish. I checked lots of Mass licenses over the years and thought I could spot a fake, but this one bamboozled me. Could be it's genuine but obtained under false pretenses. That would raise a bunch of interesting questions about who she really is and the kinds of connections she has."

I gazed out at the lake, unstirred by a breeze. Its color was the flecked gray of an antique mirror.

"What made you suspect Shawna was lying to us about who she was?" I asked him. "We agreed there was something fishy about her but . . ."

"You told me you saw her in her rowboat *arguing* with Galen Webb about approaching the dive scene. Why would she have quarreled with the constable? Why did she need to see what Bill Boone and his divers were doing?"

"You think she wanted to watch the bodies be brought up so she could be positive they were dead?"

At this, he shrugged.

"I need to call Galen and get an answer out of him," I said. "I asked him directly about the conversation with Shawna, and he refused to admit it happened."

"I don't think young Webb should be your focus. I expect the detectives will agree that the priority is finding out who Shawna

Miskin really is and what role she might have played in the deaths on Mouse Island."

"Good luck finding her now."

"Not everything she told us was a lie. Based on these tire tracks, it seems her vehicle was really being fixed, probably not by Randazza, given he had other concerns yesterday. Finding the repair shop should only take the police a few calls at most. The mechanics are bound to have the car's vehicle identification number."

"The cops can identify her by the VIN!" I shook my head in appreciation at the master class in deductive reasoning I'd received. "Thank you, Charley. Do you want me to admit you're the superior investigator? Because I will."

"If you saw fit to give your future father-in-law this dapper hat, it would be reward enough."

"It's yours, you old fart."

Glorying in his moment, Charley Stevens munched happily on a handful of blackberries.

45

We returned to the aroma of bacon frying and coffee brewing.

"That doesn't smell like Jubilee's cooking," I said.

Charley laughed. "It's not."

Ora had summoned the energy to make Stacey and me a rib-sticking breakfast before our flight south. She was inconvenienced, cooking in a kitchen not designed for someone in a wheelchair, but she seemed to be managing. I wish I could have said that the night's rest had made her look healthier. Her deeply set eyes seemed even more sunken, and there were caverns beneath her cheekbones.

"How are you feeling?" I asked.

"I think I'm on the mend," she said unconvincingly.

Neil and Jubilee hovered in the doorway, looking uncertain about the meal being prepared in their kitchen.

"I don't think I've ever had a real lumberjack breakfast," my stepfather said, which didn't surprise me.

The Stevenses, for their part, never used the term *lumberjack,* which was a midwesternism. Charley always referred to himself as a former logger or, occasionally, *un bûcheron,* since many of the lumber camps where he'd worked as a teenager had been along the Canadian border and manned by the same Québécois woodcutters who'd taught him French patois.

But lumberjack or logger, his preferred breakfast menu was the same. Fried eggs and bacon, pancakes, patties of venison sausage that they'd brought from home, and diced potatoes fried with onions in the bacon grease.

Neil and Jubilee, who adhered to secular dietary laws that were as strict as halal or kosher in their prohibitions, ate the smallest portions they could manage without insulting the cook. Stacey and I filled our faces.

"Life's too short to eat meatless bacon," was my credo.

Neil and Jubilee insisted upon cleaning up, in part (I believed) to bag up the meat scraps and grease and ritually cleanse the house as quickly as possible.

Charley and Stacey then went down to the water to go over the floatplane from nose to tail.

With an assist from me to get over the sliding door frame, Ora pushed her wheelchair out on the deck to watch the preparations. I stood beside her with my hand on her shoulder.

The Cessna 182 Skylane was the largest and most expensive plane Charley Stevens had ever owned. The Skylane supposedly seated four, but Charley carried so much backcountry gear—in the event he was ever forced down in the wild—that the cabin felt crowded with three people. Its purchase had been a concession to Ora who (understandably) hadn't enjoyed flying in single-engine aircraft since the crash that had left her paralyzed.

Both Ora and Stacey were so emotionally intuitive it sometimes seemed like they were clairvoyant. Charley liked to tease them about it: "If you two had been in Salem in the year sixteen hundred and ninety-two, you'd have been strung up for sure." But his humor belied the seriousness with which he believed in their uncanny visions.

I had once voiced my surprise to Ora that she hadn't had a presentiment of the plane crash that had changed their lives. With more patience than I deserved, she had explained that her "powers" were hardly visions of the future. They were often no more than intense, inexplicable feelings.

On the morning of the tragedy, she had been assailed by fear. She hadn't experienced a similar emotion on her earlier test flights.

She had been exhilarated, in fact. She'd tried to rationalize away the terror and hadn't spoken a word to her husband about the intensity of her fright.

"Maybe I had a feeling something bad was about to happen," she'd said. "But it seems more likely that my fear caused the crash. Don't you think?"

I had come away with a different conclusion.

Ora's powers hadn't failed her that day; she had failed them.

"I guess I should get ready," I told Ora her now.

She squeezed my hand and didn't let go for the longest time.

Upstairs, I put on a combination of clothes raided from Neil's closet and scavenged from my duffel. Because warden investigators are the detectives of the bureau, it seemed necessary that I dress up for this interview.

I ironed a button-down oxford that had gotten wrinkled in my bag and removed the creases from a pair of Levi's I'd previously worn. I borrowed one of Neil's tweed sport coats (although it was tight in my chest and shoulders) and a knit tie. I attached the holster of my SIG P226 to my belt, along with two extra magazine pouches, and clipped on the badge. Then I laced up my much-loved chukka boots.

I couldn't help but focus on my black eye in the mirror. I might shave and comb my hair and dress up in a jacket and tie, but Dianne Fenton-Whitcomb would see the tough guy beneath the dignified veneer. Having been a prosecutor herself, she would know that a cop with bruises is often a cop with problems.

"Don't you look handsome," Ora said as I returned to the porch.

I asked if I could accompany her down to the dock, and she said yes. She wanted to be there for the send-off.

Neil and Jubilee caught up with us at the lower patio.

"When should we expect you back?" she asked.

As a naïf when it came to police work, she didn't realize that a question of that kind could never be answered with confidence. The job set its own hours.

"With luck, late this afternoon."

Neil wanted to shake my hand for some reason. And then he felt obliged to shake Stacey's, too.

"Good luck, good luck."

Stacey had brought the plane in parallel to the dock so that we had only to grab a strut and step up on the float to enter. I took my seat on the right side, fastened my seat belt, and reached for the headset we would use to converse inside the cabin, since the engine was so loud.

Through the window, I watched as father and daughter spoke a few words to each other that I couldn't hear.

Stacey nodded in understanding, and then she climbed up while her dad was untying the lines tethering us to the dock.

She fastened on her own headset and adjusted the microphone, so it was pressed within a millimeter of her lips.

"We've got a good morning for this," she said. "Visibility is decent for a cloudy day. Winds are light out of the west. They'll be turning southwest this afternoon with thunderstorms possible ahead of a front. But you can focus on your interview without worrying about the flight home."

Then she went through her comprehensive checklist. I knew some of what she was doing: checking the fuel mixture, the propeller setting. Both she and her father projected such confidence and competence, it would have been easy not to notice their attention to every detail. Airplanes are fragile machines at the mercy of physical forces that test the limits of human understanding. A pilot who doesn't approach their aircraft with respect is no pilot at all.

I cast a glance in Ora's direction next. The muscles of her weary face were tight with either pain or fear.

What is she sensing?

Neil and Jubilee had joined her. Charley stood alone at the end of the dock, holding his new hat to his head so it wouldn't be blown off when Stacey started the engine.

My stepparents began to wave. This was still novel for them, watching a floatplane take off. Jubilee, especially, was beaming with childlike anticipation.

After the plane had taxied away from shore and Stacey had accelerated and the water had lost its grip on the floats, she brought us back over the house. From high above, I spotted Jubilee, alone among the foursome, still waving.

46

Just fifteen minutes later, Stacey landed at Augusta State Airport. It felt like we'd barely had time to get airborne. The Cessna was nicknamed an amphibian because, in addition to the floats, it was fitted with wheels that could be raised or lowered to land on hard surfaces: tarmac, paved roads, and even certain fields.

Despite the fact that it served the state capital, Augusta was a small airport with only two runways: a long strip capable of landing any plane in the National Guard fleet, and a shorter one perpendicular to the first.

Pomerleau was waiting for us behind the fence. She was wearing her usual black suit, which, coupled with her pallid complexion, gave her a vampiric affect. The contrast between her undead appearance and her soccer-mom van reminded me how little I knew about her life beyond the state police.

"Do I have to stay with the plane?" Stacey asked as we stepped down onto the apron where small planes parked.

She desperately wanted to watch the autopsy, never having observed one. I wouldn't characterize her as having a fascination with gore, but she had been trained in and worked for years as a biologist, before becoming an EMT, and she was not at all squeamish.

"I can call Dr. Doumit," the detective offered, "and see how she'd feel about you being there."

I glanced at the Cessna. "Will it be safe here, unattended?"

"This isn't some landing strip or flyspeck airport. Augusta has actual fixed-wing operations and real security."

It turned out that Leah Doumit was surprisingly relaxed about Stacey observing the postmortem. She had only one condition, Pomerleau told us in the car. "If you're going to be sick, vomit in a sink and not on her floor. That goes for you, too, Warden Bowditch."

The medical examiner's office was across the Kennebec River and part of a compound that included Maine's crime lab and state police headquarters. My agency, the Department of Inland Fisheries and Wildlife, was scheduled to move its own operations to a new building nearby.

"I kind of miss Augusta," Stacey said as we parked in the shady lot.

"You're joking."

"It always used to piss me off to hear people call it 'Disgusta.' Have a little civic pride, you know? It's the state capital! The seat of government. Important history has been made here."

"Such as?"

"When the legislature voted to make the whoopie pie Maine's official state treat."

She held a deadpan expression for half a minute and only lost it when I leaned over to kiss her. Gently, she touched my swollen cheek and bruised temple.

"You're not looking your prettiest, Mike Bowditch."

"I hope, as my wife, you will see past the bruises to my inner beauty."

The autopsy suite had chalk-yellow cinder blocks for walls, an ocher floor chosen seemingly for its ugliness, and lots of stainless steel. There were gleaming cabinets and carts, sinks with multiple attachments for hosing away blood and gore, and scales for weighing the organs removed from the bodies of the dead. And of course, the cold tables on which lay the naked cadavers of Kip Whitcomb and Gina Randazza. Fluorescent lights hummed above us, their stark whiteness adding to the sterility of the atmosphere and lending the corpses a waxen complexion that made their lifelessness an irrefutable fact.

"I can tell you right now that the female's larynx was fractured," Dr. Doumit told Pomerleau. "Whether it was the blow to the throat, strangulation, or forced drowning, the cause of death in her case was intentional homicide. No one accidentally suffers those injuries."

"Maybe you should do Whitcomb first, then," I said. "Whether we charge the young men in the boat with homicide or some lesser offense hinges on whether he was alive or dead when they ran over his body."

She gazed hard at me through her spatter-proof face shield. "Can you rephrase that as a question?"

"Will you perform Whitcomb's autopsy first, Dr. Doumit?"

"That was what I was planning."

The wound where Whitcomb's arm had been amputated was ragged and even more gruesome in the clinical light. The skin had been flayed from the tissue beneath. Shards of bone that I hadn't noticed protruded from the mangled flesh.

Dr. Doumit and the pathologist assisting her were dressed in identical scrubs. As always, the medical examiner began her inspection at the literal surface, surveying Whitcomb from the top of his woolly head to the pads of his toes.

She spoke in a conversational voice into a microphone. "The body is that of a normally developed, well-nourished, light-complexioned male appearing consistent with the listed age of thirty-five years. The unembalmed body weighs one hundred and seventy-four pounds with a length of seventy-two inches. Rigor mortis is present and equal throughout. Lividity is anterior and fixed, except in areas exposed to pressure. The body temperature is that of the refrigeration unit."

Disinfectant only goes so far in covering the smell of death. Decomposition begins almost immediately, starting in the stomach and colon, where the same enzymes that dissolve the food we eat begin to digest tissues left unprotected after the body stops producing mucus. In death, in other words, we cannibalize ourselves.

When she had finished with Whitcomb's front, she and her assistant rolled him onto his chest and stomach.

Dr. Doumit spent considerable time examining the skull fracture. The parietal bone had been shattered, she said. As this was the thickest part of the skull, it was no surprise the impact had dented the McAllisters' hull.

The gashes to Whitcomb's back, neck, and shoulder were parallel and deep enough to show the layers beneath the epidermis, down through the dermis and muscle fibers to bare bones.

In my too-vivid imagination, I could see and hear the rotating blades cleaving through the man.

The severed arm lay on the table beside him as if awaiting reattachment. The pathologists had removed the Rolex and wedding ring. I moved to the other side of the table, taking pictures with my iPhone for my own case file. There were no scratches or bruises on his other arm. Nor were there wounds on his face or chest.

As Dr. Doumit and her assistant began taking X-rays, I decided to step out of the room to get my thoughts together. I would return for the examination of the lungs.

It was warmer out in the hall, but I shivered anyway. The disinfectant odor lingered in my sinuses.

Stacey removed her mask as she came through the door. "Are you all right, Mike?"

"Whitcomb's body doesn't show any signs of being scratched or bruised."

"OK?"

"But Dr. Doumit tells us that Gina was attacked. So why are there no signs on him that she fought back? There should have been defensive wounds."

"She might not have been conscious when it happened. She might have been drunk or drugged."

"Who punches the throat of an unconscious person?"

She smiled up at me. "That's a question for a detective, babe. I just fly the plane here."

"There are no wounds on Whitcomb's body to suggest he tried to get out of the way of the boat, either."

"Because he was drowning," said Stacey. "Or had just drowned."

"You're missing my point. *Why* would he drown?"

"He breathed in lots and lots of water."

"I'm not joking, Stace."

"They might both have been really wasted," she said, understanding at last that I needed a sounding board. "We know they did tequila shots. Maybe he panicked after killing his girlfriend and wasn't thinking straight. That's usually why people drown; fear gets the better of them and they forget how to stay afloat. Why don't you wait for the toxicology results to come back before you jump to conclusions."

"Dr. Doumit won't get the lab results back today or tomorrow or even this week."

"Maybe Pomerleau can get her bosses to push—"

"I don't think it can wait. Something happened that night that we're not seeing."

An air conditioner in some window down the hall rattled.

"I feel like you're overcomplicating this," Stacey said. "Gina Randazza was murdered, most likely by Whitcomb. But you seem to want Whitcomb to have been murdered, too."

"It's not what I want. It's where the evidence keeps leading me."

The door to the autopsy suite opened again, and Pomerleau poked her head out. "Is everything all right?"

"Based on what you're seeing in there, Ellen, what do you think happened to Whitcomb?" I asked. "What does your gut tell you about how he died?"

She was experienced enough to know I had ulterior motives in asking these questions.

"We know he was drunk," she said gamely. "I think after he killed Gina, he must have lost it. Somehow, he ended up in front of that boat. He might already have been drowning and on his way out, but Kwan and McAllister finished the job. Homicide detectives never know every little thing that happened. What matters is we know the big things."

But we don't know the big things, I thought.

We were getting closer and closer to how they died. But we hadn't begun to approach the question of why it happened.

Pomerleau said, "Leah is about to open up his chest. If you want to watch the process, we should get back in there."

The three of us stood at the periphery while Dr. Doumit made a Y incision down Whitcomb's hairy chest and peeled back the skin. She used what looked like pruning shears to cut the ribs. I had forgotten how much this part felt like watching an animal being butchered.

The whole process seemed simultaneously exotic and familiar, for that reason. Exotic because it was a person being systematically deconstructed. Familiar because the glistening mass of organs resembled those inside the bears and moose I had cut open myself, looking for slugs fired by poachers.

The medical examiner removed the heart first and weighed it.

Then it was the moment I had been waiting for: the lungs.

First the right lobe, then the left. She spoke the weights into the microphone—815 grams and 724 grams.

"They're big and heavy," she said to us. "They're overinflated. They basically filled up the entire thoracic cavity. We call that *emphysema aquosum*. And see how the surface is marbled? That indicates collapsed alveoli interspersed with tissues that remained aerated."

"In other words, he drowned?" Pomerleau said.

"I'm not ready to say that until I can take some slices and have a look under the microscope. The challenge with drownings is that there are certain signs you look for, but none of them alone indicates pathogenic water inhalation."

"Once again in English," the detective said.

"The froth in the nostrils, the size, weight, and appearance of the lungs—everything is pointing to your victim having drowned, but as I said, I am not ready to make a determination."

It sounded to me like Whitcomb was dead when the outboard carved him into pieces. For his body to have remained buoyant, he must have drowned mere minutes before being struck.

Pomerleau stepped out to update the chief prosecutor in the attorney general's office. I had no idea what charges might be brought against McAllister and Kwan, but negligent homicide would not be one of them if Whitcomb was already dead. The Colby grads had gotten lucky—comparatively speaking.

As I followed the detective into the hall, I turned on my own phone and found a voice mail message from Rick LaJoy. While I'd been watching the autopsy, another postmortem of sorts had been taking place at the department's Sidney headquarters, where our boat accident reconstruction expert had examined the Sunsation Dominator.

"He says the 'glass shows recent scuffing. Algae takes less than a week to appear in scratches and indentations, he says, but there's no slime to be seen. Throw in the damage to the propeller, and it's obvious this boat hit something consistent with a human body. The bleach the kids used means we won't have DNA evidence, but hopefully, Dr. Doumit can match the wounds on the body to the dimensions of the blade."

It took me a minute to process what these two conclusions meant for me, personally.

My role in the case was, for all intents and purposes, over.

We had found the boat that struck Whitcomb. We were close to determining that he had been dead at the moment of impact.

I would have some additional conversations to conduct and reports to write. Eventually, I would be called to testify in court. Finch and Pomerleau still had big decisions to make about Gina Randazza's murder—how aggressively to pursue alternate suspects was first on the list. But I could metaphorically leave Mouse Island and move on to my next case.

Ellen now presented me with that very option.

"I can drive down to Medway," she told me while the air conditioner rattled. "I appreciate the offer of the plane. But I can't think of a reason you need to sit in on my interview with Dianne Fenton-Whitcomb."

"I promised to fly you down," Stacey announced, "and I'm going to fly you down."

"If you don't mind the company, Ellen," I added.

She showed one of her rare smiles. "It's bound to be better than listening to Boston sports radio."

47

Stacey brought the plane to a cruising altitude of three thousand feet.

I couldn't remember ascending to this height in a Cessna. As an investigator, I did most of my work nearer to the ground. I would go up with warden pilots and district wardens to scout for illegal marijuana grows; I often searched for evidence of poaching activity, such as shooting lanes cut in the trees and suspicious tire tracks along the wooded edges of fields. Occasionally, I would bum a ride to a far corner of the state to interview a suspect or a witness for a case.

But the ceiling was high this morning. Through the window, I watched my beloved Maine slip away behind us as we entered the airspace over New Hampshire.

We had made progress with our dual cases.

Based on a review of samples from Whitcomb's lungs, Dr. Doumit had determined the cause of death as drowning.

Gina Randazza had died of a combination of laryngeal trauma, caused by blunt force injury to the throat, and asphyxiation resulting from manual strangulation. Her hyoid bone had been fractured, which almost never happens except when a person is strangled.

I had missed much of Gina's postmortem, making calls first in the hallway and then in the parking lot, not just to the prosecutors but also to LaJoy and Boone. I thought Kathy would want to know what we'd found, too. And she did.

Watching one autopsy had been more than enough for me. Watching two had satisfied my anatomical curiosity for the day, week, and month.

Stacey had observed both with keen interest.

Although she was working as an emergency medical technician, she had previously been employed as a wildlife biologist, bush pilot, sea kayaking guide, and even the executive director of a nonprofit devoted to protecting endangered Florida panthers.

I couldn't help but wonder what a person of her many talents might do next.

"Thank you for doing this, Stacey," said Pomerleau through the intercom. "I was dreading spending the day in the car."

"Trapped with Mike Bowditch, no less."

"I'm good company!" I said.

"This airport where we're landing is super bare-bones," Stacey said. "Its website has an airport police page that is blank. I guess that means we're on our own. It's every pilot for herself at Franklin Municipal."

Pomerleau chimed in from the back seat of the plane, "The Medway Police said Franklin was the closest airport. The chief himself will be picking us up."

"You're sure you don't mind me sitting in on the interview?" I asked.

"As long as you promise not to hijack it."

"And if I can't promise . . . ?"

"Just behave yourself, Mike. I have certain information I need to get out of Mrs. Fenton-Whitcomb about her husband, specifically any history of violence. Unlike you, I don't tend to wing my interviews."

I would have felt stung if she hadn't been correct about my stream-of-thought method of questioning.

In a slow moment at the morgue, when Dr. Doumit and her pathologist were shuttling between the cadavers, I had finally told the detective about Charley's discoveries concerning the mysterious Shawna Miskin.

"That's an interesting wrinkle, no doubt about it. I'll have Finch call the local repair shops and see if they have a VIN we can track. Why didn't you tell me about this sooner?"

"I was preoccupied with my own case. And I guess I was still trying to figure out what to make of her. That ferocious argument she claimed she heard between Kip and Gina is sounding more and more suspect."

"And yet it aligns with the evidence we've found."

"The lack of defensive wounds on Whitcomb still bothers me. How can you trust anything an impostor tells you? For all we know, Shawna Miskin was the one who did it."

"I'm going to begin our descent," Stacey announced.

I felt cowed and grateful for the interruption. "Didn't we just reach our cruising altitude?"

"My dad calls flights like these *hop and skips*."

As we began our approach, I glimpsed the hard blue line of the Atlantic to the east and then the skyscapers of downtown Boston. The air above the city was brown with smokestack emissions and the exhaust from thousands of idling motor vehicles. I already missed the woods. I had left my natural element behind and was arriving in a place where I would always feel like an outsider.

Stacey radioed ahead to Franklin Municipal.

And within five minutes, we had touched down. Out my window, I saw a low-slung building and a couple of hangars and not much more.

Stacey taxied to the space where a man wearing shorts and waving orange sticks directed her to park the plane. He put chocks against our wheels to keep the aircraft from moving.

By the time I'd popped the door, he had removed his ear protectors, which hung around his neck like some sort of tribal ornament.

"Can't say we get many floatplanes landing here," he said in an accent that was closer to South Boston than Beacon Hill. "You're the cops from Maine, right? Chief Dannenhauer is inside, jawing with the manager."

Stacey cast a doubtful look at the vacant airport. "I'm going to stay with the plane."

Pomerleau hadn't invited her to attend the interview, so it wasn't as if she had many other options.

"What are you going to do while we're away?" I asked.

"Kick back in the pilots' lounge."

"Seriously."

She held up the dog-eared copy of *Persuasion*. "My mom says Jane Austen always has another lesson to teach us."

I kissed her goodbye and then climbed out into some brutal heat. Pomerleau was waiting for me on the tarmac.

The detective and I found Chief Dannenhauer easily enough; the airport building consisted of three or four rooms.

He was a balding man who wore his gray hair shaved to the scalp. He was not grossly overweight, but the ballistic vest made him look that way, and in fairness, he did possess multiple chins. His navy uniform was short-sleeved, revealing flabby forearms and thick wrists. He wore an old-school police hat pulled down low on his forehead so that his small eyes seemed to be peeking out from under the hard brim. He had a piece of red-blotched toilet paper on his cheek where he'd cut himself shaving.

"I'd expected you sooner," he said, smiling but sounding annoyed.

"Our apologies," said the detective. "We had an autopsy to attend."

"You have my sympathies."

He escorted us to a Ford Interceptor utility vehicle, one of the new hybrid versions, black with white doors.

I happened to notice that the shield emblem on the panel included the date Medway had been founded (October 25, 1713), as well as an unusual symbol.

"What does the red boot and bonnet stand for?" I was thinking of a girl heading to her grandmother's house where a big, bad surprise was waiting for her.

The question caught Dannenhauer by surprise. He studied me in his rearview mirror.

"The Red Riding Hood attire?" I said.

"It's historical. Something to do with manufacturing back in the olden days. I should know, I suppose. But you're the first who's ever asked."

Pomerleau took the seat beside the chief while I sat behind her, so the chief could see me—and I could see him—in the rearview mirror.

Ellen was eager to get down to business. "You personally delivered the death notification, I understand."

"Me and one of my lieutenants. He'd gone to school with Dianne and knew the family some, ran cross-country with her little brother. The Fentons have lived in Medway forever. This is still a small town, but we've seen more than our share of development. Good quality of life and easy access to Boston and Providence. It's a nice, safe, quiet community."

Having allowed the chief to do his bragging, Ellen returned to the questions she'd been waiting to ask.

"How did she take the news?"

"Devastated, obviously. We made her sit down first, not that standing is easy for her. You might not have heard she has multiple sclerosis."

"We heard," said Pomerleau. "We talked with her yesterday after we found her husband's body."

"He was hit by a boat in the buff, then? What a way to go. But in a way, it was pure Kip. The man was a total character. Larger than life."

"How so?"

"He was always selling something, for one thing, which meant he liked to glad-hand. When he was working as a Realtor for Sotheby's, he sold expensive properties in the area. Then he went out on his own for a while selling real estate, but he wanted to get into finance, as I understand it. He had less success in the investment business than in houses, from what people tell me."

"Oh?"

"The judge, Dianne's dad, when he was alive, forbade Kip from touching her inheritance. He tolerated Kip but didn't respect his financial acumen. Judge Fenton made it known to his friends that he didn't trust his son-in-law with his daughter's money. It kind of undercut Kip's aspirations."

Kind of? I thought.

"Not that Dianne is gullible or lacking in smarts. She was a lawyer, like her dad, but destined for politics, everyone said. Lots of people said Kip Whitcomb was beneath her. Personally, I thought they were well matched. Both were outgoing, strong-willed, energetic—until she got sick, of course. Her mom died of MS, too."

Pomerleau, to her credit, would not let any of Dannenhauer's segues derail her line of questioning.

"You said she was devastated by the news. Can you describe how she responded specifically?"

"She didn't break down, if that's what you're asking." He tapped his thick fingers atop the steering wheel. "I have to ask, what do you plan on asking Dianne?"

"For one, if her husband had enemies."

"Not since the judge died."

I wasn't sure if that was a joke.

"What about Dianne?" Pomerleau asked. "Might she have wanted her husband out of the way?"

Although the detective had asked the question, Dannenhauer flashed a glare at me in the mirror.

"The woman is disabled and housebound. She obviously had no part in her husband's death, which I understand was accidental." His eyes returned to the rearview mirror. "Isn't that your conclusion, Warden?"

"*Accidental* isn't a term I like."

His tone hardened along with his expression. "Did a boat run over the man or not?"

"A boat struck him in the water. That's all I'm comfortable saying at this point."

With a grunt that might have contained a profanity, Chief Dannenhauer hit his turn signal and pulled sharply into a school parking lot. He undid his seat belt so he could swivel his armored torso to address both of us at once.

"When we spoke yesterday, Detective, you told me that you wanted to speak with Dianne about the house in Maine and how often Kip used it. We're aware here that he was with a girlfriend who also died. *Drowned* is the word you used. Now I'm thinking something else happened. Something you haven't told me."

It was always a question when working with police from other departments—how much to divulge. Chief Dannenhauer might have had local loyalties. We had no clue how deep his relationship to the Fenton family went.

Pomerleau surprised me by taking a leap of faith. "Gina Randazza—Whitcomb's girlfriend—had contusions around her throat. The bruises indicate she was strangled."

Dannenhauer let out a blast of air through his nostrils. "And you think Kip killed her? Why the hell would he have done that?"

"That's what we hope to find out," she said.

"He wasn't a violent guy. I can tell you that for a fact."

"Someone drowned Gina," I said.

"It wasn't Kip. And I'd be careful of making an accusation against him you can't prove. The Fentons have always cared about their reputations."

48

Kip Whitcomb and Dianne Fenton-Whitcomb lived in a big, dark colonial on the Charles River. It blew my mind that this shady stream could be the same river that flowed past Harvard and MIT. Sleepy, green Medway seemed so distant from bustling, urban Boston. The Charles made the connection literal in a way that a road never could.

The lawn was professionally maintained, well watered, and shaded by Norway maples with purple-red leaves. The air smelled of freshly cut grass, the clippings of which had been removed, leaving only the good smell of the lawn. There were signs around the grounds and in the windows, too, advertising how closely and constantly the property was being monitored. I looked for and found security cameras. From the direction of the river, I heard the barnyard sounds of mallards quacking and splashing. I wondered if the ducks were watching us, too.

"Do you have many break-ins in this town?" I asked.

Dannenhauer's grimace suggested he felt insulted by the question. "No, we don't. Why do you ask?"

"All the houses we've passed have security signs in their yards. And the Fentons have cameras."

I pointed first at the doorbell cam, then at a camouflaged camera mounted to a tree branch so that it covered the front step. Most people would have missed the second one.

"This is a desirable neighborhood in which to live," the chief said. "It's right for people to want to protect their homes and families."

He turned to push the glowing bell, but before he could, the door opened. Evidently, the cameras had announced our arrival.

Inside the doorway, a fashionable woman stood behind a walker on which tennis balls had been fitted to keep it from scuffing the hardwood floors.

"Two visits in two days, Chief."

"I wish it was under better circumstances, Dianne."

"What *are* better circumstances? I've forgotten." There was the faintest of quavers in her voice.

She wore tan pants and a green linen blouse and a silk scarf around her head. Her practical thick-soled shoes seemed the only concession she had made, fashion-wise, to her disease.

She motioned us forward, into the foyer, where the chief formally introduced us, and Dianne shook our hands—her grip was surprisingly strong—and made eye contact like the high-powered prosecutor she'd recently been.

Like many people suffering from a debilitating illness, Dianne Fenton-Whitcomb seemed old and young at once. Her hair had been dyed a rich brown that was probably her natural color before MS had caused her to go prematurely gray. But her dark eyes were as alert and intelligent as the girl I'd seen in those family photos at the lake.

A black cat materialized out of nowhere and pressed his long body against the chief's leg.

Dannenhauer, I could tell from his sourpuss, was not fond of cats.

"This is Cinder," Dianne said with a wry smile. "He's the lord of the manor. We only exist to do his bidding."

The house had an old-fashioned front parlor for greeting visitors. The furniture was antique except for the mechanical recliner that rose to accept Dianne's frail body. The coffee table was barren of coffee-table books, but there was a vase full of hothouse lilies that projected a vividness that was no match for the stuffiness of the room.

My gaze went to a framed coat of arms on the wall: a white shield with a black cross and four black fleurs-de-lis. The crest was topped by a knight's helm and some heraldic vegetation I didn't recognize.

Nor could I decipher the family motto below (*Gwell angau na gwarth*), but my money was on it being Gaelic.

The chief belatedly removed his hat and set it on his ample lap.

"Thank you for making time for us," said Pomerleau. She sat upright with her legs close together.

Dianne's smartwatch glowed to life as she lifted her bony wrist. "How long do you think this is going to take?"

"We'll try to make it as quick as possible. I can't promise it'll be painless."

"Nothing in my life is painless anymore, it goes without saying. But I'm still alive and kicking. I never thought Kip would die before I did. Never in a million years. And I can guarantee you he didn't, either. The possibility was literally beyond his imagination, and my husband was a schemer, let me tell you."

She paused to take a sip of water from a tray on the table beside her chair.

Dannenhauer repeatedly cleared his throat; his big face grew red.

Dianne Fenton-Whitcomb carefully returned the glass to the table. "When will your medical examiner release my husband's body to me?"

"A few days," said Pomerleau, "likely sooner."

"Do I get him in pieces, or will they sew him up like Frankenstein's monster?"

The chief, growing ever redder, turned his hat on his lap. "If you'd like, Dianne, we can help you with the mortician and the transportation of the coffin down to Medway."

"My father passed away out of state. He was down in Texas, dove hunting. I can handle the logistics, Chief."

Pomerleau had a notebook open and a pen at the ready.

"When did you last visit Mouse Island, Ms. Fenton-Whitcomb?" she asked.

"*Dianne* is fine. The hyphen was for professional purposes. People still refer me to as Dianne Fenton. I've certainly never been *Mrs. Whitcomb*. To answer your question, the last time I visited Maine was two years ago this past July."

"But your husband continued going up without you?"

"Obviously. Kip probably went to Mouse Island half a dozen times this summer."

"Does anyone else use the house or have access?"

"No."

"Do you have a caretaker?"

"We did until this year. It was the young guy the lakes association hired to be the constable. Galen Webb. He quit abruptly this spring, leaving us without one. I'd ask for recommendations for a new caretaker if I gave a damn about the place."

Why did Galen never mention this?

"Mr. Webb had keys to the house and other buildings, I assume," said Pomerleau in a tone as flat as Kansas.

"Of course," said Dianne. "But he returned them. He sent them here by mail with a very apologetic and illiterate letter."

Had he made copies? I wondered.

But Pomerleau was determined to trudge forward. "Did your husband mention any problems you had with trespassers on the island? Did you have any break-ins before or after you lost your caretaker?"

"Over the years, of course. But nothing recent. In the interest of hurrying this along, I'm going to assume you want to ask me about the woman Kip was fucking."

"We didn't want to begin there, but—"

"I have multiple sclerosis, not Alzheimer's. I am in full possession of my faculties." She focused on Pomerleau as the only other woman in the room. "The thing they never tell you about having a disease like MS is that it doesn't just make people uncomfortable—it freaks them the fuck out. I'm like this walking memento mori. This is going to go smoother if I don't have to deal with your personal hang-ups."

"I appreciate your candor. Frankly, it's easier if we can be direct in an interview."

"You don't have to tell me. Less than a year ago, I was an assistant United States attorney, hard as that might be to believe."

It wasn't just that the room was hot, the air felt trapped.

"You said you were aware that your husband was in Maine with a woman," the detective said, making a note in her pad. "Does that mean he told you?"

"Of course not."

"Then how did you know?"

"Let's just say that Kip would have made the worst spy on the planet. He didn't know how to hide things and could never keep secrets."

Dannenhauer tried to suppress a cough but was forced to reach, too late, for his handkerchief.

Dianne fixed him with a poisonous look.

"How did you feel about his having an affair?" Pomerleau asked.

"What are you—my therapist? Look, I've effectively been on my own since my diagnosis. That's the thing about having a disease like mine. No one else can go through what you're going through, even if they're empathic, which Kip was definitely not."

"It sounds like he abandoned you."

"When he was at home, Kip devoted himself to taking care of me. He learned to cook and made me laugh and pretended to treat me like the woman he'd married. The price for his attention was that I look the other way when he went off on his 'ski trips' or his 'meditation retreats' to my family's cottage in Maine. I knew what was going on, and he knew that I knew, and it was this unstated agreement that he was free to fuck around. I couldn't be his playmate anymore, and he was a man who liked and needed a woman to go to bed with."

"How many 'playmates' do you think he had?" asked Pomerleau.

"More than a mistress, less than a harem."

"Had you ever heard of Gina Randazza before yesterday?"

"No."

"Gina's husband said Kip met his wife when he visited his house to buy a motorcycle."

"Do you think he'd be interested in buying it back? It's out in the garage. I found a picture of her online, by the way. She was the youngest one yet—that I knew about."

The black cat materialized again. I followed the white button under his raised tail as he slipped around the corner.

"The answer to your next question is no," Dianne said. "I did not resent Kip's infidelities. What I resented was this goddamn illness that made me incapable—that made it necessary for him to seek what he needed elsewhere."

Dannenhauer clutched the handkerchief to his mouth to forestall another cough.

"Can you describe your husband's drinking habits?" I said, forgetting my promise to Ellen to be quiet.

Dianne pursed her lips as she examined me. It was as if I'd been in shadow before and had stepped into the light. "I should have asked this at the start, but can you explain the division of duties here?"

"As a warden investigator, I handle boat crashes, principally those that result in injuries or death. I'm trying to establish how your husband happened to be in the water and his physical state at the time he was struck by the boat."

"By physical state—"

"We're awaiting the autopsy reports, but circumstantial evidence suggests both he and Mrs. Randazza were heavily intoxicated."

"Let me guess. Tequila? That was always his spirit of choice."

"Did he indulge in other substances that might have left him physically or mentally impaired?"

"Pot made Kip paranoid. He did coke when he was younger, but I told him he couldn't be with me and do that stuff. I had ambitions once." Dianne turned to Pomerleau. "If the warden is here to establish whether the boaters will be charged with negligent homicide, I am not sure I understand *your* role, Detective."

Instead of answering the question directly, Pomerleau responded, "Was your husband ever violent with you?"

"What kind of question is that? Absolutely not."

"Alcohol didn't make him violent, in your experience?" Pomerleau asked.

"He was the least violent man I knew."

"The detectives think Gina Randazza might have been strangled," said Chief Dannenhauer.

Dianne Fenton-Whitcomb looked appalled. "And you think my husband killed her?"

"We can't rule him out at this stage," the detective said, giving no indication of how baldly she was lying. "How about I run some other names by you? Joseph 'Joey' Randazza?"

"The cuckolded husband? I hope he has an alibi."

"Kyle McAllister?"

"No. Who is he?"

"One of the young men in the boat that struck your husband. His family owns a compound on Great Pond. And they also happen to be from Waban."

"And you assumed because Waban is twenty miles from here, we might know each other?" The idea amused her. "There are nearly five million people living in Greater Boston. No, I don't know any McAllisters."

"David Kwan?"

"No."

Pomerleau surprised me with the next names. "Rob and Robyn Soto?"

Dianne paused for the first time. Her gaze flitted about the room as if following an insect. "Who are they?"

"Real estate agents from Portland. They claim to have been engaged in a deal with your husband to purchase Mouse Island. They say he pulled out before the papers could be signed."

"Oh, them. I'd forgotten their names. Kip could be impetuous and didn't always share his schemes with me ahead of time if he feared I'd disapprove. Which I did in this case. That island belongs to the Fenton *family.* I don't know if he thought he could sneak the closing documents past me or what. He said the price the buyer was offering was absurdly high—and it was—but he had no business pulling that stunt. It was the last real fight we had, come to think of it. I've never heard of real estate agents committing murder over a deal gone bad. That sounds extremely far-fetched. I hope you have better leads."

I couldn't stop myself from lobbing out a name I knew Pomerleau wouldn't.

"Shawna Miskin."

The answer came without a pause. "No."

She's lying, I thought.

Dianne was savvy enough to know I had a reason for offering the name out of context. She understood that I was waiting to see how she responded.

"I assume she's another of my husband's girlfriends. Is that why you're asking? Who is she?"

"We don't know yet," I said, feeling Pomerleau scalding me with her gaze. "She used fake identification to rent a cottage across the channel from Mouse Island. As a former prosecutor, what do you make of that?"

"I'd want evidence connecting her to Kip before I came to any conclusions. What do you have?"

"Still early days," I said.

Dianne took a small sip of water. It wasn't obvious she even swallowed. The gesture seemed intended to stall for time.

"There was a crazy woman who came to the house once," she said. "She showed up at the door, raving about how he'd ruined her life. Kip made sure I didn't see or talk to her. He dragged her out into the driveway and yelled at her to grow up. That's all I heard. The whole situation was humiliating. Kip refused to talk about it. The worst thing was the bitch ran over my viburnum. Do you think that might have been the woman you mentioned?"

That was quite a pirouette, I thought, moving from not recognizing the name *Shawna Miskin* to telling us a detailed story of a deranged stalker showing up at the house.

"And you didn't press your husband to tell you who she was?" I asked, fully aware that Pomerleau must be desperate to get back on track.

"It was obvious who she was—one of Kip's whores." Dianne turned back to the detective. "To be clear, you're accusing my husband of having murdered this Randazza girl? That's the theory of the case you're pursuing? You and the warden came here to get dirt on Kip out of me."

"I wouldn't put it that way," Pomerleau said.

"Bullshit. You've narrowed that girl's murder down to my husband. Those other names you threw at me, they aren't real suspects." She engaged the button on her chair that caused it to rise and tilt forward. "I need to call my lawyer."

As she lunged for her walker, Dannenhauer sprang to his feet. "Dianne, please let me—"

"No!"

"This doesn't have to be adversarial," said the detective.

"Tell that to Gina Randazza's husband. You realize he is going to sue me as soon as an ambulance chaser gets to him. Kip and I kept our finances separate, but . . . I'm calling my lawyer."

"We're not implicating you in what happened, Dianne," I said.

"That's a relief!" Pushing the walker hard, she shuffled to the door. Then, leaning on the handlebars, she said, "If that Randazza tries to come after me or my money, he will regret it. I may look helpless, but it would be the last mistake he ever made."

49

We listened to her muffled steps, doors opening and closing as she moved deeper into the old building, past the point of our hearing.

Dannenhauer crossed his arms over his padded chest. “She just lost her husband, for God’s sake. What were you thinking bringing this man along, Detective?”

“That woman doesn’t need your protection, Chief,” said Pomerleau, not raising her eyes as she made additional notes in her pad. “She’s capable of taking care of herself.”

He was too chivalrous to launch a verbal assault on Ellen, so he chose me instead.

“I reprimand officers of mine who engage in acts of deliberate cruelty.”

I chose not to engage with him but rose and crossed to the family crest on the wall. The plaque had caught my eye again: the knight’s helmet above the four fleurs-de-lys. When I was a child, I had been briefly interested in heraldry and was crushed when my father had laughingly told me rednecks didn’t have coats of arms. They were lucky if they even had coats, he’d said.

Out of curiosity, I painstakingly transcribed the words *Gwell angau na gwarth* into the search browser on my phone. The words were Welsh, not Gaelic. The translation came back: “Death before disgrace.”

Charming.

And galling for a woman as proud as Dianne Fenton-Whitcomb to have been so publicly confronted with her husband's shameful conduct, I thought.

As I turned toward the door to the foyer, Dannenhauer closed the distance between us and grabbed my arm. "Where do you think you're going?"

"To find a bathroom."

"She didn't give us permission to wander around her house. How about you hold it until she returns?"

I tried shaking him off, but he only tightened his grip. "Do you want to let go of me, Chief? The bathroom is right there." I pointed across the entryway where a door stood open. "I'm not one of your officers you get to boss around. You're bleeding again, by the way."

He brought his fingertips to the tiny piece of paper he'd used to treat his shaving nick. The cut had indeed begun to bleed again, perhaps from the force of his coughs.

"Shit!"

I used the distraction to slip into the bathroom. I didn't peek in the medicine cabinets. I didn't expect to find anything of relevance in this old manse. And I liked to think I possessed some honor, still.

Returning to the parlor, I passed a bookcase in the foyer containing assorted awards and trophies received by at least three generations of Fentons. The wood had been wiped clean of dust. The glass was so clear I could read the inscriptions on the plaques and medals.

Most of them belonged to the judge. His plaques and statuettes occupied two entire shelves. A framed portrait showed him accepting a handshake from the late senator Edward Kennedy. But pride of place was given to a medal presented by the American Bar Association. I assumed receiving it had been his life's crowning achievement.

His children were also represented in the family shrine. Dianne's two diplomas from Harvard were on display, along with awards she received from the Commonwealth and the Massachusetts Bar Association, as well as a framed document from her brief tenure in the United States Attorney's office in Boston.

Her little brother, Cole Jr., was represented mostly by the medals he'd won as a junior pentathlete. If he'd graduated from West Point, he had decided to store his diploma somewhere else.

Dannenhauer had been watching me examine the contents of the cabinets. "How about you join us in the other room, Warden?"

"You mentioned that one of your officers was friends with Dianne's younger brother, Cole Jr. What do you know about him?"

"Nothing. We've never met."

"I understand he lives and works in Turkey."

"Then you know more about him than I do."

Suddenly, a voice projected through the room. It was coming from a smart speaker on a little table beside the door. It must have contained a camera in addition to a microphone and speaker. "If you're going to roam around my house against my wishes, I would like you to wait outside, please."

Dannenhauer flushed again, this time growing particularly red in the ears. His shaving nick oozed. "I'm sorry, Dianne. I've been trying to tell them—"

"Wait outside, please. My lawyer is on her way and will be here in forty minutes."

My first thought was: *Dianne Fenton-Whitcomb must be an important client to get house calls from her attorney.*

My second thought was: *I'd better tell Stacey we're being delayed.*

As I stepped into the late-summer heat, I heard a riding mower on the grounds of the next estate. The air had grown more humid since we'd gone inside, or it was just my imagination. I could smell the river through the trees.

Pomerleau drifted into the shade of the Norway maples to make some calls, while Dannenhauer returned to his cruiser. The chief sat inside with the air-conditioning running. His big, bluff face was a perfect visual definition of indignation.

Stacey picked up on the second ring. "Are you done?"

"No, and we're not going to be done for a while. Dianne Fenton-Whitcomb has summoned her personal attorney. When we let her know Gina's death was suspicious and we hadn't ruled out Kip as a suspect, her mind went immediately to the lawsuit Joey Randazza might file against her husband's estate."

"I bet the idea hasn't even occurred to Joey yet."

"I wouldn't be so sure. Criminals, even small-time criminals, see every situation as an opportunity for quick-and-easy gain. But nothing about a lawsuit would be quick. I'm guessing Dianne's attorney is first-rate, which means she knows delaying is the name of the game. Put off the trial long enough and Randazza might die in a motorcycle crash or land behind bars for possession with intent to distribute."

"*Or Dianne herself might die*," I thought but resisted saying.

Stacey said that if I had a minute, maybe I could bring her up to speed since she'd finished her book and was dying of boredom at the godforsaken little airport.

I filled her in on the interview.

"It's beyond weird that Galen didn't mention being their ex-caretaker," she said.

"Galen Webb's brain seems to operate on a different frequency from yours or mine. If he didn't consider the matter important, it wasn't important. Just like that argument he never had with Shawna Miskin."

"Who has got to be one of Whitcomb's conquests, right?"

"She seems to have rented that house for the sole purpose of spying on him. I don't see how Pomerleau and Finch can close this case until they've found out who she really is and what she was doing there."

Stacey asked, "Are you sure Dianne Fenton-Whitcomb recognized the name?"

"Yes and no," I said. "She had heard it before, I could tell. But if it's an alias taken on for the purposes of renting the house, I don't know why Dianne would have recognized it, even if it was the same woman who came to her house."

"I don't believe for a second that her husband's infidelities didn't bother her."

"Dianne Fenton-Whitcomb strikes me as too self-aware to lie to herself."

"It's not herself she was lying to, Bowditch. It's *you*."

"I think we can rule her out as a suspect, Stace."

"Listen, I'm starving, and there's not even a vending machine here. Do you think I have time to run out and get something?"

"More than enough time, sadly."

"There's a Mickey D's across the way."

I couldn't help but laugh. "I thought we weren't eating fast food anymore."

"No," she said, "it's *you* who's not supposed to be eating it, Mr. Game Warden."

Like many law enforcement officers who spend their days on the road, I frequented too many drive-throughs. I didn't want to end up like Dannenhauer, with a stomach that was on intimate terms with the steering wheel of his cruiser.

The chief had exited his still-idling Ford and was speaking with Pomerleau in the shade of a breeze-blown maple. Ellen did not appear pleased to hear his news. I signed off with Stacey and went over to investigate.

"Chief Dannenhauer is stranding us here," Pomerleau told me. "He's leaving us high and dry."

"I've got a situation back at the station I need to handle. Call me when you're done, and I'll send a unit to bring you back to the airport." He'd put on his old-school police hat and pulled it down low on his forehead so that his eyes peeked out from under the hard brim. "Or you can call an Uber."

"An Uber?"

He smiled out of one side of his mouth and touched the brim of his hat to say goodbye.

We watched the Ford circle the brick drive. Then we commenced to wait.

After fifteen minutes, I started glancing at the front door of the house, expecting Dianne Fenton-Whitcomb to invite us back inside.

After thirty minutes, I turned my attention to the road, waiting for her attorney to come tearing up the drive in a Tesla Model S.

After forty-five minutes, I started to pace the lawn.

After an hour, I began to suspect we'd been conned.

"What the hell?" I said. "Do you think her lawyer is even coming?"

Pomerleau pushed herself up off the stoop on which she'd been sitting. She tried unsuccessfully to brush the dust off the seat of her black suit. "I'm not sure she even made the call—although I can't fathom what she would've gotten out of wasting our time like this."

"There's only one way to find out." I pressed the blue eye of the doorbell again.

A minute ticked by without a response. I tried again.

"I'm sorry," said Dianne Fenton-Whitcomb's voice through the speaker. "I dozed off."

She sounded alert. And I thought I detected a trace of mockery in her voice, as if she was daring us to buy this bullshit excuse.

"I don't suppose you've had an update from your attorney," I said.

"No—wait. She left me a voice mail while I was sleeping."

Here it comes.

"She's had an emergency come up and won't be driving over after all."

Pomerleau was willing to play the diplomat one last time. "Dianne, I understand your concerns about saying anything that might be used in a civil suit against you. But we did fly down from Maine for this."

"If you'd told me what you were planning—if you'd warned me I'd need legal counsel—you could have saved yourself the trip."

"Can we at least come in to discuss this face-to-face?"

"No, but I can call you an Uber."

"There's no need to trouble yourself."

Pomerleau, who hated being played for a fool as much as I did, was already bringing up a rideshare app on her phone.

"I'm going to go out on a limb," the detective said as we followed the bricks to the road. "I'm going to say we've gotten everything we're going to get out of Dianne Fenton-Whitcomb."

"It's hardly in her interest to have her husband branded a murderer. You'd think she'd want to do everything possible to clear his name—if only to forestall a civil action."

"If she's as good a lawyer as the chief said she was, then maybe she can see which way the wind is blowing."

"What do you mean?"

"There are no other plausible suspects in Gina's murder. Joey has an alibi that doesn't look like it's about to collapse, despite all of Finch's efforts to punch a hole in it."

"What is it with your partner and those bikers?"

"The Direwolves are affiliated with the Outlaws, as you know. A few years ago, Roger's son mouthed off to one of those guys in Portland's Old Port, and he got jumped in an alley on his way to his car. The kid has had seizures ever since, and of course, he has no memory of the attack, so no one has been prosecuted for ruining his life."

It made me doubt Finch's story about his original clash with the Direwolves. He'd claimed to have stopped Randazza and his gang for speeding through Belgrade Village and then been subjected to threatening to escalate violence. But what if the detective had targeted the bikers? What if he'd been the one who'd provoked them out of pent-up personal anger about his son?

"It seems like you should have told me this earlier," I said. "Finch has a pretty big conflict of interest."

"Because the Direwolves are bikers? If the colonel pulled Roger off every case that involves a guy who owns a motorcycle, he might as well leave major crimes and take a job weighing semis on the turnpike. Despite what you and Roger Finch might wish, Joey isn't a credible suspect."

"Gina wasn't the first married woman Kip Whitcomb hooked up with."

"I'm not saying we shouldn't consider the possibility of another jealous husband."

"You just happen to think it would be a wild goose chase."

"All evidence points toward some sort of drunken quarrel that turned violent between Whitcomb and Randazza. And before you say we should take a closer look at Galen Webb because he omitted to mention he used to be the Fentons' caretaker—"

"Forget Galen."

"You're willing to do that?"

"No," I lied. "But what about our mystery woman, Shawna Miskin?"

"A woman's hands didn't throttle Gina Randazza. You're clutching at straws, Mike—as usual."

I ignored the jab. Something else had been bothering me. "I am having a problem with Dianne Fenton-Whitcomb. She started off defending her husband's character, but she stopped conspicuously short of saying he couldn't have done it."

"Maybe because she's a former prosecutor, she knows never to say never."

"Even so, it's almost like she doesn't care if Kip Whitcomb is remembered as a murderer. It seems out of character for Judge Fenton's daughter."

I was thinking of the family motto: "Death before disgrace."

"No one can blame her for Kip's actions, though," Pomerleau said. "If anything it makes her more sympathetic—and I say that as someone who doesn't particularly like the woman. Computer forensics have run through the contents of Gina's and Kip's phones, by the way. It was mostly dick pics and sexts as far as the affair went. They'd been planning the trip to Mouse Island for weeks, but she'd begun getting antsy. Gina had a feeling Joey was beginning to suspect she was running around behind his back. Kip told her she was imagining things."

'What if she wasn't?"

"Now you sound like my partner."

"Ouch!"

She turned toward the sound of an approaching car. "Here's our ride at least."

50

West of the airport, the sky was growing darker by the minute. The approaching clouds looked black and boiling. I hoped we could make it back to Belgrade before the thunderheads arrived. Stacey was a top-notch pilot, but flying in a small plane ahead of an electrical storm was an experience I'd lived through once with Charley and didn't need to repeat with his daughter or anyone else.

Stacey was sipping a soda through a straw as she finished her preflight inspection of the Cessna.

"I see you found food." I pointed to the fast-food bag waiting to be stuffed into a nearby dumpster. "What did you end up eating?"

She winked at me. "A McSalad."

Pomerleau wandered off to confer with her partner about the contents of the victims' cell phones. With no planes landing or taking off, the little airport had grown eerily quiet. Ellen seemed to be listening intently to whatever Finch was telling her.

"So, guess who's the hero of the day?" Stacey asked me. "Neil! He called in a favor with a client who's also one of his golfing buddies and owns a house on Long Pond. He's a doctor, and he agreed to have a look at my mom even though it's a holiday. Your stepdad must have saved him a lot of money in taxes."

"And?"

"She has mono! Actually, it's called *Epstein-Barr virus*."

"I didn't know an adult could catch mononucleosis."

"My dad's been teasing her, asking her who she's been kissing behind his back. She thinks she caught it from a friend's granddaughter whom she's been teaching to braid sweetgrass baskets. I guess there's no wonder drug she can take, just over-the-counter meds for the pain. I was scared for her, Mike."

"I know you were. But that's one less thing we have to worry about." The sky along the western horizon was piled high with cumulonimbus as dark as volcanic ash. "I only wish those clouds didn't look so menacing."

"If you'd come back any later, we would have had to wait out the storm."

"Are you sure we still shouldn't?"

Stacey patted the fuselage of the Cessna as if it were the flank of an old and trusted steed. "It'll be a bumpy ride ahead of the storm, but the front is moving in from the southwest, so we will have a tailwind pushing us home. And if it gets too much, I can always put us down in a lake to wait out the weather. That's the joy of flying an amphibian."

"I need to get home," said Pomerleau, approaching across the tarmac. "Please don't say, 'I told you so,' but maybe I was too quick to write off Joey Randazza as a suspect. Finch claims he's blown a hole in the alibi. He got one of the other Direwolves—the felon facing prison for possessing a firearm—to admit the New Hampshire story was concocted. He says Randazza left the White Mountains in the afternoon. So Joey would have been in Maine at the time of his wife's murder."

Stacey interrupted, "I'm going to suggest you two continue this conversation in the air."

Pomerleau paused in the door of the plane to take one last look around. "This has got to be the loneliest airport I have ever seen. Where is everybody?"

"There were a few dudes around earlier," Stacey said. "There are always old guys hanging around airports. Usually, they're friendly, though. These were just watching me."

Unless you've taken off in a private plane from a remote airport, it's difficult to appreciate how quick the process can be. A short taxi to the runway. No queueing up in a line of planes. No tower to wait for.

In less than five minutes, we were airborne.

From the copilot's seat, I had good views of the tumultuous sky. Rain slashed in columns from the leading edge of the thunderheads. I found myself holding my breath, waiting for flares of lightning.

"Shouldn't you call a tower or something?" said Pomerleau as the wind shook us.

"No need if I'm flying this low, using visual references. But if things get hairy, I'll talk to Boston Center."

Given the storm and the difficulties of conducting a nuanced conversation through headsets, we all fell into a mutually agreed-upon silence.

Our meeting with Dianne Fenton-Whitcomb was spinning around my head so fast it was making me dizzy.

She was a former prosecutor. I had anticipated a rigorous defense of her late husband's character. Was it possible Dianne Fenton-Whitcomb believed he was guilty, as Ellen suggested? The simplest, most straightforward answer is usually the correct one, argued the medieval philosopher William of Ockham.

The plane shook as turbulence lifted the left wing. The storm seemed to be catching up to us, but I knew that was merely an illusion. The airspeed indicator said we were racing along at eighty-nine knots, which was faster than the approaching weather.

"How are we doing, Stace?"

She glanced at me with a big smile. "You don't find this exciting? I live for this kind of flying."

"Just as long as we don't die for it."

"Why are you being such a worrywart today? It's not like you to be easily spooked."

"I'm not spooked. I'm frustrated by what happened to Kip Whitcomb. Something still isn't adding up for me."

Pomerleau could hear everything we were saying through the intercom. "Mike Bowditch is the only law enforcement officer I know who wishes criminal investigations were *more* complicated. I bet you do jigsaw puzzles upside down, too, right? Just for the added challenge?"

"Mike doesn't play games," Stacey said.

A strong gust hit the plane, causing us to wobble.

Pomerleau struggled to sound like she was having fun. "I've never ridden a mechanical bull, but this is what I've always imagined it feels like."

The GPS screen in the dash showed us above Boston's western suburbs. I watched the little airplane-shaped icon crawl forward.

I was thinking I'd gotten used to the turbulence when the engine made a strange coughing noise.

I noticed Stacey frown.

"What?"

The engine began to sputter like a car running out of gas.

"Is something wrong with the plane?" asked the formerly chill homicide detective in the back seat.

Stacey didn't answer. She examined the control panel. Then she wiped the sweat from her palms on her legs and readjusted her hands on the wheel. "I need to switch tanks," she said, flipping a lever.

"Why?" I asked.

The sputtering stopped, and I took a deep breath. The wind was buffeting us, but at least the engine was purring again.

"If I didn't know better, I'd say we got water in one of the tanks, but I sumped them both this morning and didn't refuel, so it makes no sense. Luckily, we have enough gas in the left wing to get us back to Belgrade."

A minute later, the mechanical cough started again.

"What's happening?" Pomerleau demanded.

"I don't know how, but we seem to have gotten water in both of our gas tanks. The engine is going to conk out any minute."

The propeller slowed and began to windmill; it was no longer powered by the engine but spinning freely.

"Make that any second." She changed the propeller pitch to high, switched radio frequencies, and grabbed the microphone. "Mayday, mayday, mayday. Cessna 177 Mike Echo. We are a Cessna 182 experiencing engine failure, twelve north of Franklin, currently at twenty-five hundred feet descending. We have three people on board."

A voice responded, "Aircraft calling mayday, go ahead."

Stacey changed the squawk to the emergency transponder code.

Pomerleau couldn't keep the fear out of her voice. "Are we going to crash?"

"Define *crash*."

51

Stacey addressed us both, her voice firm, clear, and admirably calm. "I'm trimming for glide speed. You're going to feel a wallop when I stop the propeller, but it'll lessen the drag and give me more time to put us down."

"What can I do to help?"

"I'll let you know." Then, to air traffic control: "Boston Center. Cessna 177 Mike Echo, I'm not going to make it to Crow Island Airpark. I'm putting us down in the water."

"Have you ever done this before?" Pomerleau asked.

Stacey's silence sufficed for an answer.

As part of our aborted flying lessons, Charley had walked me through the mechanics of a light aircraft, using his Cessna 182 as the example. He wanted to familiarize me with the basic elements: flaps, propeller, rudder. He showed me that the plane had two avgas tanks, one in each of the wings, holding somewhere around thirty gallons each. We could fly hundreds of miles without needing to refuel, which was why Stacey hadn't topped off in Franklin; there hadn't been a need.

I also recalled how easy it was to open a tank, especially on a floatplane that had what amounted to a built-in stepladder. Anyone could do it.

"Could the plane have been sabotaged?"

Stacey shot me a look out of the corner of her eye. "Babe, I've got a few things to deal with here. Either I land this in one piece, and we'll find out what happened, or the FAA can figure it out from the bloody wreckage."

We were descending, but it seemed like the cloud ceiling was, too, almost as if the storm were pushing us toward the ground.

The next transmission from Boston Center was cut off in mid-reply. We couldn't have been more than five hundred feet above the ground.

"All righty, then," said Stacey. "What do we have to work with here? That hayfield looks tight."

"How much room do you need?" Pomerleau asked.

"A few hundred feet."

"That pond is too small," said the detective. "That's no bigger than a football field."

"I've done made my choice, and I am sticking to it."

She spoke these words in a vaguely Southern accent. She was imitating her father, who must have known someone from the army who'd used the expression.

The pond was kidney-shaped, forested along the sound end, but marshy at the north. The wind continued to howl and gust. The swaying treetops seemed as if they were reaching up to grab us.

Stacey pulled back on the yoke. I was almost certain I heard the grasping pines brush the floats. Then the water came rushing at us fast.

Usually, the Cessna just kissed the surface, but this time, there was a jolt as the backs of the two floats plowed dual wakes through the pond. You think of water as slippery, but the friction caused us to lurch forward against our shoulder belts, even as the marsh and the trees rushed toward the nose at terrifying speed. We were moving fast when we hit the first lily pads, then the first reeds, and finally the first brittle stalks of the cattails. The brown catkins exploded into fluff that stuck to the wet windscreen as we shuddered to a halt. One of the floats had ridden up on a submerged log, so we were seriously off-kilter, but we were down and stationary and alive.

I pulled off my headset and stared at my future wife in amazement. "You knew those cattails would slow us down!"

"Well, I *hoped* they would." She still sounded cool and collected, whereas I was experiencing a sensation like low-grade electrocution. "I'm afraid we're going to get our feet wet getting out, though."

She was right about that. I popped open the door and stepped down, holding on to the wing struts to keep from sliding off since the floats were wet, and we were at an awkward angle because of the dead tree. It was hard, in the rain, to guess how deep the marsh was, but we were close enough to the forested edge that I didn't hesitate. I jumped off and sank to my thighs in the surprisingly warm water.

I found myself laughing now.

Pomerleau emerged next, smiling in a way I'd never seen from her before; this jubilant expression was one she must have saved for friends and family. "You did it!"

I offered Stacey my hand after she had secured the plane. She didn't need it. But she accepted the gesture nonetheless.

It was a short, long walk out of the marsh.

"You did it," Ellen Pomerleau kept repeating in disbelief.

Finally, we stumbled out of the pond, legs soaked and covered with muck, the three of us grinning like madmen escaped from Bedlam.

I put my arm around Stacey's shoulder and pulled her close. I could feel the energy buzzing through her nervous system. We glanced back across the water toward the pines we'd clipped coming down.

"There's no way that pond is three hundred feet long."

"Yeah, I know. But by the time I realized it was too small, I knew that if I didn't commit, we'd be toast."

"Your dad will be proud of you, Stace."

"For beating the hell out of his plane?" She gazed at the scratched float wedged against the half-submerged trunk. "I guess it could have been worse."

"That's an understatement!" Pomerleau took her cell phone out. "Whom should I call?"

The rain was coming down in sheets. Stacey wiped strands of wet hair away from her eyes. "Call 9-1-1, for a start. The air traffic controllers are going to know where we went down, roughly speaking.

And I expect we're going to hear sirens soon. But we might as well alert the locals."

"I'd suggest you call your family, too, Ellen," I said. "You don't want them getting the news you were in a crash from anyone else."

Frogs were burping and croaking as if a strange object from the sky hadn't just crash-landed into their little world. "What will happen to the plane now?"

"The FAA and the National Transportation Safety Board are going to have questions for me and my dad, starting with how water got into the tank. Someone must have sabotaged us. Probably at Franklin while I was looking for food. Probably, one of those old creeps. I doubt there's even security footage of the apron."

"It was Chief Dannenhauer who suggested we fly into that glorified airstrip instead of Franklin or Foxborough."

"You think Medway's chief of police was in on some conspiracy to bring us down? I'm sure it's just the usual place he meets small planes."

"Maybe."

"I do know for a fact that the plane didn't have water in the tanks when we left. I checked the sump this morning."

In my mind's eye, I saw her showing off the Cessna to Galen Webb when he'd visited the lake house to complain about his mistreatment by me. His father was an accomplished pilot. No doubt, the constable knew his way around small-engine aircraft.

"Besides," she added, "if someone had fouled our tanks in Maine, we wouldn't have made it to New Hampshire, let alone Massachusetts."

Stacey was speaking as an experienced pilot. I knew I should trust her judgment about what was mechanically possible. The odds were against Galen Webb being the saboteur.

The idea would have been easier to accept if I hadn't been presented, time and again, with disturbing revelations about the man's inner darkness.

52

We heard sirens and saw blue-and-red lights flashing through the trees before Pomerleau had gotten off the phone with her family. Stacey had been right about how fast our rescuers would appear.

I made my way through the forest and met the firefighters, cops, and EMTs halfway. They reacted to me, stepping into the rain-streaked beams of their flashlights and headlamps, as if I were an actual apparition: a newly minted ghost. The first responders knew how minuscule that pond was and had expected to find three dead bodies compacted inside a wrecked plane.

"You're sure none of you are in shock?" one of the local cops asked me.

"Not the way you mean. But we are confused. Where the hell are we?"

The cop showed me his shield: Sherborn, Massachusetts.

Afterward, I was surprised to look at my watch and see that it wasn't even seven o'clock. It felt like the middle of the night.

Stacey planned on staying with the plane. Investigators with the Federal Aviation Administration and the National Transportation Safety Board would have questions for her and for her dad, as well. (Having received the news from his daughter's mouth, Charley was already rushing south in my Scout.) The federal agents might have questions for Pomerleau and me, too, but we would be easy enough to re-locate. The detective understandably wanted to get home as soon as possible.

I found myself on the horns of a dilemma.

On the one hand, I felt that I should remain with Stacey out of loyalty and sheer love for the amazing pilot and person she was. But I had nothing valuable to contribute to the conversations she and Charley would have with the investigators. The probability of the Cessna having been sabotaged in Franklin were waiting.

And yet, I felt an almost magnetic pull drawing me back to Belgrade, where, I sensed, the real answers were waiting.

Someone had taken a huge risk to damage the plane. They had gambled on the Cessna going down in a crash that would obliterate the signs of their tampering. The gamble had failed. Now they would be in even greater danger than they'd been before they poured water into the gas tanks.

For the past two days, I had struggled to accept that Whitcomb and Gina Randazza had died in some drunken crime of passion. Now I had proof their murders were part of a plan laid by someone whose motives remained unclear. This person, or persons, had been careful and calculating. If Whitcomb's body hadn't drifted into the path of a superpowered speedboat, there would have been no evidence to contradict the theory of the case that the detectives were still pursuing.

Sabotaging the plane was an act of desperation.

Had I hit upon an important piece of information without realizing the danger it posed to the murderer? If so, I must have expressed my suspicions to that person or to someone connected to them. What was it I had said, and to whom? My survival might well depend on making the connection.

Wearing a borrowed raincoat, I studied the shadowy people, wondering if one of them might be the saboteur, hiding in the anonymity of the darkness and the rain.

"Am I overthinking again?" I asked Stacey when I confided these thoughts to her.

"A few hours ago, I would have said yes."

"But now?"

"The more I think about Galen, the creepier he gets. I'm not saying he put water in the tanks himself. But since the night of the deaths, he's always been on the edge of the action, watching."

"In fairness, that's the job we've asked him to do."

"The thing is he really pestered me to show him the floatplane. He kept going on about how he spent so many hours in the air with his dad and how he had a pilot's license he didn't use. He wondered if he might have a better chance of being hired by the Warden Service if he got his Single- or Multiengine Sea rating."

"It'll take more than being certified to fly a floatplane for Galen to get a second chance—especially given his behavior over the past two days."

"I wish I could be more helpful, Mike, but I'm having trouble focusing. Plane crashes will do that."

"Except we didn't crash. Thanks to you."

I reached out my arms to hold her. We were both soaking wet. She was still shivering as I kissed her goodbye.

I made my way to the road.

The Maine State Police had sent down one of their cruisers for Pomerleau. The trooper belonged to the barracks that patrolled the southern end of the turnpike. He wore a long black raincoat and a waterproof cover over his broad-brimmed campaign hat.

The detective sat in front while I sat behind the cage preventing arrested individuals from assaulting the driver. As was typical of police vehicles, this one had locking doors that couldn't be opened except by the trooper. I wasn't naturally claustrophobic, but I hated riding in the backs of squad cars.

There was zero conversation, just the burble of the police radio.

We crossed over the vaulting Piscataqua River Bridge with its green supports and its WELCOME TO MAINE sign that always felt like a homecoming even when I was many miles from my actual house.

The rain blurred the city lights of Portsmouth at the mouth of the river and the industrial brightness of the naval shipyard on Seavey Island. It was the oldest in the United States and the birthplace of everything from wooden frigates to nuclear submarines.

I leaned back and closed my eyes, thinking I might try to nap. But sleep wouldn't come.

After a while, I sat up and pressed my hand to the cage. "Ellen?

Why did you give Rob and Robyn Soto's name to Dianne Fenton-Whitcomb?"

"You heard what she said about the sale of Mouse Island falling apart."

"That must happen all the time."

"Not to the Sotos. An attorney in the AG's office told me the couple is famously litigious. If you've made a habit of loitering on the sidewalk outside their house, you should expect a process server to come knocking."

"People who sue aren't typically people who kill."

"Says who?"

"What would they have had to gain? It wouldn't help any civil action against Kip Whitcomb for negotiating in bad faith to have him out of the picture. But if Robyn didn't have a fling with Kip, I'd be stunned."

"So Rob decided to take revenge? You're really set on the jealous husband angle."

Our conversation was interrupted by the roar of motorcycle engines. The rain had slackened since we'd crossed into Maine, but the asphalt looked like wet glass in the headlights. The road conditions didn't stop two northbound bikers from flying past the cruiser at a speed I estimated as being upward of ninety miles per hour.

The muscles in the back of the trooper's neck tightened. "Unbelievable."

"That's bold," I said. "Passing us like that."

"Some of these guys have a sixth sense—they know when you're not going to chase them."

"But you might radio to a unit up ahead."

"You're assuming that they think like we do, Mike." Pomerleau rubbed the tightness from her sore shoulders. "Some people have such faulty wiring upstairs it's a wonder their heads don't catch on fire."

53

Neil was my last ride of the evening. He met me at the Augusta airport, where the trooper dropped off Pomerleau.

Three hours removed from the plane crash, the detective had recovered her characteristic sangfroid. She had refused offers of rides from her husband and her partner, saying she could drive herself home, thank you very much. Despite our recently shared near-death experience, she made no move to embrace me or even shake my hand.

Neil was waiting in his Audi for the cruiser to pull into the parking lot, and he stepped out into the drizzle before we'd come to a stop. He was wearing a light jacket, but in his happiness at seeing me alive, he forgot to put up the hood, and so his magnificent head of hair got wet. I had the sense he might hug me, but WASPish uptightness restrained him from showing his relief at my survival.

He wanted to know the details, of course, everything that had happened.

I indulged him as we headed northwest, back across the turnpike, toward Great Pond. But I only indulged him up to a point. I described the engine of the plane quitting and Stacey piloting it down into the pond like a stubby-winged glider. I omitted any mention of water in the gas tanks even as he interrogated me like the seasoned attorney he was.

A memory had returned to me the moment I sat down in the passenger seat, and I found myself lingering over it now like an object from a toy box in the attic that, a relic from childhood you forgot you'd ever owned.

As a teenager, I had been full of anger. Much of my rage was directed at my mom for divorcing my biological father and uprooting us from the North Maine Woods where I belonged. I had no interest in my new stepfather's mansion and very little initial curiosity about the nearby salt marsh or the rocky neck down the road where Winslow Homer had painted his dramatic seascapes.

One day, I'd gotten into a fistfight at school with a boy who'd been bullying a kid with developmental disabilities. The jerk and his friends had been persuading him to do gross and humiliating things (like swallowing a live earthworm) for their feigned approval. Then they'd called him a "retard" to his face. It was the first time I realized that fight-or-flight would never be a choice for me, as such. There was too much of my father in my makeup. Every confrontation would end in raised fists and thrown punches.

I'd beaten the bully bloody.

My mother couldn't face me—perhaps because the situation reminded her of bailing my dad out of jail—so she'd sent my stepfather to pick me up from the vice principal's office.

"Why are you doing this?" I'd asked him in the car.

He'd left work to get me and was dressed in a gray suit and blue tie. "Because your mother asked me to. And I love her."

Neil openly and even bravely, I must admit, refused to hide his disgust with my dad. Unlike my mother or me, he recognized the essential badness in Jack Bowditch and refused to look past it. I'd always felt that some of his resentment had rubbed off on me as the man's natural son.

"Too bad you're stuck with me, too."

"The thing about marriage is that loving her means I need to love you, too. I'm supposed to say that I hope we become friends, but I'm not sure that's possible; not because I don't like you, Mike, but because, as your mom's husband, I have a different role to play in your life. We're going to have to figure out what that role looks like. Because there are days I struggle, and this is one of them."

It was one of the most honest things anyone had ever said to me, I now realized. But for years, I had heard only the part about him not liking me.

The rain was picking up again; the wipers could barely beat time to clear the windshield.

"I want to thank you for what you did for Ora," I said.

"Oh, well, that was nothing." He seemed genuinely embarrassed.

"Convincing a doctor to skip a round of golf to examine a person on his day off? That must have taken a heroic effort. How is she doing?"

"The painkillers seemed to help a lot at first. She was doing better . . ."

"Until you heard we'd nearly crashed." I pictured the ailing, white-haired woman in her sickbed, receiving the news with horror. "The thought of Stacey being in a plane wreck must be her worst nightmare."

"Not just Stacey. That woman really loves you, too, Mike. She and Charley are two of the finest people I have been privileged to meet. You'll be lucky to have them as in-laws. I'm speaking from personal experience. Jubilee's parents think I'm a cradle robber. In fairness, I'm older than her mother."

"She's not the woman I would have expected you to marry, Neil."

"Really? Because she reminds me so much of your mom."

I thought about that as we left the road and made our way down the steep hill, which was flowing like a muddy sluiceway. My Scout was gone, of course, because Charley had borrowed it. We made a dash from the SUV to the door.

Jubilee was in the living room reading the collection of E. B. White essays that Ora had quoted from the night before. She leaped up and rushed to hug me, inevitably getting hair in my face. Her arms felt very strong.

"Ora's in bed," she told us. "Whether she's asleep is another question. You must be exhausted, but I'm desperate to hear what happened."

I feigned a yawn. "I need to take a shower first."

"You don't have to come back downstairs. I understand if you want to go straight to bed. It's good for me to be forced to wait for things."

Grateful for this, I said good night and plodded upstairs.

As soon as I turned on the light and the guest suite was revealed in all its resort-style luxury, I had that feeling of having been too long away from home. I missed Shadow terribly. Being a wolf, he wouldn't mind this rain. But if I had been there, I would have let him spend the night indoors.

In the morning, I would do paperwork while I waited for Charley and Stacey to return from Massachusetts. I'd probably have to drive the Stevenses home to their place on Little Wabassus (unless he insisted on remaining with his plane until he could fly it again, which was quite likely). But I felt happy at the prospect that I would spend tomorrow night in my own bed with my wolf dog at my feet.

I took a long, hot shower and made my way back into the bedroom and pulled back the covers. I'd just reached for the lamp to turn it off when my cell phone vibrated on the bedside table.

I didn't recognize the number, but it had a Belgrade exchange. "Hello?"

"Is this Warden Bowditch?" a woman asked in a familiar yet not immediately placeable voice.

"Yes, it is. With whom am I speaking?"

"This is Grace Webb. I'm sorry if I woke you, but I didn't know who else to call. It's about Galen."

The mere mention of his name raised hairs along my neck. I remembered the bombshell that Dianne Fenton-Whitcomb had dropped about the constable having been the family's caretaker. And again I pictured him climbing all over the Cessna.

"What about Galen?"

"He got a call a couple of hours ago. A woman said she saw lights on at Mouse Island. She said it seemed strange since the police have left. She had a feeling someone was trespassing—or worse. Galen said he'd go have a look. The wind was blowing bad, and I told him not to go, but you know how he can be. He so wants to prove himself to you and the other—"

"How long has he been gone?"

"Two hours and twenty-one minutes."

"Did he tell anyone else where he was going?"

"I don't think so."

Brave, stupid Galen Webb.

I turned off the light so I could see out the window and reached for the cord that pulled back the curtains. I blinked, then blinked again. I couldn't be sure, but there did seem to be a barely visible glow coming from the island.

"What about the name of the woman who called him?"

"I wrote it down," said Grace. "It was someone named Shawna Miskin."

54

I pulled on a pair of jeans and a T-shirt. I buckled my heavy gun belt around my waist. I laced up my Bean boots and pulled on the olive rain jacket that was part of my Warden Service field uniform. Then I put on my warden cap with the pine tree insignia above the brim. My outfit was a mishmash: neither civilian nor officer.

I had planned to stop at my Scout to retrieve a headlamp from my rucksack. Only as I stepped out into the pelting rain did I realize my truck was a hundred miles south with Charley.

Back inside, I found a small headlamp in a drawer in the mudroom. It was the kind of miniature light someone wears going for a predawn jog. I had my small but powerful Fenix, of course. The flashlight had a special holster on my belt. But I couldn't help but feel poorly equipped as I made my way down the road in the direction of the house Shawna Miskin had rented under her assumed name.

No lights came from the ranch house until I triggered a motion sensor at the perimeter. The security light shone down the path leading to the door. The sudden illumination caught me off guard.

Brave, stupid Mike Bowditch.

No one but Grace Webb knew where I was or where I was going.

I removed my cell from my pocket. The screen glowed with an image of Shadow, two yellow eyes staring out of a furry black face. The phone felt as heavy as a brick in my hand.

For much of my life, I had acted with reckless disregard for the feelings of friends and family, as if they didn't feel the pain of the injuries I had suffered or fear the phone call reporting that I had died in the line of duty.

What did I owe the people who loved me?

It shouldn't have been a difficult decision; I was simply accustomed to acting quickly without considering the consequences. It was both my greatest fault and my greatest strength.

I brought up the keypad to the phone. My finger hesitated above a name.

A minute later, the security light went off.

I shoved the smartphone back inside my jacket and continued around the darkened ranch house, triggering motion sensors, one after the next. I finished my circuit at the deck where Charley and I had interviewed the mystery woman.

As I'd expected, no one was in residence. It would have shocked me if Shawna Miskin had returned for the sole purpose of luring Galen out to the island.

What does she want with him?

Why bring him out there?

In her haste to leave, Shawna had left the rowboat tied to the dock. The oars stretched across the soaked seats. Hours of rain and waves had deposited three inches of water in the bottom of the boat.

I could have taken Neil's pontoon boat and crossed the channel fast and under the shelter of the canopy. But trumpeting my arrival on Mouse Island seemed unwise if someone was lurking there, intent on violence. Lights and sirens were for regular cops. Wardens were supposed to be green ninjas.

Besides, I had a long habit of borrowing boats that didn't belong to me.

As I bent to untie the painter, I encountered a perfect cleat knot. Shawna Miskin had acted the part of a novice rower at the mercy of wind and waves. But the person who had secured this line had spent considerable time on boats. Her seeming incompetence on the water had been another ruse.

I settled down on the wet seat. The oars knocked in the oarlocks as I positioned them. I wanted to row facing forward; I didn't like the idea of having my back to the island as I approached. The wind was pushing the waves toward the dock, so I had to dig in to turn around.

Front rowing isn't as easy as conventional backward rowing where you use your back and leg muscles to propel the boat. Instead, I had to rely on the strength of my arms, pushing against the water rather than pulling myself along.

Fortunately, the darkness wasn't absolute in the channel. The wind-whipped lake was a shade lighter than the sky above. Homes around the pond showed as smears of light, helping me navigate to a degree.

It hadn't taken me long to begin second-guessing Grace Webb. Her husband had revealed himself to be untrustworthy—a liar by omission if not something worse—and I had to consider the possibility that the call I'd received from her was a trap.

As I neared Mouse Island, I began to hear an arrhythmic knocking sound: something was bumping the dock.

I decided to risk using my headlamp for five seconds.

It was Galen's Crestliner.

The dock left the boat exposed to the rollers being pushed across Great Pond by the north-moving storm. Galen had done his best to secure it to the cleats and had dropped fenders over the gunwales to cushion the blows his hull would inevitably take as the waves rammed it repeatedly against the wood-and-steel dock.

I shipped my left oar, raising it in the oarlock so the wind and waves would push me against the dock. The impact sounded unnervingly loud. I stood up and knotted a line around the nearest cleat. Then I clambered onto the slick planks, leaving the rowboat to thud against the failing structure.

Even in the dark, with rain streaming down my brow, there was no missing the fluorescent yellow object bobbing at the bottom of the Crestliner. It was Galen's Mustang Survival vest. Water had triggered the CO_2 cartridge that automatically inflated the inner floatation chambers. Mustangs are famously rainproof and sprayproof. The constable must have been in a hurry. He hadn't anticipated that enough water would wash into his hull to set off the arming device and inflate the PFD.

My footsteps made hollow, echoey noises as I made my way up the swaying dock into the darkness of the trees.

The house ahead might as well not have existed; it would be like walking into a void. All I could do was wait until my eyes adjusted to the lack of light. I paused when I reached the shore and listened. The dripping trees made a steady patter as if the rain wasn't lessening. The waves lapped the rounded rocks behind me. I lowered my hood, hoping to hear a human sound, but detected nothing.

At my feet lay a green path. The storm had torn leaves from the beeches overhead. Some fell in clusters, attached to the tip of a branch; others were carried along singly on gusts.

The scene felt wrong.

Galen would have needed a light to get anywhere or do anything. Even if he had the best night vision in the world, he wouldn't have stumbled blindly around the island if he had a choice.

I heard a voice in my head:

Galen Webb doesn't have a lot of training for situations like this one. He has no training. Don't sneak up on him. Don't get yourself shot.

I reached for the flashlight as I took a step forward.

My foot snagged a root—or what I thought was a root—and I nearly fell over, only managing to catch myself by letting the Fenix drop. I grabbed hold of a beech branch that came near to snapping under my sudden weight.

When I'd regained my balance, I pushed the button on my cheap headlamp, and a fuzzy beam shot forward. I lowered my head to search for my dropped flashlight. Instead, I discovered a body.

Shawna Miskin lay on its back, covered in freshly torn leaves. There was a red hole beneath her right cheekbone. One of her arms lay at her side. Her sleeve had been rolled to the elbow, and I knew instinctively it was because someone had checked her wrist for a pulse.

Whoever it was hadn't found one.

The bullet had penetrated her face and her palate, likely shattering several teeth, before it tore through her hypothalamus and occipital lobe.

The blood had grown thin in the running rain, but the brain matter spattered on the pine needles told me that the slug was soft-nosed. If I turned her over, I would find a cavity the size of my fist in her skull from where the mushroom-shaped projectile had exited her head.

I snapped off my headlight and flattened myself against the trunk of the nearest large tree.

Who was she, really?

What was she doing here?

Was this a trap set for Galen Webb or a trap set for me?

Galen had been the Fentons' caretaker. He'd had an argument with Shawna he had refused to disclose to me. He knew more about the family and the island than he had shared.

Maybe he had known Shawna. Maybe he had known her very well. If his wife was to be believed, the caller had used that name, and Galen had recognized it.

But there was no way Galen could have known I had returned to the lake house. The last he'd heard, I'd been heading to Massachusetts to interview Dianne Fenton-Whitcomb. Even if he had somehow learned that we'd survived the crash, he couldn't have counted on luring me to the island.

This was a trap for him, not me.

Whatever was happening, it was no accident that Shawna Miskin had been killed on this island. The mysterious woman was always meant to die—if not here, then somewhere else. She was someone's loose end.

The only accident was that I was here, too.

55

With my back to the house, I slid down the tree until I was sitting on the wet sand and turf. I wanted as much of my body shielded as possible.

When I withdrew my cell from my pocket, the movement caused the screen to light up automatically, revealing Shadow's wolfishly handsome face.

Shit!

The phone didn't give off more than a glimmer. But the momentary illumination was enough to mark my hiding place for the person waiting in ambush.

A force jerked the glowing device from my hand. A split second passed before I even heard the gunshot. Then it was another instant before I felt the stinging pain in my fingers.

I rolled reflexively into the tree, cradling my right hand against my chest while I tried to reach with my left across my body for my sidearm. The gun stuck in the holster; it was held fast by the thumb lock designed to keep someone from pulling my firearm loose to use against me.

I was pinned down. Whoever had shot at me was standing on the porch or somewhere near the house, firing back down the path toward the water.

It wasn't lost on me that my attacker hadn't fired another shot. He was being cautious, deliberate. He didn't want people on shore awakening in alarm to the sound of a gunfight on Mouse Island.

To my right was the path. To my left were a few spindly birches and lesser pines, as well as some shrubby vegetation that provided no cover. There were clear firing lanes on my right and left, in other words. Nowhere to run, seemingly.

If I could get my gun out to fire three emergency shots—

My right hand felt like it had been stung by twenty hornets, but when I raised it to my face I detected only a little blood. I had not lost any fingers, just some skin from the force of the bullet shattering the phone in my hand.

I was glad for the big pine. Even if he had night vision equipment, my assailant couldn't know if I'd been wounded. But there was every reason to believe I was armed. He needed to act fast.

Which meant that I needed to act faster.

Keeping the sheltering tree between myself and the house, I sprang to my feet, took two long leaps, and threw myself into the shallows of the lake.

The sound of the second shot reached my ears belatedly as I ducked beneath the surface. Water rushed up my nostrils into my sinuses from the suddenness of the plunge. I hadn't had time to prepare myself for immersion.

I needed to disappear beneath the dark water before the sniper could reach the shoreline. And I had to pick a new vector from the line between the tree and the pond. Otherwise, he could guess my direction and shoot randomly, hitting me in the back without ever acquiring an actual target. Bullets, especially those fired from rifles made for war fighting, will penetrate water to a depth of several feet before the viscosity renders them nonlethal.

I needed to go deeper. I scrabbled through the sand, gravel, and weeds, ignoring the minor injury to my gun hand.

If the second bullet had struck or grazed me, I didn't feel anything yet. In my desperation to escape, my pain receptors had shut down.

At night, the shoals became as dark as the depths. I had zero visibility. But as I extended my arms and legs, I realized that I no longer felt the bottom. I changed course as I began to swim, breaking left, then allowing myself to sink. I was determined to hold my breath until I was on the verge of losing consciousness. The longest I had ever managed it was four minutes, and that hadn't been underwater with someone shooting at me.

Whoever had murdered Shawna Miskin couldn't take the chance that I survived. He had to kill me and kill me fast. Even now, the gunshots might have registered with someone ashore; a concerned citizen might already be on the phone with a police dispatcher.

Now I broke left again. The weight of my sodden clothes and boots dragged me down, not to mention the heaviness of the gun belt.

My nervous system was recovering from the initial shock and sending a broadcast along the network of nerves to my brain. The water I'd breathed in scalded my sinuses. I could feel my lungs pulling the last oxygen from the air I'd inhaled. My hand hurt.

Since I was blind anyway, I clenched my eyes shut and watched a redness spread across the inside of my lids.

I had no idea how long I'd been submerged or how far I'd swum from the island, but I had reached the limit of my endurance and had to resurface.

As my face felt the air again, I managed to take half a breath before a wave crashed over me and filled my open, gulping mouth. The chop was severe. Treading water, I kicked hard to bring my head up to look for a landmark.

I was surprised to find myself surrounded by open water. I saw no land. In my desperation, I must have powered myself out into the boating lane between Mouse and Chute Islands—the same water where Bill Boone had brought up Kip Whitcomb's corpse.

I raised one knee to untie my boot. Then I raised the other. I let the heavy boots drop into the depths.

I had lost my cap and my headlamp in the plunge.

Shrouded in darkness, with no landmarks visible, I had to make a fateful choice: Which way to swim?

I tried porpoising, kicking hard to bring my torso into the air. I saw nothing but a very distant cottage. I dropped back into the lake and held steady, treading water until I'd recovered enough energy for a second attempt. Then I breached again.

To my right was a black shape, barely distinguishable from the night itself. It had to be Mouse Island. The waves were pushing me north, I realized, past the island and toward the gap between Chute Island and Stony Point.

If I didn't return to the island, I would be pushed into deeper water, and I would surely drown. I still had my gun. And I still had all my fingers even if they hurt like hell. I began crawling back toward the island, the killer, and my fate.

56

I approached Mouse Island the way I'd left it: underwater. I remained submerged until I could touch the first rocks that bolstered its northwestern edge. Bushes overhung the pond along this side. I popped my head up beneath the scratchy branches to conceal myself while my stockinged feet felt for the bottom.

There was an upside to my situation, I realized.

The sniper didn't know my condition. I might be wounded, dying, or already dead. The current might be pushing me even now to rough water, far from shore. Perhaps I would drown, overcome by the waves and exhaustion. Perhaps Great Pond would solve his problems for him.

Or maybe I had already swum across the inshore channel and was climbing onto Shawna Miskin's dock at this very moment. Instead of having the rest of the night to effect his plan and his getaway, he might have less than an hour before backup arrived.

What he wouldn't expect, I felt certain, was that I would return to the island.

I had recovered the element of surprise.

Reaching above my head into the bushes, I used the slender branches to pull myself along until I saw an opening between the shrubs through which I could crawl.

A canoe blocked my way. It hadn't been there when we'd searched the island. I could only assume it belonged to my unknown enemy. I might have used it myself now to escape, but instead, I grabbed the stern and pulled it past me, off the raised lip on which it had been beached and into the lake. I gave it a shove so that it would drift off.

Both the Crestliner and the rowboat still offered him means of escape. But I felt secretly satisfied at depriving him of his own watercraft. If he managed to kill me, he would be in for a big surprise, finding his canoe gone.

When I was fully on shore, I resisted the impulse to rest. Because my assailant couldn't be sure I was dead, he had no choice but to hurry, which meant I had no choice, either, if I hoped to stop him.

Gingerly, I removed my sidearm from its holster. The tip of my thumb was abraded, still bleeding, and it stung when exposed to the air. But I could close my hand around the grip, and there was nothing wrong with my trigger finger.

I slid open the action, ejecting the .357 SIG caliber bullet in the chamber. I dropped the magazine to empty out any water. Shook the frame and blew a puff of air down the barrel. A pistol will fire unless moisture has gotten inside the casings and compromised the primer or the smokeless powder. But a drier firearm was a more reliable one, it went without saying.

I holstered the dried and reloaded gun and began making my way on hands and knees through the bracken ferns and over the pine needles. The soil covering Mouse Island was so thin I felt the bedrock beneath. It was amazing that trees had found enough dirt here to sink their roots.

As I neared the center of the island, I stumbled upon one of the twisting footpaths made by generations of Fentons scampering about their private playground. I risked climbing fully to my feet again, being sure to keep a birch between myself and the house. When I peered around the papery trunk, I was shocked by lights ahead. Through the windows of the cottage, kerosene lamps were blazing white.

I felt both relief and expectation.

He must have believed that I was gone, or he wouldn't have risked firing the lamps. He'd dropped his guard, giving me a chance I didn't deserve.

I moved from tree to tree until I was along the blind side of the house. The white-hot light spilled out around me, but I remained hidden in the shadows.

The wind was dying, I realized. It might or might not still be raining. The branches would shed water for hours after the front had passed.

In my desperation to escape, I had set aside the question of who my attacker was.

The sophistication of the trap seemed beyond the mental capacity of Joey Randazza. But I didn't know the man well enough to write him off. Finch seemed to think the Direwolf had orchestrated an elaborate alibi.

What about Rob Soto? The other jealous husband?

Or Galen. Try as I might to dismiss him, the angry young man kept pushing his way into my head.

David Kwan? Kyle McAllister? I really was scouring the bottom of the barrel.

Kyle had mentioned something; an offhand comment. He'd spent summers on the lake since he was a child. Attended Pine Island Camp . . .

It wasn't even a thought, just a feeling down deep that there was something significant in that remark.

In the intervals between gusts, I caught the hollow footfalls of someone moving up the floating dock toward the shore. From this angle, I couldn't see the entire path. The place where I'd found Shawna Miskin was too far from the house to be touched by light.

I no longer heard footsteps, but that was to be expected after the sniper moved onto the soft forest floor.

I pulled the SIG from its holster and raised it so that the night sights framed the broad trail.

I waited.

Had he heard me? Did he have thermal-imaging goggles that revealed the heat signature of my body, pressed against the building?

The only sounds were the boats bumping the dock, the waves lapping against the shore, the wind ruffling the treetops.

I lowered myself to a crouch and came around the steps, keeping my head down, my arms extended.

A person was crumpled on the ground at the head of the path.

Another corpse?

I took a chance that it wasn't my attacker playing possum. I knelt over a scrawny, khaki-clad man. He didn't move or moan when I touched his shoulder.

It was Galen Webb.

57

A man's baritone voice spoke from the shadows to my left. The son of a bitch had circled through the trees just as I had tried to do when I'd snuck onto the island. He'd probably used the same big pine I had used for cover.

"Throw down your gun, Bowditch. I have his Glock aimed at your center mass. I won't miss again."

It was a voice I didn't recognize. He sounded educated. And his use of the term *center mass* for the section of my torso containing my vital organs hinted he had received training in the use of firearms for self-defense.

Never give up your gun is one of the holy commandments of police training.

I remained where I was.

Suddenly, he was standing behind me. I hadn't heard him advance. He moved that swiftly and softly.

"Do what I say." I felt the muzzle press the soft tissue between my right ear and the base of my skull. The hard iron sights digging into the flesh. "Don't think you can drag this out."

"You're going to kill me without explanation?" I said, because I was determined to drag it out, whatever he said.

The words he spoke almost lightly sounded at first like gibberish. Then I recognized them: "*Gwell angau na gwarth*. There's your explanation."

The meaning behind Kyle McAllister's offhand comment suddenly made itself clear. He had referred to a Mr. Fenton, but he hadn't meant Whitcomb. *I knew him when he was a counselor at Pine Island Camp.* Kip had never been a camp counselor in Maine. Kyle had been referring to another person altogether.

"Cole Fenton," I said.

The boy I'd seen in the photo on the staircase inside, the pentathlete who couldn't make the Olympic team, the overseas knockabout and black sheep of the family—Dianne's younger brother.

The pressure of the gun muzzle lessened against my head.

"It's a shame that you didn't figure that out an hour ago when it might have saved you," he said. "Put the gun down. We're going inside. If you try anything, I will shoot you in the head."

As I climbed the stairs, I heard him snatch up my SIG.

"I know you were watching the house, Cole," I said, feeling both afraid and embarrassed at my stupidity.

He made no reply, understanding that conversation only benefited me in this moment.

"You were waiting for Whitcomb to arrive with his latest woman," I continued. "Watching and waiting in plain sight, just a man in a canoe, fishing in the channel."

The fact that I'd deduced the cover he'd used succeeded in rousing him.

"I know you're smart. But don't think you can distract me from my work. This isn't the first time I've done this."

I entered the house, where a lone kerosene lamp flickered on the table in the entryway.

"You're an assassin?"

Again, his voice betrayed his amusement. "I know how to do certain *things,* if that's what you mean. I'm well trained, and I've been at this awhile."

The foreign misadventures, the shoddy résumé, the cover working in a Turkish bank—Coleman Fenton was an operative of some sort, if not government then corporate.

"Was it family honor? Your sister told me she didn't mind her husband fucking around while she slowly dies. But did *you* mind?"

"Raise your arms. Turn around."

I refused to obey. "It was a hell of a plan. What did you do—put something in their tequila?"

"I have no issue with shooting you in the back. Don't think I'm burdened by ethical concerns."

"Of course you are," I said. "You're Judge Coleman Fenton's son and namesake."

"Turn around!"

I had finally shaken his composure, but I knew he would recover quickly.

I turned and saw a tall, broad-shouldered man in his late thirties. He had his father's thin mouth and imperious expression, his sister's heavily lashed eyes. His dark, wavy hair was long enough to part on one side. He was wearing a dark umber shirt and dark olive pants. (He knew that black makes for poor night camouflage since it hardens your silhouette.) Only his nitrile gloves and his Danner boots were black. It couldn't have been a coincidence that they were the same make and model as those worn by Maine state troopers. They'd tramped all over the island. Another set of those prints would hardly be noticed.

"You're not going to tell me why?" I asked.

"You've watched too many movies. I have work to finish. On your knees."

Again, I refused to obey.

"You didn't just want to kill your brother-in-law," I said as if I hadn't heard him. "You wanted Kip to be remembered as a murderer. So you put sedatives in something they ate or drank—"

He couldn't help but smile at my insistence at hearing confirmation of my suspicions.

"You strangled Gina to implicate Whitcomb, then tossed him into the lake to drown. Bad luck for you that a boat came along. If those idiots hadn't hit your brother-in-law, it might have been days before the bodies were discovered."

He was smug enough that he appreciated hearing that I recognized his genius. But he was intelligent and experienced enough that he never lost focus. He leveled both guns at me, Galen's and my own.

"I know you're trying to stall. But I am on a schedule. And to be honest, I couldn't care less what you think you've figured out."

"You'd better care, Fenton, because you left loose ends."

"I am taking care of them."

"Shawna Miskin was one of Whitcomb's conquests, right? But she didn't appreciate being cast aside for another woman. How did you find her? How did you persuade her to be your eyes and ears on the lake? I doubt she knew what you were intending for Kip."

"She thought they still had a future together." He caught himself and shook his head, no. He would not be drawn into a conversation. "On your knees."

I backed against the table. "No one will believe I knelt to be executed by Galen Webb. Maybe they'll buy that he mistakenly shot Shawna—"

"Have it your way," he said, raising the Glock.

"I got rid of your canoe," I said, even as his finger curled around the trigger. "I shoved it into the current after I came ashore."

He lowered the Glock. "You what?"

"You've lost your means of escape. You've lost your fall guy. Your plan has fallen apart, *Cole*."

He surprised me with a laugh.

"Webb isn't dead. He's drugged, you dipshit. When they find his drowned body in the lake, they'll think he panicked when you caught him. He shot you and took off in his boat, forgetting to attach the kill switch—"

So that was his plan: start the engine and then toss Galen off his own boat. And because he wasn't wearing his life vest or using the dead man's switch, everyone would assume the murderous constable had drowned.

"The tox screen came back. The ME found the drug you used in Gina's system."

"Bullshit. They don't screen for kratom. No one does. And a toxicology report takes weeks."

I could see the wheels turning in his head. He'd been right about my trying to stall, of course. But hearing that some dumb game warden was piecing together a puzzle he thought was unsolvable was shaking his confidence.

"You screwed up sabotaging the Cessna, too. Only a pilot or someone very familiar with planes would have known how to do that."

"Webb was a pilot," he said.

"But he had no reason to sabotage our plane. Whatever your low opinion of the Maine State Police and the Warden Service, how confident are you that no one at the FAA will realize you're a pilot, too?"

"They'll be too late."

"But your sister will be an easy target. And if this was all about protecting her—"

"What are you saying?"

"She delayed us in Medway long enough for you—or maybe you have accomplices in Massachusetts—to put water in our gas tanks. Meaning she's on the hook for attempted murder as well. It was all we talked about, Pomerleau and I, on the drive back. Why did Dianne Fenton-Whitcomb need to keep us waiting? Because she'd heard me mention your name and knew I was getting close. You failed to shield her, Fenton. Even if you get away, she won't. You've destroyed your family's reputation. I bet Judge Fenton is already screaming up from hell at your stupidity."

The smile vanished and he became the image of his cruel father as a young man. "You're an amateur at this, Bowditch. Deconstructing personalities and creating profiles is what I do for a living. You, for example, are brash, headstrong, and not as smart as you think you are. When you went into the water, I *knew* you would come back to the island. It's not in your DNA to back down or call for backup. All I had to do was wait for you to act the way you've always acted in the past."

Even as that last judgment hung in the air and he was raising the Glock for the head shot, there came a thud from outside.

Light from the house pooled around the base of the stairs.

Deeply dazed and confused from the kratom, or whatever drug cocktail Fenton had given him, Galen Webb had awakened and staggered up the path, toward the light.

Instinctively, Fenton spun around. He snapped off a shot that sent Galen spinning.

I took my only chance, grabbed the white-hot hurricane lamp from the table by its scalding base, and hurled it at the man about to kill me.

58

The lamp was not designed to be a projectile. It fell short of the target and shattered at his feet. The glass chimney broke. But so did the oil font, splashing fuel across the floorboards and onto Fenton's boots and legs.

The flame from the burner did the rest. Fire rushed up his feet and shins. In his surprise, he dropped my SIG. Most importantly, he lost focus on his adversary: me.

I threw myself across the yards between us, reaching with both hands for his right wrist. I couldn't allow him to retain control of the Glock.

But his reflexes were fast. Still distracted by the flames burning his ankles and rising from the floor around him, he withdrew his arm, brought the elbow close to the body, and squeezed the trigger.

There is a video the instructors show cadets at the Maine Criminal Justice Academy. It repeats the same situation with multiple armed officers being attacked by an assailant armed only a knife. The point is to demonstrate how quickly someone charging a man with a gun can close distances up to ten yards. In the video, most of the armed cops ended up stabbed with the rubber knife before they could even clear their sidearms from their holsters.

Fenton already had his weapon out. He didn't aim. Merely pointed and shot.

But like the knife-wielders in the video, I was too fast for him. The bullet might have only missed me by inches, but it missed.

And before he could squeeze off another round, I had plowed

into him with everything I could muster, taking hold of the hot gun barrel with my left hand. As I fell to his side, out of the line of fire, I heard the air explode from his lungs.

The force of my acceleration knocked him out of the ring of fire. He staggered, lost his footing, and fell hard onto his back. Meanwhile, he was still kicking his boots against the floor as if that flailing motion would extinguish the flames that were melting the fabric of his hiking pants and causing the molten plastic to stick like napalm to the skin beneath.

I thought I had a chance of getting the gun free. I pushed the scalding gun barrel while twisting his wrist. When this maneuver is executed well and you apply enough torque to the joint, you usually come away with the firearm.

Despite the pain, he remembered his close-combat training.

With his free hand, he grabbed hold of my left ear and twisted. The pain was excruciating. He tried to turn the muzzle of the gun toward me.

All I could think to do was bring a knee up into his crotch.

When in doubt, nothing beats a kick to the balls.

Somehow, I now found myself holding the Glock by the barrel. He'd lost hold of the grip. But before I could secure the weapon, he drove his fist into my exposed kidney.

The pistol slipped from my hand and went sliding across the floor.

I tried to rise and go after it, but he got hold of my ear again, which felt stretched to the length of a goat's. I drove my elbow into the side of his face before he could bring me in for another body blow.

Now, somehow, we were lying side by side on our backs in the burning house.

Nearby was the Glock. Nearby was the SIG.

It was a race which of us could find a gun first.

I rolled left while he rolled right. His pants were merely smoldering now. The room had filled with smoke. In addition to kerosene, melted plastic, and burned skin and hair, I smelled wood burning.

I began to cough as I scurried away, searching for the Glock. I spotted it behind a flickering line of flames. Beyond my reach.

I spun around and was surprised not to see Fenton anywhere.

I found him on all fours on the porch. In front of him lay my SIG. It must have gotten shoved outside during our grappling match.

I kicked him in the ribs, but he was too tough, and he had too much ground game.

He rolled onto his back, hooked one foot behind my ankle, and drove the other into my opposite hip. The sweep caused me to fall backward. I landed as if dropped from a window.

But instead of rising above me, he directed his attention to reaching blindly for the SIG.

I drove my foot into his face.

Blood spattered from his nostrils.

But even a broken nose wasn't enough to stop him from closing his hand around the gun. I'd never fought hand-to-hand with someone possessed of such skill and with so much willpower.

I had no choice but to roll down the stairs. The flames from the house threw an animated glow into the clearing. The swirls of smoke took on an orangish color. Out of the corner of my eye, I saw Galen Webb lying motionless behind a cloud of animate sparks and cinders.

I broke toward the dock, hoping that Fenton was too messed up to get a bead on me. Between the burns and the broken nose, and the other injuries he had received at my hands, he might not be able to pursue me. But I had underestimated him once before. It was my bad luck to have finally met someone as relentless as I am.

The house fire must have been visible for miles. The light from it spread across the calming waters and reflected off the fiberglass hull of Galen's Crestliner. The light spread out across the lake.

I heard a gunshot and threw myself off the side of the dock, not sure if I'd been hit. I resurfaced under the dock.

He had missed me again.

I heard his heavy staggering footsteps on the dock. In his place, I would have been swearing up a storm, but he must have been grinding his molars to the breaking point to keep quiet.

He would have to hang his head over the side to locate me, and I could keep diving. I could keep disappearing and reappearing. At a certain point, he would have to make a choice—either flee or be caught.

"Come and find me, you son of a bitch!" I shouted.

But he didn't. He was a cunning man and made the correct choice. I heard him fall aboard Galen's Crestliner, causing the boat to strain against its lines. Then I heard the engine roar to life.

I began to pull myself along the bottom of the dock.

I smelled exhaust from the outboard and saw the boat begin to drift away from the dock. He must have found a knife to cut it free. I glimpsed his bloody, determined face as he turned toward the steering wheel.

Then the haze coming from the burning house was pierced by a lancing white spotlight.

"Police! Do not move!" It was Bill Boone's loud voice.

"Drop the gun!" shouted Rick LaJoy.

The Crestliner continued to idle away from the dock.

From my vantage in the water, I had no view of the warden's boat. But I saw Cole Fenton perfectly as he fired a wild shot while pushing the throttle forward.

Two bullets struck him—center mass.

He fell backward over the gunwale even as the Crestliner motored away. He hadn't had time or the presence of mind to attach the kill switch to himself.

His body floated, rocking in the V-shaped waves spreading out from the still-moving, unmanned boat.

A dead man caught in his own wake.

59

I swam out to Fenton and began dragging his body back toward the dock. But I stopped when Boone and LaJoy came alongside me in the Lund. The dive chief reached down his thick arm to pull me up, and I found myself lifted from the water as if I weighed nothing. Bill Boone didn't need my help to bring in the corpse.

Fenton's bloody eyes were wide open, and no wonder. One of the big .357 caliber bullets had passed cleanly through his heart.

"I have no idea who this is," said a looming Rick LaJoy.

"It's Cole Fenton, Dianne's brother, Whitcomb's brother-in-law." My voice was hoarse from the fight and from the smoke I'd inhaled. "He planned and executed the killings."

"Well, shit," said Boone. "I don't like my wife's brother, either, but it never occurred to me to assassinate the sombitch."

"I need you to bring me to the island," I said.

"The house is fully involved, Mike," said the lieutenant. "You can't go inside, whatever evidence you might think is there."

"I'm not going inside. There are two more people on the island. One is Galen Webb. I don't think he's alive, but I can't leave him there in any case. The other is a woman who called herself Shawna Miskin. She's a former lover of Kip Whitcomb whom Fenton manipulated into acting as his accomplice. I don't think she knew what he was planning to do. Maybe she did. But she's definitely dead. I saw the bullet hole."

Other boats were beginning to appear around the lake, lights in the mist rising after the rain.

"I'd expected you here sooner," I said as we came up to the dock.

"How's that for gratitude?" said Boone.

"You can thank your fiancée," said LaJoy. "She told us to get our asses out here."

"She's what my mama called a 'three-alarm firecracker,'" added the dive chief. "You'll be lucky as hell to have her as your wife, Bowditch."

"You don't need to tell me that."

It was the second time in twenty-four hours that I had placed my life in the hands of Stacey Stevens. The first was when she'd glided the crippled Cessna to safety. The second was when I had overcome my natural impetuosity and indifference to physical danger to call her and inform her of my plans.

An hour earlier, outside Shawna Miskin's rented house, I had overcome my ego and placed a call to my future wife.

What did I owe the people who loved me? I had thought as I'd brought up my phone.

My finger had hesitated above Stacey's name.

And then I'd pushed Call.

I heard her voice again now, every word she'd spoken:

"Can I offer you one word of warning?" she'd said after I told her where I was headed and what I planned to do. *"I know you'll disregard it, but Galen Webb doesn't have a lot of training for situations like this one. He has no training, come to think of it. Don't sneak up on him. Make sure he knows it's you. Don't get yourself shot."*

"If you don't hear from me in twenty minutes—"

"I'll alert Leah Doumit to expect another corpse."

"That's not funny, Stace."

"My point exactly."

Now I hopped from LaJoy's boat onto the dock, followed by Boone. LaJoy remained behind to put in a call to public safety, informing them of the murders that had taken place on the island and the fire that was consuming a century of Fenton family history.

The air thickened with smoke as we stepped onto terra firma. The smell had taken on an odor of charred incense as the flames had leaped from the house to the drought-stricken pines. Even the heavy rain hadn't been enough to keep the dry trees from catching fire. I heard pine cones popping like popcorn. Tree trunks split as the sap boiled inside them, causing the wood to explode.

We found Shawna Miskin first. More needles had fallen since I'd stumbled over the dead woman, but now her face was coated with ash, too. The bullet wound showed as a dark spot.

"You were right about this one," Boone said between coughs. "She's deader than a dormouse."

The powerful man slung her over his left shoulder.

Instead of returning to the Lund, I was surprised to find him following me into the inferno.

"What are you doing, Bill?"

"Both of my shoulders work. You might need help with Webb."

"For Christ's sake, Boone, you don't need to show off your prowess to me."

"Prowess! Isn't that sexual?"

"Just get your ass back to the boat. I'll be right behind you with Galen's body."

He shrugged, then turned and disappeared through the smoke.

The thing about a large fire is how it renders your vision useless. The smoke stings your eyes, and the heat dries out your eyeballs. Squinting barely helps. I'd heard of smoke jumpers who've gotten turned around as they were fighting wildfires and died walking toward the advancing flames from which they thought they were retreating.

Fortunately, I had formed a good mental map of the island. I went down on my hands and knees to keep from being asphyxiated by the carbon monoxide being released from the heart of the blaze. The heat was intense, but not enough to burn my exposed skin yet, and I kept crawling until I found poor Galen where he had fallen. He lay on his side at the base of the stairs.

I took him by the collar and began dragging him over the roots and rocks because he was past caring if his skull took a few bumps.

When he twitched and let out a groan, I lost my grip.

How is he alive?

The answer had to wait. I hadn't pulled him far, not more than ten feet from the fully involved house fire. I took as deep a breath as I dared, then rose to my feet. I picked up the constable and threw him over my shoulder in a fireman's carry.

I managed to stagger another twenty feet or so when Boone reappeared.

I spat out the words. "He's alive."

"Will wonders never cease. Give him to me, Mike. Let someone else play the hero for once."

I didn't fight him this time. The dive chief was a strong dude. I followed his broad silhouette out of the smoke clouds and into the clear air above the lake.

Boone laid out Galen Webb on the boat bottom with an inflated life vest under his head for a pillow.

"Is he drunk?" LaJoy asked, casting off.

"Drugged. Fenton didn't say much, but he mentioned using something called kratom to incapacitate Whitcomb and Randazza. Webb, too, I imagine, although I'm not sure how. I saw him shot later, though. I don't understand how he's not dead."

Boone knelt over the young constable, feeling his chest for a bullet wound. He raised his face with a gleaming smile. Then he lifted one of his big fists and knocked, as if against a door, on Galen's chest. There was a hard, hollow sound.

"Plate armor," said the diver. "That's what saved him."

"Would have sunk like a stone in the water," said LaJoy.

"Good thing he didn't fall in, then," I said, remembering Fenton's plans to dump the drugged constable off his own moving boat.

Several pleasure boats floated off the end of the island, in the same shallows where we'd found Whitcomb's severed arm. The cottage owners had come out to help and were now drifting about aimlessly, waiting to be given evacuation orders. But there were no orders to be given. Mouse Island would burn to the ground.

It took a moment for me to realize that one of the boats was Neil's party barge. Ora and Jubilee were both on board and waved to me, perfect expressions of relief and joy.

I raised my face to the two wardens. "I'm wondering if you could bring me alongside that pontoon boat."

"You sure you don't want an EMT to treat those cuts and burns?" said the lieutenant. "There's an ambulance waiting up at Mosher's Sporting Lodge."

"The women on that Leisure Kraft will nurse me better than any paramedic."

LaJoy had to tell Neil to turn off his engine so we could approach safely. (As a boat handler, my stepfather was an excellent tax attorney.) The lieutenant maneuvered us into place, and I hopped over the gunwale of the Lund onto the swimming platform. Only when I raised my right hand in farewell did I note that the bleeding had stopped. It scarcely seemed possible that I might escape the events of the past days with no permanent injuries to my much-abused body.

Jubilee threw her arms around my neck when she saw it wouldn't hurt me, and when I bent over Ora's wheelchair, she pulled me down for a hug. Her face was wet from the tears she was quietly shedding.

But it was Neil's reaction that most surprised me.

He'd always been an awkward, standoffish man. I thought he would shake my hurt hand as he usually did, firmly and formally, as if we'd just completed a business deal. Instead, he embraced me around the shoulders for the first time since my mother's funeral.

In my ear, he said, "I'm so glad you're alive, son."

60

Back at the house, Ora poured me a glass of her favorite scotch while she bandaged my right hand. I usually preferred Kentucky whiskey to anything else, but the alcohol warmed my aching body from the inside out. I would be bruised and sore for days. But what else was new?

"Charley told me that, after he lost his fingerprints in the war, they grew back the same but different," she said, inspecting the finished bandage. "The ridges were thicker, he said, but they matched the ID card the army had for him."

I shuddered to think how he'd lost his fingerprints as an inmate in Hỏa Lò Prison.

Neil seemed more amped than I'd ever seen him. He was still wearing the pink sweater and wrinkled chinos he'd grabbed for his rescue mission aboard the Leisure Kraft. A strand of hair was standing up in a curlicue at the back of his head.

"Mike's been banged up so much, I worry he's going to get CTE like those professional football players."

Jubilee had changed into what I thought of as her yoga clothes. "What does *CTE* stand for again?"

"Chronic traumatic encephalopathy," I said. Then added sheepishly, "I've had conversations with my doctor."

"Stacey and Charley are waiting for our update," Ora reminded us.

She'd already called them at the motel in Massachusetts to say I was safe and to update them on the events that had unfolded that night on Great Pond.

The Glenlivet and exhaustion might have had something to do with it, but I blinked back tears when I heard Stacey's voice come over the speakerphone.

"I wish I was there," she said.

"Me, too."

"Cole Fenton was casing the island, and we had no idea. Do CIA agents really disguise themselves?"

"He wasn't CIA," Charley said, loudly enough that I could hear him in the room with her. "He was a member of the Defense Clandestine Service, from what my source tells me."

I suspected I knew who his "source" was: a man high up in the intelligence community whose missing granddaughter Charley had found in the woods when all hope seemed lost. My friend must have been on the phone immediately with the spymaster to have received this information.

I put the call on speaker.

"Well, his disguise worked against Galen Webb," I said. "The constable checked his canoe multiple times in the days leading up to the attack. If it had been me, I would have left him alone once I saw that he had a fishing license and a life jacket. But we know how gung-ho Galen is."

"Didn't you say he was the Fentons' caretaker, though?" Neil asked.

"Galen might never have had an occasion to meet Cole Fenton if he was in Turkey or elsewhere overseas. I doubt Fenton was in danger of being recognized, whatever he might have feared."

"But Galen would have seen those pictures in the house," said Stacey. "I can see where Fenton would have been worried about him putting it together."

"That young feller has moments of insight," agreed Charley. "Even if he's dumber than a bag of rocks most of the time."

"If he'd only shared the information he was sitting on from the beginning—"

But the old pilot hadn't finished his thought. "He's young and bullheaded and desperate to prove himself. Reminds me of another young man I once knew."

I blushed, and not from the scotch.

"Have you heard how Galen's doing?" Ora asked kindly.

"He has some second-degree burns from the fire, and the docs in Waterville are pumping his stomach," I said. "He mumbled something in the ambulance about Fenton ambushing him and jabbing him with a needle."

"I feel for poor Grace Webb," said Jubilee, pulling her legs up onto the couch and wrapping her arms around her knees. "The fear she must have suffered!"

Ora used her napkin to wipe the perspiration from her own glass of (medicinal) scotch. "If Galen ever earns a place in the Warden Service, she'll know what it's like to receive a call from the police saying her husband's been hurt."

"It's a call you never get used to," said Stacey over the speaker.

"No, you don't," agreed her mother.

The room fell silent.

"Do the detectives know why Fenton did it?" Jubilee asked. "Like, I'm trying to get a sense of the big picture."

"I doubt we'll ever find anything in writing that explains it," I said. "I could barely get him to say a word, no matter how hard I tried to stall."

"I thought villains always wanted to explain their genius," Neil said with a tentative smile. "Or is that only in the movies?"

"Sometimes it happens for real," Charley said. "Some men need to boast about how clever they are. Other times, it's almost a form of confession."

"Fenton had no need to boast or confess," I said. "I would describe him as exceptionally disciplined. God knows he was well trained. He was a better hand-to-hand fighter than I am. I happened to get lucky."

"It wasn't luck," said Ora. "It was providence."

Jubilee offered the inevitable platitude. "Everything happens for a reason."

My thoughts about fate were ambiguous, often self-contradictory, and made me uncomfortable when I sat with them too long. Not because I desperately wanted to believe that I had free will but because predestination suggested I might still have some unfulfilled purpose. Life had already dealt me so many terrific body blows. I feared to contemplate what might yet lie ahead.

I finished my scotch. "I think he was defending his big sister. Dianne said her father never approved of Kip, and he seems to have lived down to their bad opinion of him, especially after she was diagnosed with malignant multiple sclerosis."

"Didn't she say he was an attentive caregiver, though?" Stacey asked.

"She said she was angry at the disease," I said, "but it must have been galling to have him running around with other women publicly. I would describe her feelings toward him as . . . conflicted."

"The same could be said for most marriages," said Jubilee.

"Not all," said Ora.

I could easily imagine Charley grinning in that distant motel room.

My phone chimed. I picked it up from the coffee table and brought up the messaging app.

It was from Roger Finch. There was no text, just the image of a Rhode Island driver's license with the photograph of the woman we'd known as Shawna Miskin.

"That's her!"

"Who?" Neil asked.

I turned the phone so the others could squint at the screen.

"Her real name is Sherri McRue. She lived in Woonsocket, Rhode Island. Here's another text from Finch. She sold real estate, he says. And was divorcing her husband. Or he was divorcing her, I think Roger means."

"Maybe she and Whitcomb hooked up at a sale?" said Neil excitedly. It was the first time I could recall ever hearing the man use the phrase *hook up*.

"I wonder how Fenton found her, though," Ora said.

"Dianne said Kip had at least one stalker from his series of affairs."

"But how did *Fenton* find her?" said Charley, repeating the question that was at the heart of everything unresolved. "There's the key to it all, right there."

"Let's puzzle it out," suggested Neil.

Mysteries had ceased to be games to me long ago. My job had focused me on the real victims of crime, and once you become aware of them as human beings, it's hard to see them as abstracted characters whose deaths are fodder for entertainment.

"What does the FAA have to say about why the engine quit?" I asked Charley and Stacey, eager to change the subject.

"Water in the gas tanks," he said. "Someone opened the caps and poured in enough to cause the ignition to die eventually."

This statement affirmed for me what I had already suspected: the Cessna had been sabotaged while it was unattended at the Franklin Municipal Airport.

"Cole was in Massachusetts the same time we were?" I wondered aloud.

"He had more than enough time to drive back up to Maine after he learned Stacey landed the Cessna safely," said Charley.

"But how did he know you were going to Massachusetts?" asked Jubilee.

"His sister told him!" said good old Neil.

I stood up from my chair, feeling the stiffness in my joints. "I'm sorry, but I need to go to bed."

Everyone made understanding noises. Charley said that the feds had brought in contractors to expedite the removal of the plane from the pond (an expense for which he would be on the hook). The investigators would be done with their inspection in the morning. After they were cleared to leave, he had only to tune up the engine, flush the fuel system, and refill the dual tanks with avgas, and they'd be ready to take off for home.

"Can I speak with Stacey in private for a minute?" I said.

There were more agreeable noises as I stepped onto the porch, closing the glass door behind me. The boards were wet from the rain. Great Pond was dark again, except where Mouse Island continued to smolder. Incandescent smoke rose into a sky that was clear and cold. It was an autumn sky. I saw Orion and the other constellations, which foretold the approaching winter.

"What's wrong?" she said. "And don't say you're tired."

"It felt like Neil and Jubilee were playing a game of Clue."

"Don't be too hard on them. We've behaved the same way in the past."

"There's nothing like watching an autopsy to change your perspective on murder. Gina looked so small and naked."

"She *was* naked."

"I don't mean physically."

"There's something else bothering you—aside from having been shot at, half drowned, and nearly incinerated."

I couldn't help but smile. "Aside from that."

"So what is it, Mike?"

"Your dad's source said that Fenton was an agent with the Defense Clandestine Service. I wonder if the horse-riding accident he suffered was used to move him from regular army to the Defense Intelligence Agency. His bio reads like a series of cover stories."

"I assume the government won't confirm what Dad's friend told him in confidence."

"I'm sure you're right they won't," I said. "I can almost buy that Cole was on a mission to defend his sister's honor. The question that's bothering me is how he's connected with Sherri McRue. Clearly, he recruited her and was the one who provided her with her new identity as Shawna Miskin."

"I can see how that's problematic."

"Not if we follow this to its logical conclusion. Dianne Fenton-Whitcomb was behind the murders from the start. She initially denied knowing who Shawna Miskin was, then pivoted to a story about how one of Kip's crazy stalkers showed up at the house. Dianne must have been the one who gave her brother the name of Sherri or Shawna or whatever we're calling her."

"It's the piece that finishes the puzzle," said Stacey. "Now I sound like Neil and Jubilee. I know it's not a game."

"You're allowed to use the word. What's bothering me is I can't continue investigating. It's not my job to prove Dianne was involved or even determine how Cole did everything he did. I have to hand it off to the detectives and accept whatever decisions they make. Is there anything harder in life than acceptance?"

"Yes," Stacey said, "fighting everyone, all the time, at once."

61

Through her attorney, Dianne Fenton-Whitcomb denied any knowledge of her brother's actions. She confirmed that she and her husband had hosted him for dinner in the spring, but she claimed not to have seen Cole for months and had no idea he'd returned to the States from overseas.

A few days later, with her lawyer present, she gave an interview to a sympathetic TV reporter in the Medway house. During the discussion, she produced an email that she conveniently claimed to have found on her husband's computer from Sherri McRue a.k.a. Shawna Miskin. The most incriminating passage was put in quotes on the screen for the viewer's benefit:

> "Don't think you can ruin my life without paying the consequences! I have nothing left, Kip. NOTHING! Do you realize how dangerous that makes me to you?!"

Dianne admitted her brother had always despised her husband as being a grifter and unworthy of her. "And Cole was right about Kip's character in the end, though it doesn't excuse what he did."

The interviewer asked how her brother had found an accomplice in Sherri McRue.

Dianne claimed she had no idea.

Personally, I thought the better word to describe Sherri/Shawna's role in the plot was *pawn.* Before she died, she must have willingly accompanied Cole Fenton out to the island in his canoe. Had she known she was paddling to her death? Did she even care by that point?

The interview portrayed Dianne Fenton-Whitcomb as a brave woman cut down in her prime not just by disease but by domineering men and conniving women. She looked every bit the suffering martyr in the wheelchair they'd found for the segment. Given her mobility a week earlier, I assumed the chair was a prop, and yet there was a shadow behind her eyes I didn't recall from having sat across from her in the parlor.

The Maine Office of State Fire Marshal found a charred pistol amid the wreckage of Mouse Island. It was a Beretta Model 70 chambered for .22 long-rifle bullets and fitted with a silencer. The magazine was fully loaded. Cole had only ever used the Glock he'd taken off Galen.

The marshal also located the remains of a duffel that held three melted cell phones, all cheap prepaid models. The data on them was irrecoverable due to fire damage, and the other items in the bag were so badly burned they were unidentified, although one might have been a small glass container for holding pills or liquids.

Fenton's canoe washed up on Otter Island, north of Mouse. It was a 1980s-era Old Town with no provenance.

Deputies responded to a report from Rob and Robyn Soto of a Jeep abandoned in the woods of the former Camp Machigonne. They had no idea how it had managed to bypass the chain gate unless the driver was gifted at picking locks. Inside the Jeep were a tent and a sleeping bag, a 2.5-gallon jug of spring water, several boxes of energy bars, and nothing else.

The vehicle identification number matched a Wrangler that was supposed to be on the lot of a used-car business in Somerville, Massachusetts. The owner said he hadn't realized it was missing. Nor did he claim to recognize Cole Fenton when shown a picture of the man. Somerville police said they had been investigating the business for running multiple scams, including rolling back odometers and washing titles of vehicles that had been salvaged from flood zones. The Wrangler wasn't the first vehicle to disappear from the lot without having been reported.

Neither the Defense Intelligence Agency nor any other department of the United States government made any statement on the matter, presumably because there was no proof that Coleman Fenton Jr. was anything but a cybersecurity officer at a bank headquartered in Istanbul. I did note, however, that the Turkish government expelled several U.S. State Department employees in the weeks following the murders. I was sure the timing of this act was merely a coincidence.

"I don't care if Dianne Fenton-Whitcomb is arrested," I told Pomerleau.

"I have to admit that's a shock, coming from a founding member of the Justice League of America."

"I don't see what good will come of it."

"Joey Randazza doesn't deserve justice?"

"Gina does. But you know as well as I do how effectively lawyers can stonewall. And even if you get lucky and find enough evidence against Dianne to secure an indictment, it will be years before the case goes before a judge and jury."

"I'm starting to feel like Mike Bowditch was replaced by an alien body snatcher."

"Malignant MS is a death sentence. It might take months, or it might take years. But Dianne's not getting away with anything. I'm guessing that was their fallback in case things went crosswise. Cole would take the rap. She would maintain deniability until the end comes. In this case, that's probably the best we can do. But if you and your partner decide to keep going, I'll do everything in my power to help."

"That sounds like the warden investigator I know."

"Middle age is making me pragmatic."

"Just as long as you never become fatalistic, Mike. It's one of the saddest things that can happen to a good man. Expect a call from us about Dianne Fenton-Whitcomb."

Meanwhile, back in Rhode Island, journalists found Sherri McRue's cuckolded husband a willing interview subject, eager to vent his anger at his late wife for trashing her career, incinerating her marriage, and abandoning their two young boys for a worthless womanizer like Kip Whitcomb.

"She was delusional," the balding, bespectacled Mr. McRue said.

"I no longer recognized Sherri at the end. I have been told by the FBI that the real Shawna Miskin was a girl her age who had died in childhood. My wife wouldn't have known how to use a dead girl's identity to get government identification. She had to have had help. I think she stopped being Sherri some time ago. The woman her family is mourning isn't the person those forest rangers found on that island."

If I could have a dollar for every time I was referred to as a *forest ranger* in the news, I could have built my own summer palace on Great Pond.

I had better luck concluding my investigation of the hit-and-run boaters.

Three witnesses, all high school students from nearby Oakland, came forward belatedly, saying they had been partying on board one of their dads' boat when they were approached by the Sunsation Dominator. The girls swore that Kyle McAllister was incoherently drunk and that David Kwan had been driving the cigarette boat. This encounter had taken place less than an hour before the collision. It wasn't hard evidence that Kwan was at the controls at the time of impact, but it probably would have persuaded a jury.

Luckily for Kwan, there would be no trial. His lawyer struck a deal with the Kennebec County District Attorney's Office to plead guilty to the misdemeanor charges of operating a watercraft at unsafe speed and filing a false report. The DA was convinced by the recent graduate's lack of a criminal record, stellar academic achievements in college, and letters from his professors testifying to his sterling character.

I did get one last text from David Kwan demanding to know whether I had been the person who'd contacted the investment bank where he was scheduled to begin his internship. Evidently, the offer had been rescinded based on information provided to the partners from Maine law enforcement. I felt no obligation to confirm or deny the accusation and subsequently blocked his number.

Kyle McAllister received no punishment after he checked himself into a ninety-day drug and alcohol rehabilitation program at McLean Hospital, outside Boston.

"His mother and I are relieved our son has admitted he has a problem and is getting the help he needs," was the totality of the statement delivered by the family's attorney on behalf of Kyle's father.

Galen Webb wrote me a long letter that combined gratitude for having saved his life with an apology for having withheld information from the investigation in general and me in particular. The email was riddled with spelling and grammatical errors the way a block of cheese can be riddled with blue mold:

I fucked up, I know I did. I should have told you about being there care taker but I thought you wouldn't let me play a role in the case and I needed to prove that I was up to the job and it was a mistake for the wardens service not to hire me. All I wanted was a chance to prove myself and now I'm done and won't ever be a constable again even. I knew that Shawna woman was hiding something important and I thought maybe I could solve it and prove myself and you'd let me apply again or even just hire me because Id solved it.

I'm really sorry for not being honest but my motivation wasn't bad just misguided, my wife Grace says. I know you risked your life to save me and that is a debt I mean to repay no matter it takes a year or fifty years. May God bless you and yours, Warden Investigator Bowditch and watch over you as you go about your work punishing the wicked and unrighteous because I sincerely believe your work is His work.

I wrote him back with one question: "Why did your polygraph exam suggest you were lying about the kid you hit with your car?"

The answer was slow coming:

Because I don't know if I could have avoided killing him, OK? It was dusk and maybe if I'd been paying better attention or hit the brakes sooner. And I know I got special treatment on account of my dad being friendly with so many cops. I felt guilty and now people think I'm a liar or worse too. Every night I pray to the Lord Jesus Christ to have that day back to do over again. But He just comes back with the same word, "Atone"! It's why I feel divinely called to become a warden. It's why I mean to repay my debt to you no matter how long it takes or what it costs me.

I feared Galen's vow to repay his debt would hang over me more as a threat than a promise, but I wrote back accepting his apology and making clear that nothing he'd done would have warranted the death Fenton had planned for him, so I hoped he would stop kicking himself and devote his energies to being a better husband and father and let the career take care of itself if it was meant to be.

Despite myself, I couldn't help but share the letter with Bill Boone, who remarked, "That boy doesn't know whether to check his ass or scratch his watch."

Kathy Frost shocked us by asking if she could bring Boone with her to our wedding. We agreed, of course, provided she also brought Maple.

"I'm not sure how much cornpone I can stomach, but Bill's a funny guy," Kathy said, perhaps a little embarrassed to be dating again. "It's amazing how far a sense of humor can get a man."

The ceremony was held outside my house so that Shadow could be present, although he spent most of the nuptials growling in the background at Maple, who, despite her training, paid anxious attention to the meager fence separating her from 140 pounds of half-wild wolf.

"Here we go," Stacey whispered as we passed through the crowd behind our flower girl, Logan Cronk's little sister Emma, who was scattering asters to make a path for us.

"Here we go," I said.

The Reverend Deb Davies, one of the Warden Service's chaplains, officiated, but I chose not to wear my dress uniform, opting instead for a dark suit while Stacey went barefoot under her simple wedding dress. (Jubilee kicked off her own shoes in a gesture of solidarity.) It was a small ceremony, just our family and closest friends clustered under the spreading branches of an ancient red oak from which a few scarlet leaves had begun to fall. Gus the raven even made a flyover. No church could have stirred our spirits more deeply than those woods on the coast of Maine, where the only incense was the smell of birch smoke coming from the stove inside, and the burble of the Ducktrap River down the hill the only music we wanted or needed.

After Stacey and I had exchanged our vows and kissed and were presented to our guests as our new selves, the cheers and whistles set the wolf to howling. I knelt beside Ora's chair to receive her now-healthy embrace, and when I stood up as their new son-in-law, Charley threw an arm around my shoulders in a half bear hug and exclaimed:

"Took you long enough!"

Author's Note

No matter how many books you write, each one is its own thing. It may have its unique genesis in some chance meeting, some casual remark, or some scrap of information read, then forgotten, then remembered. And when you are finished with the writing, it can be hard to transport yourself back to the time when the idea was slowly taking shape, before you recognized it as a novel in embryo.

Which is to say I can't remember when *Dead Man's Wake* announced itself to me as the next book I needed to write. And yet here it is, and I hope you have enjoyed it.

Somewhere along the line in its composition, I began to realize that I needed to learn many things to tell the story that wanted to be told. I found myself buying and reading references on arcane subjects. *Boat Accident Reconstruction and Litigation* by Roy Scott Hickman and Michael M. Sampsel and *The Water's Edge: A Manual for the Underwater Criminal Investigator* by Mike Berry were particularly useful for this one.

More helpful still were the people who lent their experience and expertise to me, especially Maine game wardens John MacDonald and Jeremy Judd, pilot (and early reader) Mat McConnel, author and Belgrade booster Maureen Milliken, and all-around resource person Jessica Hollenkamp. Peg and Ron Churchill will not recall hosting me at Bear Spring Camps in Rome some years ago, but *Dead Man's Wake* would not exist had I not made a choice to stay there to try my luck at pike fishing and absorb whatever good energies remained from E. B. White's fateful visits.

On the topic of White, I am sincerely grateful to Allene White (his daughter-in-law) and Martha White (his granddaughter) for granting me permission to quote from his classic essay "Once More to the Lake," set on Great Pond. It goes without saying that passage is the best thing in this book.

I want to thank my other early readers, Eric Hopkins, Nancy McConnel, and Kristen Lindquist, who is not only my wife (I love you, K), but my best critic.

I owe a deep debt to Sander and Erin Van Otterloo for inviting me to write at their lake house so that I might get right the sights, sounds, and smells of a mid-Maine pond at summer's end.

Thank you, as always, to my parents, whose love and support constitute the bedrock for everything I try to build. I love you, Mom and Dad, Roger, Pam, and Alicia. Just as I love all you Doirons, Nagles, Oenemas, Chababs, Hendersons, and aforementioned Van Otts.

I am grateful to Ann Rittenberg, whose good work on my behalf sometimes seems the literal definition of "tireless."

To my team at Minotaur and Macmillan Audio—Andy Martin, Kelley Ragland, Sarah Melnyk, Paul Hochman, Steve Erickson, Sam Glatt, Amber Cortes, Sarah Grill, and Hannah Pierdolla—you guys rock. I especially want to thank my editor, Charles Spicer, not just for acquiring *The Poacher's Son* but for shepherding the entire series of fourteen books (and counting) into print. Mike Bowditch, as we know him, would not exist without you, Charlie.